DANA HAWKINS is a caffeine-fueled writer of contemporary romance stories, including *Not in the Plan*, *In Walked Trouble*, *So Not My Type*, *The Ex Effect*, and *Any Girl But You*. After living for twenty years in Seattle, she recently trekked back to her hometown in Minnesota. She is a huge romance-genre book nerd and borderline obsessed with happy-ever-afters. As a mom of three humans and one Saint Bernard, she spends her days chasing after kids and various animals, neglecting her last remaining bamboo plant, and searching for the perfect coffee mug.

My Girlfriend is Not the Father

DANA HAWKINS

ONE PLACE. MANY STORIES

HQ
An imprint of HarperCollins*Publishers* Ltd
1 London Bridge Street
London SE1 9GF

www.harpercollins.co.uk

HarperCollins*Publishers*
Macken House, 39/40 Mayor Street Upper,
Dublin 1 D01 C9W8
This edition 2026

1
First published in Great Britain by HQ,
an imprint of HarperCollins*Publishers* Ltd 2026

Copyright © Dana Hawkins 2026

Author asserts the moral right to be identified as the author of this work.
A catalogue record for this book is available from the British Library.

ISBN: 9780008779801

This novel is entirely a work of fiction. The names, characters and incidents portrayed in it are the work of the author's imagination. Any resemblance to actual persons, living or dead, events or localities is entirely coincidental.

All rights reserved. No part of this publication may be reproduced, stored in a retrieval system, or transmitted, in any form or by any means, electronic, mechanical, photocopying, recording or otherwise, without the prior permission of the publishers.

Without limiting the exclusive rights of any author, contributor or the publisher of this publication, any unauthorized use of this publication to train generative artificial intelligence (AI) technologies is expressly prohibited. HarperCollins also exercise their rights under Article 4(3) of the Digital Single Market Directive 2019/790 and expressly reserve this publication from the text and data mining exception.

Printed and bound in the UK using 100% Renewable
Electricity by CPI Group (UK) Ltd

To my forever. Thank you for supporting me in all of my dreams, no matter how big or small they may be.

PART ONE

Chapter 1

Lucy

Lucy Green palmed a needle the size of the baton she used to twirl in her high-school marching band. A hot sting of bile snaked up her oesophagus and bubbled in her throat, threatening to launch. Droplets of cold sweat pricked her neck. She stared at the doctor. 'I'm sorry. Did you say I have to stick this in my butt?'

Doctor Olson, a kind woman with salted grey hair and crinkles around her eyes, smiled. 'Not technically *in* your butt. More … outside of the butt. The nurse will draw a bull's-eye around the outer butt cheek and upper hip area to ensure you don't hit a sciatic nerve. We want to make sure you can walk during this pregnancy.'

Her tone made this statement sound like a cute, tongue-in-cheek joke. But Lucy knew the doctor was dead serious. Lucy's gaze flickered between the fathers and the hormone drumstick in her hand. She exhaled a shaky breath and forced a brave face so her bestie, Drew, and his husband, Mason, wouldn't catch a whiff of her nerves.

At least she wasn't dating, because between a semipermanent

bull's-eye drawn on her ass, the extreme amount of hormones she was about to take, and the inevitable morning sickness, she could probably take home an award for the *World's Least Desirable Single*.

'Okay, gotcha.' Lucy sank back into the cushy leather couch – one perk of seeing a doctor at a swanky Minneapolis fertility clinic instead of the local medical group.

Doctor Olson reviewed the computer screen. 'Any side effects from starting birth control?'

Growing up as president of the Certified Lesbian Association, never in Lucy's wildest dreams did she think she'd ever take The Pill. 'A small headache, but not too bad.'

'That should go away by next month but keep me posted.' Doctor Olson's index finger scrolled the computer mouse. 'And how are your periods? Regular?'

Lucy shot a glance at Drew, who seemed as cool as he'd always been since meeting him twenty-five years ago in kindergarten. He ran his fingers through his ginger-red hair and gave Lucy a quick grin.

Mason, however, stiffened a little more – if that was even possible. Mason once mentioned that the female body was like the Bermuda Triangle meets a black abyss – fascinating, but something he had no desire to explore. If the words 'heavy flow' left the doctor's mouth right now, he'd probably collapse.

'Yep, so far, so good,' Lucy said.

'Great.' The doctor tapped the keyboard. 'This will give you a leg up when the IPs choose the egg donor.'

So many terms. IPs, GCs, egg donors, pre-birth orders. Lucy's head swirled, but she did a quick calculation. IPs equalled Intended Parents. Aka the fathers. Aka the two men in the doctor's office who now knew everything from her weight to her sexual history (less activity than she wanted, *cough, cough*), and that she was not nearly as cool with needles as claimed when they started the surrogacy conversation years ago.

'Dads.' Doctor Olson folded her hands and glanced at Lucy's friends. 'Questions for me?'

Mason shook his head, not one speck of his perfectly coiffed jet-black hair moving. He thumbed the tip of his heavy, dark designer frames back into place and glanced at his husband. 'Drew?'

'Just confirming, if Lucy gets sore, she can shoot the injection into her thigh?' Drew said.

'That's correct, but not always advisable.' The doctor shifted towards Lucy. 'I'm going to be honest. The thigh is going to hurt. If that's your injection site, you need to heat, massage, and ice.'

Cool, cool. Lucy hoped her expert-level poker face didn't break. She resisted the urge to peek at Drew, knowing he could decode her micro-expressions in a snap.

'Okay, friends. If there are no further questions, sit tight.' Doctor Olson adjusted the stethoscope around her neck and stood. 'The coordinator will arrive shortly. I'll see you next month.'

The heavy door clicked shut and Drew blurted out, 'Oh, my hell.' He scooted in next to her on the couch. 'I had no idea it was so big.'

Too easy. 'That's what she sa—'

'Nope, no jokes. I'm serious.' Drew tugged on his designer jeans, his freckled white face turning more pale than normal. 'I'm sick to my stomach. That needle is no joke.'

'Lucy, are you okay with this?' Mason scratched at his dark, permanent five-o'clock shadow scruff. 'You can still back out.'

'Guys, seriously? Stop. We've talked about this for a million years. I'm not backing out.' She could hear how her voice sounded – calm, confident, light-hearted. Basically, the exact opposite of the monstrosity occurring inside her. She shoved her shaky hands under her legs. 'Besides, that bride of Satan's needle won't start for a while, so we're good.'

Lucy couldn't help but notice the quick, worried glance Drew shot at Mason. *Ugh*. Her dirty-joke-telling, drag-show-watching, chocolate-stealing bestie had flipped into an overbearing, protective dad the moment she had said 'yes' and it made her itchy.

'Well, hellooooo there!' the ultra-bubbly coordinator announced as she bounced through the door.

The men sat up straight like when Sister Katherine stomped in during seventh-grade algebra for a pop quiz. Lucy got it. She was nervous as heck, too. Even this deep into the surrogacy process, they could still be denied at any point.

'I'm Kendra. Such a pleasure meeting you all.' She propped a tablet in her lap. 'Ready to review a few things?'

Not really. The image of the needle had burrowed deep in Lucy's mind, and she wasn't sure she could handle any more surprises. Still, she plastered on a smile for Drew and Mason's sake. 'Yep! Looking forward to learning more.'

'Open up your calendars, please.' Kendra pressed her stylus pen to the screen. 'We need to complete the MMPI psychological exam, and then a follow-up with the doc. Does Friday the twelfth work for everyone?'

Lucy flipped through her calendar app. 'Can we take this over lunch?'

Kendra chuckled, then zipped her mouth when she looked at Lucy's scrunched eyebrows. 'Oh sorry. I thought you were kidding. No, you'll be here at least four hours.'

'Four hours?' Lucy glanced at the men. 'For a personality test?'

'It's more than an internet test to see if you're an introvert or extrovert. God, I love those things. They always seem to be so accurate, right?' Kendra set down the pen at the edge of the desk. 'But this one is in depth, really getting into the heart of who you are, what you need, all that good stuff. Afterwards, you'll have a dedicated ninety-minute session just for you, and another session with you and the dads.'

Drew's eyes widened. 'I think we know everything about each other already.'

'I bet you know lots, but this will dig deeper.' Kendra turned to Lucy. 'You still don't have a significant other, correct? Nothing has changed since we asked you earlier this year?'

Geezus. Maybe a bullhorn could announce her status to people across the hall. Parade her around with a flashing neon sign that said: *Lucy Green. Single ... still!*

'Nope, no significant other, unless you count an extremely needy rescue pup.'

'Great.' Kendra smiled and poised the pen over her clipboard. 'That sure is convenient, isn't it?'

Convenient was never a word Lucy would use to describe her perpetually single status.

'We'll need you to sign an affidavit stating that information,' Kendra said.

'Stating I don't have a girlfriend?' *So embarrassing.* 'Why?'

'Surrogacy affects the partner almost as much as the surrogate.'

'Really?' Lucy said, feeling dubious.

'Well, they won't get swollen ankles, heartburn, or morning sickness, obviously.' Kendra grinned. 'But we need to confirm their beliefs will not contradict our goal. Or if they have to make any difficult medical decisions on your behalf, we file the necessary legal paperwork. They'd also need a medical evaluation to check for any STIs or communicable diseases they could pass on to you, and thus the foetus. But of course, the real reason is to make sure they'll feed you soda water and saltines when you throw up for those first few months.'

Lucy's stomach flipped.

'Now, even being single, we still strongly caution you to be careful with any sexual partner, of course, but it's required that you refrain from having sex at least six weeks prior to implantation.' Kendra's thumb flipped through the paperwork. 'Have you secured lawyers?'

Mason raised a pristinely manicured hand. 'We've narrowed the list down to a few that specialise in surrogacy law. Quick question. Is there any leeway in the rule regarding lawyers from the same law firm? We found a couple we really like from the same office.'

'No, sorry.' Kendra frowned. 'We must protect the gestational carrier's interests, without influence. Lucy has one hundred per cent control over her body this entire time and can make *whatever* choice is right for her, no matter what that choice may be.'

Kendra's tone flipped to firm, and Lucy appreciated the intention behind the words. Since day one, this message never faltered. Lucy knew the dads trusted her. But as hyper-prepared and organised as the men were, no doubt they had a bit of reluctance giving up all control until after the birth.

Mason tugged on his crisp tie. 'Of course. Not a problem.'

'A few more medical evaluations, the psych exam, obtaining lawyers, and we should be good to go.' Kendra turned her focus to the dads. 'You can evaluate egg donor files right after we receive a passing psych exam score.'

'Send the ones that look like Mason,' Lucy cracked and nudged Drew with her elbow.

'Jerk,' Drew whispered.

Kendra's smile dimmed. 'You know you can't see the donor, right?'

Oh no …

Several seconds passed as the dads communicated between themselves with their eyes. 'We can't?' Mason finally asked.

'You're allowed access to their childhood picture, but not an adult photo. We don't want people to pay for pretty babies. Can you imagine the lawsuits if we allowed that?' Kendra chuckled, then cleared her throat. 'Besides, the vast majority of egg donors remain anonymous.'

Lucy could almost see the men's wheels turning. No doubt they'd had visions of everyone involved in their baby's conception – including the egg donor – at a yearly summer picnic, filled with mini-gourmet sandwiches and a tasteful mimosa bar, swapping the same birth story year after year with attendees. Well, adjusting seemed to be a common theme in this process. They wouldn't see or meet the egg donor. And Lucy had to make friends with the bride of Satan's needle. Great.

For the rest of the appointment, Lucy scribbled the med schedule, pros and cons of acupuncture, and starred a reminder to take baby aspirin in her 'Get a Baby Up in Here' personalised notebook. After stuffing the pamphlets in her purse, she, Mason, and Drew left.

Stepping outside, the humidity slapped her in the face. 'Gross. I'm melting.'

August was peak heat season for Minnesota, and she was fully over having perpetually damp skin. She'd run out of baby powder to use in her bra, and any moment now she was going to have an unfortunate chafing episode. Maybe this afternoon she'd walk the lush green path lining the St Croix River and stop at an ice cream shop in downtown Stillwater to combat the heat.

'Just wait until you're carrying an extra thirty pounds.' Mason beeped the car lock. 'I'll make Drew tail you with one of those mist fans.'

She groaned.

'Bring it in. Group hug time.' Drew opened his arms and engulfed Lucy. 'You still good? Need anything?'

She pushed a gentle hand against his chest. 'You've got to stop asking me that, or I'm going to ask for something that's seriously bananas.'

'Anything. Anything you want.'

The sincerity in Drew's eyes almost killed her. From the moment she agreed to be a surrogate, the power dynamic in their relationship had shifted. She went from being the bestie, the jokester, the 'you're so not a third wheel' third wheel to someone Drew and Mason felt like they owed. They didn't understand she was doing this as much for herself as for them.

'Hmmm.' She strummed her fingers against her chin. 'A date

with Demi Lovato, a Ferris wheel in my backyard, and for you to get a massive chest tattoo that says "Lucy: Still Better Looking Than Me".'

Drew rolled his eyes. 'I'll work on the Ferris wheel.'

'Come on, Drew. I have to get back to work. Those bridges aren't going to build themselves.' Mason chuckled at his all-too-common civil engineering joke and held the door open for his husband. 'Lucy, we'll text you later.'

'Byeeeee!' She hoisted herself into her truck and headed for Stillwater. One quick stop at the grocery store before spending the day binge-watching *Schitt's Creek*, eating terrible food, and having a glass of wine while she still could.

Lucy plopped the canvas bags and her purse on the counter and loaded the fridge. Even though a night of nothing but salted chips and cheesy dip sounded good, in a moment of excellent judgement, she had forced herself to buy a few veggies to offset the preservatives.

She stuffed the bags together and grabbed her purse to toss in the closet.

Oh no.

No, no, no, no. The purse was too light. Her fingertips rummaged through the bag. She patted her pockets, scanned the floor, and bolted back to the car. Crap. Did she seriously leave her wallet at the store? In the cart? Did it fall out in the parking lot?

Every pore brimmed with sweat as she swerved through traffic. Her mind raced with things she had to do if it was gone: cancel credit cards, new licence, call the bank, new insurance cards … her stomach knotted. *Unless some good Samaritan turned it in …*

Ten minutes later, she barrelled through the store entrance and up to the customer service counter. 'I think I left my wallet here. Rainbow-coloured, trifold. By any chance, did someone turn it in?' She tapped her fingers against her thigh.

The uninterested teen shuffled his hands underneath the

counter, then pulled out the wallet. 'This?'

Oh, thank the holy dancing queen gods. Good people still existed. 'Yes! Whew, am I right? What a nightmare that would've been.'

A blank stare met her.

After a quick scan, she saw that not only were the credit cards still there, but so was the cash. She death-gripped the wallet against her chest but refrained from smooching the material. 'Do you know who returned it?'

'Yeah, I think she might still be here. Tall lady, purple hair. Kinda hard to miss.' He shrugged.

Lucy stretched her neck. The grocery store was small enough, fewer than twenty aisles. She'd scoot through a few and see if she could find this woman. If not, the wallet-finder had a bucket of good karma coming her way. Lucy peeked down the cereal aisle, bread aisle, and froze when she reached the spice aisle.

'Kinda hard to miss' was the understatement of the century. Six feet tall, legs from here to heaven, shaved hair on one side, deep purple hair on the other, full-sleeve tattoo. Freaking beautiful.

The woman scowled at the sauces.

Lucy gulped. *I'm going in.*

Chapter 2

Jade

Was this place actually serious? Jade shuffled the sauces and crouched to see if anyone had stuffed sriracha behind the BBQ. Nope. Not behind the mustards, relish, chilli sauce, nothing. *What in the actual fu–*

'Um, hi.'

A timid voice cut into Jade's not-so-timid internal monologue about the moral failings of the supply chain bosses who had somehow not procured the best condiment on earth.

A doe-eyed, pink-cheeked woman with long, wavy chestnut-brown hair stared at Jade. Her neon pink shirt caught Jade's attention. Rainbow letters spelling 'Queer AF' paraded across her chest. Jade's eyes lingered. On the cute message, of course. Not on the way the fabric hugged her full curves. Or … mostly on the message.

The woman jerked her thumb behind her shoulder. 'The guy up front, he told me where to find you.'

Jade stood up straight, towering over the woman by a good six inches in her own estimate.

'I mean, I asked him where to find you.'

Hmmm. Now I'm intrigued.

The woman cleared her throat. 'Sorry, um, did you find a wallet?'

Jade's frown from the sriracha debacle switched into a grin. *Lucy.* Once she said 'wallet', it only took Jade a moment to connect that this woman was the same one on the driver's licence she peeked at earlier. 'The rainbow one? Yeah, I did.'

'Oh my God, you're seriously an angel.' Lucy folded her hands in front of her chest. 'I was freaking out! Ugh, I can't believe I left it here. I thought for sure someone would've stolen it, and holy extra-chunky guacamole replacing everything would have been such a massive pain in the booty.'

Jade propped the plastic grocery carrier on her hip. 'The booty, huh? Wouldn't want that.' She took a bit too much pleasure in the pink that brushed Lucy's cheeks. 'Don't worry. I only pocketed a fifty. I left everything else.'

'Perfect, so you didn't find the hundred-dollar bill. Good to know that my hiding spot still works.'

'You have one of those too? I thought I was the only one.' Jade had no actual bill-hiding spot, but this woman's scattered, excited voice was doing something to her insides. Coming off a not-so-great day, and an even worse last two years, this was a refreshing breath of glittered air.

Lucy dodged an oncoming cart. 'My dad always told me, keep a hidden twenty-dollar bill, and always have a quarter in case you need to make a call.'

'Jesus, how old are you?' Lucy looked to be in her early thirties like Jade, but one could never tell these days. 'A quarter? I thought payphones were obsolete in the last twenty-five years.'

Lucy strummed her fingers on her cheek. 'Clearly my anti-wrinkle cream is working.'

Jade switched the carrier to her other hip. 'I have a confession to make.'

'I knew it.' Lucy twisted her mouth. 'Were you going to hold a knife up to my wallet in a ransom pic?'

Oh boy. She's really adorable. Stop this conversation immediately. 'No. I peeked at your licence. I was going to find you on social media and shoot you a message that I turned it in at the counter, in case you didn't remember where you lost it.'

'You looked at my licence? So, you know what my middle name is?'

Jade chuckled. 'Is that your *actual* middle name?'

'Sunshine?' Lucy nodded. 'Sure is. My parents … they're a unique bunch. Not sure how they thought Lucy would go with Sunshine, but here we are.'

'Well, it's definitely original.'

'Not quite as original as your purple hair, though.'

Jade patted the side of her head. 'Purple? This is called Midnight Amethyst, thank you very much.'

'Well, it's very cool.' The playfulness in Lucy's voice faltered to soft, and Jade lapped it up. Lucy dug the tip of her chequered Converse into the metal shelving.

'Have you ever coloured yours?'

Lucy tucked a lock behind her ear. 'No. I mean, not really. I tried highlights a few years ago. But really, I'm about as boring as they come.'

Nothing about this woman was boring. Something tugged at Jade not to end the conversation. Maybe because it was the first non-client and non-family conversation she'd had in a year? Maybe because she needed a distraction from what was happening at work? Whatever the reason, it felt … *nice*.

'Well' – Lucy waved at the mustard and ketchup behind Jade – 'I didn't mean to interrupt you and whatever street fight was about to happen with the sauces.'

'Ugh. My angry face. Sorry. They're out of sriracha for the second day in a row. And how's a girl supposed to eat her eggs, you know?'

Lucy grimaced. 'You put sriracha on your eggs?'

'You don't?'

Lucy shook her head. 'Born and bred central Minnesotan here.' She stuffed the wallet under her arm. 'Pretty sure I don't use sriracha on anything.'

Okay – her giggle, a little high-pitched and nasal, was adorable. Jade needed to jet the hell out of here before they chatted any longer. She had a life plan – a very long, thought-out, therapy-guided life plan – which did *not* include talking to a cute, charming stranger. She had learned her lesson, hard. 'In Chicago, I used it on everything. Eggs, veggies, pizza.'

Okay, maybe just a few more minutes …

'Chicago, huh? What brings you to Minnesota?'

Running away from my past, seeking an unattainable new future, burying my memories in a different state. 'I opened a salon.'

Lucy lifted a brow. 'Oh really? Which one?'

'Jade's on 7th.' She pointed at the store entrance like there was an open window but quickly dropped her hand.

'Are you Jade?'

'Yep.'

Lucy shuffled her weight between her feet. 'Your place is the one by the bubble tea shop?'

Jade nodded.

'I should stop by.' Lucy tugged at the bottom of her strands. 'I haven't cut my hair in over a year.'

Jade slapped her hand against her heart. 'Nails on a chalkboard, saying that to a stylist.'

'Is it better or worse than scraping a fork on glass?'

'What sort of sociopath are you?' Jade's smartwatch timer beeped. *Dammit.* But also, probably saved by the bell. 'Speaking of hairstyling … I have a perm to do. I should head back to the salon.'

'*Head* back to the salon.' Lucy tapped her wallet against her thigh, a smirk rising. 'Is that a play on words?'

Jade chuckled. 'No, but it should be.'

'People still do perms?'

'You'd be surprised.' Jade grabbed a wasabi-based seasoning that would do in a pinch and set it in the basket. 'Well, Lucy Sunshine Green. It was nice to meet you.' Jade wanted to tell her this was the best convo she'd had in a long time and ask for her number. Which would be ridiculous, of course. Chicago-gate was barely eighteen months old.

No, she was tired. Overworked. A tad horny. That was all.

'You too, Jade's on 7th.' Lucy inched back. 'Thanks again, seriously. You've restored my faith in humanity.'

'Don't give me that much credit. I might trip a toddler on the way out just for fun.' Jade winked.

A wink. Really? What in the hell am I doing?

Lucy lifted her hand in a sort of awkward half-wave goodbye, spun on her foot like a slightly uncoordinated dancer, and speed-walked from the aisle.

Jade strained her neck to see if she would turn back and give a wave.

Nope, nothing.

Good. No look back was good. Jade had moved here for several very specific reasons – to settle into her single life and shield her recently mended heart from any potential heartache, to open a business, and to rediscover her damn self. Not to flirt with the cute woman in Aisle Five.

She self-scanned a can of tomato soup, an apple, two chocolate bars, and the wasabi sauce – a lunch of champions if she said so herself – and raced back to the salon.

Sunbeams ricocheted off the sea of foiled hair, and the scent of bleach wafted into her nose. Seeing all ten chairs fully occupied in the middle of the weekday did something sparkly to Jade's insides. If she were more on speaking terms with her family, she'd snap a picture and send a group text.

'There you are.' Mrs Dieterman folded the lifestyle magazine in her hand and set it on the side table. 'Thought you forgot about me.'

'I would never. You're my favourite.' Jade slung Mrs Dieterman's jacket around her forearm. Eighty-five degrees in August, and she still brought a light coat. Jade held out her arm, and Mrs Dieterman gripped her, shaking a bit as she stood. After making their way across the sand-coloured mesquite hardwood floor to Jade's station, Jade spun the black leather chair and eased her into a sitting position. 'Would you like coffee, extra sugar, splash of cream?'

'That would be delightful.' Mrs Dieterman tilted her head and Jade fastened a smock. 'Got any of those tea cookies?'

'Just for you.' Which was not a lie. Jade had them on opening day, along with champagne, a charcuterie board that cost almost as much as her rent, and an espresso stand. Mrs Dieterman walked in and downed five cookies. Jade promised to have them on hand for when she visited – which turned into a strict weekly shampoo set, monthly trim, and every other month perm.

Jade grabbed a mix of yellow and blue rods – never again making the mistake of using all yellow like back in her early hairstyling days. The client had stomped out with a scowl, a few choice words, and what looked like a poodle on her head.

The back-room door flung open and Shayna, Jade's top stylist, flew through, balancing colouring bowls, brushes, and a smock.

'Whoa? When did you do that?' Jade circled her hand towards Shayna's face, which sported fresh, sharp, razor-edged blond bangs. 'I leave for twenty minutes and it's a whole new you.'

Shayna tossed the items in the sink and pinched the edges of the hair grazing her red chunky frames. 'You like it?' She dipped her head and looked in the mirror. 'You don't think I look like Thelma from *Scooby-Doo*, do you?'

First, Thelma was the cutest of the detective squad if Jade said so herself – not that she'd say that to her employee. Second, Shayna was a natural pale blond, with such fair skin that it sometimes looked translucent. And she was never without deep red lipstick and black pencilled-in brows. So no, she looked nothing like Thelma. 'You mean because of your glasses and bangs? Nah. But it looks great. Nice change.'

'Cool, thanks.' Shayna grabbed a stack of sanitised combs from the drawer. 'My next client is gonna be late. I'm grabbing a bubble tea. Want one?'

'Dear God, yes. Thanks. I have some cash in my drawer.' Jade popped a small chunk of granola in her mouth. 'You're the best.'

'I know …' Shayna laughed and floated out as quickly as she floated in.

Among the zen-like atmosphere of the salon, with its cream-coloured walls, tan and white stone accents, and more plants than the local nursery, Journey's greatest hits thumped through the salon speakers and Jade's mind drifted. *Lucy Sunshine Green. Hmmm.* She added the activator and neutraliser to the tray, and pictured the cute, flustered woman waving her rainbow wallet in the air like some sort of lesbian fairy. Not that she'd normally guess someone's identity. Especially with femmes. But Lucy's 'Queer AF' T-shirt gave Jade the intel she needed.

Why had that conversation been so refreshing? Jade talked to people all day. She even enjoyed most clients. But this felt … *different.*

The bucket of rods clicked as she walked. She handed the coffee to Mrs Dieterman, who responded to her first sip with a sharp wince.

'What happened to a splash of creamer? Tastes like you dumped the whole carton in there.'

Dammit. She was totally doe-eyed, distracted in the back room. 'Oops, sorry. Must be the chemicals getting to me.' *Or maybe a random stranger with great hair and a pouty mouth?* 'I'll make you a fresh one.'

'Nah, this is okay.' She took another sip. 'So now, where did I leave off last week?'

Jade separated Mrs Dieterman's hair and clipped strands to the side. 'You were telling me about your grandson going off to college in the fall.'

'Oh yes. So, he chose Iowa. Can you even believe that? He's gonna take classes in the middle of a damn cornfield.'

'That's not true.' Jade spritzed her hair with water, layered the tissue, and wrapped the rod. 'Iowa is a thriving state. Des Moines is beautiful. Great food, culture …'

'Pfft. Nothing like my homemade dumplings, that's for sure.'

She sliced the next section of hair. 'You're gonna miss him, huh?'

Mrs Dieterman rolled her eyes, but fessed up a short while later that, of course, she was going to miss him, and even though you weren't supposed to say it, he was one of her favourite grandkids. Jade warmed at the words, thinking briefly of her own feisty grandma back in Chicago.

Jade continued to spray, wrap, and roll as Mrs Dieterman went through the lives of each of her grandchildren since their last visit. *Spray, wrap, roll …* She fought hard against zoning out with the methodical motions.

Activator applied, shower cap fastened, drier set, and Jade cleaned her station. She strolled to the front and joined Amanda – receptionist extraordinaire – to review the daily client list.

Amanda peeked up from her personal laptop propped next to the salon computer, no doubt studying for some exam Jade couldn't even fathom taking. When Jade first hired her, Amanda spent every second of downtime dusting, rearranging products, even sweeping up for the stylists to keep herself busy during the slow times. When Jade learned Amanda had a full online college credit load for a criminology degree, she offered salon downtime to study.

'Fun fact.' Amanda stopped tapping the keyboard and patted the side of her hair. Today, she had her edges slicked into a row of swirls at the crown of her head with her hair pulled up into an Afro puff. Amanda wasn't a hairstylist, but she had some serious skill when it came to doing her own hair. 'Do you know a body will decompose slower in water than the air? *Slower*. Who knew?'

Jade ran her hand under the till in search of a highlighter. 'Fun fact, huh? Thank you for using your personal laptop to google this stuff. All I need is the FBI raiding my salon thinking I'm planning a murder.'

'That would be awful if a murder happened here. Awful.' Amanda's lips tugged into a smile. 'But in case it did ... you know you'd have to call me, right? For educational purposes, of course.'

'Of course.' Jade pulled out the vendor documents from the folder and tapped them against the counter. 'I just think every few days you should sanitise your algorithm. Search cute baby elephant videos or new vegan ice cream shops or something.'

'Oh! Yes.' Amanda smacked her multilayered ring hand on the desk. 'Elephants cause how many deaths per year? I bet more than we think.'

Jade shook her head with a grin. 'Do you really need this information for your degree?' What she would've given to have the smarts and confidence Amanda had at her age. Jade's life probably would have looked different. Juvenile mistakes – vanished. Heartbreak – gone. She would have entered her marriage with an analytic mind and solid research, not with stars in her eyes and a foggy brain. And she would have saved herself a hell of a lot of heartache.

Amanda's marble-decorated nails – that probably took hours for her to design – clicked against the keyboard. 'You never know. I won't be left hanging if this is on a test.'

'Be honest. You're the one sitting in the front row of the class, aren't you?' Jade pictured herself in high school, sliding into the very back seat so she could doze off if needed without the teacher noticing.

'Hell, yes I am. I want to hear everything the teacher has to say.' The salon phone rang. Amanda reached to pick it up as Jade returned to the computer.

A rebooking request for one of Jade's regulars caught her attention. She scrolled through the screen to see if he had rescheduled when Amanda tapped her arm.

'It's for you.'

Jade didn't have time to chat with a client or vendor. She had to check her schedule, take a bite of yogurt, and return to Mrs Dieterman. 'Can you take a message?'

Amanda shrugged. 'They said it's urgent.'

Jade clocked the time. Six minutes before rinse time. Urgent or not, Mrs Dieterman's hair had to be neutralised, or the rods would pop off with a very undesirable chemical haircut. She tucked the phone under her chin. 'This is Jade.'

'Hey, it's me.'

That voice. Jade's heart stopped beating for so long, she was sure she'd pass out. Darkness filled her periphery.

'Can we talk?'

'I told you to never contact me again.' Jade slammed down the phone, hot air shooting from her nostrils.

Amanda's wide, dark eyes searched Jade's. 'Everything okay?'

Nothing about hearing that voice was okay. Jade's stomach knotted so tight, she thought she might be sick. She exhaled a shaky breath and gave Amanda a quick nod. 'Yeah, just a vendor who won't take no for an answer.' She stormed away before Amanda could call her out on the obvious lie.

Chapter 3

Lucy

The canvas bag of cash piled in front of Lucy gave her a split-second pause. A scruffy, grey-haired man refused to loosen his grip for a solid minute. A gentle cash-hostage-negotiation followed until Lucy offered a soft smile and leaned forward. 'You don't have to give it to me if you don't want to.'

She had a fleeting urge to scold the man, however, for stuffing it in his mattress all these years. What if his house caught fire? What if it was stolen? What about the interest rates! Those thoughts popped up as quickly as they exited. After working at the bank for over a decade, she'd seen it all. As her old boss always said, *Follow the bank teller golden rule: Their business ain't none of yours.*

Once the man released his precious cargo, Lucy hip-bumped her work wife, Erica, as she made her way to the cash sorter. Erica blew at her sharp black fringe to keep it from swinging into her chunky brown glasses and gave Lucy a quick, knowing grin. When Erica started five years ago, she and Lucy bonded over vanilla yogurt, a love for crap reality television, and a deep affinity for customers like the man who had just handed her a bag of cash. Lucy told Erica most everything – but for some reason had not told her about the interaction at the grocery store with Jade. And right now, Lucy didn't want to do a full self-reflection deep dive as to why not.

The clicking of the cash sorter sounded. She removed another stack and tapped it against the table. *Whoosh, whoosh, click.* A curled-up five-dollar bill stuck to a twenty. She scraped a tiny piece of tape off the edge of the bill and flattened it against the counter as her mind wandered back to Jade.

More than a week had passed since Lucy ran into Jade, but somehow, Lucy thought about their interaction every night. And most mornings. She'd even stopped by the grocery store a few times, hoping to bump into her. Which was kind of pathetic since their conversation had lasted less than five minutes. But she felt a smidge better that at least she hadn't slipped into any sort of serious creeper-stalker territory and refrained from walking by Jade's salon. For now.

The hormones were already affecting Lucy's brain, obviously. Wait – nope. Besides The Pill, she hadn't started injections yet. And yes, maybe Lucy had been single for the last five years, and maybe she was a tad lonely – but still! It's not like she hadn't seen other attractive women in those five years. So why did the image of the six-foot-tall, purple-haired queen refuse to disappear?

It's not that she didn't want to date. But she'd lived in Stillwater, Minnesota, her entire life and was pretty sure she knew every single queer woman within a thirty-mile radius. And dating sites were like a weird meat … er … peach market, and she hated swiping to find a mate. She didn't even like the internet that much. Her dad always said she was an old soul wrapped in a millennial body. Which was both true and not true. Frank Sinatra wasn't spinning in the background on a vintage record player and she didn't smoke cigars (gross). But she found comfort in driving around in her four-speed stick-shift, canary-yellow 1990

Ford pick-up over a more modern car. Phone conversations beat text messaging. Fishing over dancing. Knitting over bar hopping.

And the women these last few years seemed to want *more*. More excitement, more flare, more jet-setting, more ... everything. She didn't need more. She had Chucky, her rescue dog, Drew and Mason, and her dad.

After printing out the receipt for the man, she explained how to open a savings account, and escorted him to the new-account office. She peeked at her watch – *sweet*! Break time. She was hungry as hell. Unfortunately, she had already snuck her quota of cookies from the lobby earlier today. She rounded the corner and ran into her manager, Pamela. Literally. Boobs-to-boobs. Thank God Lucy's double Ds cushioned the impact, but still. *Ouch.* 'Ugh, sorry!'

'You scared the crap out of me!' Pamela slammed her hand against her chest and laughed. 'I'm not a young woman anymore, Lucy. You have to be gentle with me.'

'Um, aren't you like only five years older than me?' Lucy readjusted her purse strap. 'And sorry. Break time, and I'm freaking starving.'

Pamela dropped her cell into her suit jacket pocket. 'Real quick. Just checking if you saw the email from the director about the–'

'Yep. Done, responded, and filed.'

'You're amazing. And the quarterly report for the small business div–'

'Sent thirty minutes ago, uploaded, and I bcc'd you.' Lucy got an extraordinary amount of satisfaction from her boss's sigh of relief.

'Did you happen to review the audit about the new—'

'Accounts opened last week and compared them against our projected prospects? Sure did.' Lucy dug her keys from her purse. 'I need to validate one thing, and you'll have it this afternoon.'

Pamela gripped Lucy's shoulder as she passed. 'What would I do without you?'

'Cry into your daily sugar-free vanilla coconut latte?' Lucy called out as she bolted down the hall.

'True story.'

Lucy waved behind her head. 'Be back in an hour.'

It'd be great to say that Lucy was on top of details like this because being a responsible employee, one her manager leaned on, one that leadership mentioned at team meetings as a 'stellar example', gave her a strong sense of personal satisfaction. And sure, a little bit of that existed. But in reality, she'd been gunning for a managerial position for the last two years, and was inching closer to cinching that deal. Rumour on the street was that the regional branch manager put in for retirement at the end of the year, and Pamela was a shoo-in for that role. Which left Pamela's local manager position open. Which *then* left Lucy dreaming that next year at this time, her name would be on a shiny bronze plaque in the lobby, welcoming in all the customers.

At her car, Lucy held the door open to release a mushroom cloud of trapped heat, tapped the seatbelt to make sure it didn't fry her skin, and took a U-turn out of the parking lot. NSYNC (*don't judge*) blasted on her playlist, and after grabbing a huge deli-meat sub – yet another thing she'd soon have to temporarily say goodbye to – she pulled into the pharmacy for a few items. Of course, she gravitated towards the cleaning aisle. So many products, so little time. Lavender, grapefruit, grease-cutting power with an organic super oil!

Her phone buzzed. She pulled it from her purse and grinned at the icon of Drew's face.

'Dude,' Drew said.

'What's up?' She propped the phone on her shoulder and reached for an all-natural pet-odour eliminator.

'I think we found the donor.'

'What?' Her breath locked in her throat. They found the donor ... *already*? The surrogacy coordinator said this could take months. *Months.* Not like forty-seven seconds. *Breathe, breathe. This is good news. Great, actually. Right? Right.* 'Are you serious?'

'Yep. Mason and I just met up to review more profiles and ... this one just stood out. We both agreed this is it. And, guess what? She's a ginger! Or at least that's what the profile stated.'

'Shut up,' Lucy said and dropped the cleaner into her basket, hoping that the bead of sweat gurgling beneath her pores wouldn't spring across her forehead. She swallowed and pushed out a grin, even though Drew couldn't see her. 'That's perfect!'

After Mason's apparently superior sperm beat out Drew's during the swimming test, Drew thought he had to give up his dream of having red-headed children. Not that this guaranteed mini-strawberry shortcakes, but it was certainly a shot. So really, this was actually perfect and exactly what her bestie hoped for. It was just all so ... fast.

'I'm thinking tomorrow I can swing by and pick you up for the psych appointment.'

She shifted the phone to her other hand and continued scouring the cleaners, doing everything she could to ignore her palpitating heart. 'Why's that?'

'I checked out the Google Maps street site, and parking looks limited. And with Bertha–'

'Betty Yellow.' She corrected him on her truck's name, as per every conversation ever about her vehicle.

'Just not sure you could back that beast up into a tiny spot.'

'I could back my beast up into any tiny spot,' she said with a terrible growl. *Nope.* 'Ugh. Why does it always sound so good in my head but never coming out?'

'Oh, Lucy-goosey. Someday your humour will land.'

'You suck.' She glanced behind her to make sure she wasn't holding up anyone who needed supplies. 'Fine, you can pick me up.'

'Seriously, when are you going to get an electric car? The amount of gas–'

'The amount of mining it takes to get your battery for your electric car–'

'*Fair.*' He chuckled. 'Call you later. I have to go back to coding all the things.'

'Better you than me.' How Drew received so much satisfaction working with software was beyond her. He explained many, *many* times what he did at work, but her eyes glazed over after about twelve seconds of him rambling about the interworkings of JavaScript and Python.

Okay, so another huge milestone was checked off the baby list. The coordinator told Lucy she'd have fluctuating feelings, sometimes moment to moment. Happy, terrified, anxious, thrilled. But right now, they all seemed to hit at once, making her dizzy.

After taking a moment to recoup, a smile crept onto her face. *We're getting close.*

She tossed her phone into her purse and moved to the self-checkout. *Shoot. Baby aspirin.* She wasn't even pregnant yet, and her forgetfulness was teetering on an all-time high. She pivoted, searched a few aisles, and stopped. Smack dab in front of her was a display of sriracha.

She had an idea.

Chapter 4

Jade

Amateur hour. For freak's sake. Jade scrubbed the red dye off her hands. How, after doing hair for almost twelve years, did she apply colour without her gloves? Red colour, no less, one of the most potent pigments. She didn't want to leave her client hanging, so when she realised her mistake, she slapped her hand with a towel, put on gloves, and finished applying. Thirty minutes later, after saturating the last strand, the dye had seeped into every pore and was surely making its way to her internal organs.

Her focus had been off this week. Even Mrs Dieterman called her out for not paying more attention to her stories. Hearing her ex-wife's voice for the first time in almost a year had rattled Jade to the core. She hated that Elizabeth's voice still held power over her, this draw to the life Jade left behind, to the shattered dreams that were once so profound. A year and a half ago, when she signed the divorce papers and packed up her belongings for a new life in Minnesota, she didn't think she'd hear from Elizabeth again. Ever. In fact, she *prayed* she wouldn't hear from Elizabeth again. She needed to cut her ex-wife out of her life completely, because Jade knew herself – a moment of weakness reminiscing about some rose-coloured memory would unravel all the healing work she'd done on herself.

It wasn't vindictive on Jade's part. Not at all. It was simply that Elizabeth had made her choice. A distinct, bold, hard-lined decision that didn't include Jade: after eight years of marriage, Elizabeth decided she wanted to start a family.

Jade didn't.

She never had, and she'd been upfront about that with Elizabeth from the start. She'd thought they were eye-to-eye, heart-to-heart, and then … and then the love of her life, her person, her *wife*, drew an impossible line. The ultimate ultimatum. And in the aftermath, Jade knew she'd never be whole again. The pain was guttural, the type that buried deep into your bones and infected everything. Even now, the wounds had healed as much as they could, but the scars would be there forever.

But the worst part of it all, as much as she ached to hate Elizabeth, she couldn't. Part of her soul had been branded by her ex, and Jade wasn't sure that she'd ever be able to fully let her go.

Jade grabbed a fresh box of latex gloves from the cabinet and ripped open the top as painful memories of her marriage flooded through her. Elizabeth had begged, pleaded, bribed, and borderline threatened to have a baby with or without Jade. Jade didn't budge – she *couldn't* budge. She had never wanted to be a mother. Being an aunt, great. Motherhood, no.

What hurt the most was that Jade and Elizabeth had been on the same page since freshman year of college when they first met. Careers, early retirement, travelling the world – *that* was their future. A family was never on the cards. And then – *wham*.

After months of begging, haranguing, and outright disparaging Jade for her 'cold heart', Elizabeth finally said she'd take care of the baby on her own, and Jade could just be there for moral support. 'You don't even have to change a diaper,' Elizabeth had yelled outside their locked bedroom door as Jade buried her face into a pillow. Even though Jade had no motherly bones in her body, she knew that was a terrible way to raise a kid.

That Dark Night flashed in her mind – the moment she knew their relationship would never recover. A document slapped on the table. Elizabeth crossing her arms. Jade bursting into tears.

Not divorce papers. Or at least not yet. No – they were *adoption* papers. Elizabeth had gone ahead and applied for adoption on her own. She said Jade could be with her on this journey, or not.

Jade left their home a week later.

The next several months, Jade downward-spiralled through bouts of anger and self-doubt. Her only relief came from her hyper-fixation on building up her salon. She spent eighty to ninety hours a week for those first few months getting Jade's on 7th off the ground. Blistered feet, bloodied hands, nearly falling asleep at the wheel on the drive home … everything was a welcome distraction from the ugly truth: Elizabeth hadn't chosen her. Jade wasn't *enough* for her wife. Her self-worth faded, slipped between her fingers. For months, she battled to regain some sense of value. A year plus later, she wasn't sure if she had fully succeeded.

The magenta soap suds swirled down the drain, and Jade wiped her hands. Her fingers would stay pink for a few days, but after some hefty exfoliation, the dye would fade. She zoned out, staring at bottles of colour. 'What am I doing …' she mumbled and tapped her fingers against the ceramic counter. Oh yeah, coffee for the client.

Admittedly, hearing Elizabeth's voice wasn't the only thing pestering her brain. She'd perked up one too many times when the salon phone rang, scoured the upcoming appointments log, and not-so-casually asked Amanda, 'Any new clients this week?' hoping she'd see Lucy's name. A strange tug-of-war between relief and disappointment occurred every time a new client was someone other than Lucy. And the relief was a much safer emotion to process.

'Here you go.' Jade brought her client a coffee and chocolate and set the timer. 'Forty-five-minute processing time. I'll be back in a bit to check on you. Need anything else?'

The client shook her head. Jade gathered up her tools and returned to the back room. While she ran the brush and bowl under the water, Amanda popped in.

'I'm so irritated right now,' Amanda said, her dark eyebrows scrunching. 'The delivery driver just said I looked like Halle Berry.'

'Yikes,' Jade said through gritted teeth as she stuffed the brush into the drying rack. 'I mean. She's beautiful, but you're twenty, not fifty. I literally just saw her on this amazing program talking about menopause. And you don't even look like a *young* Halle Berry. Maybe he meant Halle Bailey?'

Amanda rolled her dark brown eyes. 'Like, why say anything at all? Whatever. Anyway, he dropped something off for you.'

Jade tightened the top of the developer bottle and set it on the shelf. 'Shipment doesn't come in until tomorrow.'

'It's not shipment. It's a basket. Kind of … a random basket.'

The twinkle in Amanda's voice piqued Jade's ears. 'Random basket?'

Amanda inched closer with a grin. 'All I have to say is I am *soooo* curious what the thought process was behind the selection. You know, in my forensic psychology course, we're examining motivations for certain behaviour. Tomorrow, I'm looking up what would compel someone to send … that.' The phone rang and she bounced away.

I'm so confused. But also, so damn curious. Jade pushed through the swinging door, smiling at a client in Shayna's chair. When Jade rounded the corner to the reception desk, she stopped.

Facing her was a lovely wicker basket with three bottles of sriracha, a chocolate bar, and a … *huh?* … bottle of organic eucalyptus lemon cleaner. She picked up the card tucked in the middle.

Jade–

Funny story. I stopped at a pharmacy, and they had a huge display of sriracha! Who knew you can get aspirin and an (apparently) delicious sauce at a drug store? Not this gal, that's for sure. Wondered if you found any, so I thought I'd get some and put it in a thank-you basket. But then I thought, a thank-you basket should also have chocolate. But the chocolate seemed weird in the mix, so I thought I'd throw in this cleaner, which is also kind of weird, but whatever. It smells amazing, by the way. Anyway, this is the longest note in the world to say thank you again for returning my wallet. Cheers! ~ Lucy Sunshine Green

The flutter in Jade's chest shot straight to her head. She flipped over the card. Huh. No phone number. Maybe that meant Lucy didn't want Jade to contact her. Or maybe she wanted to leave her number but didn't want to be presumptuous. But Jade had to thank her for the thank you, right?

She cracked open the cleaner and sniffed. A burst of citrus and spring floated to her nose. Okay, wow. It *did* smell heavenly.

Amanda dipped her head towards the bottle. 'Dang, that smells good. But, what the hell? Sriracha and cleaning products?'

Jade bit back the smile forming and tucked the note in her back pocket. 'I found a lost wallet at the grocery store the other day, and the wallet owner just sent a thank you.' *Maintain calm demeanour.* Despite being nearly fifteen years younger than Jade, Amanda was one of the most intuitive people Jade had ever met. And Jade was in no shape to describe the surprising goosebumps on her neck, nor the reason the sensation scared her so much.

Amanda twisted her lips. 'Well, it's definitely an odd mix, but I can get behind that.'

Odd, but also kind of perfect. Lucy was sweet. With her intense work schedule and strict policy of not getting too friendly with clients, Jade hadn't made a single friend in town. She'd made that mistake a few years back. And when one of her stylists royally screwed up an ash-blond balayage on Jade's friend, Jade defending her employee ruined their relationship.

Oof. Now what? Lucy wasn't a client, so Jade wouldn't be breaking any personal protocols by reaching out. But this was Stillwater, not Chicago, and even though Jade had been here for a year, she wasn't privy to all the cultural and societal norms of the small-ish town. Would she be considered a grade-A creep if Jade found Lucy on social media and shot her a message? Back home in Chicago with a population edging towards three million, that was the norm. But here, when you have a legitimate chance of running into that person several times a year, that might be totally frowned upon.

And does she want to contact Lucy? Yes. But also ... no. It had been a long damn time since tingles fluttered in her belly the way they were now, and as warm and fuzzy as they felt in there, bouncing around, they also made Jade's stomach knot.

Jade stood at the counter way too long staring at the assortment, like somehow the sriracha bottles had a magical genie stuffed in there, and if she rubbed the side, the mythical entity would tell her what to do. Finally, she walked the basket to the break room, set it on the counter, and contemplated – *hard* – on her next move.

Chapter 5

Lucy

There is something wrong with my mind.
Lucy clicked the pencil against the desk. *Yes, yes there is.* She smirked, but quickly made an effort to look more serious, not wanting to create any flags for the MMPI exam proctor. Every so often, he'd scribble something on his clipboard, and she vowed to try to get a good peek at his notes later and see what he wrote.

She checked 'no' and moved to the next question.

The surrogacy coordinator was not kidding – this exam was like giving mental birth. The name alone, the Minnesota Multiphasic Personality Inventory, was intimidating enough. Her brain hurt, her fingers were cramping, and she kept thinking each question had a double meaning.

She stretched her hands above her head. The industrial clock in the stuffy room clicked slowly, each second dragging. She gripped the desk and twisted. *Ah* … a chorus line of cracks flew up her spine. *Come on, come on, focus.* The test was important – one of the last things needed before getting the final stamp of approval to move forward with the embryo implantation. She needed to buckle down and stop staring at the clock. It wasn't even a timed test, so why did she care how long she'd been in this boiler room?

Memories of stressing over cranky-butt Professor Waddle's English exams flooded her. So many rules for the English language. Using commas to set off conditional clauses, predicates, dangling modifiers—

And ... her focus had slipped. Again. She'd clocked nearly ninety minutes by now and was ready to bust out of this joint. She smoothed the last page against the table and gripped her pencil. The second she marked down her final answer, she was shooting up from her seat and practically sprinting towards the door.

Freedom! The hallway provided a burst of air-conditioning reprieve. The fans were probably lowered in the exam room to make people sweat, another devious physiological mind trick to ensure honesty while answering the questions. She leaned against the wall and fanned her face with her notebook. A door down the hallway opened. Mason stepped out of the waiting room and into the hall with Drew lagging a few steps behind. *Overachievers.* They all took the test at the same time, but just like finals week, the guys had finished in half the time she did.

'All done?' Mason's signature, ultra-starched button-down with a tasteful navy diamond pattern moved with his body like cardboard as he approached. She had no idea how the man sat in an office doing whatever it was civil engineers do without feeling suffocated by luxury polyester and spandex.

'*Finally.*' She pushed herself off the wall. 'I'm so tired. I'm not going to form a single coherent thought after that exam, and the doc's going to reject me during our session on account of me being a bumbling idiot.'

'No, she's not.' Drew held out a bag of smoked almonds and a bottle of water. 'Eat up. We're about to head into the final quarter.'

'I cannot believe you're making a football reference. My dad would be so proud.' She popped a few almonds in her mouth.

'How did you answer the question about if you ever feel like swearing? I said yes, but what if they think I have anger issues?'

Drew wrapped his arm around her shoulder and guided her to the office. 'No one is going to think you have anger issues. I answered yes to that, too.'

She nodded and buried the urge to ask the men how they answered each question. They were so close to the finish line, and if she did something to screw this up for them, she'd never forgive herself.

Mason held the door open, and Lucy stepped into the cosy office with dark green walls and light wood accents.

'Hi, Lucy. I'm Doctor Nelson. Good to meet you.' A petite woman with black curly hair and a dusting of grey shook Lucy's hand, then waved to the couch. 'Go ahead and take a seat.'

'We'll be in the waiting room,' Mason said, easing the door closed. 'I confirmed upon check-in that they'll come get us about halfway through.'

Of course he did.

The large taupe couch with its firm-looking back and slim armrest was not nearly as inviting as the cushy one at the fertility clinic. Lucy sat on the furthest edge and rested the water bottle on the cedar coffee table.

Dr Nelson pulled out a three-ring binder and angled a ballpoint pen over a page. 'Let's get started, shall we? Lucy, you're single, correct?'

Seriously, from now on she's gonna wear a T-shirt emblazoned with this phrase and arrows pointing at her face. She nodded, and the doctor checked a box.

For the next hour, Dr Nelson asked every invasive question possible. Periods, history of mental illness, if she struggled with depression or anxiety. 'Only when *The L Word* wasn't picked up for another season.' Lucy chuckled.

The doctor did not.

Dr Nelson asked about the worst fight she and Drew ever got

in (when he said she couldn't wear flats with her prom dress), if she had ever witnessed concerning behaviour between Mason and Drew (only when Mason claimed ABBA was superior to Fleetwood Mac), and how she felt when she was ten and her mom passed away.

Okay, that one was hard.

Dr Nelson lowered the clipboard to her lap. 'Let's talk about the meaningful relationships you've had in your life with women.'

'Like, women I've dated?' Darn her cheeks, warming as usual. She wanted to clap her hands, thank the doctor for her time, and moonwalk out of the room without another word. Lucy's life skill was chatting – with friends, customers, co-workers. But talking, *really talking*, felt about as comfortable as a pap smear.

'Yes. Partnerships. Any domestic issues, threats, cheating, trust issues?'

'No, not at all.' Lucy twisted the cap off her water bottle. 'I don't really click, romantically, with anyone.' She stuck her tongue against her cheek. 'Wait! I'm not lonely or anything. Do not write that in your little surrogacy Freudian manifesto book there.'

Dr Nelson's face showed no reaction. 'Have you *ever* connected, romantically, with anyone?'

A long moment passed where Lucy thought about stretching the truth. What would this doctor think when Lucy admitted that no, she hasn't connected with anyone ever? Surely, one would think by the time they hit their thirties, this would've happened. And yet … here we are and nada. Zip. Zilch. 'Honestly, no.' She thanked the stars that Drew and Mason weren't here listening to the emotional complexities around her non-existent love life. 'But if I said that to anyone, they'd look at me like I'm some lonely maiden destined for a life of solitude and a litter of cats, which is totally not true. First, I hate cats. Second, I have a really full life. I've got Drew, Mason, my dad, my dog. I'm good, really.'

'Would you consider yourself asexual?'

Lucy's head snapped back, and she pointed a thumb at her chest. 'Me? This girl right here? Heck no. I *love* sex. Give me all the sex.' *Oh God*, she did not just say that. She's pretty sure she may shrivel up at the edge of this fancy couch and die from embarrassment. But her brain was mush – she had only a few cells left after taking that SAT-on-steroids.

Dr Nelson flipped to a new page. 'Do you fear getting close to women because your mom passed?'

Damn. Lucy didn't feel like diving into ancient history. Her mom had died twenty-two years ago. Her dad put her in therapy for a year. End of story. 'No. Of course not. I was a child when my mom died. It barely … affects me.'

Why would she even say that? Her stomach soured at the lie. Since she was ten, rarely had a day gone by that Lucy hadn't thought about her mom. And if a day did pass when she didn't think of her mom, she practically choked on the guilt. Sometimes the pain of her mom's absence cut so deep, she would grab her mom's old scarf, douse it with Obsession for Women – her mom's favourite perfume – and sniff it until her nose burned.

Of *course* her mom's death affected her – but that didn't mean Lucy wanted to talk about it. Nope. No matter how skilled the therapist, they would not extract any more words than were strictly necessary for this assessment. These memories, these feelings were hers to keep, held close to her heart, protected in an internal time capsule. No one would ever understand what it had been like for Lucy to lose her hero. Not even Drew.

She crossed her arms. 'I thought this was to assess my mental stability for carrying a baby for my friends, not about my love life.'

'This meeting is to assess the entire individual to make sure you have the proper coping mechanisms during this journey, and the right support in place for potential postpartum depression. We want to protect you and the fathers and prevent separation anxiety or regret when handing over the newborn.'

Regret? *Not gonna happen.* 'I've never wanted children.'

'Why is that?'

Lucy flashed three fingers. 'Poop, puke, and more poop.' Fine, the reasons were deeper than that. And yes, she was in a therapist's office, divulging at least some of her deep, dark secrets. But talking about the fact she lacked the emotional capacity to care, and the amount of nurture it would take to have a child, might be counterintuitive to trying to prove she could squeeze a baby out for her friends.

The doctor studied Lucy. 'When you're feeling anxious or overwhelmed, what is your go-to coping mechanism?'

Lucy stared at the window blinds, ran her tongue against the ridges of her teeth. 'Ah, I guess rewatching my favourite shows, reading, knitting, spending time with my dad. I'm an eighty-year-old wrapped in a thirty-two-year-old body. Just slap a cardigan on me and you wouldn't know the difference.'

Dr Nelson gave a gentle smile but remained silent for several long moments. 'Would you say you use humour as a coping mechanism?'

Geezus. Man, this doc was going for the jugular. 'Would it be better if I was sitting here cantankerous and crying?' Lucy didn't like her tone towards the doctor. But the question was valid.

'Not at all. Just trying to dive into the inner workings of Lucy Green.'

Another hour flew by as Lucy answered life history and family questions. Dr Nelson shook her pen, scribbled, and grabbed a new one. 'Let's talk separation anxiety. How will you keep detached from the foetus?'

Lucy breathed out as heat swept her face. 'I don't think it'll be an issue.'

'How so?'

Lucy wrapped her foot around her ankle. She opened and closed her mouth several times before any words formulated. This question was not a shock. She had anticipated it and even prepared a little. But saying it out loud made her wiggle in the seat. 'I'm going to say something that might disqualify me completely. Like, seriously.'

Dr Nelson placed her hands in her lap with zero expression. 'This is the time to get it out. Please share.'

Here goes nothing. 'There are times that I am *so* not worried about connecting with Drew and Mason's baby that I feel like I'm a psychopath.' She breathed in and exhaled a hefty breath. 'Like, I want it to be healthy and whatever. But I really struggle to make, like, real connections with people. I don't think that will change just 'cause it's a bunch of growing cells housed in my belly.'

Dr Nelson nodded but remained silent.

'Honestly, Drew and my dad are really the only people I feel anything … deep for. Please don't say that to Mason.' She could picture Mason's sweet, analytic soul breaking down what that meant and taking it as a personal blow, not realising that Lucy's lack of fuzzy, close feelings had always been *her* issue, and not a reflection on others. 'It's sort of been the crux of my relationship issues. One common theme from break-ups is that the women I dated felt like I could take them or leave them. And it sounds really crappy, but they weren't wrong. I was never disrespectful, obviously. And we seemed to enjoy each other's company. But when it was over, I just sort of moved on without looking back. I wasn't really sad about it.'

Dr Nelson nodded. 'Good news. You're not a psychopath. But it sounds to me like you tend to dissociate.'

Lucy tugged at her skirt. 'Oh, great. I saw a movie like that once. Does that mean I have multiple personalities and murder people while sleepwalking?'

The doctor smiled. But no laughter.

'Tough crowd,' Lucy muttered.

'Dissociation or *multiple personalities*' – Dr Nelson air quoted – 'at least in the way you are speaking of, is not what this is. What you're talking about is lacking the ability to feel intimacy. And that's not always a bad thing. In this case, being a surrogate, it may actually help you.' She looked at her watch. 'Time to bring in the fathers.'

Lucy shuffled to the middle of the couch, then the end, then stood. The men probably wanted to sit together, which meant she had to choose which side to sit on. Which would be Drew, of course, but she didn't want Mason to feel bad. Mason was sensitive and kind, and the last thing she wanted was to highlight her allegiance to Drew. *Or am I overthinking this??*

When the dads entered the room, she stepped to the left, then turned and stumbled a few inches. 'Um, do I sit in the middle of you two, or side, or–'

'Why don't you sit in the middle?' Mason lowered himself into the right corner.

Drew took a seat on the opposite end, and she plunked down between them.

Dr Nelson crossed her trousered legs. 'How did you all meet?'

Kindergarten, a shared love of Cheerios, art, and dinosaurs.

'I met Drew at our Catholic school when we were six. Instant best friends, even though he stole my grape-scented pencil.'

Drew pushed up the sleeves of his lightweight Henley. 'You're such a liar. You know Jenny Reed took it, but you were crushing on her and couldn't see past the lies.'

'I was six!' Lucy elbowed him in the arm. 'And when Drew and Mason started dating junior year, Mason became a close second bestie.'

Drew lifted a finger. 'But I'm still number one.'

'Yes, Drew. You are the one and only forever.' Lucy groaned. 'I have my half-heart best friend tattoo with your name to prove it.'

Dr Nelson's eyebrow flicked, and she scribbled. 'Do you really have matching tattoos?'

'Sorry, don't write that down. I'm kidding.' Lucy waved her hands. 'For his twenty-fifth birthday, I got a temporary one as a prank and told him it was real.'

'We did go the next year and actually got tattoos.' Drew lifted his jeans to show a Gemini zodiac sign on his ankle. 'But not matching.'

The doctor glanced at Mason. 'Did you get one as well?'

'Absolutely not.' Mason chuckled. 'Nope, I leave the shenanigans up to these two.'

The visual of perfectly sanitised, manicured, and polite Mason getting his body inked by a burly bear with a nose full of piercings almost made Lucy crack up. She snapped her stretch watch band against her wrist to keep her composure.

If Lucy thought they had already gotten personal this past hour, she had no idea how much deeper they were about to dive. The doc bombarded her with so many questions, she felt like the little metal ball in an arcade pinball machine.

'If you're in a horrible car accident, do the fathers have permission to keep you alive until the gestation date?' (*yikes, um ... yep*)

'If the fathers decide they don't want the child anymore, do you still waive rights to adopt?' (*of course*)

'Are you okay being interviewed by media?' (*sure*)

'If the fathers divorce, do you waive your rights to testify in a custody hearing?' (*definitely*)

'Do you agree to sign a form stating you will withhold from having sex with a biological male?' (*um, duh*)

'If you have a vaginal birth, can the husbands watch the baby eject, or do you request they stay at your shoulder?' (*The money shot? Hmmm. Need to think about this one.*)

Lucy glanced at both men. Drew was twisting his wedding band, and Mason was a statue. She stared a moment longer just to confirm Mason blinked.

Dr Nelson closed the binder and held it against her chest. 'Do you have any concerns about being a gestational carrier for Drew and Mason?'

Lucy's chest filled with warmth. She had so many questions about life, didn't always know the direction she would take, or what her future would hold. And even though admittedly, there was still a part of her terrified of *having a freaking baby*, she'd never doubted that Drew and Mason would be amazing fathers. 'None whatsoever.'

Dr Nelson nodded and her gaze passed over the men. 'Gentlemen? Any concerns about Lucy being a gestational carrier for you?'

'No.' Drew's and Mason's voices rang in unison.

'Okay.' Dr Nelson stood and rolled the chair under the desk. 'I'll write up my assessment, review your MMPI, and send the findings to the fertility clinic. I'll also include the confirmation from today that all final medical decisions, as to what happens with Lucy's body, including termination, are her sole decision. You'll need to file that paperwork with your lawyer prior to implantation.'

Lucy thanked Dr Nelson for her time and followed the men to the elevator in silence. Their faces looked as emotionally fried as she felt.

When Lucy and Drew had casually floated the idea of surrogacy ten plus years ago, she could never have predicted the amount of effort that would go into the journey. She was so focused on the medical part of it – how she would *get* pregnant. For the last two years, when they dived into more serious discussions and research, she had no clue the amount of talking she'd have to do. Honestly, it was all exhausting. After she gave birth, she was going to take a weeklong vacation to a bunker in the forest. Alone.

The car ride home was quieter than usual. After Drew and Mason dropped her off, she waved while they backed out of the driveway, then jiggled her key into the door.

Chucky hoisted himself up with his arthritic legs and trotted over to her, his tail wildly wagging. 'Hi, baby! Were you a good boy?' After showering him with belly rubs and ear scratches, she made a sandwich and plopped on the couch. Chucky nestled himself next to her.

She grabbed her phone for her obligatory five-minute check-in with her dad. When she was younger and he was working shifts at the post office, he took his break precisely at the time when the school bus dropped her off, and he'd call her on the house phone. If she didn't answer by the second ring, there'd be extra chores for her that evening. He'd ask her the same three things: how was school, did you eat, do you have homework. When she moved out after high school, she called him once a night and always asked him three random questions.

He picked up on the second ring.

'Did you order the extra sheets for the guest bed, did you take your blood pressure medication, and did you see that the Vikings are going to suck in the fall?'

'Yep, yep, and you're wrong.' A heavy breath sounded over the phone, and she could just imagine him sitting in his favourite chair for their chat. 'You had your fancy shrink appointment today?'

'Sure did.' She withheld telling him that no one used the word 'shrink' anymore.

'Well, I figure they found you completely unfit, and you all can knock this nonsense off.'

To the outside world, his words might seem harsh, but she knew his heart. She kicked off her slippers and tucked her feet under her legs. 'If that happens, you have to tell Drew.'

'Hell no. That boy used to be so scrawny. Such a little shit. Now he has muscles for days. If I told him that, he'd probably throw me over his shoulder and toss me in the cornfields.' The sound of her dad gulping back a drink echoed through the phone. 'Guess you better stick with your plan then, huh?'

'Guess so.' Chucky nudged Lucy for more rubs. She obliged. 'On Sunday, you want rhubarb pie, or should I bring some bars?'

'Bring the ones with the cornflakes and peanut butter on the bottom,' he said. 'Time's up. Gotta go feed the chickens. All righty.'

And with that, per Dad MO, he clicked off without saying goodbye, which was fine enough for her tonight anyway. She needed to veg out after today. Her tongue felt raw, and her brain was crispy. She turned on the TV, but choosing something to stream right now sounded awful.

Maybe a brain-dead quick scroll through social media would help her achieve optimal zone-out status. She opened an app, looked at the gazillion notifications from not opening the app for six months – and noticed the little message icon flashing.

She tapped, and a picture popped onto her screen: the gift basket she'd sent to the salon earlier today. Lucy perked up. Her chest perked. Her freaking skin perked.

I was confused at first. Sriracha makes sense. Chocolate, always a crowd pleaser. But the eucalyptus spray, I didn't understand. Until I did. Heavenly. I've sprayed it over the whole salon, my car, my boots, and am currently contemplating taking a bath in it. Anyway, just wanted to thank you for the gift. Hope you have a great weekend! ~Jade

Lucy read the message more than a dozen times. She could leave it right there, smile at the kind note, and then go to bed. Done. But …

'What do you think, Chucky? Thoughts on the matter?' She rubbed his scruff.

The dog cocked his head. Clearly, no help at all.

Lucy raised and lowered her twitchy thumbs over the screen so many times that she was pretty sure her fingers were going to cramp. *What do I do?* Let this go, or take a chance? She kept looking at Chucky, and then back at the phone, hoping that one of them would give her the clarity she needed. After exhaling a full breath, she straightened her back and tapped the screen.

Chapter 6

Jade

Jade ripped off her bra and threw it in the corner, the clasp hitting the bare, stark-white bedroom wall with a ding. At this moment, she wanted nothing but to launch herself superwoman-style onto her bed and not move until she'd slept for a solid twelve hours.

Owning a business was everything she'd dreamed of. The salon had done well its first year, turning an actual profit, which was already much more than the 'experts' (her judgemental-as-hell parents) had predicted. She'd already done more than what her ex said she could do. Even more than what Jade herself thought possible. Starting next year, assuming things kept going well, she should even be able to offer health insurance to the dozen stylists in her salon – a rarity in her field.

Owning a business was also everything nightmares were made of. While the clients and staff were amazing, the invoices, taxes, banking, supply lists, back-orders, auditing, inventory … not amazing. Everything about this owning-your-own-business world was an Amy Winehouse beehive-level learning curve. During her marriage, Jade hadn't filed a tax return, looked for insurance, or opened a credit card account on her own. She hadn't even so much as paid a bill, as her wife took care of all their finances. And now, juggling a full day of hairstyling followed by two hours of paperwork at night, well … it was picking at her sanity.

Jade turned over and flung her wrist over her eyes, willing herself to stand so she could brush her teeth and slip into pyjamas before she fell asleep. She peeked at the clock resting on her nightstand. 7:07 p.m.

'Power through,' she mumbled and propped to her elbows, and then to a sitting position. She exhaled.

A sea of numbers and paperwork was soon drowning her. Sometimes Jade shot up at night, sweating, trying to remember if she'd forgotten to pay the electricity bill, or the colour distributor. She hated herself for the fleeting desire to ask her ex for help. Elizabeth was always so organised, so controlled, so ten steps ahead of everyone. Graduated early, promoted early, rose in the ranks at the communication firm where she worked in record time. Vowed to be the youngest VP in the history of the company, and then made it happen. Jade had no doubt that whatever Elizabeth put her mind to, she'd succeed at. But even though Jade scrambled and hustled, she always felt like she was lagging.

After wiggling back into the headboard, she pulled her laptop onto her lap and scanned her emails. She opened her reports from the previous month and reviewed the types of services the stylists performed, as well as which stylists brought in the highest profit margin. She squinted, hoping to concentrate on which sale she should run to move product without dipping too much into the profits. Walk-ins vs appointments, perms vs colours, backbar stock vs sellable product … she ground a knuckle into her eye socket.

A ping sounded, signalling a direct message, but she ignored it. Talking all day, being 'on', depleted her. Right now, she didn't care who it was, though her brain did flag the warning that it could be Elizabeth trying yet another avenue to contact her …

Funny how dynamics changed in a relationship. For years, it was Jade trying to contact an unreachable Elizabeth. Jade liked to blame Elizabeth for the demise of their marriage because she wanted to be a mom. But truthfully, their marriage had cracked years prior. Elizabeth was a star, and she shone the brightest in the room – any room. Hyper-driven, successful, beautiful. *Loud.* 'She sure is the life of the party, isn't she?' Jade's mother would beam, staring at Elizabeth with the pride that Jade craved. Jade was pushed to the side, not heard or seen. Her wife took up all the space, and there was none left for her. Sometimes Elizabeth would forget to text her back, or show up late for dinner, and more than once she forgot their anniversary because work or something else besides Jade took precedence.

Of course, at first, Jade excused it all. She loved Elizabeth so hard that she convinced herself Elizabeth's scraps were enough. But after a few years of telling herself that the morsels of time Elizabeth flung her way were enough, something in Jade broke.

She would never forget the odd behaviour that became her wake-up call. One evening, after Elizabeth was late for dinner again, Jade had stepped away from the now-cold pasta primavera to take an 'important' phone call from a phantom number. She faked the conversation all the way to their bedroom, where she closed the door, then sat shaking on the side of the bed, feverishly asking herself *What the hell am I doing?*

Another time, Jade struck up a conversation with a stranger at the bar. Elizabeth was right next to her as Jade laughed loudly with the stranger about something inane, her back to Elizabeth. *What the hell am I doing?* she asked herself again.

But this time, she had an answer. Obviously, she wanted to prove how independent and cool she was. Obviously, she wanted to show her wife that if Elizabeth could mingle at parties and ignore Jade, well, Jade could ignore her too.

That night, as Jade lay next to her sleeping wife, everything inside her screamed for more. She wanted more than scraps. She *deserved* more than scraps. Instead, she had let herself slip away. The strong, confident Jade of the past didn't exist anymore. Somehow, in her marriage, she'd become needy and small – and full of shame.

Now, a year later, Elizabeth seemed determined to talk. And Jade wasn't having it. *You didn't want me then. So, you can't have me now.*

So, no, Jade wouldn't peek at the social media message.

Right now, she had to figure out why Shayna, who was the top earner at the salon last year, had dropped in her commissions. In the beauty industry, business could be fickle, and fluctuations were normal. Everyone wanted to be beautiful right before holidays, school, and before the summer. And summer months were slow.

But Shayna had progressively dipped over the last several months. Jade scrolled through the logs, auditing until she was damn near dizzy, noticing more '*R' next to clients' names than she'd seen all year. The dreaded '*R' for 'redo'. The worst four-letter word in a salon's vocabulary – fixing a client's hair for free when they left unhappy. It happens to all of them, from time to time. Jade had even done one last week for a client who added teal highlights. Jade had warned her that the colour literally slides off the hair, and she shouldn't shampoo every day. But the client came back a week later upset about the faded green strands, so Jade slapped on more colour and ate the cost.

But according to this audit, Shayna's re-dos had been increasing. A lot. *Shit.* Thankfully Shayna's clients were loyal and had not complained to Jade. But if word got out that Jade's salon was slipping in quality, it could spread through the town like embers in a dry forest. And not only were there more re-dos, but she was also seeing fewer clients per day than normal. Jade's chest squeezed tight, constricting her air, and she slammed her laptop shut. After the bad break-up Shayna had a few months ago – which clearly affected her work performance – the last thing Jade wanted to do was to point out a slump and lag time between clients and offer some demeaning coaching for her former top stylist. But she had to.

Another cell phone ping. *Maybe it's not her ex ... Could it be Lucy?* A quick burst of hope bounced through Jade, cutting through the stress-inducing salon thought cycle, but she pushed it away as quickly as it arrived. She'd messaged Lucy three days ago about the gift basket and never heard back. Which was just fine with Jade. *Sort of.*

With her growling belly clamouring harder than her tired eyes, she forced herself down the hall to the kitchen for a snack. As she sank her teeth into a PB&J, she blinked at the tiny pink floral pattern covering the kitchen walls. *Oof*, that wallpaper needed to be ripped down and repainted. Maybe in a soft blue-grey. Or red. Or literally any other colour. The landlord had offered to pay for supplies if she did the work. When she moved in, she thought she'd only be here for a year before purchasing a home. Now, with no home purchase in sight, she'd just signed another yearlong lease and still wasn't feeling remotely settled. Maybe she should take her landlord up on that offer and try to make this place feel more like her own ...

Focus, focus. Jade stepped towards the bedroom to review the digital inventory list, then pivoted sharply and marched into the bathroom, deciding that a bubble bath with her rain sound machine and candles was exactly what she needed.

She dropped her clothes, wrapped a towel around herself, and ran the water. Lavender and mint-scented bubbles filled the tub, and she breathed in. She leaned against the door and flipped on her socials while she waited for the tub to fill. Her heart skipped and stuck in her throat when she saw a DM from Lucy.

> Lucy: *I'm pretty sure there's an actual warning label on the bottle that says 'do not use cleaner as a bubble bath'. You think the eucalyptus lemon smelled good? Definitely try the grapefruit one. I contemplated*

taking a tiny taste until every Mr. Yuck sticker from my childhood flashed through my mind, warning me not to eat the cleaner.

Jade smiled at the message and cracked her thumb knuckles.

Okay. I will add this to the long list of things that I should not do, per childhood programming: walk on the sidewalk, eat my veggies, stay in school, and ignore bullies (terrible advice by the way). I think I'm batting at about 50%.

The skipping in Jade's heart upgraded to thumping when three bubbles appeared on the screen.

Lucy: *Veggies are disgusting, bullies should be throat punched, and sidewalks are overrated.*

Jade: *Veggies are disgusting? For real, or just kidding?*

Lucy: *No, for real. Oh, wait. I do like corn on the cob with butter and salt. Does that count?*

Jade: *Corn is like the bottom of the barrel of all the veggies.*

Lucy: *I'll chow down a Caesar every once in a while. Dripping with dressing and a half-pound of cheese, of course.*

Lucy: *Oh wait, let me guess. You eat veggies regularly, get three squares a day, and practice gratitude meditation for thirty minutes every morning.*

Jade: *One out of three isn't a bad guess. I'm vegetarian.*

Lucy: *Wait, really? No.*

Jade: *Yep, since I was fifteen.*

Lucy: *Oh, you poor thing. Does that mean no burgers, no steak, no nothing?*

Jade: *That's what that means.*

Lucy: *Growing up, we basically had slabs of meat and something resembling a veggie for dinner. I even used to hunt with my dad but couldn't actually pull the trigger. Never mind that it was freaking cold and kind of boring.*

'Oh shit!' The water sloshed onto the floor and Jade flung her phone to the side. The towel dropped to her feet as she dashed to the tub. *Crap, crap.* She cranked the water off, lifted the plug drain with a gurgling pop, and frantically grabbed any towel available to sop up the wet floor.

'Hello? Hello?'

What the hell? Jade jolted at the sound of the voice, looked at her cell facing sunny-side up with Lucy's tilted head filling the screen. *Ack!* Jade threw the towel over the phone. 'Oh my God! Did I butt-dial you?'

'Well, not sure if you used actual cheeks, but you did video call me.'

That did *not* just happen. *Oh my dear God, please can a crater come swallow me whole?* Heat fanned Jade's face. 'You saw my boobs!' She wrapped a robe around herself and lifted the towel from the phone. 'I think I might die, now. You might need to call me back at my funeral.'

Lucy's hand covered her mouth. She giggled and shook her head. 'I didn't see your boobs.'

'Yes, you did.' Jade wanted the tub to fall through the floor and take her with it. 'Pretty sure you got my left tit in a weird angle. The left one isn't even my good one!'

Laughter rang through the phone. Now pink flushed Lucy's pale cheeks. 'I promise you I didn't. I wasn't even sure how to answer the video call – I've never used video calling over social media. Anyway, when I did, the screen went black.'

'Oh, whew.' Jade was pretty sure Lucy was lying, but for right now, she'd take the gift. Honestly. How does stuff like this even happen? 'I was about to get in the tub, and it overflowed, and I tossed the phone. Must've hit the button.'

Lucy propped herself up to a sitting position. 'You didn't put the eucalyptus cleaner in there, did you?'

'No, not today. Although you were right – that stuff smelled amazing. But I did add lavender and mint bubbles.' Jade hiked up her robe, careful not to flash the goods at Lucy, and sat on the edge of the flat-lipped tub. She slipped her feet into the tub. *Oh ... heavenly.* The warm water seeped its heat into her sore muscles. 'I have a vanilla candle buried somewhere in the closet that I was thinking of lighting, but it seemed too complicated.'

'Good choice.' Lucy grinned. 'Too many scents and soon you'll smell like an indecisive twelve-year-old leaving a mall perfume shop.'

A loud snore boomed through the phone.

'Was that you?'

'No. It's my dog, Chucky.' Lucy lowered the phone screen to a sleeping, fluffy golden dog on the floor. She ran her fingers across the dog's back.

Jade swirled the water with her feet. 'He's sweet. What kind of dog?'

Lucy shrugged. 'Not sure. They think he's a Shar Pei, golden retriever mix. He wandered onto my dad's farm about four years ago. No tags, no nothing. Poor thing was super dirty and skinny. I searched for a month for the owner and no one came forward, so I got to adopt him.'

Adoption. Hearing the word shouldn't make Jade's shoulders stiffen. 'Lucky pup.'

'Ah, I'm the one who's lucky. I think he's the only entity in my life that can handle me on a regular basis.' Lucy gave him one more scratch. 'And he's such a good guard dog. Watch this. Chucky – serial killer at the door. Get him!'

The dog peeked up with one uninterested eye and went back to sleep.

'Anyway,' Lucy said, 'I better let you get back to your eucalyptus-cleaner-free bath.'

'Suppose so.' *Don't do it, don't do it, don't do it.* 'I know it's super last minute, but … Want to grab a drink later tonight?' *Holy shit, why did I just do that?*

Jade could see Lucy's smile drop and throat roll with a swallow. 'Oh, sorry, I have plans.'

Whew. Saved. 'Of course. People with lives usually have plans on a Saturday night.' Jade forced out as self-deflecting of a chuckle as she could. 'Well, have a good n–'

'How about coffee in the morning?' The words seemed to tumble out, and Lucy pulled in her lips.

Jade stopped breathing. She wasn't ready for this. She was not even remotely at a place in her life where she could have coffee with a cute, sparkly woman that she thought about a little too much. *Say no, say no.* 'Sounds great.'

What in the absolute hell am I doing? When Jade hung up the phone, she was filled with so much regret for saying yes, that she nearly called back. But, instead of making yet another rash decision, she slipped her entire body into the tub and sighed.

Tonight, regret.

Tomorrow, she'd decide if she'd go through with meeting Lucy or not.

Chapter 7

Lucy

Lucy exhaled to try and calm her racing pulse. She still had an hour before she was meeting Jade for their coffee *non-date*, but at this rate, she'd probably keel over with a heart attack before she arrived.

She hadn't slept well the previous night. Who knew that a shot of adrenaline from talking to a bathrobe-laden Jade would produce the type of dreams she had? She really needed to get out more. Perhaps have some meaningless sex with a random stranger to release some tension. It had been a while since her last hook-up – inching towards six months or so. Probably time to rev things up before she entered celibate purgatory with the impending inception.

Lying to Jade was probably not a great way to start a friendship. When Jade asked her out for a drink, Lucy said she had plans. She didn't. At least, besides sending stupid memes and reels to Drew, binge-watching *Schitt's Creek* – again – and rubbing Chucky's belly. The problem was, when Jade asked, Lucy froze. Did she mean a date? Maybe? No. Lucy shook her head to snap out of the down-pouring of thoughts. The decision to ask Jade for coffee was impulsive. But so far, Lucy had no regrets.

She did *kind of* wish she'd said yes to the original offer of drinks last night. I mean, really – Jade had just asked for a drink. That was it. Why did Lucy go and get all up in her head about it? Sure, Jade was beautiful, had legs for days, and seemed kind-hearted, but Lucy didn't know her very well. Not well enough to warrant all this overthinking. *Right?* Right. So, her belly really needed to stop twisting so ferociously.

Itchiness invaded her body. First her arms, then her neck, then her legs. What if Jade really liked her? She might want to move in, get married, and get another rescue pup. Lucy would have to turn her down, then smile when she ran into her in town. She could already see herself giving Jade an awkward one-arm hug with a solid pat on the back and making a mental note to avoid whatever area they ran into each other for the rest of time. Like the grocery store. Lucy already knew they shopped at the same grocery store, so she'd have to go to the other one, which was a very inconvenient ten extra minutes away.

Spinning. She was spinning.

She dabbed her make-up brush into the palette and added a pop of colour to her eyes, walked under a spritzed perfume mist, and brushed her teeth a second time.

A low bark sounded in the kitchen. Chucky's tail wagged as he stood at the sliding glass door, watching the squirrels run up the maple tree. She crouched down. 'Be good while I'm gone. No ragers. Got it?' She scratched his ears, refreshed his water, and hopped into her truck for the drive downtown.

Even after a lifetime of being here, downtown was still one of her favourite places on earth. From the quaint art shops to indie bookstores, from the ma-and-pa restaurants to the specialty ice cream shops, downtown was the heartbeat of the city. In the summer, it filled with an energetic life – lots of people strolling store to store, handwritten chalk signs on the sidewalk touting the sales of the day or an art crawl announcement, the buzz of excitement as tourists took in the view of the water and bridge.

Lucy cranked down her windows as she navigated Betty Yellow through town. The warm air smelled of minerals from the Croix River and smoke from local pubs firing up their grills for the day. Riverboats were lined up on the water, waiting for the Stillwater mix of tourists and locals to join for a jaunt around the river.

The sidewalks were full of shoppers carrying bags and pushing strollers. Lucy waited at the crosswalk as a mom scooped a child in her arms and scooted as the light turned from yellow to red.

After pulling into a parking spot, Lucy shook the gear into neutral and killed the engine, then flipped down the mirror to check that no mascara flakes had fallen. *Okay, okay. I got this. It's just freaking coffee.* She rolled her shoulders, slammed the heavy truck door, and dashed across the street.

Not a date. Not a date.

When she turned the corner, her breath hitched at seeing Jade sitting inside next to the large window of the coffee shop, sipping from a mug and scrolling through her phone. Lucy stopped dead in her tracks and a stroller nearly banged into the back of her ankles. Not a date, but *uff da*. Jade was beautiful. Obviously, Lucy knew that from the interaction at the store and from the video call last night. But did she somehow forget how Jade's sharp jawline seemed to highlight her smooth, porcelain skin? How her apple cheekbones popped under that lavender purple hair? Lucy gripped the front door and breathed in through her nose.

The shop was loud and festive, with the buzz of conversation and the metallic clicking of silverware against plates and mugs. Freshly brewed coffee and buttery dough scents filled the air. A rainbow flag adorned the exposed brick from the early-nineteenth-century building, and the sun shone through the large windows, reflecting off the shiny, hardwood floors.

Lucy bounced over to the small white two-seater table where

Jade was sitting, definitely not *not* noticing her long, bare legs accentuated beautifully in cut-off denim shorts. 'Hey!'

Jade set down the mug and stood. 'Hey, you.'

Hug or no hug?

Jade fiddled with a trio of rings on her index finger.

Lucy bounced on her toes. She wanted to hug Jade. She was a self-proclaimed hugger. She squeezed most anyone she'd met more than once. But their face-to-face meeting in the grocery store was the only time they'd met in person. She probably shouldn't feel drawn, magnetically, to touch her. *Pull it together, Green.* 'Gonna grab a drink. Need anything?'

'Nope, I'm good. I just got a salted maple latte. Incredible.'

'Oh, that sounds amazing. Okay, be right back.' Lucy had apparently forgotten to breathe in the last minute, because as she turned, she sucked in a sharp breath like a drowning woman. Fighting off a touch of light-headedness, she headed to the counter.

The rustic chalkboard menu listed a gazillion items she wanted, and hardly any she could have. In preparation for pregnancy, she'd stopped drinking almost all caffeine last week. Her gaze stopped at the 'Sweet & Salty' drink. *Perfect.*

After grabbing the cup from the pick-up station, she returned to the table, and slowly slid into the chair, careful not to spill.

Jade peeked at the mug. 'Oh, what's that?'

'Salted hot chocolate.' Lucy took a sip. The whipped cream melted on her tongue and the rush of chocolate hit her brain. *Yum.* Who needed caffeine when you had this?

'No coffee?'

She tipped the cup to her mouth. 'Nope. Laying off the caffeine for a while.'

'Why would you do something so terrible?' Jade smiled.

Oh boy. She had a really great smile. Soft mouth, straight white teeth, a small dimple on the corner of her left cheek. 'Saving the coffee bean plants, one cup at a time.'

Now was not the time to talk about the surrogacy. It was hard to gauge how people would react, or if they would treat her differently, or if they would think the whole process was bizarre. Lucy hadn't broadcasted it to hardly anyone besides her dad. And although he was supportive –he'd practically helped raise Drew when they were kids – he was obviously worried. 'Your heart's gonna break when you gotta hand over the kid,' he'd said. The words came from a good place, but his comment stung.

The limelight made Lucy uneasy. When Lucy needed help ironing out some kinks around HR time off and insurance, she reluctantly, pre-emptively told her manager Pamela about the surrogacy – who'd immediately fawned over Lucy like she was some local superhero – and Lucy couldn't handle it. She ended up shutting her office door, a rarity, and buried herself in paperwork for the rest of the afternoon.

Drew fawned. Mason fawned. No reason for any other potential fawning.

'Is the salon open today?'

'We're closed Sundays.' Jade picked at a rhubarb scone and popped a piece in her mouth. 'Isn't Sunday the day of rest?'

Lucy smacked her lips, unsure how to read the serious expression on Jade's face. Lucy was opened-minded about everything but wasn't sure about getting too close with folks who had fundamentally different beliefs than her own. 'I'm gay,' she blurted. 'Like *super* gay.'

'Super gay, huh?' Jade said with a glint in her lovely eyes. 'I didn't realise there was a step up from being just regular gay like me.'

The confirmation that Jade was queer tickled something inside Lucy. She sipped on the hot chocolate and swallowed back all the Dr Nelson-style invasive questions she suddenly wanted to lob at Jade about her relationship status.

'I was kidding about Sunday being the day of rest.' Jade plucked another chunk of scone. 'Well, sort of. I close the shop that day, but that doesn't mean I rest.' She chuckled. 'I usually use Sundays to catch up on all the shit I neglected the entire week. So, it's more like errand day. Clean-house day. "Drown myself in paperwork" day.'

The shrill sounds of metal chairs moving against the floor and the raucous voices of a loud group of teens taking selfies at the table next to them made Lucy scoot her chair closer to Jade. Or at least that was what she told herself. 'Is there a ton of paperwork?'

'So much paperwork. And I'm just not a numbers person. I honestly don't understand how *anyone* could like numbers.' Jade shivered.

The sun beaming through the floor-to-ceiling windows caught the amber highlights nestled among the green in Jade's hazel eyes. Her mascara-free eyelashes were thick and black and the soft crinkling around the edges showed years' worth of smiles. *God, she's pretty.* Lucy lowered her mug. 'I love numbers.'

The corner of Jade's lip curled. 'No. You can't actually. Right?'

'For real. I really do. I work at Inspire Bank.'

'No way.' Jade wiped the foam from the corner of her lip. Her plush, lovely, *full* lip.

Lucy tried not to stare.

'What do you do there?' Jade asked.

'Account manager. But every week, I'm a teller for a few hours. I love being an account manager, but it turns out I really missed the quick, snappy interactions with customers.' Lucy peeked outside at the folks walking on the sidewalk, their sun hats planted firmly on their heads. The summer traffic was heavy. A horn honked loudly – a rarity for Stillwater's typically polite drivers. Lucy settled back in her seat and finished the rest of her hot chocolate as they chatted about work, clients, and horrible haircut stories. Apparently, the mullet was making a comeback.

'I feel bad that we've taken this table for so long.' Jade wadded a napkin in her hand as Lucy glanced at her watch and did a double-take. How had a whole hour gone by already?

She looked back up at Jade, her heart plunging at the clear sign Jade was done with the non-date.

'Want to walk down by the river?' Jade asked as she stood.

Lucy's heart sprang back up in her chest – a foreign sensation, but not entirely unwelcome, and she rose from her chair with a smile. 'Sure!'

The door jingled as they exited, and Lucy pulled her sunglasses out of her purse.

'The heat finally broke.' Jade stepped to the side to avoid an oncoming family marching towards them.

'Such a Minnesota thing to say. Do they do that in Chicago?'

'Talk about the weather? Of course, we do. That's not exclusive to Minnesotans. Although, folks around here seem a little obsessed with it.' Jade pushed the button at the crosswalk and waited. 'People here also seem to have more time, or *take* more time, I guess. The pace is slower. I'm kind of starting to fall in love with this town more than I ever dreamed I would.'

The light turned green, and the crosswalk countdown flashed. Lucy loved living in Stillwater. Hot, cold, it didn't matter. The city was thumping, thriving, filled with cute shops, amazing food, and lush scenery. A Midwestern city that gave off a coastal-town vibe. A trolley bumped by, ringing the bell as it passed, and they moved towards the river. The faint sound of a violin playing on a street corner wafted through the air.

'Have you ever been on one of those?' Jade asked, nudging her head to the river where crew members dashed around a riverboat setting up tables, likely getting ready for a lunch tour, or a private reception.

'A riverboat? Yes, lots of times.' This used to be an annual thing Lucy and her dad did and she loved it. Stillwater is such a vibrant, radiant town from the street. But seeing the city from the river, looking out through the white pines, sugar maples, and oaks, was an entirely different experience. Serene, meditative, peaceful. Every boat ride, whether on a riverboat or canoe, rejuvenated Lucy's soul. She made a quick pact with herself: if this budding friendship with Jade fully evolved, she'd show Jade the city from the water.

Lucy looped her thumb around the edge of her purse and slowed her pace. 'Do you miss Chicago?'

Jade kicked a small rock on the sidewalk. 'Parts of it, yes. Parts, no. I miss my friends. My parents still live there, but we're not really close. I have two sisters and some nieces and nephews, but they're a few hours outside of Chicago. I love them to death, of course, but we all have such busy lives that I didn't see them that much. I talk to my younger sister Bethany the most. Probably because she doesn't have any kids.' Jade chuckled. 'That sounds terrible, but I just mean that she has way more time than my older sister, who's always juggling the kids and her job. And Bethany's getting her PhD, so she has intense periods of work time, but then chunks of downtime during breaks. I usually just wait till she reaches out because I never know when those times will be.'

Lucy knew what she was asking with the 'miss Chicago' question, but either Jade didn't pick up what she was throwing down, or she didn't want to answer. 'Anyone, um, special back home?' *Yep, as subtle as a hand grenade.*

Jade cleared her throat and took so long to respond that Lucy rolled her lip into her mouth and almost apologised.

'Not anymore.' Jade ran her finger through her lavender hair and focused on the ground. 'You?'

Lucy shook her head. 'Not ever.'

Jade didn't ask any follow-up questions, *thank God*. Because really, how do you go about explaining that fun little morsel to an outsider who probably couldn't understand the innerworkings of Lucy's … unique … brain. Lucy motioned to a black iron park bench overlooking the water. With the sun hitting the soft ripples, the water seemed to dance with sparkles. A silence spread between them for a while. Not uncomfortable or awkward, more like they were mutually drawn into the river's hypotonic pattern. But then, the conversation fired back up, and they spent the next hour talking about favourite movies, the best local restaurants that Jade hadn't tried yet, and a dozen other lighter topics. And definitely – quite obviously in Lucy's humble opinion – no other conversation about past relationships, or lack thereof.

'I should probably get back home and take care of my Sunday work,' Jade said after a pause in the conversation.

Lucy rose, more reluctantly than she should. The past several hours were some of the best she'd spent in a long time, and she wasn't ready for them to end. Then again, Sunday was visit day with her dad, and if she arrived too late to help him with chores, he'd retaliate and cook her Sunday-night steak well-done.

When they reached the parking lot, Lucy stopped outside of her truck.

Jade's eyes scanned the vehicle. 'This is yours?'

'Betty Yellow.' Lucy patted the tailgate. 'My longest relationship. I've had this baby since I was eighteen. My pops gave it to me, and I just can't let it go.'

'Your bumper sticker! I'm dying.'

Lucy cracked a grin at the familiar sticker. *Yes, I have a truck. No, I won't help you move.* 'I had to get it. Everyone thought it was so impractical driving this beast around until they needed to borrow it to move furniture.'

Jade skipped her fingers across the lettering on the tailgate. 'Well, I love it. Ms Betty Yellow. I think it's pretty perfect.'

'You do?' Why did this make her feel so warm? Of course, Lucy loved Betty Yellow – this baby got her through the roughest of snowstorms and could carry Chucky, fishing gear, and supplies when needed. But Jade's approval felt validating somehow. It struck something in Lucy, deeper than expected, but she'd process why later.

'I really do. Reminds me of, like the good old days, I guess. Nostalgic. Like an old TV show you loved as a kid.' Jade peeked at her watch and frowned. 'Thanks for the fun morning. Really, it was amazing to get out of the house.'

'Definitely.' Lucy shifted her weight between her feet. So, was this it? Should she ask Jade for her number? Or was messaging on the social platforms good enough for now? For the first time in a gazillion years, she didn't feel like bolting after a non-date.

Whatever. She needed to admit this. This felt date-ish.

And *now* ... she wanted to bolt.

A date was too real, too much, too intense. She'd been on dates before, but this tugging in her stomach, this heart-skipping, this longing sensation to hear more about Jade, to brush her fingertips against her hand to see how soft the skin was, to not let her just walk away – it felt new. And scary. And, truthfully, it didn't make sense. Lucy had so much going on in her life. Right now was the absolute worst time in the history of all time to embark on anything.

Jade pulled her hands out of her pocket. 'Can I give you a hug?'

Her voice was softer than Lucy had heard all day, and Lucy soaked up the vulnerability in the tone. 'I'd love one.' She stretched on her tiptoes and held her arms open, and oh boy. This woman could *hug*. Her slim arms were much stronger than Lucy expected. Citrus and sage hovered on Jade's skin, and the combo was downright yummy. Lucy pressed into her and inhaled one more time before she forced herself to break from the warm grip and opened the truck door.

Oh God, now what? Lucy really didn't want this moment to end, but also, one million per cent needed it to end. She stared at her purse and chewed the inside of her lip. 'I, uh ...'

Jade stood there. Waiting. Maybe expectant, maybe curious, but her smile twitched into a grin. 'Yes?'

So much heat. In her cheeks. In her chest. Travelling down in a zip to her belly and settling there, uncomfortably. *Breathe, breathe.* 'Do you want to exchange phone numbers? I mean, we can totally keep chatting on the app, if you want to keep chatting that is, but you know ... you never know when you'll have a sriracha emergency ... and what if there's a time that you stop at a store and see like a lemon, eucalyptus, *and* lavender cleaner, but there's only like one bottle left, and I'm not sure if I'll see the message ... or ...'

The hint of a smile on Jade's face turned into a full, prominent, glowing one if Lucy said so herself, and a moment later, they swapped their phones and typed in their contact info. Finally, Lucy snapped her seatbelt and fired up Betty Yellow. 'Take care. I guess we'll chat soon?'

Jade stepped back and held a hand up in a quiet wave. 'Yes, we will.'

As she pulled out into traffic, Lucy's shoulders slumped. She didn't want to leave as much as she didn't want to stay. The pregnancy countdown clock ticked away, and the very last thing Lucy should – or even could do – was get involved with anyone.

But Jade was *freaking awesome*. Sweet, kind, smart as hell. Owned her own business, for God's sake! She probably had her shit completely together, whereas lately Lucy felt like a duck frantically paddling in a stream. She hoped Jade had at least bought her façade of being ultra-chill.

And that soft mouth, though. *Damn*. The beautiful shape, that glistening, full bottom lip. She wanted to pull that lip into her mouth and ... *stop*. No. She wasn't doing this. She wasn't going to entertain anything. All of these thoughts were completely useless because she couldn't get involved with anyone. Legally, she'd already signed that she was, in fact, single, and she'd stay celibate until after implantation. How would that be to kick off a new relationship? 'Hey, there, you mind if we swing by the lawyer's office to update my statement, then make a quick pit stop at the doctor's to make sure you don't have any STIs? Cool, thanks.'

Ugh. Although the statement of singlehood had more to do with marriage than defining a dating relationship, but *still*. Awkward.

After she picked up Chucky to take to her dad's farm for the day, Lucy's belly slowly unravelled from its knotted state during the scenic drive. After contemplating all the scenarios, by the time she reached the farm, she knew exactly what she needed to do when it came to Jade.

Which was nothing at all.

Chapter 8

Jade

Jade probably shouldn't like the smell of ammonium as much as she did, but she couldn't help it. As Shayna applied activator on a teen getting a soft spiral perm, Jade withheld from taking a deep sniff as she walked by.

Deep down, even though she didn't want to admit it, she probably just wanted a distraction. A little singed nose hair to provide a big, fat distraction, because it was Wednesday afternoon, and she had checked her phone no less than twenty times since Sunday to see if Lucy had messaged.

She hadn't.

But neither had Jade.

It wasn't like Jade hadn't thought about picking up the phone and sending Lucy a message. But every time she did, she wondered why Lucy hadn't contacted her. Maybe Lucy hadn't felt the zings Jade did as they sat by the water and watched the riverboats. Maybe Lucy hadn't felt distracted like Jade as she thought about the soft slope of Lucy's neck, her smooth pale skin, those chestnut waves rolling against her collarbone peeking from her shirt.

Maybe Lucy wasn't damaged like Jade, with the hovering ghost of an ex-wife, reminding her what happened when you let your guard down and opened yourself up.

Of course, Jade had hoped Lucy would reach out. Then again, this was what she should have expected, right? To be met with what she'd always been met with when she opened up a bit, shared a bit, *trusted* a bit: nothing.

On her way to the front of the shop, Jade tossed the empty perm box for Shayna, who mouthed a silent 'thank you' while her client chatted on. She'd been thinking so much about how to broach the whole 'mentorship' conversation with Shayna and couldn't land on a way to not make it seem condescending for a seasoned stylist. So, she did what she did best – complete avoidance of the subject.

At the reception desk, Amanda handed Jade a thick folder.

'Hey, I printed out the last six months of sales for you,' Amanda said. 'You know the trees are weeping right now, right? You can see all this online.'

'I know, I know.' Jade sifted through the salon junk drawer for a red pen, welcoming a distraction from thinking about Lucy, even if it came in the shape of her archenemy – numbers. 'But isn't it easier sometimes to just read things on paper?'

'Nope.' Amanda lifted her water bottle with *allegedly* written across the front. Jade had bought the bottle for Amanda on a whim last year when she visited a small shop in North Minneapolis, thinking it fit Amanda's criminology, analytic mindset to a T. 'I was born in a digital world, woman. I'm not even sure if I know what paper is.'

Jade lifted a brow. 'Are you saying ...'

'That you're old? Never.' Amanda's sly smile spread. 'Just 'cause you were born in the late nineteen hundreds doesn't mean old. It means ... seasoned.'

'Late nineteen hundreds? Such a terrible thing to say. True, but terrible.' Jade grinned through her scowl and moved to her back office.

With a break in clients, she needed to dive back into figuring out why Shayna had dropped so much in sales. Was it just due to the dreaded re-dos? Was she working fewer hours? Taking longer per client to complete, thus serving fewer clients weekly on average? Once Jade had a solid understanding, she could figure out how to help her.

She fanned the paper across the tiny oak desk. *Deep breath in, deep breath out.* Numbers had always intimidated her. She was a visual learner – an artist, really. Someone who wanted their clients to feel beautiful and seen. Studying numbers, trends, and earning fluctuations was not her area of expertise. And had Amanda not brought Shayna's downslide to Jade's attention a few months ago, Jade may not have even noticed. Other stylists had been steadily increasing their sales, offsetting the loss, so profits had appeared to be stable.

The red pen hovered over the paper, and she circled the areas when Shayna dipped most significantly, and definitely noticed she was seeing a quarter fewer clients every day. Because Shayna always had someone in her chair, Jade didn't notice that she'd been blocking an hour for a haircut, or three for a basic colour. *Hmmm. Okay ...* Perhaps the day of the week played a role? Or the time of day? Jade was a morning person. By evening, she was useless. But, it had taken her a few years in the business to realise this. Maybe Shayna's sales dipped on Wednesdays after Taco Tuesday. Or maybe it had nothing to do with days and times, and she had something personal going on besides the break-up a few months ago, which would be a delicate issue to address. As an employer, it wasn't Jade's place to pry. But Jade also had to figure out the best way to guide Shayna – and protect her business.

A quick knock against the door jolted Jade upright.

'Phone's for you.' Amanda handed her the receiver and shut the door behind her.

Jade tucked the phone on her shoulder. 'This is Jade.'

'Will you please give me five minutes?'

Her heart hammered at the voice. *Elizabeth.*

Couldn't she take no for an answer? Every attempted contact felt like Elizabeth was scraping at a barely healed scab in the centre of Jade's chest. All those years, did Elizabeth feel a fraction for Jade as to what she felt towards Elizabeth? If Elizabeth did, she'd know how hard this was. Every phone call, every sought-out communication, sprung up flickers of memories, flushing Jade with the type of nostalgia that she didn't want to wade through. Their wedding day, the glorious two-week honeymoon where days passed when they didn't leave the bed, when they bought their home and took their sweet, sexy time christening each room. The way they laughed, and hugged, and clung to each other. And then ... the way their relationship frayed until it snapped, until Jade was a shell of her former self.

Maybe the calls weren't enough to be considered harassment. But enough was enough. 'Stop calling me.'

'Please, this is important.' The familiar firmness that had helped Elizabeth land multiple promotions at her communications firm echoed through the phone.

Jade breathed through the rising fire in her chest. 'Is it anything about the sale of the house, taxes, or divorce papers?'

'Well, no, not exactly ... but I really want to talk.' The firmness softened.

Jade slumped into the office chair. 'Honestly, I can't do this. I really can't.' Damn. Her voice was already cracking, which she *hated.*

All her strength had depleted when her marriage ended. It took over a year for Jade to rebuild emotionally, to regain her power. The nights filled with bawling on the shower floor, hitting her pillow, or drinking one too many glasses of Merlot until the ache disappeared were barely in the rear-view mirror. Every time Elizabeth contacted Jade, her mended heart verged on splintering all over again.

'Please,' said Jade. 'Can you just do this through a lawyer?'

'We are not those people, Jadey.'

The hair sprung up on her neck. 'Don't call me that.' How dare she resort to the sweet names they used during their marriage? Elizabeth had made her choice. Loud and clear. She didn't get to use emotional manipulation right now to get Jade to talk.

Funny how during their marriage, Jade was the one begging Elizabeth to talk. Share something, *anything*, about her feelings. Elizabeth was great talking about work, meetings she had, presentations she gave, the new promotion dangling in front of her face. But never about feelings or relationship issues. Never about the fractures in the foundation of their relationship that teetered on cracking under the weight of their unspoken issues.

Elizabeth cleared her throat. 'We don't need lawyers to have a friendly conversation.'

'This isn't friendly.' Jade propped her elbow on the desk and rested her forehead in her palm. 'Stop calling. Please.'

Hanging up was harder than it should've been. She didn't miss *her*, exactly, but she missed having someone to come home to. Honestly, she'd been missing someone during the last several years of their marriage, too.

Elizabeth was hyper-focused on her career, and then on becoming a mom. The loneliest Jade ever felt was during her marriage. She pictured them at their shabby-chic white kitchen table, eating in silence while Jade scrolled through hair videos and Elizabeth typed on her laptop. Conversations overflowed with 'fines': How are you? *Fine*. How was work? *Fine*. How are we handling the plethora of problems in our failing marriage? *Fine*. A sporadic, kiss-less, few-times-a-year sex life. Sleeping back-to-back afterwards, missing the warmth of her wife's dewy skin against her chest. Feeling she wasn't enough – not *good* enough, or *interesting* enough, or *smart* enough, to hold her wife's attention.

Jade leaned back in her chair and stared at the ceiling when her cell phone buzzed. She ripped it from her pocket. If it was her ex-wife calling her cell from an unblocked number, she swore she was going to smash it with a hairdryer–

Oh. Lucy. Not Elizabeth.

Some of Jade's anger faded as curiosity took its place. 'Hello?'

'So, wait. You're a vegetarian from Chicago. Which means you've not had a Chicago-style hotdog in, like, fifteen years?'

Lucy had gone completely radio silent the last several days, and now she was calling to ask Jade about hotdogs? The similarities with how Elizabeth would vanish, then return as if nothing happened, weren't lost on Jade. But ... Lucy wasn't Elizabeth. Lucy was sweet and cute, and a perfect distracting ray of light. And at this moment, Jade was hungry for a distraction.

She lifted her body from slumping to sitting. 'Closer to twenty years.'

A sound like *umphh* came through the receiver. 'And you haven't had a Chicago-style pizza, either, I suppose. Which is apparently the best thing on earth.'

'Well, I've had it with cheese.'

'Doesn't count unless there's a pound of pepperoni on top.'

'I beg to differ.' Jade plucked a rubber band out of the rainbow cup holder and stretched it between her fingers. 'Is this what you're doing, sitting at work contemplating the food choices of a native Chicagoan?'

'Well, I'm on break, at a sandwich shop, so I'm not really at work.'

'Are you eating pastrami?'

'I'm trying to be respectful of my new vegetarian friend and not telling you how delicious my lunch is. It's, um, filled with sprouts and apple slices.'

'Sprouts and apple slices equal salted meats. Got it.' Jade twirled in her chair and checked the time. Mrs Dieterman would be here any moment, but this totally out-of-the-blue conversation was springing Jade out of her funk. 'How did you know I'd be free right now? That I wasn't with a client?'

'Oh, that? I installed cameras in your ceiling to watch your every move. Cute outfit, by the way.' Lucy coughed. 'Gah. Too stalkery. Super groan. Things I think are funny sound totally wrong the second they fly out of my mouth. Honestly, I wasn't sure you'd answer.'

Because she hadn't tried calling or messaging sooner? Because they'd both gone radio silent? Because Jade thought more about their coffee time than Lucy did? Jade wasn't sure she wanted to know. 'So … why did you call?'

The sound of Lucy swallowing liquid came through the phone. 'Earlier today a couple came in needing someone to notarise their divorce papers. It was awkward and awful. At the end, I said, "Hope to see you again soon." I really said that. Like literal facepalm moment.'

'Oh man. Miserable for everyone involved.' Jade clocked the time. 'And that made you think of me?' Was she some sort of divorce magnet? Maybe Lucy did have cameras installed here and just heard the belly-churning conversation with Elizabeth.

'Ha. No. I mean, I thought about calling Drew, but he's such a dude, and wouldn't really care as much. I figured I would call you, purge my sin out exorcist-style on your voicemail, and just go from there.'

A knock on the door jolted her upright. Amanda poked her head in. 'Mrs Dieterman's here for you.'

Jade nodded and stood. 'I have to go get my client.'

'Oh, for sure. Sorry about the randomness. Talk to you later.'

'Wait!' Jade swallowed. *Come on, it's not that big of a deal. Breathe out the shakes.* 'Can I call you tonight?'

Too many moments passed. Jade scratched at the back of her neck.

'I'd love that.'

And with those words, lobbed much softer than Jade expected, her heart soared.

Chapter 9

Lucy

'Do you want me to grab a chunk of your fat and stick it in for you?' Drew's voice was kinder than his words. He cocked his head and gazed at Lucy's bare belly before his eyes turned wide. 'I didn't mean that.'

'Such a jerk-hole.' Lucy ground her elbow into his ribs. She brought the paper instructions up to her nose and reread. Again.

The past two weeks had flown by with a barrage of appointments, final stamps of approvals, and late-night chat sessions with Jade. All legal papers were finally signed, the egg donor prepped and now … shots.

And not the tequila kind.

The fluorescent light in Lucy's bathroom radiated some sort of deep red heat that burned into Lucy's chest. She grabbed the binder with the med schedule and fanned her face. 'We got this, right? I mean, we really got this. This will be way less painful than when we got our tattoos.'

Drew dug an alcohol pad package from the box and laid it

on the bathroom counter. 'God, I hope so. I almost passed out.'

'Oh stop! You so didn't.'

Drew grinned, the skin around his light green eyes creasing. 'I really did. I didn't want to tell you, though, 'cause you were chatting it up the whole time like you were getting a mani-pedi, and I almost threw up. I couldn't let you one-up me. But needles … I had no idea I feared them until I did.'

Chucky, excluded from the action, whined at the door, but Lucy couldn't risk any floating dog fur settling into her skin and erupting into some kind of infection. Although with the amount of antibiotics the doctor put her on prior to the embryo transfer, she was probably good.

She picked up the tiny syringe and felt the weight in her fingers. In the doctor's office, she'd practised on a silicone ball. But this was all real. *So freaking real*, and she released a shaky breath. *Thank God* the extra-duty butt ones didn't start for a few weeks. She lifted her tank and saw Drew's face go white. 'You know – you don't have to watch.'

He hooked his finger in his collar and tugged. 'You're having my baby. The least I can do is help you shoot up.'

'That just sounds so wrong.' She wiped the alcohol wipe across her belly, the cool tingle flushing her skin. *Inhale, exhale*. Now or never. She pinched her belly. The back of her throat moistened with a hot, metallic film, and she swallowed. She exhaled and … *Bam!*

'Oh. Not bad. Here, let me stick you.' She held the needle out. Drew flew back into the door, his hand slapping against his heart. His face turned as red as his hair, and she was sure his freckles were going to pop right out of his cheek skin. 'I'm just kidding! Seriously. I would never stick you with a used needle. A new one … maybe. Just for solidarity purposes.' She tossed the syringe into the sharps container. *Not as bad as it could've been.*

He chuckled and settled his gaze on Lucy. 'Are you okay? Do you feel weird?'

She wobbled and gripped the side of the counter. 'Actually Drew ...'

'Oh God, what? What?'

'I'm sorry. That was so not funny. I'm *fine*.' And she was, physically of course. The needle barely hurt. But it seemed every single step made everything more real, and this was no exception. God, she was so excited. All these years of talking and planning and prep, and they were so close. But – and she avoided Drew's gaze even thinking through this because he'd pick up on it via some super freakish osmosis or something – she was scared. What if it worked? What if it didn't? What if she was sick, or the baby got hurt, or she accidentally did something and destroyed her best friend's dreams? 'You've got to stop doing this. Please, make fun of my shoes. Or my hair, or wardrobe or something. My choice in music–'

'Terrible. Truly.'

'Nineties pop is not terrible.' She opened the door and leaned down to scratch Chucky, who had resigned himself to lying on the floor, in the dog equivalent of a pout for leaving him out of the party.

Drew followed her into the kitchen. She pulled down a box of crackers and held them out.

He waved the snacks away. 'It's just so weird, right?' He swung his hands in between the two of them. 'Freaks me out a little bit.'

'That I'm going to be housing your baby?'

'No, not that.' He leaned back against the counter, his soft cotton-tee stretching against his crossed muscular arms. 'I worry we're going to lose "our thing". Since we were kids, it's been Drew and Luce against the world. And now, all we talk about is, you know, lawyers and transfers and ovulation.'

She popped a cracker in her mouth and dusted off her hands. She'd been meaning to talk to him about Jade for a while now but stopped herself every time she started – which scared her. Lucy told Drew everything. Almost daily, she'd give an excruciating play-by-play of the tiniest interactions. Sometimes she'd snap her fingers near his face because his eyes had glazed over. But Jade, she'd kept to herself.

Lucy knew why. These sensations, the rush she felt when they spoke, the way she kept thinking about how the sun had highlighted the green speckles in Jade's eyes during their non-date at the coffee shop, the smell of her citrus sage perfume – which Lucy had searched for at the mall a week later ... She had feelings. She *never* had feelings. And she had no idea what to do with them.

'We do have something to talk about besides the pending alien about to inhabit my belly.' She busied herself digging out more crackers. 'I sort of ... met someone.'

Drew's mouth dropped. 'Met someone? Couch time.' He pointed to the living room. 'I'm grabbing root beers.'

She slumped down onto the sofa and Chucky burrowed into her feet. Like Chucky was a living sensory toy, she ran her fingers through his fur and massaged his ears, until her heartbeat calmed.

Drew returned and handed her the soda. 'Spill the details.'

'It's not what you think at all. She's a friend.'

'You have lots of friends.'

Technically, she had lots of *acquaintances*. But she didn't correct him. She popped the top and the fizzy bubbles burned down her throat as she took the first sip. Her legs seemed to have a mind of their own as she squirmed and shifted in her seat. 'She's really nice, funny, just moved here last year from Chicago. She owns Jade's on 7th.'

Drew's eyebrows scrunched. 'The salon with the Pride flags?'

'Yep.' She tucked a leg under her butt. 'Anyway, we met a few weeks ago for coffee and, uh, we chat occasionally.'

'So just friends?'

Her face turned pink. Drew could for sure see right through her fake nonchalant nod.

Drew sat back and crossed his arms. 'So, this *friend* ...' He cleared his throat. 'What does she think about you getting knocked up in a few weeks?'

Lucy flicked at the top of the can with her finger. 'I didn't tell her.'

'You haven't told her.' He cocked his head. 'You meet a *friend* for the first time in forever, and you haven't told her? Why not?'

Well, when he says it like that, in that tone ... Maybe it sounded worse than what she originally thought. Lucy loved Drew. *Loved.* Obviously. But she wasn't quite sure she wanted to open up to him fully about the thoughts swarming through her head these last few weeks. She'd never had these sparks before, and honestly, *selfishly*, wanted to hold them tight. They seemed fragile, delicate somehow, like cupping your hands around a candle in a windstorm, and hoping the flame remains.

How would Jade react if she told her? Think Lucy was some sort of holier-than-thou person who needed some praise? Maybe Jade would think it was gross, or weird, or that Lucy was 'too much'. Or maybe ... Jade would be supportive and kind and wonderful, and honestly, Lucy wouldn't know what to do with any of these outcomes.

'No. I still haven't told anyone except my dad and my manager.'

He lowered his pop. 'Seriously?'

She shrugged and resumed petting Chucky. 'Yeah. I don't need people all up in my business. Can you even imagine the amount of questions? And then they'll ask how we conceived and when I tell them to shove it where the sun don't shine, they're going to think we screwed. *Ewwwww.*' For a hot minute, she thought of telling people exactly how she would conceive, but that was almost as invasive as just letting them think she and one of the dads had humped. Curious about implantation, friends? Behind door number one we've got menstrual cycle matching, and hormones, and progesterone, and fallopian tube checks, and the mother of all plungers during a pap, and egg extraction, and ...

'People are definitely going to think we had sex. Gross.' He gnarled his lip. 'I mean, *you're* not gross, but …'

'I know. I get it.'

'Are you ever going to tell her?'

She'd thought about it. Lucy and Jade messaged every night, mostly sharing work stories, or little anecdotes from their day. Jade had sent a few vegetarian recipes, and Lucy sent a picture of a half-eaten, surprisingly delicious vegetarian breakfast sandwich from Starbucks. But the last two times Jade had asked if she wanted to grab dinner or coffee, Lucy came up with a flimsy excuse. 'I don't know. I mean, if we keep hanging out, probably. She's gonna notice when it looks like I swallowed a basketball and have two broken ankles.'

Drew set his can on the coffee table. 'It's your body, your choice.'

'Damn right, per our signed legal document, thank you very much.'

'What I mean is that it's your choice to tell whomever you want, if you want, whenever you want. But you know once I announce it to my family, they'll take out a billboard over 494, so she may find out eventually, anyway.'

She knew this was true. Drew's family was not quiet. Stillwater was not a small town, but it wasn't huge either. Word would get out, and Jade could find out from someone who *wasn't* Lucy. Which … She should probably try and control the narrative. 'You and Mason are still waiting for second trimester, right?'

'Yeah, just in case …'

She hated the crack in Drew's normally ultra-confident voice, but she felt it too. Lucy was not a praying kind of woman. But there have been more than a few nights right before she fell asleep where she whispered to the universe that she hoped everything turned out healthy and safe for the future little nugget. 'Nope. You're not jinxing anything.' She patted him on the leg. 'Everything's going to be fine.'

An hour later, after Drew had left to meet Mason for dinner, Lucy picked up her phone and grinned at an unread message from Jade. At some point she shouldn't get flutters this intense, right? One would think after weeks of chatting, the thrill of getting pinged would dissipate. Indulging in these little zings and zangs was fun, at least for now. But she really needed to pull herself back, and keep her mind focused on the mission at hand.

Although, a few texts couldn't hurt ...

Jade: *Do you remember in high-school chemistry when we learned about color molecules?*

Lucy: *No, but why?*

Jade: *I have a redhead who wanted to go platinum blond in one sitting.*

Jade: *Told her no. Impossible. Her hair will fall out, so she finally agreed to do it in multiple appointments.*

Lucy: *So, what happened?*

Jade: *She is currently cat-pee yellow/orange and I'm trying to do some semipermanent toner on her, so I don't ruin my reputation around town.*

Lucy: *Oh no haha. You got this.*

When Jade didn't respond, Lucy shoved the phone in her back pocket and took out the recycling. She pictured Jade at work, laughing with clients, her sleeved-tattooed arms working the round brush as she styled someone's hair. She wanted to be wrapped in those strong arms again. She hated that she'd rejected

Jade's last two offers to get together. But these emotions were unfamiliar, and her brain wouldn't settle.

And it wasn't just that she was unsure of what to do with these feelings. Lucy had also signed documents stating she wouldn't engage in sexy nefarious acts, and that a partner wouldn't interfere with the surrogacy process. The doctor, therapist, coordinator, even the legal secretary had all seen Lucy's sworn statement of singlehood.

Lucy wasn't a relationship guru or anything, but it seemed obvious that no one would want to date her with the promise of nothing but hand holding, cuddling, and witnessing morning sickness in their future. It was like there was a pending doom of rejection hovering in the air, before they'd even got started. And sure, although Lucy had never experienced this in her life, she wasn't totally obtuse in thinking that the fear of rejection was uncommon when you are in the beginning stages of developing feelings. But this seemed like a guaranteed way to snuff the flames before they even had a chance to burn.

Her phone pinged.

Jade: *What are you up to?*

Lucy: *Drew just left. About to dive into a bag of chips and sour cream and watch* Golden Girls.

Jade: *I LOVE* The Golden Girls. *Which one are you?*

Lucy: *Really? I figured you knew me a little better by now. Rose, of course. You?*

Jade: *Dorothy*

Lucy: *No nonsense. Kind of salty. Love it.*

Lucy: *What are you up to tonight?*

Jade: *On a Saturday night? Going home. Taking a bath. Passing out by 10.*

Lucy's heart skipped a beat. Should she? No. Yes? Maybe. Gah! They were just friends. They both had the day off. They loved *Golden Girls*. This was *fine*.

Lucy: *Want to come over?*

And then she dropped the phone like it was burning her palm and rubbed Chucky's fur until her breath evened. *I cannot believe I just did that ...*

Chapter 10

Jade

Jade finished cleaning and closed the shop in record time. She normally liked to take a shower after a long day of work. But it was already seven, and she had to swing by the grocery store before going to Lucy's. She made a quick call to her sister Bethany both to check in on how her summer grad school classes were going, and to distract herself from the perma-tingle in her stomach during the drive. Thirty minutes later, she pulled into Lucy's driveway.

Whoa. This woman really, really liked lawn ornaments. And hanging things, and butterflies.

The small white rambler-style home was cute. A cedar fence surrounding an overgrown garden, hanging plants, a swinging bench on the front porch, a one-car garage. The front step creaked under her foot as she made her way to the door. She inhaled and lifted her fist to knock, but the door swung open.

A fresh-faced Lucy in a T-shirt and black cotton skirt opened the door with a wide smile. Her long brown hair cascaded down her shoulders. Jade figured she had mentally exaggerated how beautiful Lucy was. That somehow, the vision of Lucy in the coffee shop with her pink mouth and curvy body and those dark brown eyes Jade wanted to swim in was enhanced in her mind.

She was wrong.

'Hey! You found it okay.' Lucy bounced up for a hug, and Jade was caught off-guard. 'Oops. I'm a hugger. Sorry.'

Jade squeezed tight and pretended that Lucy's apple-scented shampoo wasn't having the effect on her that it was.

'Rooooroooo …' A moan echoed behind Lucy.

Lucy stepped back and held the door wider. 'Yes, my little man. Chucky, meet Jade.'

The sweet golden-haired dog with a wrinkled face and patches of grey on his scruff looked up at Jade. She crouched, held out her hand for him to sniff, then scratched under his chin. 'Glad to finally see you in person, Chucky.'

She took another step. The house was even cuter on the inside. Hardwood floors, a large, overstuffed couch, a huge wooden coffee table with a smattering of books, remotes, and chargers. The walls, in soft orange and yellow, were surprisingly colourful for Jade's taste, yet they suited the space. A small kitchen island, a tiny circle table, and so many dog toys it looked like Lucy ran a doggy daycare. Pictures of what she assumed were family and friends had been framed and hung in what seemed like no particular way.

Jade lifted a bag. 'Cheese, crackers, cookies. And grapes. 'Cause, fruits, you know?'

'Let's make sure Chucky doesn't get into those,' Lucy said as she closed the door. 'He's a sneaky little old man. Grapes will make him do unsavoury things to the floor.'

Jade slipped off her shoes.

'You can keep shoes on, unless you want your socks covered in dog hair. I sweep every day, but by the end of the night my feet look like Snuffleupagus from *Sesame Street*.'

Jade followed Lucy into the kitchen and set the bag on the island. 'I haven't seen that in forever. The shaggy monster?'

'Yep.' Lucy opened the fridge and pulled out a few items, as Jade tried to get a handle on her heartbeat that was thudding so loud in her ears, she was sure that Lucy could hear it.

Stop freaking out. This was a friendly get-together, nothing more. They'd been talking daily for a while now and had built such a casual rapport. So why did being inside Lucy's home, with its warm feel and even warmer smells, seem anything but casual? 'Can I help with something?'

Lucy bumped the door closed with her hip. 'Nope. Take a seat. Can I make you a drink?'

'What do you have?'

'How does homemade strawberry lemonade sound?'

'Like actually homemade?'

'Yep. Stirred it from the powder myself.' She grinned and plopped strawberries in a colander. 'I'm sure I have some vodka in one of the cupboards if you want a shot.'

A drink sounded kind of nice, but Jade needed to remain on her A-game tonight. Her nerves were already shooting through her, and after a few drinks she'd either get super anxious, want to dance on the kitchen floor, or fall asleep. None seemed like appropriate options. 'Thanks, but if I have one, then I'll want two, then I won't be able to drive home, and I don't think we're quite ready for a sleepover yet. I don't even have pyjamas.'

If she didn't know any better, she could have sworn that a blush swept Lucy's cheeks.

Jade sank into a barstool, sipped the lemonade, and watched Lucy's delicate fingers arrange the cheese slices, meat, and crackers on the plate. She spread jelly on top of the brie and stuck a knife in the middle of the cheese.

'That's quite the spread,' said Jade. 'I usually end up with PB&J or leftover Thai for dinner.'

'Thai does heat up pretty nice. But I like this stuff. Cooking, having friends over.' She folded a piece of prosciutto. 'I'll make sure my meats don't touch your cheeses.'

'Glad you'll be keeping your salty meats to yourself.'

Lucy stopped mid-slice and started giggling. 'Oh my God, why does that sound so dirty? My maturity level is perpetually stuck in junior high.'

Can she be any more adorable?

The sugary strawberry lemonade slid down Jade's throat, and she stood to look at the backyard. A hammock swung between two trees, a wind chime flickered golden magenta with the evening sun, and leaves swayed in the late summer breeze. The entire yard looked like relaxation, and she verged on asking if she could come over and take a nap there someday.

Chucky whined, and Jade turned back to Lucy.

'I know, Chucky. Here.' Lucy tore off a small chunk of mozzarella and held it in her palm. 'The vet fat-shamed my dog. Chucky's supposed to lose like three pounds, but I just can't do it. He loves treats, and he only has a few years left. I want to make them as happy for him as I can.' She washed her hands and returned to the platter. 'And honestly, when I'm a senior, no one better take away my snacks.'

Jade helped Lucy carry the food into the living room and took a seat next to her on the couch. She cut a chunk of brie, spread it on a cracker with pepper jelly, and told Lucy about the hair catastrophe from earlier.

Lucy chatted about having their quarterly practice today for what to do during a robbery.

'A robbery?' Jade hated the thought of Lucy in danger. 'Has that ever happened before?'

'No, even though we do get some sketchy people in there sometimes,' Lucy said. 'But I'm much more likely to get in a car accident on the way to work.'

They continued to talk for almost an hour, with *Golden Girls* playing in the background, when something inside Jade started to tug at her. She should probably tell Lucy she was previously married. At this point, it was starting to feel like she was lying by withholding the information. On the other hand, talking about her ex always plummeted whatever good mood Jade had. And so far, tonight was the most relaxed, fun evening she'd had in a long time.

'Have you ever been married?' Jade casually plucked a grape off the vine and chewed slowly, trying to act calm despite her pounding heart.

'Nah.' Lucy grinned and plucked one for herself. 'I don't think marriage is on the cards for me. You?'

Not on the cards? What exactly did that mean? Even though Jade wanted to know more, now was the perfect opportunity to come clean. 'I got divorced last year.'

Lucy stopped chewing. She began again and swallowed hard. 'Really? Can I ask what happened?'

Realised love wasn't enough. Lost my identity in a relationship. Wanted fundamentally different things. 'Why ruin a good *Golden Girls* marathon with all of that?' Jade tried to chuckle, but a sort of awkward cough escaped instead. After all this time, she thought she was ready to talk about her ex. She wasn't.

Lucy shifted back into the couch and tugged her legs to her chest. 'I'm so sorry. Ms Prying McPryerton. None of my business.'

'It's all good.' Jade waved the words away. 'So, you don't think marriage is on the cards for you?'

'Nah. I don't like people.'

Jade laughed. 'I don't think I have ever actually met a warmer person in my life.'

'It's all a cover. You have no idea what I do when the clock chimes midnight.'

'That could be terrifying or sexy depending on how you look at it.' The word 'sexy' rolled off her tongue in more of a growl than intended, and the room heated. A commercial played on the TV, interrupting the moment. *Thank God.* Jade took the opportunity to hop off the couch.

She wasn't ready for whatever was happening here.

But her mind struggled to transfer that message to the rest of her body.

'I should get going.' She piled the napkins and glasses on the tray and scurried to the kitchen. She had to get out of there, stop being so close, stop talking so openly to this woman who made her laugh, forget about pressures of work, forget about the pain in her past. She needed to stop looking at Lucy's soft mouth, and her pretty fingers, and the long slope of her neck, and she *definitely* needed to stop wondering what her skin tasted like. The memory of her divorce was still raw, and she knew that opening herself up to Lucy invited in the possibility of getting hurt.

Yep, she had to leave. Now.

Lucy joined her and set the rest of the plates in the sink. They both stood in silence.

Was she thinking the same thing as Jade? That she should leave … or that she should stay?

Lucy rested her hand on top of Jade's. 'I'm really glad you came over. It's been a long time …'

'Since you tasted salted meats?'

'Oh my God, I'm never living that down.' Lucy laughed and their eyes locked. Really, really, locked. Lucy's gaze dipped and lingered on Jade's mouth.

The moonlight settled on Lucy's soft amber waves. Jade took in her round cheeks, her smooth, full lips, the way the top of Lucy's neck flushed with rose. God, she was irresistible. Her pulse thudded in her chest, a steady thump that moved, louder, and more intense, until it reached her ears.

Screw it. Jade bent her head down and pressed her lips against Lucy's, softly. Lucy's warm lips parted, moved, and pushed back. She tasted like grapes and lemonade and hope. Jade laid a palm on Lucy's hip and tugged closer.

Lucy whipped her head back and fumbled on her feet.

'Holy shit! I'm so sorry.' Jade slammed her hand against her mouth. 'I should've asked … I should never presume–'

'No, no, it's me. I ... can't.'

The heat from the kiss catapulted to the heat of embarrassment. How had she misread the signs so badly? Jade wanted to bolt from the house. This was so mortifying. And now she had probably destroyed the first friendship she'd made in years. 'Truly, Lucy. It's me. It's been a long time since I ... What I mean is, I totally misread—'

'I'm pregnant.'

Jade cocked her head. One, two, three full seconds passed as Lucy's eyes grew wider and she bit on the corner of her lip.

And ... Jade burst out laughing. Pregnant? 'Oh my God! You kill me.' She put her hand against her chest as her belly quivered. Lucy's humour was one for the record books.

Lucy's gaze flicked back and forth, and it took several moments too long for Jade to realise Lucy's mouth was absent of a smile.

Wait. No. *What?* Jade's laughing halted. She scanned Lucy's face. 'What?'

'I guess I'm not *technically* pregnant.' Lucy fiddled with her fingers. 'But I'm in the process of being a surrogate for Drew and his husband.'

No. Wait ... no. Shit. Jade's mouth opened. So many thoughts tumbled through her brain, but she couldn't lock on a single one. She swallowed what felt like a boulder and stepped back. 'Wow. I guess that's ... a big deal.'

And then, suddenly, questions sprang into her mind, filling the shocked emptiness. Questions, like 'so does this mean you are going to be a mom' and 'why' and 'what does this mean for our budding, ah, friendship?' But no. She couldn't voice any of that. Those questions were all too invasive – or selfish.

'Yeah, I guess it is a big deal.' Lucy cleared her throat, oblivious to the storm inside Jade. 'I actually haven't told anyone except my dad. Well, besides the lawyer, doctors, surrogacy coordinator, receptionist, and my manager. Other than that ...' She grinned and swiped her hand across Jade's. 'If this is all not too weird for you, then I'd love to, ah, continue what we started here. Not to be all, technical or whatever, but I can't do *everything*. But I can do some PG-13 related items …'

Jade couldn't contain all this information. The image of Elizabeth stomping into their kitchen saying she applied for adoption flashed through her mind. Even though it wasn't logical, even though the situations were not the same, Jade couldn't stop her chest from filling with a mist of betrayal.

She and Lucy had been chatting for weeks, and Lucy never once brought this up. All the times when Jade said, 'what were you up to today', had it slipped Lucy's mind to mention that she was having a *baby*? Lucy didn't owe Jade anything, per se. But wasn't Jade worthy of a little honesty?

After all the work Jade put in to rediscover herself, her worth, and once again the steadfast conviction that she wanted absolutely nothing to do with mothering or raising children, Jade felt her face heat. *This is what happens when I let my body instead of my brain do the thinking!* She wasn't ready to date yet. Or sleep with anyone. And she especially wasn't ready to be with someone who'd be totally focused on something else, and once again Jade would have to elbow her way into their world and take the scraps.

Sure, the irritation of all this landed unfairly on Lucy, but Jade couldn't help it. Her back stiffened. 'I don't think this is a good idea anymore.'

'It's not like anything is broken down there.' Lucy chuckled. 'It's all in working order. Even the doc says so.'

I need to leave. Jade wanted to smile but didn't. Lucy's grin faded as Jade reached for her bag on the counter. 'Thanks for the food. And I guess, um, congratulations.'

Run. Run fast and far and do not look back for anything. Jade bolted to the door. When her hands gripped the knob, she took a breath and glanced back at Lucy, who was chewing silently on her lower lip. 'It was really nice getting to know you, Lucy.' The words felt like sandpaper against her throat, and she swallowed back the sickliness rising in her belly. 'Good luck with everything.' She shut the door, ran to her car, and refused to look back.

And she barely made it to a stoplight when the hot sting of tears formed behind her eyes.

Chapter 11

Lucy

The sting of rejection softened a few days after Jade's abrupt departure. A full week down, and it had almost completely disappeared. *Almost.* Lucy shooed away all thoughts of Jade and blamed the longing on being extra horny from the hormones.

But Lucy missed their conversations. Sure, she and Drew talked daily, but it wasn't the same. And yes, she had other people in her life, co-workers, acquaintances – but none that she wanted to sleep with. *Ugh.* Whatever. It was a fun few weeks, and now her friendship with Jade was done. And that was that.

The clock showed it was break time. *Finally.* She was tired. She'd been putting in some extra hours this past week both while troubleshooting a few account issues and making sure she stayed on upper management's radar that she was a top contender for the expected manager spot next year. It sucked thinking this way, but it was reality – pregnant women were often not viewed as leadership material while pregnant. And if all goes well next week with the embryo transfer, in a few short months she'd start showing. She couldn't afford that any of them would forget that she locked in new accounts quicker than anyone else at this branch.

Lucy gathered her lunch bag and purse and swung by Erica's office. 'Hey, lady, we still want to go for our walk over lunch?'

'Ugh, sorry. There's an issue with the Minneapolis branch, and I've got to do some heavy audits before we close,' Erica said, barely looking up from the screen. When she did, though, her fingertips stopped clacking against the keyboard and she pushed her slipped frames back up her nose. 'Hey, you good? You don't look like your usual chipper self.'

Lucy never told Erica about Jade. Sure, Erica was her work wife, but their relationship was strictly nine-to-five. And now was not the time to talk about this low ache in her chest from how things ended the last time Lucy and Jade talked. 'Yep, I'm good. I'll catch ya later. Let me know if you get caught up and we'll sneak in a fifteen-minute walk this afternoon.'

As she pushed open the door, sunshine and a slight breeze reached Lucy's face, and she took a moment to breathe in the fresh, non-air-conditioned air. Fall would be here soon, and beautiful days like this would be scarce. She plopped down on the park bench in the bank courtyard space. She was just digging out her lunch when her phone rang. For a split second, her heart leapt – her phone rarely rang. *Jade?* Her dad called, but never during the workday. Unless someone was in the hospital, he always said 'no personal calls until after five'.

Lucy pulled the phone from her purse to see Drew's name flashing on her screen. *Not Jade.* She swallowed back the slight disappointment and pushed out a smile, instead. 'Why are you calling? We have a strict texting-only friendship.' She sank her teeth into a turkey and provolone sandwich.

'I know. I'm nervous and I hate I can't be there.' Drew's voice was breathy. Most likely he was in the middle of his noon speed-walk. 'I cannot believe they're sending me halfway across the country for the next three days when all of this is happening.'

She tried not to roll her eyes. A bit of her missed the old Drew – calm, funny, dirty-minded Drew. His perfectionism was one for the record books, but he'd always directed it at himself, his studies, or his job. He'd taken on a whole new level of obsession since this baby journey began.

'Dude. For real. You already said this. Like a million times. I'm fine, okay.' Lucy dragged the napkin down her face. 'You'll be back in time for the transfer, so we're totally good.' Even though the transfer should be the biggest of the big deals – when they actually implant the little nugget in her belly – that part was so deeply clinical and informal that Lucy wasn't even worried about Drew or Mason being there. Apparently, it took hardly any time at all, like five, ten minutes, and then they sent her on her merry (*hopefully pregnant*) way. It would take longer to find a parking spot for Betty Yellow.

And then, nothing except for shots for weeks until she peed on a stick to see if it took. *And then ...* well, then, the fun began. Baby. In the belly. *Holy freaking cannoli.*

'But if something happens ... if the bottle breaks, or the syringe pops off, or if you hit a nerve–'

'Whoa.' Her spine stiffened. 'You think I'm gonna eff this up, don't you?'

'What? I didn't say that. No, I don't. I just–'

'You're a control freak. I know you not being here is killing you. I promise I'll be fine. Chillax.' She bit into another corner and wiped her lip with her pinkie. 'I can record a video for you to watch.'

'Of you injecting? No, thank you. I want to maintain a healthy sex life with Mason, and the image of your white ass burned into my brain will not contribute to that.'

'My smooth, beautiful, plump white ass, thank you very much.' She revelled in her friend chuckling on the other side. 'If you were with me in person, though, it'd be the same. You'd be scarred for life.'

'Nope. Video makes it weird and creepy. In person is clinical.'

'Whatever.' She cracked open a bubbly juice and took a hearty gulp. 'You excited about your trip?'

'A software convention is *not* a trip. Imagine being surrounded by the most humourless humans alive. Boring as hell. But! I forgot to tell you they're going to have a keynote speaker on system architect design within an agile framework utilising the technology of …'

Lucy fought to pay attention to what her friend was saying but quickly lost the battle. Her eyes followed a blue jay hopping from branch to branch until Drew's throat-clearing snapped her back to reality.

'Anyway, Mason texted that his flight changed, and he's coming back early tonight from Phoenix, so if you need him to help, let him know.'

'I think he'd rather die.' She gathered her items to find shelter in the shade. 'But it might be kind of funny to watch him squirm.' The picture of a shaky-handed Mason holding a needle over her butt made her crack up.

All this was nerve-wracking, of course, and even though she didn't want to admit it to Drew – no reason to freak him out more than he already was – she hadn't been able to sleep the previous night, plagued with thoughts of the injection. What if she did actually screw it up? What if it hurt as bad as she thought? What if she had some sort of allergic reaction to it, and no one was there to call 911. She breathed out, and after chatting for a few more minutes, she felt better. Drew dropped the call to finish his speed-walk and she dropped in search of chocolate she could swipe from the lobby.

A few hours later, as she packed up her items at the end of the day, Erica knocked on her open office door. 'Happy hour tonight. Everyone's coming.'

Lucy powered off her computer. 'Oh dang. I can't. I have plans.' *To inject myself with progesterone.*

'Oooh, what's her name?' Erica winked and tossed her large tote purse over her shoulder.

Jade. 'Stop it.' Lucy forced a giggle. 'Her name is Chucky, and he is the neediest child in the world.'

Erica shook her head. 'Remind me never to get a dog. If you change your mind … shoot me a text and I'll save you a spot.'

On the drive home, Lucy couldn't shake thoughts of Jade. Should she reach out? She really missed their conversations. Besides Drew, she hadn't had in-depth conversations with anyone else. Wracking her brain, she couldn't even think of an ex-girlfriend she'd talked to at the level she and Jade talked. And yet … when Lucy was honest, things went south.

Yes, she had the itch to call Jade. But also, Jade was the one who had upped and left, as if Lucy had said something offensive. Maybe she should've told Jade about her surrogacy arrangement sooner? But also, was she obligated to tell everyone everything about her life the moment they met? Honestly, how would she have even slipped that into one of their early conversations? *'So, have you eaten at the new ramen place? I'm going to be a surrogate. Do they put the eggs in the soup like the other place?'*

She eased up to a red light in front of her favourite indie bookstore and the new do-it-yourself ceramic place that she still hadn't checked out, and debated for exactly five seconds if she should hop over to the left lane to drive down 7th Street. She'd never admit it to anyone, but she'd driven on 7th twice this week and once the previous week to see if she could spot Jade. And she went to the grocery store where they met, even though she didn't need to buy anything. But only once. When she didn't see Jade in either place, she felt a rush of relief mixed with disappointment, which was unsettling and confusing, then went home upset with herself for being a creeper.

This was silly. They'd only known each other for a few weeks. The slight knot, deep in the corner of her chest, was clearly from the hormones. She turned Betty Yellow into her driveway, killed the engine, and stepped into the house.

The air conditioning blasted her face. How had she forgotten to turn that down this morning?

Chucky trotted to her, tail wagging. She tossed her keys and bag on the side table and bent down to scratch his ears. 'Come here, baby. Were you a good boy today?'

A note on her kitchen table caught her eye.

Your house was too damn hot for the fat dog. I turned the air conditioning on higher. Also, I gave him two turkey sticks and some cheese, so lay off the treats – Dad.

'Can't save 'em all. And I ain't got the energy to help,' he had said when she rescued Chucky. And then he proceeded to stop by every day to visit.

She dug out her 'save pile' wicker basket from the coat closet and set the note on top of the stack. A few more cards and notes and she'd have to buy a bigger basket. She never considered herself a hoarder, but since she was younger, she couldn't bear to throw away any handwritten notes from anyone.

After taking Chucky for a walk, she snuggled on the couch with him at her feet and reread the instructions for the progesterone shot. Gnawing on her cheek, she read again. She sniffed her fingertips. Was she dirty? Probably. Dealing with cash that had changed a million people's hands by the time it reached her bank might carry some sort of funky embryo-stalling germs. Even with the alcohol wipes the doctor gave her, she definitely shouldn't take that chance. She needed a shower.

The heated water beat down on her back and shoulders, and she kept peeking at her butt cheek. *Whew. Still there.* Every shower since the doctor's office visit, she was convinced that the injection spot circle the nurse drew last week would slide right off her skin and swirl down the drain, but that baby had barely faded in seven days.

Finished with her shower, Lucy towelled off and grabbed the supplies. Twenty minutes to go before injection time, but a little practice stab wouldn't hurt. She propped herself up on the bathroom counter and twisted. Jesus, this was an awkward-as-heck angle. She fisted her hand and pretended to poke herself.

Her belly gurgled and her mouth grew hot. She threw on her bathrobe and moved to the kitchen, shaking out her tingling arms. Bouncing on her feet for a few moments seemed to calm her limbs. After guzzling soda water, her belly soothed.

The minutes ticked by as she paced the house. *Come on, come on. Game time.*

She returned to the bathroom with a trotting Chucky following at her heels. A vision of golden dog hair floating off Chucky and burrowing into her injection site filled her mind. *Nope, no way.* She was *not* adding golden Shar Pei DNA to her body. She guided Chucky outside the room. 'Sorry, boy. This is a solo act, my friend.'

After singing the national anthem a full three times while washing her hands, she hopped on the counter, cleaned her skin with the prep wipe, and twisted like a contortionist. Good grief. She really needed to consider taking up Pilates.

'Come on, Green. You got this.' *Shoot like a dart, break the skin, do not angle, do not hit the nerve ...*

Sweat beaded on her upper lip. The syringe in her palm was *just so big.* Sweat now popped on her forehead. *I got this, I got this.* The belly shots she'd been doing these past few weeks were a piece of cake. But this baby-arm-sized syringe pulsating in her palm was a beast.

She swallowed sticky saliva and swiped the sweat on her lip with her hand. Dammit! She rewashed her hands, Cirque du Soleil'ed herself into position, re-wiped the alcohol, and poised her fingers.

One, two, three. She jabbed, and her arm froze. What in the hell? She lifted and jabbed again. Her arm apparently had a mind of its own. It had stopped an inch before it broke the skin. She squinted. 'Come on!' Lift, freeze, lift, freeze.

Her stomach turned. Forty shot attempts passed. She blinked away the black spots filling her vision and opened the door. Chucky lifted himself. 'Ruuu?' he asked.

'I had the same thought.' She paced the hall, the kitchen, and back. Her doctor had warned her about this, but she had thought it was funny – at the time. A drawn-out speech about the mind-body connection, and how the brain sometimes halted the body when trying to inflict pain upon itself. The concept sounded so alien – that her brain could stop her from injecting.

But she had just experienced this phenomenon, and now she felt completely out of control. Like a sports player psyching themselves up before a big play, she jumped up and down. She kicked the air conditioning on two degrees lower and rolled her neck.

She could do this. *Had* to do this.

Hands washed, skin wiped, awkward position resumed. And her arm stopped. Every damn time. Lucy checked her watch. She was already nearly an hour past when she was supposed to take the shot. And even though the doctor said she had a window of time, she wanted to do everything perfectly.

And this was absolutely *not* perfect.

Her lip trembled. Sweat trickled down her spine. She could not get sweat into the syringe. Who knows if sweat mixed with progesterone would screw something up and stall the meds getting into her body? She tried one last time.

Shit.

'Think, think …' What were her options?

The dads. Drew was gone, and Mason was just arriving from his Phoenix flight. The soonest he'd even get home was still a few hours away.

Her dad. No. Her pops loved her, but she didn't think he could stomach shooting her in the ass.

Erica. She wasn't the best option as Erica didn't know she was a surrogate, but desperate times called for desperate measures. Lucy grabbed her cell and dialled.

'Lucy Lu Lu Luuuuu.' Erica's muffled voice was hard to hear over the thumping music.

'You still at happy hour?' *Please say you're just driving with the music blaring.*

'You won't believe this. The veep showed up, bought everyone shots, and is paying for all of our Ubers. Even *Linda* is drunk! Ha. Good thing tomorrow is Saturday. Wish you were here … Wait, one sec.' The sound of a phone shuffling echoed through the receiver. 'Sounds like we're heading downtown to the Irish pub. Most epic happy hour ever! You sure you can't come out?'

Lucy grinned through her words to keep from crying. 'Nope, sorry. Next time though.' *And by next time, I mean in about twelve months from now.*

After ending the call, she leaned against the wall and squeezed her eyes tight. One option remained, but she did not want to do it. No, that was an understatement. To the depths of her core, she absolutely did *not* want to do it. She looked at her unstabbed hip, her belly that carried the hopes and dreams of her best friend, and the cell phone in her hand. She had no other choice. Her fingers shook as she scrolled through her contact list.

'Hey. Sorry to bother you,' she said and sucked in a deep breath. 'I really need some help.'

Chapter 12

Jade

Jade took a moment to process Lucy's voice. It sounded smaller than she'd heard before. When she saw Lucy's name on the screen, Jade thought for a hot second that she had called Lucy by accident. Ever since she'd stormed out last week, she'd been feeling terrible. Every day Jade had wanted to pick up the phone and explain her feelings, but she felt like such a shit that she couldn't bring herself to contact Lucy.

'Are you okay?' Jade asked as she propped her phone on the holder and pulled out of the salon parking lot.

'I'm hard core on the struggle bus. One-way ticket to Failure Island.'

She moved into the left lane. 'What's wrong?'

'I know this is really weird, and well, things didn't exactly end as peachy-keen as they could've last time we talked, and trust me when I say that you are my *very, very* last resort, although that sounds super mean, and I don't mean it like that–'

'Jesus, just spit it out.'

A large exhale filled Jade's ear. 'Can you please come over? I'm, um, having a bit of a … medical issue.'

The small crack in Lucy's voice gripped Jade. She whipped a U-turn at the yellow light and accelerated. 'I'm on my way.'

She was less than ten minutes from Lucy's house – plenty of time to really feel like crap about how she left Lucy's place. Lucy deserved an explanation. It wasn't like they were dating or anything. But they had gotten close, and for Jade to stop all conversation in a snap after Lucy shared something vulnerable wasn't fair.

Although Lucy hadn't reached out either.

But … now she had. *Grrr*. Should Jade break down and tell this woman about her trust issues, and self-doubt, and imposter syndrome, and that she really liked Lucy, which scared her, and that was why Jade was so weird, and that her ex had broken her, but really, she was equally to blame for the brokenness, and she really wanted to keep kissing her last week, but now she was overthinking and …

Or maybe she should just keep her mouth shut. *Solid plan.*

She pushed the gear into park and made it up the porch in two steps – long legs for the win. She knocked and Lucy whipped open the door, a rose-gold robe snugged around her body, her hair wrapped high on top of her head, her face flushed.

She was seriously so damn pretty.

'I'm so sorry.' Lucy pulled Jade in and shut the door behind her, her voice rushed. 'And I'll explain in a bit, but I'm on a huge time crunch, and, um, are you scared of needles?'

Needles? Jade held out her arms, her full-sleeve tattoos on display. 'What do you think?' She grinned. 'I live for needles.'

Lucy exhaled. 'I have to give myself a shot, and I can't. I'm freaking out, but I don't want to freak out. The last thing I need right now is to increase my blood pressure and reject this shot, but I'm already over an hour past the time I'm supposed to take it, and I can't.'

Jade nodded. She wasn't totally ignorant about what it took for surrogacy. When Elizabeth had originally brought up having a baby, she rambled on about the IVF process. As much as Jade tried to ignore her wife at the time, some of the information had sunk in. 'You need me to shoot you?'

Lucy's mouth twisted, and she glanced at the floor. 'I mean, if you don't mind?'

This was going on the top five list of odd requests. Not as odd as when a man came in and asked her to dye his pubes magenta. But still, odd.

Lucy's pleading face struck a chord deep within Jade and suddenly, she wanted to scoop Lucy into her arms. Jade's superpower had always been staying calm in the face of a storm. That was how she'd handled things when one stylist accidentally clipped a kid's ear, or when she had a screaming toddler in the chair. Her motto: Calm in the moment. Freak out after.

'No problem at all. Where's the medication?'

A sigh of relief released from Lucy. 'Really?'

Sure, Jade had never stuck anyone with a needle and the thought was nerve-wracking as hell, but was that going to help the situation? No. Lucy already looked like she was about to fall on the floor. Jade nodded.

Lucy led the way to the bathroom.

Whoa ... it must have been thirty degrees colder in the house than it was outside. Jade shivered.

'Sorry,' said Lucy. 'I was sweating like a damn pig.'

'Hi, Chucky,' Jade said as she passed the dog, who peeked with one eye, and returned to snoring in the corner on the dog bed.

In the bathroom, Jade glanced around at the dozen alcohol wipes, packages, and syringe, and took a breath. *Wow. Okay.* The moments prior to Lucy calling her must've been chaotic as hell. Jade wished she had a few moments to gather her thoughts, but Lucy looked like she was on the verge of a meltdown. Jade exhaled quietly and rubbed her palms together. 'Tell me what I need to do.'

Lucy bit the side of her lip. 'So, you have to shoot me in my upper ass area. Here.' She pointed to her side. 'Sorry. This is going to be awkward. The nurse drew a circle, and as long as you get it in there, it won't hit a nerve. Or … shouldn't.'

'Got it.'

'And you have to hold it like a dart at a ninety-degree angle. You've played darts before, right? So, you have to pop it like that. Not too hard and not too soft. You don't want the needle to break off in my skin, but you need it to puncture. And wash your hands, like really good. Wait, did you just come from the salon? I wonder if you have any little hairs on you.'

Jade looked down at herself. Considering how much clipped hair she pulled from her bra every night, the probability was high. 'Probably.'

'I'm being ridiculous. A shower is too much to ask, huh?' Lucy forced a smile as if she was joking, but her eyes looked like she did, in fact, want Jade to take a shower.

'I have a cami on. I'll just take off this shirt.' She lifted her top over her head and caught Lucy's eyes. Did her eyes just flicker down? Maybe. *Doesn't matter.* Natural reaction when someone partially disrobes in a tight quarter that was quickly heating.

Jade scrubbed her hands with the ferocity of a surgeon and watched Lucy in the mirror, sticking out her right leg while parting the robe.

'Ugh, sorry, so weird.' Lucy shoved the fabric between her legs. 'Trying not to flash the full kitty, you know?'

Jade tried. She *really tried* not to look at Lucy's beautiful, pale, round thigh highlighted by the curve of her ass. Now was not the time to admire anything, even though there was so, *so* much to admire. 'You ready?'

'Yes. Oh boy, I'm nervous. Okay, breathe, breathe. You'd think with all the therapy, I'd be prepped. I really thought I was. But here I am fumbling around like a drunk teenager. Wait, that was a weird analogy. Scratch that. Okay, I'm wasting time. I'm ready.' Lucy stuck the syringe in the rubber top, flicked at the air bubbles, then handed it over. After she wiped the skin with alcohol, she placed her palms flat against the counter and braced herself, her ass cheek lifted and facing Jade.

Jade popped the top off the syringe. 'I'm going to put my hand on your hip to steady myself, okay?' She tried to control the shake in her voice. She pushed out a soft grin, trying to portray more confidence than she felt. With this monstrous needle now in her hand, she was not nearly as calm as she hoped.

The mirrors fogged a little, no doubt because of the humidity in the air mixed with their combined nerves. She spread her fingers against Lucy's soft hip. *Concentrate.* The sensation of Lucy's silky skin under her fingertips spider-webbed up her arm. Was the rest of her body as soft as this? Jade wanted to shake herself. This was so unprofessional. Granted, she wasn't a nurse, but it still seemed unethical to have Lucy in such a vulnerable position, while having unholy thoughts. 'I'm going to count to three.'

Lucy nodded and held her breath.

'One–'

'Shit!' Lucy yelped.

'All done.' Jade topped the orange cover back on the syringe.

Lucy yanked gauze from the pile and slammed her hand on the injection site. 'You said count to three!'

'The anticipation is the worst. When I got my nose pierced, the guy did that to me, and I was so grateful.' She laid the covered needle on the counter. 'You mad or relieved?'

'Relieved.' Lucy dabbed her skin and peeked at the gauze. Seemingly satisfied, she tossed it into the garbage and the needle into the waiting sharps container, and dragged her fists up and down her hip. 'The doc said my muscles would stiffen if I didn't massage. I've always wanted rock-hard thighs, but not like this.' All colour drained from Lucy's pink cheeks and she gripped Jade's forearm. 'Sorry. I, uh, think I need to sit down. Whoa. I feel like a freshman who just tapped her first keg.'

Jade gripped her arm. 'Puke or dizzy?'

'Just dizzy.' Lucy stumbled out of the bathroom and squeezed Jade's hand until they reached the couch. 'I think I'll be fine. The doc mentioned this might happen, but it should pass pretty quick.' Lucy plopped on the shot-free side and continued massaging. 'Anyway, thank you for coming over. I know it was super out of the blue; it's just Drew's gone for a few days …'

Definitely Jade's signal to leave, right? But she couldn't just walk out. What if Lucy fell on the floor and smacked her head? Was Chucky doggy-trained to call 911? Jade somehow doubted it. She needed to chill for a little and make sure Lucy didn't pass out. 'I'm starving. I would never normally ask someone if I could raid their fridge, but–'

'You literally just shoved a needle the size of a light post in my ass. You can eat whatever you want.'

Jade lifted her brow. 'No salty meats, though.'

'That will *never* get old.'

At the fridge, Jade shuffled a couple of leftover containers to the side and opened the drawers. 'Can I bring you something to eat?' She pulled out an orange, a yogurt, and a cheese stick. She wasn't even that hungry and didn't want to waste Lucy's food. But the lingering awkwardness from the last time they hung out was still in the air, and she didn't know if she could just come right out and say she was going to stay and monitor.

'No, I'm good.'

With snacks and water in hand, Jade made her way back. She sat on the very edge of the couch by Lucy's purple-glitter-covered toenails, as Chucky eyed the cheese stick in her hand. 'Here, maybe just take a few sips of water.'

Lucy lifted herself, emptied the glass, then lay back down. She titled her head to the ceiling. 'You know, I haven't gotten drunk for almost a decade.'

Jade opened the cheese stick and Chucky leapt up like he heard a gunshot. In a millisecond, his eyes were wide, tail wagging, and he'd pressed himself directly against Jade's legs. She peeked at Lucy, who nodded. Jade broke off a chunk and laid it in her palm. 'A decade of no drinking? Why?'

''Cause this.' She waved to her face. 'I was like twenty-two, maybe twenty-three, and devoured buttery nipples all night—'

'Not a bad way to spend a Saturday.'

'The shot! Butterscotch liquor and Irish cream.' She pinched the bridge of her nose and shifted. 'We were at a casino and the carpet's diamond pattern started spinning ... and oof. Let's just say I ruined my shirt, a pair of shoes, and the security guard put on latex gloves before kindly escorting me out. Never again. I *hate* being dizzy.'

'Oh, no.' Jade smiled and tore the top off the yogurt. She dug her spoon into the cream, and several moments of awkward silence stretched between them. She probably should call out the elephant in the room, but it was the mother of all uncomfortable conversations. 'Hey, um, I'm really sorry about the last time I was here.'

Lucy slowly sat up and propped herself on her elbows. 'That was a sucky night. But honestly, I probably should have told you sooner.'

'You don't owe me anything. I barely know you.'

Lucy looked down at her fingers and took a breath. 'Why do you say that?'

'That I barely know you? Because it's true. We only met like a month ago.'

Lucy's beautiful amber-dark eyes tapered. 'Do you only think of how well you know someone by the length of time you've spent with them?'

Hmmm. How did other people measure the amount of knowing someone? Jade had known her parents her entire life and barely knew them. But she'd known Amanda for less than a year and felt like Amanda understood her better than most. She thought she knew her ex-wife better than anyone, but it turns out she didn't know her at all. 'I guess? I mean, how else do you know if you know someone?'

Lucy sat all the way up and crisscrossed her legs. 'It took until I was in my twenties before I felt like I knew my dad. I've known co-workers and other friends for years, and they don't know I'm going to be a surrogate. They've certainly never seen my butt.' She tore a chunk of orange from the peel and nibbled. 'I don't normally get to know people on any sort of deep level, and I feel like I know you. At least, I know you enough that I was pretty confident when I called you for help, you'd come over.'

Hmm. This was a lot to take in, but Jade saw the logic in Lucy's words. Jade scooped the last bite of yogurt and set the container on the coffee table. 'Your co-workers don't know you're going to be a surrogate?'

Lucy shook her head. 'No. My dad, the fathers, and my manager all know – and my manager just knows because I had some questions about health insurance.' She shifted on the couch and covered her leg. A soft tendril fell from her messy bun and grazed the top of her collarbone.

Jade pretended not to notice.

'Is this your first time taking a shot?'

'I've done them in my belly, but the needle was so much smaller. Like the size of a flu shot needle. I didn't think I would freeze. Months and months spent prepping, and I just failed.' Lucy's eyes flickered down before she reached for another orange slice.

Zero reason existed for Lucy to feel bad. Even though her body pushed her to reach out and touch Lucy's leg, Jade refrained.

'Five years ago, my ex-wife bought us tickets to sky dive,' Jade said. 'It was a lifelong dream of mine. I took the classes, prepared myself – I was so damn excited. Went up to the plane, stood at the door, and literally became immobile.'

Lucy's eyebrows knitted. 'Such a bummer. Was she pissed?'

Jade chuckled. 'You have no idea.' Jade left out the part where she and Elizabeth drove back home in silence. But the level of disappointment radiating from her wife was nothing compared to the self-loathing Jade felt. By that point in their relationship, it felt like Jade did something at least once a week that let her wife down.

Lucy's eyelashes grazed her cheeks as she looked down. Suddenly, Jade had so many questions. Had Lucy ever had her heart broken? Who was her first love? Why did there seem to be a flicker of sadness behind her eyes even when she was giggling?

'I'm feeling better.' Lucy stood up and readjusted her robe.

If that wasn't an invitation to leave, Jade didn't know what was. Her heart dropped to her toes. What was she thinking, anyway? Because she performed a kind act, she was now some purple-haired knight in shiny cosmetology armour, and therefore deserved more of Lucy's time?

Jade gathered her things. She couldn't help but take one last look at Lucy in her pink robe with her toes sticking out. She moved to the door, ignoring the way her belly churned, ignoring the way the robe wrapped around Lucy's curves.

Lucy bounced on her tiptoes and chewed the side of her lip. After a moment passed, she gripped the front door and swung it open. 'Thanks again. For real. Super, super cool of you to help me.'

'Of course.' The warm night air engulfed Jade as she walked to the car. On the drive home, her mind wandered to what a strange, and yet almost familiar, evening it had been. As awkward and odd as the last hour was, it also wasn't. Which was confusing as hell, and she didn't know how to decipher the conflicting feelings.

She rolled up her driveway and pushed her car into park when her phone pinged.

Lucy: *You saw my butt.*

Jade grinned.

Jade: *In all fairness, it was more butt-ish. Just the side. And I wasn't looking, anyway.*

Lucy: *Rude.*

Jade chortled. She actually wanted to say that she shouldn't have looked but did, that touching Lucy's skin was electric, and Lucy smelled nice, and her house was homey, and Jade kind of wanted to curl up with Lucy's chunky knitted blanket and fall asleep next to the dog.

Instead, she hovered her fingers over the screen.

Jade: *Goodnight.*

And that little tingle that Jade had been fighting with, trying so hard to ignore, sprung back up. But this time, no matter how hard she tried, it refused to disappear.

Chapter 13

Lucy

Ouch.

Two a.m. on Saturday, and Lucy woke up with a thudding pain radiating throughout her leg. She heaved it into a different position. The leg felt less like a limb and more like a wooden tree trunk attached to her hip. She fisted the knot and, for the second time in twenty-four hours, her chest tightened. How the hell was she going to inject herself for the next several weeks? Sure, she had melted into a pile of goo with the calm and extremely sexy way Jade took charge, but she couldn't ask her to just drop everything to come over every night until Drew got back into town next week.

The ache lessened and Lucy must've dozed off because she woke up to a whiny Chucky. She threw a robe over her pyjamas and stepped outside as Chucky zoomed past her on the lawn. The morning sun warmed her face; the dewy grass squished beneath her bare feet. Her purple nail polish peeked out between the grass blades as she spread her toes against the earth.

Of course, soon, being barefoot in the grass wouldn't be safe.

After going down a destructive internet search on everything pregnant women should avoid, from alcohol and cat litter to deli meats (*that one really sucked*), she starting double-clicking on the *super* scary articles. Apparently, bare feet on grass could lead to an infection. Manicures could lead to a staph infection. No sushi, of course (no fair). No colouring her hair. No soft cheeses, nail polish, household cleaners, coffee … the list went on. After the embryo transfer, she'd have to travel in a latex body suit and eat only organic veggies to make sure she kept the embryo growing.

Well, one more week of enjoying feeling the earth on her feet for almost a year. She might never move from this spot.

She yawned and pulled her phone from her pocket.

Drew: *Hey, can you call me when you wake up?*

She dialled. 'I'm up.'

A rustling sounded over the phone. 'You know, most people start with a hello, or hi, or hey. Not, I'm up.'

'I'll add that to my long list of things I should do to make me seem human.' She watched the dog chase a squirrel up a tree. 'What's up?'

'Just checking in. How are you feeling after the shot last night?'

More emotions than she wanted to share. A little scared. Sore. Kind of enamoured with Jade. And feeling a little skittish about essentially kicking Jade out last night so quickly. But Lucy had come down, hard, with a case of rescue romance after Jade saved her from shot hell, and Lucy needed some space so she didn't do something stupid.

The only message she'd sent the previous night to Drew was: '*Shot one down. Just like that time senior year when we got into your dad's disgusting cinnamon whiskey.*' No reason to rattle the Drew-cage and tell him she hadn't actually been able to do it on her own.

'Good. A little sore.' She wiggled her toes against the grass. 'I'm going to have Chucky crawl on me for a paw massage.'

'Nice. Time for him to be useful.' A sound like a suitcase zipper sounded over the phone. 'Question. Mason looked through the weekly invoice and you never charged us for the two doctor visits last week.'

She slouched down in the wicker patio chair. 'I have like a gazillion sick hours at the bank. I'm not going to charge you for those hours. I use or lose them.'

'You *have* to charge us. You're already doing so much and–'

'We've talked about this. Seriously. It's like I'm double-dipping. Which is great if we're talking chocolate fondue, but not as fun with your and Mason's money.'

A hefty sigh sounded through the phone. 'But it's in the paperwork and the last thing I want to be in is a breach of contract and the lawyers get involved, and then the clinic gets involved, and then something happens.'

The unusual panic in Drew's voice gave her pause. 'Hey, sorry. You're right. I just feel guilty taking your money.'

'It still blows my mind that you feel guilty about anything. Sister Katherine would be so proud.'

Back in the parochial school days, Sister Katherine had been the main guilt enforcer, pounding into the children's heads that they should constantly think of all the terrible things they'd done that week and seek forgiveness. Thankfully, Sister Esther was there to offset with a stash of butterscotch candies and sunshine stickers.

'Do you remember that time she whacked Jordan on the knuckles for talking back?' said Lucy.

'That kid was a dick, though. Still is. Remember when he tried to sell me some weird ass skin moisturiser a few years back?'

'Oh God, I forgot about that.' Chucky trotted up to her with a toy frisbee in his teeth and dropped it at her feet. She tossed it and he tore around the yard.

'Hey, after the embryo transfer, you want to hit up Luigi's the

Second? Mason and I were thinking that'd be a perfect sort of "pre-celebration" spot. Although we all know how superstitious he is, so we won't actually mention that. We'll call it a post-appointment dinner.'

She threw the frisbee again. 'Wait, they opened? I thought that wasn't until next month?' Luigi's had been their favourite pizza and pasta joint for years, and she and Drew had been counting down the days until the second location opened.

'Yeah, they opened last week. How did you forget?'

How did she forget? She pushed a thumb into her forehead. Ugh, she was so scattered lately.

'I've gotta run. Gonna have some breakfast with my boss. I might need you to rescue me. If you get a text that says X, call me five minutes later and tell me that there's an emergency. I'll love you forever if you do.'

'You already do love me forever,' Lucy said. 'But deal. I got you.'

After fully exhausting Chucky, she returned to the kitchen and popped a pod into her coffee machine. Soon, the freshly brewed scent filled the air. Cutting down from a four-cup-a-day habit was tougher than she'd expected, but with the transfer only a few short days away, the moments of enjoying even the occasional fresh cup were ending. The doctor said she could have one cup a day, or even switch to decaf, which she scoffed at (because, what was the point?). Ultimately, she wasn't risking Drew and Mason's kid coming out with an extra toe because she needed her morning espresso.

A few hours later, after a trip to the doggy park and a quick stop at the grocery store where she did not, under any circumstances, walk every aisle hoping to see Jade, Lucy pulled into her dad's home.

The home conjured up complicated feelings, and each time she pulled up the long gravel driveway, she never knew which feeling would emerge. The summer after she graduated high school, her dad had bought this chunk of land and moved into a trailer on the property while he built a modest, one-level home among the trees and fields. Lucy suspected her father had wanted to move right after her mom died but didn't because he also wanted to offer Lucy some sense of stability.

He rarely talked about her mom, or at least never initiated the conversation. Lucy struggled for years to reconcile what that meant, feeling like a nuisance when she asked about her, feeling guilty for how much she thought of her, and feeling angry that he seemed to just *move on*. Although he never dated anyone else, everything else just seemed to continue. As if she were never here. Not until Lucy was an adult did she understand that was how her dad coped.

That first year, he hugged Lucy when she cried, probably trying his very best with words like 'Let's focus on happier things. Want some ice cream?' Sometimes it seemed he wanted to pretend his wife's passing had never occurred. That instead of being truly gone, she was just 'somewhere else'. He didn't remove any pictures of her, redecorate, or even so much as remove her random bags around the house filled with cross-stich supplies and overflowing with yarn.

But when he moved into this home, he stripped everything of her mom away, as if she had never existed.

Though this house had never felt like home to Lucy, she had to admit it had grown on her these last fifteen years. A white house with black shutters and hanging plants lining the front porch. Surrounded by standing gardens, strawberry bushes, and mismatched lawn furniture. Perched bird feeders and birdhouses scattered the yard. She appreciated that the place was her father's fresh start, but while sometimes that made her happy, sometimes it made her sad.

As she killed the engine and watched her father pull weeds from his vegetable garden, a dull ache filled Lucy's chest. So many times over the years she had wished her mom was here – when she aced an impossible science course, graduated, was promoted at work, or when she first got her period. Now was one of those times. Her dad had the emotional intelligence of a pineapple, and she always leaned on Drew for moral support. But she couldn't talk to Drew about all her feelings about surrogacy. He was on code-red high alert with anything she said, and if she said the wrong thing, he might dive into a tailspin of despair.

For once, she wished she had a partner.

Her father crossed the driveway to her truck. 'Unless I'm losing it more than the average bear, you're here on the wrong day,' her father said, fisting a large chive bunch in his gloved hands. The front of his work jeans had stains from years of effort and garden dirt.

'Come on, Chucky.' The heavy truck door squealed as she opened it, and Chucky ran out to terrorise some bunnies. 'Yeah, I was taking the boy out for a country drive, and we thought we'd stop by and make sure you're fully hydrated and staying out of trouble.' She bet good money her dad knew she was lying – she rarely stopped by unannounced. But right now, she needed her pops.

His red cheeks showed beneath his two-day-old, salt-and-pepper scruff. He tugged off his muddied gloves and waved her in. 'Well, come on then. Better get some lemonade.'

Inside the house, he dropped the chives into a small bowl and washed his hands. 'Hot as the devil out there today.' He took off his brimmed hat and dried his hands and face with a towel.

'What are you going to make with the chives?' She dug in the fridge for lemonade.

'Found a recipe in a magazine at the barbershop. Potatoes and chives. I almost ripped it out when I remembered I could take a picture with my phone.' Sunlight burst through the blinds and Lucy snapped them shut. Her dad slid a stool out from under the table and slumped down. After gulping back the lemonade Lucy handed him, he wiped his mouth with his wrist and eyed her suspiciously. 'Hope you're not looking for steak tonight, 'cause

I just took them out to defrost. Won't be ready until tomorrow.'

She'd never dream of ruining their Sunday-night steak routine. 'Nope, we're still on for tomorrow.' She sipped her drink and watched Chucky from the window roll in the dirt. Ah, the life of a dog – carefree, consumed with chasing, playing, and sleeping. She was a tad jealous of her canine companion.

Her dad stood, grabbed a cookie tin from the cupboard and pushed it towards her. He said nothing, and she appreciated it. She plopped her head into her hand and zoned out, her eyes lost in the view of the field outside the window, nibbling at her favourite sweetened shortbread.

'I took the first big shot for Drew. Remember, I told you after the belly shots, I had to do the huge one?'

Her dad leaned back in the chair and tapped his fingers on the bottom. 'Well, you're still walkin', so must've been okay, huh?'

She shrugged. 'I had to have a friend come over and do it.' Her father broke his usual stoic face with a slightly raised eyebrow, and her ears turned warm. 'Uh, I had a hard time doing it myself this time. I'll totally get it tonight, though. I just got spooked.' The words rushed from her lips. *Hopefully*, she'd get it tonight was probably more accurate. She really did need to do this on her own. They had only a handful of days prior to transfer, and then the entire first trimester, where she'd have to stick herself. But the thought of Jade being there last night, her firm hands steadying Lucy, the concern flushing Jade's face that she seemed to try to hide but couldn't … Lucy guzzled half the lemonade and avoided her dad's gaze.

He turned to watch Chucky barking at a branch. Several long moments passed until he folded his arms and took a quick breath. 'Your mom hated needles.'

A shot pierced Lucy's chest. Maybe her dad was more intuitive than she thought, and knew she needed something, even the tiniest morsel, to connect her with her mom right now. 'Oh, yeah?' *Play it cool. Too many questions and he'll bolt.*

He grabbed a cookie from the tin but only played with it in his palm. 'You know, when we went to the hospital to have you, she was so damn worried about needles she refused to get the spinal shot. What do you call it?'

'Epidural?'

'Yeah, that. She took twenty-two hours of labour, crawling on her knees, me rubbing her back, hot towels, everything. Damn near broke my hand when she was squeezing it through the contractions. But she couldn't stomach the idea of letting someone stick that thing in her back.' He cracked off a piece of cookie and chewed. 'She was the strongest woman I knew.'

A small, dormant hole within Lucy seemed to fill. Her dad abruptly stood, and she knew the conversation was done. After giving him a moment, she met him at the sink and leaned her head on his shoulder.

'Your mother may have been the strongest woman I *knew*,' he said quietly. 'But you got her beat. Proud of ya, kid.'

Warmth flooded Lucy. So few words and yet, this was exactly what she needed. She leaned up and kissed her dad's rough cheek.

He grabbed his gloves and clippers. 'Come on now. Your fat dog is going to eat all my strawberries if we don't get out there.'

She swallowed down the knot in her throat and followed him outside.

The afternoon sun cast a golden hue through Lucy's window and reflected against the TV. She was halfway through a murder-mystery marathon, which had taken a weird, dark turn that was making her more emotional than usual. She turned the channel to a *The Price Is Right* marathon to cleanse the creepy vibes. A pink-haired woman who vaguely resembled Jade jumped up and down before spinning the wheel.

Lucy grabbed her phone and eyed Chucky, who was snoring at her feet. 'What do you think, bud? Should I go for it?'

Green eyes, purple hair, and a perfect heart-shaped mouth

had captured her thoughts since yesterday and she couldn't shake the images. The memory of those long, strong fingers gripping her naked hip had almost kept her up as much last night as the knot in her side, and even though the moment had theoretically been so deeply *non*-sexual, somehow she couldn't stop replaying the image.

She was *so close* to being implanted. For the next year she'd likely be pregnant, and then postpartum. That was the plan, the same plan they'd had for years. And she was so freaking excited about the plan.

So yeah, it made no logical sense for her to pick up the phone. She bit her lip as she typed the message. Her stomach fluttered. She hit send.

Chapter 14

Jade

The hair cuttings tickled places where they shouldn't have even fallen. Jade flapped her shirt to release some of the embedded strands, then ran a sticky brush over her tank and bra to catch a few more stragglers. She'd cut straw-dry hair before, but this last client had an unfortunate perm on top of an even more unfortunate bleach-job (not from Jade's salon, of course), and the hair had shot like thumbtacks into her skin.

The back-room door swung open, carrying the buzz of hair dryers and conversation, and Amanda peeked in.

'Hey, Mrs Dieterman called. She's running a few minutes late.' Amanda tapped her fingers against the door frame. 'Also, your last client of the day just cancelled.'

Normally, that would've irritated Jade, but today she welcomed the news. She hadn't slept well last night, what with the visions of needles and a soft pouty mouth swirling in her brain. The idea of leaving early, grabbing some takeout, and taking a bath sounded exactly like what the hair doctor ordered.

'Want me to check if someone in the books next week wants

to take an earlier appointment?'

Jade tore off the sticky paper from the roll and tossed it into the trash. 'Nah. I'll just take the rest of the night off.'

'Suspicious. You okay?' Amanda raised a perfectly shaped black eyebrow. 'Ohhhh, do you have a date? Saturday night and all.'

'Yeah. With myself, Netflix, and a bath.' Jade left the part out about including a new vibrator in her evening plans. She and Amanda were tight, but she wasn't about to violate *that* boundary. As chummy as they were, there was still an employee-employer relationship to consider. 'I'm too old to go out on a Saturday night.'

'You're a hottie. You know that, right?' Amanda pumped rose-and-herb-scented lotion in her palms and handed Jade the bottle. 'Probably inappropriate for me to say, since you're my boss and all, but whatever. Seize the moment, woman. You aren't going to be in your thirties forever.'

Inappropriate or not, Jade warmed at the comment.

'Hey, favour to ask you,' Amanda said as she stuffed the last of the dirty towels in the washing machine.

'Sure, what's up?'

'You okay if my aunt meets me here after hours and I use your station to do her starter locs?'

'Yeah, of course.' One of the benefits she had for her employees was the ability to use the salon after hours for family. Amanda didn't have a licence and technically, Jade could get in a little trouble for having an unlicensed employee working on hair. However, she never once heard of a cosmetology board member slapping a fine on a salon owner for free after-hour services. 'You're a nice niece. You might want to have Uber Eats on speed-dial since you'll be here for a few hours.'

'I was thinking maybe we'd order pizza and make it a whole family affair. I think I'm gonna have my mom come help if that's cool.'

'For sure.'

'Thanks, lady.' Amanda grabbed a few water bottles from the fridge and bounced out the door.

Jade double-checked her tray. Spray bottle, rollers, and freshly sanitised combs. Check. Often, auto-pilot took over, and she returned to her station carrying supplies that she forgot she even loaded.

With an unexpected reprieve, she grabbed her phone from her pocket and peeked. Her heart leapt when an unread message from Lucy popped up.

Lucy: *Hey, do you have plans tonight? Wondering if I can take you for dinner?*

Dinner. Maybe this message was a gratitude offering since Jade helped Lucy yesterday. Maybe Lucy was asking for a date. Maybe Lucy was bored and just checking if her friend wanted to hang out to help pass the time.

Jade wasn't sure which one of these scenarios sounded better. Or worse. Too many thoughts swirled in her mind, and after staring at the message one too many times, she slipped the phone back in her pocket without responding. Does she want to have dinner with Lucy? Yes. *Should* she have dinner with Lucy? Honestly, she didn't know.

The back-room door swung open and Shayna bounced in, her sky-high, ultra-snug ponytail flapping behind her. The hairstyle looked damn good, but Jade couldn't help but wince at the inevitable pounding headache Shayna would have by the end of the shift.

At six feet tall, Jade was used to being the tallest woman in the room. But Shayna was a fan of platform heels, and the ones she had on today nearly put her eye-to-eye with Jade.

'You must have a spine of steel.' Jade glanced at Shayna's shoes. 'I'll never understand how you don't jump into an ice bath as soon as your shift ends.'

Shayna reached for colour and developer. 'Who says I don't?' She squeezed a dollop of deep red into a bowl and mixed. 'I was born in heels.'

A conversation had to be had. Shayna's profit's downward spiral was ongoing, and Jade knew they had officially reached the point where she had to address the situation. She pulled in a deep breath. Elizabeth always said that Jade's greatest fault was avoiding hard conversations – that she bottled everything up and stewed until she boiled over. She should just come out and casually ask if Shayna was okay.

'Are you okay?' Shayna asked as she plucked foils from the box. 'You look like you're off in la-la land.'

Ugh. Beat me to it.

'Oh yep!' Jade's words were way too chipper. She was the boss, dammit. This was her salon, her employee, her profits. She needed to just spit it out. 'Off to see if Mrs Dieterman arrived.' Her face heated. She'd address the Shayna situation later. Right now, the text message from Lucy was playing in a constant loop, and she had to figure out what to do. Besides, if something was happening, a busy Saturday afternoon was not the time to have a heartfelt and possibly upsetting conversation.

Definitely not avoiding. Definitely.

Jade pushed the door open with her hip and smiled as her client walked through the door. 'Mrs Dieterman. Looking as beautiful as ever.'

Mrs Dieterman scowled. 'Well, now I know you're full of mouldy baloney. My shampoo set cannot keep up with the humidity, and I refuse to go to church tomorrow looking like a raggedy doll.'

Jade set the supplies on her station and held out her arm.

'You don't eat fish, right?' Mrs Dieterman gripped Jade's arm and shuffled to the shampoo bowl. 'I forget if you vegetarians count that as meat. You know, in the church, we don't count fish as meat. You can have that during Lent on Fridays and it's okay.'

'Good to know,' Jade said with a smile at the random food fact. Does Lucy eat fish? Can pregnant women eat fish? There are so many rules, she imagined, with pregnancy and eating, but she had no reason to dig into those. *Wait ... what did Mrs Dieterman ask?* 'Oh, uh, no, I don't eat fish. Why do you ask?'

Mrs Dieterman sighed as Jade lathered the suds and scrubbed, rubbing softly on the top, and harder on the nape. 'Mr Dieterman went with our oldest son fishing today in Brainerd. Last summer, they came home with almost fifty pounds of fish. They said this year they're expecting to get *more*. Who can even eat that much? I figured I'd beer batter fry them and bring you some. You could probably use some meat on your bones.'

Normally, any comment about body or sizes, or someone being too fat or too thin, made Jade cringe. But Mrs Dieterman got a pass – it was clear in her tone it was more motherly love than societal judgement. As Mrs Dieterman continued chatting about the best spots for walleye, Jade's mind wandered. Dinner. Tonight. Was this *dinner* dinner? Or was this just grabbing some takeout with a friend. And if it was 'dinner' dinner, was Jade actually ready for that?

Back at the station, Jade grabbed the rollers. Crap. Wrong ones. How the hell did she do that? She scurried back to grab the right ones and took one more glance at the text ... *wondering if I can take you for dinner*.

Okay, that was definitely more than takeout. Jade took a second to pinch the tip of her nose, separate the flush of tingles from the coiling belly, then returned to Mrs Dieterman.

'I don't think I ever asked how you and your husband met,' Jade said as she rolled. 'Was it love at first sight?'

'I'll tell ya – I told him it wasn't. But I knew he was the one, even though we were only fourteen when we met.'

'You've been together that long?' *Incredible.* Meeting your soul mate so young and sharing a lifetime of experiences, knowing everything about each other, loving each other ... a dream come true. Being a divorcee fresh into your thirties – not a dream come true.

Amanda set a cup of coffee down in front of Mrs Dieterman. Jade mouthed her quiet thanks. She was all Lucy-distracted from the adrenaline-inducing text message and had totally forgotten the drink.

'Thank you, dear.' Mrs Dieterman took a small sip. 'We had this boy in our school. Pretty new, moved from a different county. Kinda different from the other boys. Really shy. The kids picked on him and pushed him around. But not my husband. One day, the boys were really laying into him. My husband has always been a little quiet. I'm the talker. But we were chatting outside of school, and he was real distracted. And then he excuses himself, walks right up to the bully and socks him one, square on the chin. And I knew right then and there he was the guy for me.'

Jade chuckled and divided the next section of hair. 'You knew he was for you because he could throw a punch?'

'Oh, heck no. The hit barely fazed the bully, and he got my husband back ten times more. But the bully never bothered that boy again, and it made me realise my husband was a good person. He stuck up for someone who couldn't stick up for themselves. So, I say, find a mate who's a good person.' She adjusted in the seat. 'Now, last time I was here, I forgot to tell you about my youngest granddaughter. Oh boy, did she get herself into a pickle this week …'

After the final roller was tucked away, Jade moved back to her office to take a break. Mrs Dieterman would be under the dryer for a decent chunk of time, and she could use this time not only to get caught up on paperwork but also to decide what she was going to do about dinner tonight.

She sifted through a stack of mail on her desk when a letter caught her eye and her breath hitched. *Elizabeth.* Whatever it was, she didn't want to see it. Besides calling, Elizabeth had sent emails, which Jade used all brute force in the universe to delete without reading. But a letter seemed so formal. Legal.

Thinking of their time together still made her belly thicken, although the pain of the break-up had vanished. She didn't want to open the envelope. But she had to see what the letter said.

She ripped it open.

Jade, I hope all is well with you. I will keep this quick. I have tried countless methods to get a hold of you and cannot. So, a letter it is! Please. I need to talk to you to discuss an urgent matter. Will you call me? Thank you. – Liz

Shit. Jade closed her eyes. Whatever Elizabeth needed, it must actually be important. Jade had to deal with this, whatever it was. And even though she had lingering bitterness towards Elizabeth, she cared for her former in-laws. If this letter was about them, she wanted to know.

Jade picked up the phone. Elizabeth answered in one ring.

'Elizabeth.' Jade held her voice firm, professional, and short.

'It's so good to hear your voice,' Elizabeth said, and Jade could tell by the sound of her voice that she was smiling. 'How are you?'

'Cut the bullshit. You don't care. What do you want?' Maybe a little harsh, but pleasantries were the last thing Jade needed right now.

'That's unfair and you know it. I will always care about how you're doing.'

Several long moments passed without another word, and Jade's chest heated. Why was Elizabeth clamming up now? Was she waiting for Jade to ask probing questions and pull it out of her? Jade didn't have time for this. She needed to free herself, sage the air, and move back to thinking about Lucy. 'Just spit it out. What's so urgent?' A moment passed, and Jade contemplated actually hanging up the phone this time. But that might lead to more letters, and Jade would rather deal with this now and be done than prolong it.

'I hate to do this, but I need a favour. A huge one.'

Jade almost laughed. During their marriage, it was painfully obvious that Elizabeth didn't need one single thing from Jade. After the honeymoon period wore off, Jade felt rejected, useless, dismissed. She was never the top priority – or any priority at all, really. She slumped on the chair and drummed her fingertips on the desk. 'What do you need?'

'I need you to write a statement testifying I'll be a good mother.' Elizabeth's powerhouse voice sounded meek and rushed.

'You're fucking kidding me.'

'Please.' The pleading was a rarity. Jade had only heard it once or twice during their relationship – the last time was when Jade slammed her car door and took off for Minnesota.

She assumed that Elizabeth would have already gotten a kid by now. Sure, Jade had no idea how long the process took. But well over a year and a half had passed since the 'I filed for adoption knowing that it meant saying goodbye to you' bombshell.

None of this made sense. Of all the people in the world who could testify on Elizabeth's behalf, why choose Jade when they didn't even part amicably? 'I don't understand.'

Elizabeth exhaled a long breath. 'The first adoption agency had some issues. You remember them, right?'

Remember? It's why they divorced.

'Without boring you to death on details, I applied with another agency, and our divorce obviously came up in the background check. And my God, they are thorough. I swear they were about ready to ask me for my blood type and previous sexual partners. Remember when we applied for our first mortgage and how much documentation we had to supply? That times ten.'

Jade couldn't help but flash back to the place where the newlyweds with knotted stomachs and sweaty palms jumped, skipped, and damn near bulldozed through every hoop imaginable to get a first-time home buyer loan. 'I'm still not tracking. Why me?'

'The adoption lawyer felt a statement from you – my ex – declaring I'd be a good mom, that I don't have any anger or substance abuse issues, et cetera, would strengthen my case.' The silence that followed was long. 'Please, Jade. I wouldn't ask this unless it was absolutely critical.'

Jade wanted to yell *You destroyed our marriage for this!* She didn't want to help Elizabeth. Jade owed her nothing. But deep down, somewhere low and uncomfortable, Jade knew that if Elizabeth put half as much effort into *being* a mom as she did *becoming* a mom, she'd nail it.

Jade pushed back from the table, her chair screeching against the floor. Her chest was hot, tight, and her breaths felt like sludge in her lungs. She needed to leave the space, step into the sunshine, and end this conversation. After one more quiet plea from Elizabeth, Jade squeezed her eyes shut. 'I'll see what I can do.'

Elizabeth sighed. 'Thank you, sincerely. If there's anything I can ever do for you—'

'There's not.'

A pause followed. 'Well, thank you again. I hope you're happy, Jade. Truly. I miss you. More than you know.'

The words depleted the surrounding air. Jade hung up without responding, paced the small office, and fanned her face. Dammit. She needed to purge Elizabeth. After swallowing back a full glass of water, she powered on her laptop and hit the keyboard with the fury of a million bullets.

To whom it may concern,

Elizabeth Fleming and I were married for eight years, together for eleven. We divorced amicably after a fundamental difference of opinion. Throughout the marriage, and divorce, Elizabeth always held herself with integrity and fairness. She displayed empathy and kindness as we went on our separate life paths.

Please use this as the strongest recommendation I can provide in support of Elizabeth's application for adoption.
Sincerely, Jade Hudson

She slammed the laptop shut, wrapped her arms around her bent legs, and dropped her head onto her knees.

So many moments passed that Jade started to get a kink in her neck. She breathed out, exhaling the final string tying herself to Elizabeth, inhaling what felt like a new, clean slate, the beginning of something different. Soon, a grin spread at the lightness in her chest.

She was officially free. She grabbed her phone and typed.

Jade: *Just to set expectations, is this your nice way of asking if I'll pop you in the butt again?*

Lucy: *Well, when you put it like that ...*

Lucy: *I wanted to thank you for coming to my booty rescue last night. And if that leads to another popping, well, then so be it.*

Jade: *Are you still scared to do it on your own?*

Lucy: *Yes.*

Lucy: *But that's not why I am asking you for dinner.*

The spring in Jade's chest amplified into a full backflip, topped with a somersault. But then it nose-dived.

She could do dinner. She was an adult, just like Lucy. They both had to eat, and it might be nice not to eat alone. They had great conversation, and she liked Lucy's company. Jade even liked her dog, and she was *not* a dog person. And this whole interaction with Elizabeth had not rattled Jade, at least not as much as she thought. *Right?* Yes, she was pretty sure. She felt better, not worse, and maybe having dinner would be just what she needed to prove, to herself, to the universe, that this 'Elizabeth' chapter in her life was officially closed.

Jade: *Dinner sounds great. Pick you up at 6?*

A few hours later, after Jade's last client left for the day, she tore out of the salon and flew down the road. Pulling up to the stoplight, she tapped her fingers against the steering wheel. Her skin still itched from the haircut earlier in the morning. She needed a hot shower and a fresh change of clothes before her date tonight.

It's not a date. It's not a date.

She couldn't date Lucy. Lucy was about to get pregnant, for God's sake. If an award existed for the literal worst time ever to fall for someone, pretty sure it would be on the cusp of that someone getting knocked up.

But she could have dinner, stare at Lucy's cherry lips, and indulge in her bubbly personality. And then shake it all off and commit to being friends.

Damn her legs tingling with the idea of spending more time with Lucy. Later, Jade needed to have a serious sit down with her body and tell it to stop doing all this fluttery bullshit. Because one thing was absolutely clear – she could not allow her feelings to mess with her good judgement.

Chapter 15

Lucy

Lucy hopped on one foot to pop on her sandal and then scurried to the entryway mirror. She flattened her palm across the stomach of her sundress. Light pink was a gamble. She wasn't the most elegant eater in the world, and it would really suck if she spilled spaghetti sauce on the front.

The clip holding half her hair felt like it was ripping out strands. She unclipped, wrapped, and re-clipped. The mirror confirmed she'd wasted her efforts – her wavy locks were springing in all the wrong directions. She tossed the barrette on a side table, smoothed her locks, then peeked out the window. No sign of Jade yet, although she wasn't due for a few minutes. Lucy had tried to distract herself – errands, house cleaning, doggy playtime, and yet, these last two hours had dragged by at the speed of a glacier.

The sound of crunching gravel made her chest flutter. *Breathe.* Why was she so damn nervous? She didn't even want to answer her own question – she knew why. She hadn't had feelings for someone in forever. Truly, forever. Sure, she'd liked people in the past, had a few relationships, had some amazing sex. Okay, and mediocre sex with a terrible kisser once, but she didn't want to dwell on that now.

This whole-body flush feeling was so out of the norm that she felt like she was being lust electrocuted. She was jolty and shivery and didn't know what to do with this burst of energy.

And it was all a little scary. After they'd kissed a few weeks ago, and Jade stopped talking to her, it stung. Bad. Lucy would probably need to address that at some point but didn't feel like ruining the time they were about to spend together.

She opened the door. Um – wow. Jade was *killing it* in skinny ripped denim, sandals, and a snug, white button-down shirt, showing a peek of deep cleavage. Lucy ripped away her gaze. Jade strolled up to the porch, so effortlessly cool, her purple undercut with fresh lines carved in the right side. Lucy gnawed on the inside of her cheek to refrain from whistling.

'That dress is super cute,' Jade said as she stepped onto the porch. Chucky nudged himself past Lucy and pushed against Jade's legs with his tail wagging.

Lucy made an awkward curtsy, then straightened. 'Thanks. Chucky helped pick it out. He was like ru-roa, that one, and threw a paw.' *I did not just do a terrible imitation of Scooby-Doo. Pull it together.*

'He did great,' Jade said, petting Chucky's scruff.

Seriously, breathe out the nerves. Tonight was just a typical Saturday night and Lucy was just having a casual dinner with *freaking beautiful* Jade. No biggie. They'd shared a quasi-meal before on her couch. They chatted all the time. They were friends for God's sake. Her thumping heart needed to chill.

Lucy tossed her matching cotton-candy pink purse across her shoulders and scratched behind Chucky's ear. 'You be good. When I come home, I better not find that you brought over any bitches.' She cracked herself up and glanced at Jade. 'I can say that word 'cause–'

'Female dog. Got it.' Jade chuckled and held open the screen door. 'Ready? I can drive.'

'You drove over here. The least I can do is drive us there.' Lucy followed Jade down the porch steps to the truck. 'Besides, Betty Yellow likes having guests. Makes her feel useful.' She opened the truck door for Jade and released a trapped cloud of heat and humidity. With her long ballerina legs, Jade hopped into the raised truck without needing the step like Lucy did.

Lucy shifted into reverse and tossed her arm behind the seat as she backed down the driveway. Her eyes flickered to Jade, whose glossy grin made Lucy want to melt.

'You drive a stick-shift?'

Lucy pushed the gear into first, then second, as she gained speed. 'Yep. Love it. I don't think I would do an automatic.'

The evening sun blazed through the window and illuminated Jade's face. 'Why?'

So many reasons. Lucy always struggled to explain why things from 'back in the day' were so comforting to her. *Saved by the Bell* episodes. Obsessing over Rachel and Ross. Perfecting the 'Bye, Bye, Bye' dance – which she was damn good at, if she said so herself.

'A sense of power, maybe? My dad taught me when I was super young, like twelve or thirteen. He didn't want me to get stranded if there was only a stick-shift option available. I think since he was raised in the no cell phone, no internet era, he forgets I could just call an Uber.'

'Such a dad move.' Jade flattened her arm against the window edge. 'Sounds like he loves you a lot.'

'Yep. I think I earned the whole "daddy's little girl" title.' Lucy shifted lanes. 'So, you drive a Prius, huh? I think we need to come up with a name for it. Since it's all New Agey and has fancy things like a back-up camera and moon roof, we need a good name. Flashdance?'

'Flashdance? For my car?' Jade chuckled. 'Um … not sure that works.'

Lucy tapped the steering wheel. 'Sparkles? Galactic? The Milky Way?'

'The Milky Way? Nope, hard pass.'

Lucy grinned. 'Oh, oh! How about Starlight? You know what, I'm actually not even going to give you a say in this because you clearly have terrible taste. Starlight it is. You're welcome.'

Jade laughed again, a sweet, full laugh, and Lucy soaked up the sound. 'Starlight is perfect.'

Fifteen minutes later, Lucy backed Betty Yellow into a parking spot with the ease of a NASCAR driver and hopped out. She raised her hand in salute to shield her eyes against the bright evening sun and followed Jade. A garlicky, meaty haze enveloped them before reaching the door. She filled her lungs with the savoury scent. 'Yum.'

'My God, how much garlic does this place use?' Jade opened the door for Lucy.

Chivalrous. I like it. 'So much. We have to promise we'll both eat it, so we'll neutralise each other's stinky.'

Jade grinned. 'Deal.'

The Italian restaurant was hopping, and thankfully when Lucy called earlier, they had a reservation available. She had an 8 p.m. sharp (no pun intended) date with a syringe, and even though she normally wouldn't have made a reservation, tonight she couldn't chance an hour wait for a table.

A hostess escorted them past the massive wine display, plants, and paintings of Italy, and sat them down at a red-and-white-chequered table. Delicious smells filled the air – hearty tomato sauce, sage- and fennel-stuffed sausage from a table near theirs, and the restaurant's signature fresh baked bread. Clanking dishes and laughter surrounded them, and Lucy thanked the heavens they'd got a quiet-ish booth in the corner.

After debating which meal sounded the best and placing their order, Jade sat back in the chair and scanned the room. 'This place reminds me so much of one of my favourite spots back home – a ma-and-pa Italian place right outside downtown. I had the best manicotti of my life there.'

The server set down a wooden platter with a small loaf of crusty bread and pointed at the four dollops of butter in front of them. 'Honey, fig, garlic, and plain.'

'We made a pact, right? I'm starting with garlic.' Lucy tore a chunk of warm bread and spread a hefty pat of butter on the pillowy interior. 'Would you ever move back to Chicago?'

'Hmmm. I don't think so. I loved the city. *So much.* It has everything one could ever want, but there's nothing there for me anymore.' Jade picked up the knife to cut herself a slice.

Lucy sank her teeth into the perfect combo of crunchy exterior and soft interior. 'Don't you have family there?'

'Yeah, my parents.'

Lucy raised her eyebrows.

Jade slathered a combo of honey and fig butter on half and garlic on the bottom half. 'Let's just say I have a very complicated relationship with my folks.'

'Oh yeah? How so?'

'My parents are pretty successful. My mom's a VP at a telecommunications company and my dad's a lawyer. And they always expected that I would do something ... great, I guess. My older sister's a doctor. My younger sister is at Harvard earning her PhD in history. And, well ...' She gave Lucy a lopsided grin. 'Here I am.'

'And here you are ... what? A successful business owner?'

'Thank you.' Jade chewed slowly and swallowed. 'I thought I'd go to school for graphic design, maybe go work at some big firm. But I hated it so much that I dropped out my sophomore year.' She added another dollop of butter to her slice of bread. 'When I told my parents I was going to cosmetology school, they freaked out. They couldn't fathom why I would go to "beauty school". They said they wanted me to be as successful as possible, and cutting hair was not sustainable. Of course, the whole spiel was for *my own good* – and then they said they were cutting me off.'

'What?'

'Yeah. I was on my own, and they wouldn't help pay for a

single thing. They even kicked me off the family cell phone plan. So dumb.'

Ouch. Lucy loved her dad, and she might not always get the emotional support she needed, but she was always her dad's number one. She couldn't imagine a world where she didn't feel one hundred per cent supported. 'I'm sorry. That sounds really, really hard.'

Jade shrugged. 'I don't know. I mean, so many people have it worse, you know? Who am I to grumble that my rich parents didn't give me enough? I'm a walking billboard of privilege. I hate even complaining about it.'

'Someone will always have it harder. Doesn't diminish your reality, or your struggle, you know? You had to fight for what you wanted. That's real.' Lucy added an extra helping of fig butter onto the bread. 'Also, how do I not know this stuff about you already? I mean, I've seen your boobs for God's sake.'

'I knew it!' Jade laughed.

'I'm totally kidding. I swear I didn't!' Lucy was still pretty bummed she hadn't gotten a sneak peek.

Jade fiddled with the straw in her sparkling water. 'What about you? Do you have family in the area?'

The server set down the plates, the steam rising from the pasta. Lucy twirled the noodles on her spoon and felt a sliver of honesty edging its way upwards. 'My mom died when I was ten. Bike accident.'

'Oh, wow.' Jade's words were soft.

Lucy wanted to suck back this conversation. She didn't talk about her mom, ever. And yet, just saying that piece was stirring something.

'My dad is around, and we spend a lot of time together. I sometimes wonder if my dad and I would be as close if my mom were still here. Oh gosh, that probably sounds awful. Obviously, it's not like I'm *glad* my mom died, but I lucked out in the dad department. You'd like him. He's a grumpy old man.'

'I love that you guys are there for each other.' Jade scooped up tomato sauce with a chunk of bread. 'Can I ask you a question?'

'Sure.'

'What made you decide to be a surrogate for your friend?'

The question was hefty, although not unexpected, and Lucy wanted to give Jade a longer answer than she could probably formulate coherently on the spot. 'You're not going to ask me how much they're paying me?'

'That's none of my damn business.'

Something about Jade's response warmed Lucy. 'Very few people in my life know I'm doing this, but I've gotten the same two questions from all of them: How much are they paying you and how's it going to happen?' She bit into a spicy sausage and swallowed. 'I think they assume Drew and I are going to bang it out in the bedroom with blindfolds on.' She shuddered. 'Gross. Dudes.'

'True.' Jade laughed and tipped her glass in solidarity. 'I knew the surrogacy process was a ... process. But it's even more than I realised. The shots, meds, appointments and things.'

'During one appointment, they shot dye up my fallopian tubes, and I got so sick. And the doctor was super cute and I *Exorcist*-style projectile vomited all over her.' Lucy slammed her hand on her mouth. 'Oh God, we're eating. Sorry.'

Jade laughed and waved her hand. 'You probably wouldn't believe this, but a few times a year, some customer at the salon pukes. It's gross, but it doesn't gross me out to talk about it.' Jade pulled the straw to her lips. Her eyes were twinkling. 'So, what did the doctor do?'

'Funny enough, it wasn't so much what the doctor did as what Drew did.' Lucy grinned with the memory. 'He turned as white as the lab coat and stumbled from the room. The doc was a pro, though. Returned a while later in fresh clothes and did the transvaginal ultrasound.'

Jade winced. 'Yikes. That doesn't sound fun.'

'She dug out what I swear was a twelve-inch dildo. I totally panicked so I threw my hands up and said, "Wait, you gonna buy me dinner first or what?"'

Jade muffled a laugh with her fist. 'Oh no, you didn't!'

Lucy lifted an eyebrow. 'She didn't find me nearly as amusing as I found me.'

Jade chuckled, then dunked the bread into her sauce and stared out the window while she chewed. 'I bet the dads are super grateful for you.'

'They are, but I'm so grateful for them.' Lucy twirled the pasta on her fork. 'It's hard to explain, but sometimes I feel like I get more out of this than they do.'

'Well, they get a baby, right?'

'Okay, fair. But … how do I say this without sounding like a Mother Teresa wannabe?' Lucy strummed her fingers on the table, her silver rings clicking. 'Have you ever paid for coffee for the people behind you in a Starbucks drive-thru?'

Jade cocked her head. 'Um … Yeah?'

'Tell me what it felt like.'

'Hmmm.' Jade shrugged. 'An adrenaline rush, maybe? I remember flying high for an hour after, wondering if it made these random people's day. And then hoping they weren't assholes.'

'Oh, good point – wouldn't it be the worst to waste a good deed like that on jerks?' Lucy wiped her mouth with the corner of the napkin. 'But yeah, so buying that coffee just makes you feel good, right? Picture that feeling, times a thousand, for *years*. Sometimes I think it's more me doing this for *me* because of the jolts I'm getting.'

A few beats passed, and Jade blinked at the window. 'I think I'm slowly starting to get it.'

They spent the next hour eating a raspberry-and-chocolate-filled torte and laughing over embarrassing stories – Lucy had a million of them, Jade not quite as many. As the hour went by, the more they talked, the more Lucy's eyes travelled to Jade's mouth, to the curve of her shoulder, to the creamy outline of her nape. Her laughter filled the room, her words filled Lucy.

What was Lucy thinking? She signed an affidavit claiming to be single. Yes, yes, the essence of the affidavit was in regard to marriage, or a live-in partner, but *still*. She didn't fully understand these feelings. And she was two seconds away from getting pregnant. Pregnancy might bring forth her best self, or her worst self, but it would certainly change her in some way. Any relationship she started now would be doomed.

Maybe the impending pregnant-hood was affecting her more than she realised. She really thought she had worked out most of her issues in therapy ... not to mention years' worth of long conversations with Drew and Mason. But never during those conversations did it occur to her that her solitude, and not just that but her *joy* and *comfort* in solitude would be rattled. Was it Jade? Was being on this journey alone scarier than anticipated? Was this like a panic crush right before the inevitable?

On the way to the parking lot, Lucy stuffed her hands into her pockets – bless the designers who finally added pockets to dresses – to keep from brushing herself against Jade. But her hand kept inching out, apparently with a mind of its own, wanting to touch her.

Situated in Betty Yellow, Lucy pulled the truck out of the parking lot and down Main Ave. She didn't want the night to end, but she needed it to end. Time alone to process would help provide clarity as to why she *so badly* didn't want the evening to end.

Jade cracked the window and glanced at Lucy. 'You ready to take the shot on your own?'

'Um, yep.' Darn her shaky voice.

'If you want, I could be there for moral support. And if you can't do it, I can stick it in.' Jade chuckled. 'That sounds terrible.'

Lucy's face flushed with relief. 'If you wouldn't mind, or ... if you don't have anywhere else to be.'

Jade laid her hand gently on Lucy's knee.

The warmth spread up Lucy's thigh and down to her toes, leaving a delicious, heated imprint.

'There's nowhere else I want to be.'

Chapter 16

Jade

A rush of electricity coursed through Jade from touching Lucy's knee, and it took a moment for Jade to withdraw. She was drunk off Italian food, flawless conversation, and Lucy's cupid bow mouth, and couldn't control her actions. The car turned warm, even with the air conditioning on, and Jade rolled up her sleeves to cool down.

Lucy's chest lifted. She bit her lip and jolted forward with a metal crunching sound. 'Grinding gears like an amateur. There goes the transmission.' She grinned. 'Too much spaghetti.'

Dinner had been as close to perfect as Jade could have imagined. She had expected it would be smooth – after sticking Lucy with a needle yesterday, Jade knew her on a totally different level – but it was hard to know exactly how people would act on a first date-*ish*.

Not a date. Not a date. But it *felt* like a date. Jade had dressed up like it was a date – as had Lucy. And now Jade really, really wanted to do what people sometimes do *after* a date.

They pulled into Lucy's house, the last sliver of fuchsia evening sun warming her skin.

Lucy held the front door open for Jade and the sound of a trotting animal on hardwood floors grew louder. 'Hi, baby. Were you a good boy?' She bent down for snuggles. 'I need to fill his food and water.'

Jade's eyes skipped through the gazillion framed photos lining the wall. Most were candid shots of Lucy at various ages on a boat, fishing off a dock, some with a school in the background. One particular photo caught her attention: Lucy with rain boots, a hoodie snugged over her head, and a massive smile, standing next to a man with crossed arms and a deep frown.

'Who's this?' said Jade, nudging the frame with a finger.

Lucy approached and looked over Jade's shoulder.

Sweet vanilla and jasmine scent wafted to her nose, and Jade's heart pounded a little harder. *Play it cool*, she told herself.

'The stupidly handsome ginger is Drew,' said Lucy.

'He's cute. Total Prince Harry vibes.' Jade peered closer. 'He looks pissed.'

'He was.' Lucy grinned and ran a finger across the framed photo. 'A few years ago, we tried camping for a weekend. He dropped like a thousand bucks for tents, cooking equipment, sleeping bags, everything. It rained almost the entire time, and he kept whining that he should've spent the money on a luxury resort. Mason and I were cracking up so hard, and Mason snapped a photo. Poor Drew. He's too pretty to camp.'

Jade's gaze flashed to the photos of multiple women, and a tiny tinge of jealousy bolted through her. 'You have so many–'

'Friends,' Lucy said. 'These are all friends, or co-workers.'

Jade laughed. 'Sorry. I didn't mean to, you know, insinuate–'

'That I'm a hussy?'

'No one says that word anymore.' Jade grinned and stepped back from the wall. 'Besides, I'm all about free love. Women's empowerment. Sleep with whomever you want.'

'Oh, my.' Lucy fanned her face like a joke, but her eyes shifted to Jade's mouth and lingered. She cleared her throat.

'Although sometimes I feel like I should take my own advice.' A heat flushed Jade's chest, but maybe now was the time to get all these sorts of things out into the open. 'It's, um, been awhile.'

Lucy's eyebrow arched. 'Oh yeah?'

'Yeah. Not since my ex-wife. And before that, I was scattered at best. Would you think less of me that I've slept with exactly three people in my life?' The air seemed tight, at least to Jade, but Lucy's face showed nothing but a soft grin. Jade wasn't some college kid bragging – or not bragging, she supposed – about conquests. And yet, there was something maybe a little depressing that she never put herself out there more both before she got married, and after her divorce.

'Less of you? There is probably nothing you can say that would make me think less of you unless you tell me you're a cat person. 'Cause, *what*?' Lucy chuckled, but she still had that look, the one that seemed to be staring directly into Jade's soul, the one that was hungry and waiting, and Jade's body churned in response. 'Want something to drink? Lemonade?'

Whew. Something needed to break this moment. Jade's toes were tingling, and even though it wasn't unpleasant, it freaked her out. She needed to take herself into the bathroom, give her body a stern scolding, and splash some icy water on her face.

Lucy was going to have a baby. Jade wanted nothing to do with babies. *She had left her damn wife over a baby*. Moments like this needed to stop. She stepped away from Lucy. 'No thanks. I've reached my sugar limit for the night.'

'No such thing.' A timer shrieked and Lucy's head snapped to the sound. Her shoulders lifted with a deep inhale. 'Shot time.'

'What do you need me to do?'

'I think just moral support.' Lucy pulled the bottle from the cabinet and rolled it between her palms. 'And if I can't do it, then you can take a stab at it. Get it? *A stab.*'

Jade groaned. 'Yep, got it.' She followed Lucy to the bathroom, as Chucky pulled himself away from watching the yard and followed the women down the hall. 'Why are you rolling the bottle?'

'It heats the oil in the meds, so it's easier to inject. Or at least that's what they told me. But I call bullshit. Last night it felt like super glue was pushing through my veins.'

Jade shuddered at the visual.

Lucy closed the bathroom door behind them. A thud hit the floor. 'Chucky gets so moody when he's not invited to the party.'

The bathroom was a decent size, but between Lucy's vanilla scent and the way her ample cleavage peeked out from her sundress, the room felt a heck of a lot smaller. *And warmer.* After scrubbing her hands, Lucy hiked her dress up past her hip, hooked her finger on the strap of her black underwear, and lifted it higher.

Jade stopped breathing. She whipped her head to look somewhere else, *anywhere else*, besides the smooth skin and curve of a beautiful, perfect ass that was *so close.* 'Alcohol wipe?'

'Yes, please.'

Jade grabbed the wipe and met Lucy's eyes in the mirror. A look – a *curl-the-toes, heart-patter, hot-neck* look – passed between them.

'Looks like my Sharpie circle is still intact.' Lucy's words were rushed. 'I might need to re-outline my bull's-eye later this week. I've been too scared to exfoliate, but I don't want to get all flaky and crunchy.' Lucy filled the syringe and contorted her body. She held the needle away from her hip as her lips pulled tight. Her nostrils flared with each heavy breath.

Jade wished she could strip that fear away. She tiptoed behind her and touched her shoulder. 'You got this.'

Lucy nodded. 'One, two, OWWW!' She leapt from the counter. 'Christ, that hurts.' She pressed a gauze strip on the entry point, her cheeks morphing from white to pink. 'I did it! Oh, my God. I can't believe I did it!'

God, she's beautiful. 'You should be proud! I've never injected myself, but I'm sure it's hard.' *I really need to get out of this small space.* 'Do you think you should lie down in case you get dizzy again?'

'Good idea. I need to lie in the bed. I have to massage my leg for like a hundred hours or it gets super stiff.'

Jade followed Lucy out of the room. 'Did that happen yesterday?'

'Yep. I seriously got so stiff. Like I'd been dancing the running man all night, forgetting that I'm thirty-two and not sixteen. I woke up and my leg was all "Bam, sucker! Take that!" It hurt *so* bad.'

Jade couldn't help but laugh at Lucy's animated words and air punches. 'Oh no. Hopefully tonight isn't as bad.' Jade stepped over a sleeping Chucky in the hallway. 'Well, I should probably head out.'

Lucy stopped. Her eyebrows squished together. 'You don't have to leave yet. I know this probably isn't the most exciting Saturday night of your life, but maybe after I'm done, we can watch a movie or something?' Lucy's cheeks turned pink.

Jade needed air. She needed to not be walking this closely to Lucy, who smelled so good and looked so delicate while also looking so fierce. The sense of urgency in Lucy's voice shouldn't affect her this much. And she definitely shouldn't be this conflicted over staying or leaving.

'So ... bedroom?' Lucy asked.

Jade swallowed. 'Bedroom it is.' The air felt like sludge in her throat. Lucy didn't mean *bedroom* bedroom. Jade knew that. She simply needed to lie down more comfortably to massage a leg. So why did *those words*, coming from *that mouth*, make her pulse *do this*? 'Hey, that lemonade sounds good right now. Cool if I grab us some glasses?'

'For sure.'

The air in the kitchen was breezier, *thank God*. Jade fanned the bottom of her shirt to cool her sticky skin and dug into the fridge. Exhaling, she calmed her racing heart, expelled the vision of black lace, and returned to the bedroom with two glasses. She stopped in the doorway. 'Wow. This was not what I was picturing at all.' Her eyes travelled over the soft grey pallet-wood accent wall, the wrought-iron bed, the rustic nightstands, and two single grey-scale abstract paintings, one on each wall.

'Be honest. Were you picturing it more like a rainbow unicorn exploded?' Lucy pulled her knee into her chest and ground her fists into her thigh.

Jade set the drinks down and returned to the doorway. She could not let everything about tonight – about the last month – fuzz her judgement. Sure, Lucy was amazing. But she was about to embark on a life-changing journey, one that Jade couldn't be part of. Right? *Yes, er, no. Definitely, no.* 'I just didn't expect it to be so, I don't know, calming in here. Not that the rest of your place isn't calm. It just has a lot of–'

'Stuff?'

'More like a lot of colour. And stuff, but not in a bad way. Like a homey way.'

'I wanted my bedroom to be super peaceful. No TV. No heavy colours, just calm.' Lucy patted the top of the soft cream comforter and wiggled back into the mattress. 'You can sit here.'

Jade tucked a leg under her butt and sat, wincing along with Lucy as she pounded her leg.

'Most times, I feed off energy and a sprinkle of chaos. But at night, I like the quiet.'

Jade rested a palm on the bed. 'I did the same after my divorce. Downsized everything.' The physical pain of the divorce had been gone for a while, but talking about it still felt like a chokehold. Memories of shoving clothes, a favourite pillow, and boxes of hair products into her car to make the six-hour trek from Chicago to Stillwater flashed through her mind. 'I didn't even need a moving truck. There's something liberating about a fresh start. You know, leaving all the crap behind.'

Lucy swung her leg higher and shook out her hand. She exhaled and continued to rub. 'Was it hard to date after your divorce?'

Jade shrugged. 'Wouldn't know. I haven't done it.' *Except for maybe tonight.*

Lucy's eyes grew wide. 'Was it a terrible break-up?'

'Aren't all break-ups terrible?' Jade skipped her fingers across the ivory cable-knit blanket draped across the bed. 'It wasn't the break-up that was bad. It was the relationship. The break-up was the relief.'

Lucy stretched her leg and returned it to the bent position. 'Is it too personal to ask what happened?'

'I've stuck a needle in your butt. I think we're past too personal.'

Jade loved to think the reason they divorced was because Elizabeth wanted to have kids. It sounded so simple that way. But if she was honest with herself, their issues ran so much deeper – and had started so many years earlier – than the bombshell that Elizabeth had detonated during the last six months of their marriage. Jade drew in a deep breath.

'Where do I begin? I met her freshman year of college. She was a couple years older than me, and she shined. She was super driven. Super determined.'

'Sort of like your parents, huh?' Lucy asked.

'Yes! Just like my parents and sisters. And it was … I don't know. Seductive? Does that make sense? She always carried a promise of a better tomorrow. Like, once I graduate, this will happen. Or once I get my MBA, or land my job at the premier Chicago firm, we'll do this. But with every milestone, it's like … the distance between us grew.'

Lucy remained silent.

'At a holiday party a few years back, I left to get us some drinks. When I returned, she was in a circle with her co-workers laughing about some office jargon and said something like, 'Jade's just a hairdresser. She wouldn't get it.' And I literally shrank. Like, I'm six feet tall, but felt like the smallest person in the room.'

The image of that night was forever seared into her brain. Jade had pivoted, stormed into the lobby, finished both drinks, and scrolled vegan recipes on her phone for over an hour before Elizabeth even realised she had never returned. At home that night, Elizabeth said Jade was overreacting, she always overreacted, and Elizabeth hadn't meant it like that, *obviously*. But then soon, Jade stopped getting invited as Elizabeth's plus-one, stopped being told about work, stopped being engaged with. Until Jade became a ghost in her marriage.

'Something like that would've gutted me. I'm so sorry. What an awful thing to say, especially from someone who's supposed to love you the most.' Lucy stroked her hand across Jade's knee, then pulled her hand back to resume her thigh massages. 'Did you ever call her out?'

'Yeah, sometimes.' Jade stared at her leg where Lucy's touch still lingered and wondered how someone's fingertips could carry that much warmth. 'I don't know how to say this without sounding whiny. I'm sure there were plenty of times that I wasn't a peach to be around. But she needed her co-workers, her friends, her managers. She didn't need me. Everything else – *everyone* else – was more important. It's not like I was jealous. I just felt …'

'Invisible?'

Lucy's soft words hit hard. *She understands.* 'Exactly.' Jade stopped stroking the blanket and sat higher. 'Jesus. No more sob story. What a mood killer.'

'What? Like this is not the sexiest thing you've ever seen, me rubbing a lump out of my swollen, stiff thigh?' Lucy flexed and shook her fingers.

Sympathy flushed through Jade for Lucy's delicate fingers. 'Need a breather? I can take over for a while.'

'No, you don't have to do that. My hand's just getting a little tired.' She rotated her wrists until it cracked. 'I'm playing Russian roulette with my muscles to see which will cave first.'

'I really don't mind. I've got titanium fingers.'

Lucy scrunched her nose.

'That sounded really, really weird.' Jade chuckled. 'What I mean is, I've given at least ten scalp massages a day for the past fourteen years. My fingers are the strongest part of me. I got this.' She hovered her hands over Lucy's thigh. 'I mean, it's no big deal for me, but I don't want to rub without permission.'

Lucy released her hand. 'Please, be my guest. Rub away. My hand is so flippin' tired.' Lucy scooted herself sideways, her pink sundress getting tangled with the blankets. 'This is why I sleep naked. All the fabric gets twisted and uncomfortable.'

It was clear she wasn't trying to be sexy as she flipped over, huffed, and shimmied the dress straight. But it was too late. The image of Lucy sleeping naked had burrowed itself inside Jade, probably for all eternity. She exhaled slowly through her nose and tried to think friend-only thoughts.

Lucy tucked a pillow on the edge of the bed, backed her butt up to Jade, and shifted her leg. After some finagling and a few grunts and giggles, Jade scooped Lucy's thigh onto her lap and pressed her palm with slow, circular strokes. 'How's the pressure?'

'Good.'

The muscle was knotted – Jade could feel it right away, a knob beneath the skin. But if she could work it out, Lucy could sleep pain-free tonight. 'So, you've never been married.'

'Nope. Never in my game plan.'

'No?' Jade pushed her knuckles into Lucy's leg and waited for her muscle to tense. When it didn't, Jade continued. 'Never found "the one"?'

'Never even found a maybe.' Lucy rested her hand next to Jade's leg. 'It's hard for me to connect with people. I love Drew. I tolerate Mason.' She chuckled. 'Just kidding. I love him too, but even with Mason, who I've known for a hundred years, I don't fully connect. And I've dated a lot, but I guess it always just fizzles out.'

The words were hard to comprehend. Lucy had a natural

warmth to her. To Jade, she seemed like the type of woman who would comfort a crying kid, bring soup to a sick neighbour, or walk out of an animal shelter carrying an armful of elderly cats. Not connecting didn't seem part of her DNA. 'Did you ever have your heart broken?'

'Never.' Lucy's hand crept closer. 'I missed them for a while, but it was more about missing having someone around. Not always missing *them*. Does that make me sound like the most awful, terrible person ever?'

'It sounds honest.'

The silence that followed was more comfortable than awkward. *Is Lucy bonding with me?* Maybe Lucy struggled to connect with people, but this right here, this entire last month, felt like a deep, growing bond. And every second spent with Lucy, or thinking of Lucy, made Jade's heart and mind dash in totally opposite directions.

The rush Jade got when she and Lucy talked sparked all her dormant cells. But fear seeped in when Jade felt herself opening up. An urge to wrap Lucy in her arms and taste her candy lips elbowed Jade daily. Lucy's leg muscles loosened beneath Jade's touch. She was kneading Lucy through the thin dress, but soon Jade's mind travelled to what was underneath. All she wanted was to hike up the skirt, give her a proper massage, and feel her utterly melt. She swallowed and breathed through her racing pulse.

'This feels really good,' Lucy murmured.

'Good.' Jade's fingers stretched, and Lucy wiggled back, her backside nearly flush with Jade. The tiny hairs on Jade's neck stood on edge, and she wondered if Lucy felt the same charge.

No, stop. She was helping Lucy alleviate pain. Being a friend. Listening. This wasn't …

Oh shit. Maybe this was. Lucy wiggled back a little more, a soft moan escaping, and inched up her dress. So subtle, it could have been waved away.

But not subtle enough.

Jade added a second hand, her heartbeat pounding through her chest, reaching her neck. Lucy's soft sigh and quiet stirring wet Jade's mouth. Lucy tugged up her dress, higher, a few more inches, and shifted. Her ass was now nearly in Jade's lap, and Jade's breath hitched. She licked her lips, her fingers aching to touch flesh.

Another tug of her dress, another wiggle, and *finally*, bare skin flashed under her thumb. Jade swiped the skin, once, twice, and Lucy's moaned intensified. 'This feels … amazing.'

Jade didn't say anything. Half of her wanted to bolt out of this room, still her heartbeat, slow her thoughts. The other part wanted to reach underneath the dress, to inhale Lucy's scent. She tugged the dress higher, her full hands on Lucy's bare, silky thigh, the skin so perfect, so smooth under the pads of her fingers.

'Do you want to touch me?' Lucy's voice, low, husky, in a whisper.

'Yes.' Jade's words were breathy. Her pulse thudded in her ears. Her mouth ached. But her heart wasn't ready. She wanted to, *my God* she wanted to, but this was more than sex, and she knew it.

'I want you to touch me.' Lucy scooted back and hiked her dress up, until the whisper of lace peeked through.

Elevated breaths filled the room. Jade slid her hands higher. It had been so long since she touched someone like this, with intention, with hesitation, and heat rose between her legs. She clenched her thighs. Maybe they should stop, but God, it felt so good to feel the shakes, the urgency running through her veins.

But it wasn't smart. Not now.

Lucy pushed herself into Jade, reached behind her, and stroked Jade's thigh. Jade's pulse moved to her neck and her breaths came heavy. She grazed Lucy's shoulders and watched greedily as a trail of goose bumps rose on Lucy's arm. A chill ran through Jade, her hands hungry, her mouth wanting to taste Lucy. She gripped Lucy's hip and pulled her into her, hard. Jade drank in the sensation of Lucy, burrowing back into her, a moan releasing into the air.

Beep, beep, beep, beep, beep! The timer on Lucy's phone screeched and rattled against the nightstand.

Lucy froze.

Jade froze.

Lucy's chest rose and fell. She broke contact, and Jade's skin turned cold. 'I'm so sorry.' She slapped the alarm off. 'I want to … I just don't think … I mean, with the pregnancy …'

Jade was empty, sad – and still fighting with arousal.

But also, so very relieved. 'I know.' Her words were nothing more than a whisper. Her chest felt like it was bound in rope, squeezing out her limited air. A few deep inhales later, she slowed her pulse. She gently tugged Lucy's dress back down and covered her leg.

Silence filled the room. Jade held still, so did Lucy. So many seconds passed that Jade wondered who'd break first.

Lucy turned, and laid her head on Jade's lap, her shoulders hunched. *Defeated?* Jade stroked her hair until her pulse normalised. All of this sucked. Why couldn't they have met a year from now? Or when they were teens like Mrs Dieterman and her husband, or before she and Elizabeth met? The unfairness of the situation made Jade want to punch the universe in the face and storm off.

Lucy exhaled a shaky breath. 'Friends?'

Her timid voice was barely about a whisper.

Friends was safe. Friends made sense. Friends hurt a little but was the only logical choice. They couldn't do this. Maybe someday in the future, maybe not. But for certain, not right now.

Jade battled back the urge to cry. 'Friends.'

Chapter 17

Lucy

The room was so still that Lucy could hear her friends' breath. Never had she been so silent in her life. Never had Drew been so silent in his life. And definitely never had five minutes passed by at the speed of a sloth.

A month after starting the shots, and three weeks to the day after the transfer, the three of them stood there, silently. If someone peeked through the window, they'd probably think a group of friends had gathered for a seance, to worship the power of a digital stick. She, Drew, and Mason were crowded into the bathroom and staring at the pregnancy test lying on the bathroom counter. All their hopes and dreams, and serious amounts of cash, held in the balance by a plastic stick.

'We should look away, right? Let's look away.' Drew chewed on his pinky nail. The last time Lucy had seen him do that was when he was waiting for Mason to call him back after their first date. 'Let's go into the hall.'

Mason tugged Drew's finger from his mouth. 'This is going

to be okay. If it's negative, we still have three other embryos we can use. After that, we try again.'

'We should've implanted two.' Drew shoved his hands in his pocket, then pulled them back out. 'What were we thinking?'

Um, nope. She had *never* signed up to carry twins.

Mason stood in front of Drew and put his hands on Drew's shoulder. 'Babe. We didn't want to try for twins, remember? What if both took?' He pulled Drew in for a hug.

This moment was definitely for the dads. Lucy wanted to give them distance, *should* give them some distance, but also had the deep desire to elbow both so that they'd make some room for her to join their hug circle. When thinking of this moment, she didn't expect to feel so empty. But for the first time in this journey, she felt like an outsider, watching a movie on how a family prepares for life-changing news. She could've stepped into the next room, and her besties wouldn't have noticed.

It wasn't jealousy she was feeling, per se. Nor loneliness. No … the feeling engulfing her was something different, something relatively new, something she didn't yet have a label for and needed to process. A longing tugged at her, a sort of wistfulness, like an unfulfilled wish … *Oh.* She did know what this was.

She wanted a partner.

And she knew which partner she wanted.

But everything was so complicated.

She and Jade had grown close, and Lucy really, *really* liked her. And deep down? Lucy knew it was more than *like*. She felt it, she knew it, but she'd never whispered those words to another person besides her dad and Drew. And she certainly wasn't in the headspace to do it now.

Lucy had signed an affidavit declaring her singlehood. She had signed a medical document stating she'd refrain from sex before implantation – although based on Jade sleeping with fewer people than she could count with on one hand, the chances of an STI were slim. But in any case! Here she was, hopefully, about to be confirmed pregnant.

The timing was terrible.

But ... was she using timing as an excuse? And even if she was, was that a bad thing? I mean, if she could focus on the excuses, and the reasons they *couldn't* be together, due to the journey she was about to take, maybe this twisty, twirling, 'keep her up at night' feelings would disappear.

Ugh. Too many thoughts were running through her head. She was just crouching to rub Chucky's ears when the sound of a buzzer cut through the silence.

Oh boy, here we go.

'Ready?' Mason asked, waving his arm towards the bathroom.

Drew exhaled, his cheeks nearly matching his fire-red hair.

Lucy's gut constricted and the back of her throat itched. The room looked a few shades darker than even a moment ago, as she flickered her gaze between the guys standing with straight lips and twisted eyebrows.

Even Mason looked nervous. Stiff, normally calm and 'cool as a Sunday morning breeze' Mason had a flushed face. All year, she had thought about this moment. Drew would sprint across the room, nudging her out of the way in his excitement to see the results, prompting a fatherly scolding from Mason. Instead, they all stood there, frozen and unbreathing.

Finally, Lucy broke and shuffled down the hall.

The pregnancy stick held years' worth of dreams and work. If it showed positive, their lives changed immediately, forever. If negative, they'd be crushed. No one reached for the bathroom door handle.

'We got this, right? Come on, guys. Let's do this.' She tried to be chipper. She really did. But her voice fell flat, and she gulped. She opened the door and squeezed her eyes shut.

The men stood behind her, silent. The only sounds were the

ticking analogue clock in the living room, Chucky snoring, and Lucy's own heartbeat, thudding in her ears.

She blinked at the test. She should breathe now, right? Oxygen was necessary for survival. Finally, a sharp breath pinched her chest, and she stumbled a few inches to the side.

'Pregnant!' Drew screamed, throwing himself into Mason's arms before pulling Lucy in. Everything blurred as they stumbled back into the hall, as sighs of relief and squeals filled the air. 'Oh my God, we did it! Do you feel different?'

'From thirty seconds ago?' Lucy hugged them, expensive cologne, mint, and sweat mixing in her nose. 'Nope. Still feeling like the same sexy beast as always.' She was pretty sure that she'd kept her tone jovial, but she sure wasn't feeling jovial underneath the façade. Thankfully, the men didn't seem to notice.

For the past two years, she'd thought about this moment *so* many times. What she'd feel like, if her heart would explode. If her ears would ring. If she'd scream and jump on the counter, or lie down immediately, put her feet up, and swear off anything non-organic. She'd thought her mind would swirl like a burst of confetti in the wind, or that she'd cry from happiness as the joy poured from her. But never once had she predicted the emotional state she now found herself in.

She wanted to cry. And not the good kind of cry either. Not the 'we've worked so hard and finally made our dream come true' cry. Nope, this one was the straight-up 'sad for myself, want to wallow in a bathtub' cry.

She should be feeling happy, right? Elated, excited, or any other possible positive emotion. Or heck – she'd even take nerves, terror, *something*. She watched the men hug. Drew wiped tears, Mason whispered in his ear, and they kissed. They didn't mean to make her feel isolated, of course. But watching them be so adorable and snuggly together, her stomach sank.

Drew reached out an arm for Lucy, once again gathering her in, and squeezed. 'I can't believe this is real. It's real, Luce! Everything.

We did it.' He pulled back and clapped his hands together. He looked so happy. So earnest. 'I love you. You know that?'

Lucy smiled. She wanted to wrap herself back in his embrace, have him tell her everything was okay, they *got* this, and what she was experiencing was totally normal. 'I love you, too.'

Mason rubbed his palms together, his throat bobbing. He was always the pragmatic one in the relationship. The man had Hilary Clinton-like nerves of steel, never showing real ups or downs. But the light reflected a mist in his dark eyes Lucy had never seen before. *Uh-oh*. Lucy wasn't sure if she could handle Mason's emotions when she could barely handle her own.

'Lucy,' he said, his voice cracking, 'I ... there's so much ... I, we, can never repay–'

'Oof. I have to use the bathroom. Sorry. You think 'cause I just peed on a stick I'd be fresh out, but here it is, gurgling around the 'ole belly.' She shooed them away before they could question what in the hell she was even saying.

The bathroom door clicked shut. She rested back against the wall and blew upwards as she fanned her face. What if they had misread the stick? Were they absolutely sure a 'not' wasn't floating above the word 'pregnant'? The men would be devastated. They had read it correctly, right? She quickly unwrapped another stick to test again, just to make sure.

While waiting for the secondary test, she squinted at the word, focusing on the plus sign with 'pregnant' right underneath.

Three solid moments passed. Dizziness kicked in, a fog in her vision out of nowhere. She planted her palms on the counter to catch herself.

Holy shit. I'm pregnant.

She flumped on the toilet seat and dropped her head into her hand. *I'm pregnant.* Deep breath in and out. In and out. Every potential missing emotion from the last ten minutes slammed into her at once, like a boxing speed bag. Happy, scared, sad, elated, terrified.

Terrified rose to the surface.

Had her mom ever felt this way? She bit back tears and tried to picture her mother's reaction when she found out she was pregnant. She hadn't had this many questions about her mom in forever and was hungry for intel. Was she scared? Happy? Sad? Was her dad in the room with her? Did her parents try for her or was she a surprise?

Heat filled her face and chest. She splashed cool water on her cheeks and breathed through her nose. Tugging up her shirt, she ran a palm down her stomach. She angled to the side, then the other side, then back again, inspecting for any sign of pregnancy. She poked her index finger into her fleshy belly, but nothing. A touch on the curvy side – it would probably take a while before she saw anything.

But seeing something or not, surely her body should feel different, right? Sore boobs. A rounder stomach. Unruly hair sprouting from somewhere. Anything? Granted with all the fancy math with pregnancy, she'd only be considered six weeks at this point, but still ... shouldn't something signal that this was reality?

I'm pregnant. Yes, they'd been prepping for almost a year. And been talking about it for two thousand years prior. She thought she knew what she would feel like at this moment, but until it happened, obviously she didn't.

A knock sounded on the door. 'Luce? You good in there?' Drew asked.

'Yep, good! Just one more sec.' Her brain was murky and fuzzy, and she needed the men to leave so she could process what the hell this wet throat, short breath situation was all about. She'd never describe herself as stoic, but she hadn't cried since she was a kid. And now, all she wanted to do was sob.

She loved Drew. She loved Mason. But she didn't want to do this alone.

She needed more.

This moment was huge, and yes, she had the guys, but she

needed to share it with *her person*. With someone more than her dad, who'd only give one or two supportive comments. Someone other than the superficial relationships at work, or cousins who were busy juggling careers and families. She couldn't have her mom. The pit grew, deep, swallowing her whole.

She wanted Jade. No, wait. She *needed* Jade.

Once the secondary test showed the positive lines, she flung open the door and faced an elated Drew, whose face dropped. 'Oh God. Are you having second thoughts?' He held her shoulders and Superman-laser-gazed into her eyes.

She struggled to maintain eye contact. And she hated herself for putting the slightest doubt into his mind. She refused to ruin this moment for him by having a rare heart-to-heart and revealing all the sad feelings she wasn't supposed to be having.

'No, stop it.' She swatted at his hand. 'I'm totally fine. It's just all super emotional right now. I'm sure it's all the hormones and shots and … well … this.' She waved her hand over her stomach.

'Same.' His chest lifted and he eased out a breath. 'I can't believe we did it.'

Mason rounded the corner and rubbed his hands together. 'Okay, what do you need? Food? Let's go for dinner and celebrate!'

The last thing she needed at this moment was dinner. Ugh, what she would give to be in the mood to celebrate what was so deeply deserving of celebration. She hated that this moment was not what the dads planned. But she knew herself well enough to know that tonight she couldn't take a loud restaurant and the men gushing. The energy she'd spend to fake it would make her crack. She yawned and threw her hands over her head. 'Ah. I'm so tired. But you guys go. Go celebrate. Snap me a gram-worthy pic.'

Drew cocked his head without a word, knowing damn well she loved food as much as she loved Chucky, and rarely gave up the opportunity to eat out. 'No way. This is a group effort. Come on. We can go to the cities, stay local, seriously whatever. We *have to* celebrate. This is huge.'

Ugh. She didn't want to ruin this for him. 'A woman in my condition cannot just go traipsing around the town.' She added a British flair to her voice in an attempt to cut the questioning look. 'Seriously. I really, really want you guys to go enjoy this huge moment, but I'm dead tired from today.' She refrained from pulling out some emotional baby-puppet strings and saying something like she was worried about overexerting the growing cells.

Her efforts must've worked because Drew and Mason eyed each other with raised shoulders.

'Cool?' She moved into the living room and plopped on the couch. Chucky nuzzled up to her legs. She stroked his fur, which held a superpower level of calming antidote, and soon she relaxed.

Mason's forehead creased as he stared at Lucy. 'We need to do something for you. Anything you want.'

This notion of Mason 'taking care of his family' and 'repaying debts' – even though she'd explained to him a hundred times it wasn't necessary – was clearly killing him. His face screamed 'help me help you'. She had to put him out of his misery.

'Oh! I know. I will love you forever no matter what, but I will double love you if you can run to the store and get me one pint of Chunky Monkey, and one pint of Chocolate Truffle.' Her stomach was turning so much that the idea of ice cream made her queasy. 'Is that okay? I don't want to hold up your dinner plans.'

Relief flushed Mason's face. 'Absolutely. Want salt and vinegar chips, too?'

She grinned. 'You guys seriously know me to a terrifying level.'

'Drew, you coming?' Mason asked as he stuffed his phone and keys into his pocket.

'Nah, I'll stay with Luce until you get back.'

For the first time ever, a slight thread of disappointment weaved through her. *Go with your husband!!* she wanted to scream. Her thoughts couldn't process with him here.

As Mason's car backed out the driveway, Drew sank into the couch and slung an arm across the overstuffed pillow. 'Thanks for sending Mason on that mission. I think he would've crumbled without some kind of assignment.'

'No idea what you mean.' Her voice dripped with sarcasm.

He tapped his fingers against the back of the couch, his freckles spreading as he smiled. 'Well, Luce, like it or not, we're bonded for life.'

She smiled at the sweet sentiment. To her, though, the pregnancy wasn't what bonded them. It was him biking over in the rain with his rickety green ten-speed the night her mom died and staying with her all night. It was her clinging to him like he was a lifesaver when they snuck his dad's old DVD of *Blair Witch Project* and scared themselves to death when they were twelve. It was him buying her strawberry cotton candy when he was at the fair while she was grounded and tapping on her window to sneak it to her.

The pregnancy was just another layer of lifetime bonding glue.

'You gonna tell Jade?' he asked.

Even though Lucy and Jade were hard-locked in the friend zone, she and Drew had talked about Jade a lot. A few weeks ago, they all finally met at a bowling alley and the guys liked Jade immediately. Which was not a surprise. Anyone who meets Jade loves her in a snap. Jade and Drew bonded over the buffalo cauliflower appetisers (what's the point unless it's chicken, Lucy had complained). And Jade and Mason hit it off when they both refused to wear the bowling alley shoes and droned on about various communicable diseases.

'Are you cool if I tell her, like, right away?' Lucy asked.

Drew tapped on his crossed leg. 'It's your story as much as it is ours. Please don't forget that. Your body, your choice, on *everything*. Including who you want to tell and when.'

'As notarised and filed with two different law firms. Got it.' She grabbed the remote. 'GiGi's?'

'Your obsession with *The Golden Girls* is for the record books,' Drew said. Chucky snorted at the perfect time, drawing a giggle from Lucy. 'Do you think you'll change from your self-proclaimed Rose to Dorothy or Blanche while rocking your pregnancy?'

'Maybe I'll become Sophia. Who knows?' Lucy cracked a grin and tapped the power on. The moment Drew shifted his focus to the television, her mouth faded into a straight line. She wasn't sure if she'd change characters, but one thing was certain. Things were already changing.

An hour after the guys left, Lucy's heart leapt at the sound of a knock on the door. *Skipped heartbeats aren't good, right?* She'd probably already damaged some of the belly cells.

'Hey, you! Missed you.' Jade stepped into the house and wiped her Doc Martens on the mat. Her hair had switched from lavender to a mix of deep cinnamon and sunset gold. Lucy decided on the spot that no colour in existence could look bad on Jade.

'Hey!' Lucy reached up for a hug and squeezed. 'Missed you, too.'

'I was talking to the dog.' Jade set her keys on the side table.

Lucy groaned. 'And here I was about to tell you how much I love the new hair colour, but I'm withholding my compliment 'cause you suck.'

Jade patted the top of her head. 'Fall colours. Gotta keep up with the trends. And if I want to make my end-of-the-year goal, I need to encourage my clients to spice up their colour routine.' Jade scratched behind Chucky's ears. 'So, what's up? You said I had to come over right away.'

'Um, pretty sure my text said if you had nothing going on, you could come hang out.' Lucy dug out the tub of Chunky Monkey, Jade's favourite, and offered her a spoon. Lucy preferred Chocolate Truffle, but she loved the little routine they'd built of sharing bites out of the same tub. And yes, it was dumb, and yes, so very sixth grade of her, but it forced their heads close together, and Lucy could indulge in the fantasy of Jade leaning in for a kiss.

'Fair.' Jade leaned against the counter and crossed her ankles.

She dug into the ice cream and wrapped her full lips around the spoon. Lucy ripped away her gaze.

'So, I've got something to tell you.' Lucy placed the spoon on the counter.

Jade's smiled dropped. 'Yeah?'

Today was a freakishly warm mid-October evening, but everything was so hot. Lucy's cheeks burned, and the ice cream was not helping cool her mouth down enough. 'I'm, um. I'm pregnant.' Saying the words out loud to someone else landed her reality with a thud. *I'm actually, genuinely, not hypothetically, for real this time pregnant.*

Jade's eyes went wide, and her chest lifted like she sucked in a breath but didn't release. Lucy couldn't interpret anything behind her expression. After what felt like the longest few seconds of her life, Jade pulled Lucy in for a tight hug.

'You're going to be the best damn oven that bun has ever seen. I'm so happy for you all.' Jade stepped back and stared at Lucy's belly. 'Why do I have a weird urge to touch your stomach? Don't let me be one of them.'

'One of who?'

'You know, the people that feel entitled to rub a woman's belly if she's pregnant.'

'You can rub this bad boy anytime.' Lucy patted her stomach. 'It doesn't even belong to me. Property of two queens from the Greater Twin Cities area.'

Jade shook her head. 'Everything about that statement is so wrong.' She grabbed the spoons and ice cream and jutted her chin towards the sliding glass door. 'Want to sit outside?'

Like Pavlov's dog, when Lucy unlocked the door, Chucky dashed outside and tumbled in the grass. A smattering of moths flew in the moonlit air. Lucy followed Jade to the swinging bench and tucked her legs under her butt.

Everything was different. Lucy knew it would be, but it was really, really different.

The rickety wooden seat swung in a hypnotic rhythm as silence filled the space. Jade dug into the dessert and took a hefty spoonful. 'Okay, tell me everything. How did the dads react? Total freak-out? Was Mason super chill? Did Drew bawl? Or in a shocking twist, the other way around?'

Lucy was in a dream. That's what this was ... Jade was here, next to her, but she was foggy and fragmented. She needed to tell Jade how she felt, how she loved that Jade was here, but she wanted Jade here *with her*. Not as a friend, not as a buddy. Lucy wanted her arms, and love and heart, and why did this all have to crash on her tonight of all nights?

Jade's words lingered in the air, just like the moths, and she continued peppering Lucy with questions about how Lucy's dad felt, how Lucy felt, if she felt anything different in her belly. Lucy's gaze floated to the north star. She mumbled responses but couldn't form anything super coherent. The star seemed to flicker broader, wider than she'd seen before, and she wondered for a moment if that was her mom winking at her from wherever she was.

A spoon waved in front of her face, and Lucy blinked back to reality.

'Hey, you good?'

No. 'Yep.' She was lost, scared, and felt more alone than she'd ever felt before. But she was also happy. She needed physical touch right now more than anything, but Jade normally shrank back when Lucy reached for a hug. Lucy wanted to hear everything would be fine. She wanted Jade to snap her out of whatever was happening right now.

The bench stopped swinging. 'Are you crying?' Jade's gaze flashed across Lucy's face.

'Nah, must be the allergies.' Her eyes filled, threatening to overflow. One more word and Lucy was sure the salty-tear floodgate would fly open.

Maybe Jade could sense this, or maybe she needed touch as

well, but she inched towards Lucy and draped her arm across the back of the swing. Lucy gratefully accepted her silent invitation and snuggled against her chest. She melted into Jade's comforting embrace, indulging in her warm body and musky citrus scent. Moments passed in silence, the only sound, the chain squeaking against the swing, and the grass squishing under Chucky's rolls. The fear and trepidation within Lucy seemed to drift away, and her stomach loosened. She wasn't sure how long they sat there, but the moon moved behind the trees. Finally, an exhausted Chucky flopped on the deck.

'Thank you for being here,' Lucy whispered. Jade planted a kiss on her head, and Lucy savoured the soft touch.

Jade patted Lucy on the arm and gave her a gentle squeeze. 'I will always be here.'

Lucy wasn't sure what power those words held, but her chin trembled against their intention.

Chapter 18

Jade

Jade pulled into her driveway and leaned against the headrest. The obnoxious Halloween decorations on her neighbour's lawn were only exasperating the stress headache she'd been grappling with for the past hour. Orange and purple blinking lights draped their trees, tombstones lined their lawn, and the plastic dancing zombies were kind of freaking her out.

Halloween decorations shouldn't make her this irritable, but here she was, swearing at the scarecrow poking out from the garage. She whipped open her front door, slammed it shut, and tossed her bag on the floor. She was being unreasonable. Her flared nostrils and pounding chest and constricted heart were all stupidly unreasonable.

Lucy. Is. Pregnant.

Why were Jade's insides pretending like she didn't know this was going to happen? For months, she'd thought about this daily. But now that it had happened, her stomach was knotted so hard that she needed to sit.

The refrigerator kicked on, a low buzzing sound as it churned its way through the cooling cycle. *Food.* Maybe she needed food. She stared at the rows of takeout inside the fridge, and the lone bagged salad. One box, she didn't even remember ordering. She popped open the top and gagged. 'Gross.'

Netflix proved to be an unworthy opponent for her antsyness. She clicked off the screen after scrolling through a gazillion shows. 'What the hell's my problem?' she muttered into the void.

No response was returned. But she didn't actually need a response. She knew.

Against all better judgement, she'd fallen, hard. She'd tried to keep her distance, but that hurt worse. A month ago, she had decided she wanted Lucy in her life. But not *being* with Lucy chipped away at her soul.

Leaning into the couch, Jade lifted her head and pinched the bridge of her nose. Should she do some Pilates? Meditate? Chop some onions to help drudge up a good cry?

She had withheld physically from Lucy, as much as possible. Their physical contact had mostly been scattered hugs or Lucy's go-to show of celebration – the dreaded fist bump. But Lucy was so damn affectionate – linking their arms when they walked or just reaching out to touch Jade's arm. Of course, that's just who Lucy was. She acted the same way around Drew and Mason. She was a lovey, gooey, joy-filled person. And Jade may have misread those signs.

Yes, they'd kissed last month. But even Lucy joked the shots made her extra horny, and she would've humped anything with a heartbeat. She had told Jade she felt no intimacy with sex, almost hinting that she and Jade could get it on without repercussions. But Jade was wired differently. Sex equalled intimacy equalled love. Only once in her life had she slept with someone she didn't have real feelings for, and it was miserable. The morning after, she left feeling empty and icky. Just because Lucy could shut it off, didn't mean Jade could.

A piece of her – a small, vindictive, angry piece – wondered if

Lucy was love-gaslighting her. Lucy was so warm, but Jade wanted more than snuggles. And every time she worked up the courage to say something, she froze. But now she'd lost her chance.

Lucy was pregnant.

Jade kicked the side of the coffee table, knocking her pinky toe just right. 'Fuuuuu!' She jumped, the burn shooting up her foot. The house was trapping her. She needed to escape and let her mind settle. At this rate, she'd be up until 2 a.m., pacing the house like a madwoman until she collapsed into bed. After tugging on her light jacket, she stepped outside. The crisp fall air still held a hint of warmth from earlier. She hopped into her car, shifted into reverse, and took off for anywhere but here.

When she was with Elizabeth, isolation consumed her. Elizabeth was the star, and Jade gravitated towards her like everyone else did. For more than a decade, Jade maintained few friendships. The salon co-workers rotated in and out. Clients were clients. The type of deep, fulfilling friendship like she had with Lucy, didn't exist. She opened up to Lucy about almost everything.

But she couldn't talk *to* Lucy *about* Lucy.

The city zoomed by as Jade drove. Random streets turned into eerie cornfields. She whipped a U-turn near a rustic barn and drove to the edge of town. Civilisation squinted into focus as billboards and a gas station flickered past her window. A neon pink 'open' sign flashed above an 'all day breakfast' and 'homemade pie' sign. Maybe a rhubarb pie à la mode and a steamy cup of diner decaf would do the trick.

The bell jingled above the door. Bright fluorescent lights bounced off the red booths and silver-backed chairs. The scent of burnt coffee grounds and fryer grease filled her nose. She squished into the slightly sticky chair at the bar next to the old-fashioned malt machine with stacked tin cups, and rotated the menu designed as a tiny jukebox. This place was perfect.

A woman wearing a name tag reading 'Bunny' approached. She pushed a dusty-blond tendril that had come loose from her floppy bun behind her ear and picked up the pair of glasses hanging from a pink chain around her neck. 'Hey there, what can I get ya?'

Heartache cake, perhaps? 'What's the best pie you've got?'

'Well, the best pie we've got today is strawberry rhubarb, but that's because it was made fresh this morning. The cherry's my favourite, but it's a day old at this point.'

'Perfect. I'll take the strawberry rhubarb à la mode and a cup of decaf, please. You got oat milk by chance?'

The woman raised her eyebrow.

'Never mind. Black is good.' Jade had far surpassed her sugar intake for the day, but this was exactly what the Misery Doctor ordered.

Several bites of phenomenal pie later, offset by the bitter coffee, and Jade's thoughts still wouldn't relax. She was in love purgatory and didn't know how to escape.

Choice one, do nothing. That was the smart and reasonable option. She flipped open the queer dating app she'd signed up for a few months after her divorce. Pic after pic she swiped, hoping something would give her a spark. But each impersonal profile, or dreaded mirror selfie, sank her spirits further. She knew what she wanted, and it wasn't contained within this app.

'Can I get ya anything else?' Bunny asked as she stacked Jade's silverware on top of her now-empty plate.

'No, I'm good. Thanks.'

Bunny ripped off the ticket. 'Pay whenever you're ready. No reason to rush outta here if you don't want to.'

It's like it's written on my face. 'Thanks. Where's the restroom?'

Bunny pointed to the large metal sign on the wall that said 'Restroom this way'. Jade nearly facepalmed herself. She followed the antique licence plates, Coca-Cola and Dr Pepper tin signs, and posters ranging from Marilyn Monroe to Elvis, until she reached the bathroom.

A few minutes later, Jade stared at herself as she washed her hands. Mirrors surrounded her at work. But it had been forever since she'd really looked at herself.

Fine lines had emerged around the edges of her green eyes, and … she rather liked it. Ageing was a gift. But the bags, she could do without, as they reflected the last few years, the sleepless nights, the burden of running a company.

The hours spent thinking about what a life with Lucy would look like.

Jesus. Jade needed to snap out of this. Make a decision, stick with it, and be done. She crumpled the paper towel and tossed it in the wastebasket. It was already past ten, heading dangerously close to her bedtime on a work night, and she wasn't going to solve her love woes in a small-town diner on the outskirts of town.

She tugged her purse across her shoulders and exited the bathroom when she did a double-take at a couple sitting in a corner booth. 'Mrs Dieterman?'

Mrs Dieterman jolted her head upright. 'Jade, dear. What in the world are you doing here?'

Contemplating the biggest decision/non-decision of my life. Trying to pinpoint the exact moments when my feelings shifted so profoundly that my heart filled and then broke.

'Needed some late-night pie.'

Mrs Dieterman gestured to the man sitting across from her. 'This is Mr Dieterman.'

The soft-grey-haired man with curled shoulders and a smattering of brown age freckles on his cheek lifted himself to stand.

'Oh please, don't get up.' Jade waved him back down. 'It's nice to meet you. I've heard so much about you.'

'Sure is nice to meet you.' He shook her hand with a snug grip. 'My wife here talks about you almost as much as the grandkids.'

'I hardly believe that.' Jade grinned. 'What are you two doing out at this hour? Or is this a common occurrence?'

'Well, I'd love to say this was a date night, but sadly we just came from Rochester for a wake. My nephew.' Mrs Dieterman stirred the coffee and clanked her spoon against the mug. 'Can you believe it? Only fifty-two years old, brain aneurism. He just passed on Monday.'

Jade's heart dropped. 'I'm so sorry to hear that. Fifty-two? That's so young.'

Mrs Dieterman patted the booth next to her. Jade accepted the invitation and slid in next to her.

'We hadn't seen him in years, but it's real sad all around.' Mrs Dieterman pooled syrup on the side of her plate and dipped a chunk of pancake in it. 'His mother could barely stand, she was so distraught. Doesn't matter how old your baby is; losing a child is every mother's nightmare.'

Jade was glad she'd never know that type of deep devastation and recommitted on the spot to never have children.

'So, you're the one that keeps my Clara here looking so beautiful?' Mr Dieterman smiled as he fumbled with the creamer seal.

Jade had the urge to reach out to pull it off for him as his thumb shook, but she refrained. 'I only maintain what she was born with.'

He finally tugged open the creamer and splashed the minuscule amount of liquid into his mug. 'Clara's been a looker since the day I met her. You ever heard of love at first sight? I'll tell ya, it was love at first blink.' Mr Dieterman spent the next ten minutes rehashing the story of how they met, the details only slightly shifting from Mrs Dieterman's version. Somehow, as Jade listened to his warm words of adoration, comfort washed over her. After sixty years of marriage, these two still looked at each other like *that*. She and Elizabeth only had those eyes for the first two years.

Jade showered him with questions, asking what their school was like and if Mrs Dieterman had the same feisty personality back then as she did now. Mrs Dieterman cracked a joke about getting frisky during a dance after the girls were allowed to enter the boys' gym, and he talked about him and his buddies helping decorate that day, just to get closer to the girls. A yearning filled Jade, and she wanted to cry at the sweet story.

'You know I made him wait a whole year while I played hard to get?' Jade shook her head. 'I *wasted* that time. And seeing our grandnephew today just ...' Mrs Dieterman waved her hand.

The words hovered, heavy in the air.

'Do you have someone special?' Mr Dieterman asked.

How to answer that? There *was* someone special, but she didn't *have* someone special. Jade bit the inside of her cheek. 'Well ... I mean, I have someone I care about ...'

Mr Dieterman set the fork against the plate with a *tink*. 'Do they know?'

'Marlon, now that ain't none of our damn business.' Mrs Dieterman swatted at his hand. He shrugged and dug back into his meal. Mrs Dieterman glanced at Jade and leaned towards her. 'I tell ya, it might have been all those years ago, but I wish I could get that year back. I'd never want to waste this precious gift of time. The second I knew he was the one, I shoulda told him, right then and there. Ya never know what could happen.'

The words hit, hard. The pie from earlier rumbled in Jade's belly. Mr and Mrs Dieterman spoke facts, and Jade needed to listen. During her marriage, she'd chased and waited, chased and waited. She never felt settled, whole, or complete. And she didn't need someone to do that for her, but dammit, she *wanted* someone.

'I need to head out.' She shook Mr Dieterman's hand and patted Mrs Dieterman's forearm. 'Thank you for the chat. And I'm so very sorry about your nephew.'

The temperature had dropped another degree while Jade was inside. She made her way to the car, the noise from the highway sounding faintly in the distance. The smell of moisture saturated the air, and before she left the parking lot, rain started spitting on her.

Streetlights blurred as her mind swirled. Visions of Lucy and pregnancy and broken marriages and broken vows and hope and love flashed at the same speed as the rain pellets. The image burned in her brain of Lucy's thigh wrapped around her, that snort-giggle that made Jade laugh every time, that sweet mouth and the deep kindness behind those eyes. How energy burst through Lucy, exploding out of her as she twirled through the living room, spilling popcorn as Chucky lapped it up.

Tears brimmed, then fell, and Jade swiped them away with her sleeve.

No more waiting, no more silencing herself. Forget the pregnancy. Forget the fear. She was not letting another minute go by without saying how she felt.

The rain beat harder, the swoosh of the wipers matching the swoosh in her stomach. As if on auto-pilot, Jade pulled down Lucy's street, her heart thudding in her chest. She leapt out of the car, not daring to waste one more second. Jade had to tell Lucy how she felt, and if Lucy didn't feel the same ... well, she'd still stay. She wanted Lucy in her life, even if it could only be as friends. But she really, really wanted to be more than friends.

The stairs were slippery as Jade leapt up to the door, the rain now pelting against the gutter. The *ting ting ting* matched her pulse that had now skyrocketed to her head. She lifted her hand to knock but froze. It was after eleven. Lucy was pregnant. Maybe it could wait.

Jade didn't want to wait. Dammit. She hadn't thought this through. She could text her, see if she is awake. What if Lucy rejected her, right here, tonight?

But what if she felt the same?

Texting. Yes, that was good. Jade pulled out her phone, fingers shaking, when the porch light turned on and illuminated the deck. The front door swung open. Somehow, Jade was shivering even as adrenaline pumped through her veins.

'Jade?' A confused-looking Lucy tugged her robe across her

waist. 'Are you okay? Come in! Come in.' She dragged Jade inside. 'You're wet. Are you freezing? Let me grab you a tow–'

'I can't do this anymore.' Tears brimmed, fuzzing her vision. 'I just can't. There's so much I want to say. I thought I was okay with all of this, and I am, but I'm not, and I'm really freaking out right now, and I'm usually the calm one ...' Fat tears rolled down Jade's cheeks. Her ears were ringing; her mouth turned dry.

Lucy's eyebrows folded into themselves, worry lines cutting across her forehead. 'I'm so confused. Are you okay? Are you in trouble?'

Jade needed to breathe, but the words were heavy and thick and not coming out right. She was ruining this moment, if this could even be called a moment. Everything could crash and burn and die, or it could go amazingly. She shouldn't wait, but now she wanted to wait, because exposing herself like this terrified her. 'I can't do this anymore, Lucy. I can't pretend to be your friend. I don't *want* to be your friend. You've grabbed my heart and held it and squeezed it and– I'm not making any sense.'

Lucy stepped back, silent, her hand draped across her mouth.

'You're everything I think about. You have this halo around you, these, like, slices of light and joy and loveliness and shit. I just– Okay, I'm going to say it, because I'm not wasting one more day without you knowing how I feel. I want to be with you.' Jade swallowed. 'There, I said it. And if you want to be friends, it's okay, even though that's not what *I* want, but I will respect whatever you say, because you are–'

Lips pressed against hers, warm and intentional.

Jade melted into the soft embrace and pressed back. Her breath constricted. Did this mean Lucy felt the same? Or was this a pity kiss?

Lucy gripped her cheeks and stood back. The amber in her eyes sparkled in the low lighting as her gaze flickered to Jade. 'You're not just saying this?' Lucy's voice was quiet, almost shattered.

'No, I'm not. And I don't know what this means for us, or you, but we can figure it out, right?' She'd never been so hopeful in her life ... while also wanting to run and dive into the cornfields. Even with Elizabeth, Jade never remembered feeling so jittery, so alive, so *terrified*, all at once.

Lucy approached her again. Slowly. Warmly. She wrapped her arms around Jade's waist and laid her head on her chest. Jade kissed the top of her apple-scented hair, breathed her in, moulded herself into her. *Does this mean Lucy feels the same?* Jade stood still. Lucy was holding her, clinging to her, so motionless that Jade almost wondered if Lucy had fallen asleep against her.

'We're gonna figure this out,' Lucy whispered.

'Yeah?'

'Yeah.' Lucy released and stretched on her tiptoes, closing the gap between their mouths. She pressed against Jade's lips again, kissing her, firm, full, sweet. 'I want to be with you, too.'

After spending the last year thinking something like this would never happen to her again, Jade bit back tears. She found the person she wanted to try again with, and her heart overflowed with gratitude.

Chapter 19

Lucy

Is this real?

Lucy pulled herself away from Jade's lips. She needed to read Jade's face again, study her eyes, confirm she didn't just wake up in the middle of a dream. After the devastating 'let's just be friends' conversation almost two months ago, Lucy had tasted heartache for the first time in her life. And she never wanted to feel that way again.

'Are you okay?' Jade pulled Lucy's hands into hers.

Yes and no. When Jade showed up on her doorstep a few minutes ago, wet and frantic, Lucy absolutely did not expect Jade to say what she said. Yes, Lucy wanted to hear those words, and she felt the same. But finding out she was pregnant the same day as finding out about Jade's feelings … the room was spinning. Her *heart* was spinning.

'Can we sit?' Lucy moved to the couch without waiting for a response. When Jade joined her, Lucy tugged the blanket across Jade first, then rested it in on her lap. 'Do you want a dry shirt?'

Jade shook her head. 'No, it's fine.' She inhaled through her nose and slowly exhaled. 'I'm so sorry. I shouldn't have dropped this on you tonight. You've had a huge day, but I just couldn't wait.'

Chucky eased himself into the corner and slumped back down to sleep. Lucy tugged on her lower lip, willing herself to speak. The last few months of getting to know Jade had shifted everything Lucy knew to be true. She'd never seen herself with a partner. She assumed she'd go on random dates until she died, and receive her joy from friends, her dad, and her dog. And now, the real possibility of a future froze her.

'What are you thinking?' Jade reached back again for Lucy's hand, her delicate fingers padding the top of Lucy's hand.

Lucy's fingertips interlocked with Jade's, soaking in the safety and security of her touch. 'I'm terrified, honestly. I've never had this before. I've never even wanted it. And now that it's here, I guess … I just don't know what to do.'

Jade's eyes flickered down and several moments passed. 'I'm really scared, too. After Elizabeth, I said I would never open myself up again. Ever. The pain was too much and I lost my identity, you know? I was no longer a person; I was just one half of a couple. And I don't want that to happen again.'

Speaking about the divorce was rare for Jade, and Lucy leaned into the words. She couldn't understand the pain of losing love and then opening yourself up to it again, but she could relate to the overwhelming pain of losing someone you loved when her mom died. She played with the top of Jade's fingertips and let the words sink in. 'I can't guarantee if we do this that it won't happen. I've never been in a real relationship before. I don't know all the rules and what to do, and what it will look like with this …' Lucy waved her hand against her belly, pulled in a full breath of air, then released it through her nose. 'But there's no one else in the world I'd rather try this with than you.'

A soft grinned curved Jade's lips. 'Yeah?'

Lucy nodded, a low, steady heartbeat tapping against her chest.

'Yeah.' She scooted closer to Jade, cupped her cheeks in her hand, and swiped her thumbs over Jade's face. Oh, her face was so soft. How had she never felt her skin before? Delicate, porcelain, perfect. She pressed her lips against Jade's. Gently at first, feeling her mouth warm. Jade parted her lips, opening Lucy's mouth up with hers, and pushed back with her velvety tongue.

Okay, maybe this was real.

Jade was the one to pull back this time, her gaze intent on Lucy. Her mouth opened like she wanted to say something, but instead, she captured Lucy's mouth again. Gripping the back of Lucy's head, Jade deepened the kiss. Her plump lips filled Lucy's mouth. Lucy grazed her tongue against Jade's, relishing the taste of strawberries and coffee. Jade sucked on Lucy's bottom lip, shifted her other arm, and tugged Lucy closer. Deeper, with more intention now. Lucy smiled into the kiss, dizzy and gasping.

The only sounds were the patter of rain against the window, heavy breaths, and Chucky snoring. He snorted and Lucy snapped her head to the side. 'God, he's a buzzkill.'

Jade grinned, her reddened lips highlighting her blushed cheeks. 'Oh, Chucky.'

Dog or not, Lucy had waited too long for this moment to let anything get in the way. Before she could let logic sink in and mess with the pheromones, she grabbed Jade's hand. 'Do you want to move to the bedroom?'

'You have no idea how much I want to.' Jade hopped up and threw the blanket on the couch.

Lucy had some idea. She refrained from sprinting down the hall, her fingers intertwined with Jade's. Once inside, Lucy shut the door behind them both. 'Chucky's gonna have to stay in the living room tonight.' She pulled Jade in for another kiss.

Oh wait. Lucy was being super presumptuous. Just because Jade confessed her feelings didn't necessarily mean she wanted to sleep with her. Or did it? Should she ask? Or was that like the romance kiss of death?

'What's wrong?' Jade stepped back, her eyebrows creasing. 'Are you okay?'

God, I'm the worst. I am overthinking everything and ruining this moment. Lucy was the queen of casual sex, never mixing emotions with the bedroom, and it worked. But this was so different. What if feelings interfered and made activities worse? What if it made the sex so much better that she became co-dependent and ridiculous, and started chasing Jade everywhere she went?

'I'm fine. Totally good. You? Everything good?' Lucy's words came out hushed and frantic and definitely not sexy. She pinched the bridge of her nose. 'I'm swirling. Totally overthinking. And ruining the moment.'

Jade hugged Lucy tight against her chest and kissed the top of her head. In a snap, the scent of rain-misted clothes mixed with Jade's citrus musk filled Lucy, and she melted into the embrace. Maybe she didn't know how this would go. But she had Jade with her, sharing this, powering through the fear together.

Lucy lifted her head, brushing her lips across the top of Jade's cleavage. Slow and steady, she inched her way up, the sweet, salty skin rich under her tongue. Her fingers gripped Jade's waist as she trailed kisses from the base of her neck, to below her ear lobe, to her jawline.

Hands rested on her hips, strong, pulling Lucy towards Jade. They slid up higher, up her back, behind her head. Jade reached down, capturing Lucy's mouth. Gentle kisses firmed, pushing, and soon Jade owned Lucy's mouth. Lucy's legs felt nearly useless, and she leaned against the wall for support. She breathed into the kiss, feeling light-headed and dazed, and Jade's arms flexed, supporting her.

I am safe. God, Jade's mouth tasted so good, her tongue so strong yet soft, a perfect balance of needing and wanting. Jade parted Lucy's leg with her own, her thigh pushing against Lucy's centre, and Lucy's breath hitched.

'Is this okay?' Jade asked, her fingers hovering on the outside of Lucy's robe, one hand dancing on top of Lucy's naked thigh.

'Yes, yes, perfect …' Lucy murmured as the touches against her skin sent jolts through her body. She cupped Jade's ass … *oh my gosh*, perfect, sweet, beautiful ass … and moved closer. The friction wasn't enough. She needed more. She wanted it all.

Jade stopped and dropped her hands.

Oh no. 'What? What's wrong?'

Jade exhaled a shaky breath. 'The paperwork … you told me that one time about signing paperwork that you wouldn't have sex with anyone … oh shit. I want this so bad. But is this illegal or wrong or whatever?' Even as Jade spoke these words, her face said, *Dear God say this is okay*.

'We're good, we're good. Don't stop.' Lucy pushed her mouth back on to Jade's. 'That was only before I got pregnant. Now that I'm here … anyway, just don't stop.' Paperwork be damned. She'd explain the logistics tomorrow. Right now, no more clinical talk. She wanted Jade. *Bad.*

Full moonlight filled the room; breaths permeated the air. Lucy tugged at the bottom of Jade's shirt, lifting it higher, her finger scraping against her naked belly. Jade's stomach quivered in response. She threw the T-shirt to the corner and tugged at Lucy's robe.

'Can I touch you?' Jade's words were hoarse, raspy, needy.

Lucy moved her mouth to Jade's ear. 'Yes … I want everything.'

The robe opened and Jade's palm skimmed up Lucy's thigh, higher, higher, moving to her centre, hovering. 'You're so beautiful, Lucy … your skin … I can't …' Jade pressed her palm on top of Lucy's centre, and pushed *just enough*, just right, until Lucy's legs verged on giving out completely.

'Bed,' Lucy commanded and dropped her robe.

Before Lucy had even lain down, Jade kicked off her jeans. Her chest lifted and lowered. Her eyes skimmed every inch of

Lucy, taking a mental tour, inventory, her lips parted with want. 'I can't believe this is happening.'

Lucy propped up on her elbows, meeting Jade's gaze. 'Me, neither.' They had only just begun, and already this was better than Lucy ever had, better than she ever envisioned. She was naked, exposed, more vulnerable than she'd ever been, yet the safest she'd ever felt. Was this how other people felt? How was she so lucky to be feeling this want, this full-body desire, with someone she cared about so much? Tomorrow, she would do some gratitude prayers. Tonight, all she wanted to do was fill herself with Jade.

As Lucy ran her tongue up Jade's cleavage, across her throat, she mixed it with kisses and hot breaths, and Jade shivered under the sensation. She gripped Jade's ass, tugging her leg between her thighs, then moved her hands to unclasp Jade's bra. After tossing it aside, she hovered her mouth over Jade's breast. 'Good?'

Jade exhaled, dragging Lucy into her. 'So good.'

When Lucy's mouth met Jade's nipple, Jade gasped, her shoulder crumbling. Her tongue swept Jade. The need to sample every part of her, to take the most luxurious journey, to show her how much she cared and wanted and believed in her, consumed Lucy. Fingers and mouths moved, lips on body parts, soft moans filled the air.

Jade lowered Lucy, resting her against the pillow. Her palms slid down Lucy's face, her neck, her hands filled themselves with Lucy's breasts. 'I … can't … it's so good … you're so fucking perfect.' Her mouth moved, a perfect combination of licking and sucking, as Lucy's eyes fluttered closed. If the apocalypse happened right now, she'd die happy. This was heaven. Jade was heaven.

Hands trailed, moving, heavy breaths flowed. Lucy hooked her fingers on Jade's underwear and tugged, the pads of her fingers aching to feel Jade from the inside. Jade slipped out of her remaining clothes and rolled to the side. When Lucy shifted to face Jade, her skin blushed, feverish. She wanted more.

Jade's fingertips found Lucy and touched her outside, the softest of touches.

'Mmmmmm ...' murmured Lucy. How could something that was a whisper of a graze make her feel like this? All curled toes, skin on fire, tingles shooting up to her scalp. And then ... *oh God* ... Jade dipped two fingers inside. Each glide, each motion showed Lucy how much she was wanted, how much Jade felt the same.

Lucy wanted to do the same, needed to do the same, but her thoughts were fuzzy. 'It's so ... good ...' she mumbled incoherently as she lifted her hips, matched Jade's rhythm, and gripped Jade's forearm. She rocked against her touch when Jade lowered herself, never breaking stride, never faltering.

Jade's mouth hovered over her core, breath joining in the motions, and then ... *oh yes* ... then skilled lips and tongues and fingers moved together. Lucy gasped. Everything was so right, she felt needed and appreciated and beautiful. Her thighs tightened around Jade's perfect, perfect motions.

How was Jade reading Lucy's body, her movements, her breaths so seamlessly? More pressure, less pressure, faster, harder, slower – Jade knew. Lucy's breaths were heavy, her moans louder. The trembles started deep in her abdomen. 'Right there ... more ... please ...' A whimper escaped as the trembles grew, heavier, fuller, so close. More kisses, more glides, a thumb added to the outside and *oh ... yes, there*. Her insides clenched, her thighs shaky and quivering. 'Oh fuuu ... yes!'

Finally, release. The wave hit, hard, high, heavy, and strong. Lucy's heartbeat slammed against her chest.

Jade stayed until the shakes stopped, then gently lifted herself off Lucy and lay to her side, stroking her hair.

Lucy couldn't move. She was boneless and limp but ached to do everything to Jade. When her breathing calmed, she whispered into the air. 'Two more minutes ... and I cannot wait to do that to you.'

PART TWO

Chapter 20

Lucy

So. Much. Vomit.

Lucy rested her head against the porcelain god which had become her new best friend these past two months. Sweat beaded on her neck and her hair stuck to it like putty. The inside of her nose stung, a wretched feeling like she dived into the deep end and chlorine shot up her nostrils. She hurled again, then felt gentle hands sweep her hair away from her face and snug it into a firm grip.

Lucy was too sick to even be surprised that someone had walked into her home without her knowledge. 'Whoever said morning sickness ended after the first trimester is a liar on every level.' She gasped as she stood on wobbly legs, grabbed a rag from the linen closet, and ran it under cold water. The wetness against her cheeks and neck cooled the heat from the nausea. 'I didn't even hear you come in.'

'Couldn't hear me over the hurling, huh?' Jade filled a glass with water and handed it over, their routine over the last two plus months since becoming a couple.

Some new couples went wine tasting and tried out new restaurants. In their dynamic, Jade rubbed Lucy's feet and ran to the store when Lucy ran out of Tums.

'Aren't you still in your first trimester, though?' Jade asked. 'You only peed on a stick like, what, two and a half months ago?'

'No, I'm in the second trimester.' Lucy gargled and spat. 'Because we did IVF, they considered me two weeks pregnant when I left the office the day of implantation.' She added toothpaste to the toothbrush and grinned at Jade's tilted head. 'So, when I took the pregnancy test three weeks later, I was considered five weeks when it showed positive.'

Jade scrunched her eyebrows, then slowly shook her head. 'Nope. What do my teen clients say? The math isn't mathing. I know you're the numbers person, but that literally makes no sense.'

Pregnancy and timelines and inception and all the other stuff that Lucy had studied over the last year didn't make sense to her either. Who knew that everything revolved so closely around *weeks*. Everyone wanted to know how many weeks she was, how many weeks until birth, how many weeks along could she be if something happened with the foetus and it needed to come out early. 'We'll discuss later after my urge to puke goes away.'

Jade washed her hands and studied Lucy in the mirror. 'You have that glow. You know, the one pregnant women have.'

Lucy looked at her puffy, flushed face, unsure whether to laugh or cry – which had become a common emotion combo these past few months. 'That's only because my cheeks are red from being nauseated.'

Jade gave her a playful smack on her butt. 'Oh my God, stop. I'm serious.'

'Do you still think I'm the sexiest woman alive?' Lucy asked through a mouthful of toothpaste.

Jade laughed. 'The absolute sexiest. Lesbian scout's honour.' She held up a peace sign. 'Besides, your boobs look amazing.'

Lucy tugged her shirt tight. 'They do, don't they?'

One unforeseen side-effect of pregnancy for Lucy was she really did feel sexy when she wasn't nauseated. She felt powerful, invincible, but also sometimes fragile, and the blend made her realise her body could do more than she ever thought possible. She even couldn't wait for her belly to pop out more than its current state, which only looked like she ate one too many eclairs at the holiday party.

Lucy followed Jade out of the bathroom as Chucky trotted next to them. These days, she relied on Jade more than she ever thought she would. Man, did she really, *really* rely on her. The first few weeks of their newfound relationship, they were inseparable. Jade took days off work, they spent hours in the bedroom, shower, kitchen, living room – and once they tried to play out Lucy's high-school fantasy of getting freaky on the car's backseat. As spacious as the Prius ('Starlight' as Lucy maintained and Jade had yet to adopt) was, Jade's six-foot frame just couldn't make it work, and Lucy laughed from the depths of her soul at the clunky failed sexual encounter.

Last week, they exchanged holiday gifts, Jade gifting Lucy a tiny gold charm bracelet and a blanket imprinted with Chucky's face, while Lucy got Jade a monthly home box subscription from a gourmet vegan cheese and crackers shop. And two nights ago, they spent New Year's Eve in, playing Pictionary and charades with Drew and Mason, and downing several bottles of sparkling apple cider while Lucy whined that she couldn't have any of the salted meats on the charcuterie platter.

Lucy knew every part of Jade, from the sprinkling of angel kiss birthmarks directly below her left hip, to the curve of her backside, to that tiny scar on her ribcage from a childhood playground accident. She knew Jade's sweet spot, the dip right behind her ear lobe that made Jade squirm, how much pressure to use, how deep, for how long, when to move, and when to remain perfectly still. They were totally in sync.

But their relationship was more than the phenomenal sex. When Drew and Mason took a weekend trip last month, Lucy had some scary spotting. Jade rushed her to the ER and waited for hours until they got the 'false alarm' and 'this is normal' thumbs-up from the doctor. When her dad – and apparently Jade's new best friend as they hit it off immediately – needed a hand on the farm and refused to let Lucy do any heavy lifting, Jade helped.

The initial rush of being in a new relationship had settled, and a few months in, Lucy was happy. Even more, she was *content*. For the first time in her life, she had a real, live, honest-to-goodness girlfriend and it was awesome. Relationships were *so much easier* than she thought they'd be.

'Want something to drink?' Lucy asked as she scoured the fridge.

'Nah, I'm good.' Jade sank onto a barstool and rubbed Chuck's head. 'There'll be plenty tonight.'

Tonight? What's tonight? Lucy shut the door with her hip and faced Jade.

Jade's chin dipped. She ran her fingers through her mermaid-blue hair, a short pixie cut Lucy was still getting used to, and exhaled loudly through her nose. 'You forgot, didn't you?'

Ever since getting pregnant, Lucy felt like the foetus amoeba was chomping away at her brain. She was in a state of perpetual brain fog, with only sporadic moments of clarity. She felt like she was living between being severely undercaffeinated, a head cold, and not getting enough sleep. Drew, who was reading *What to Expect When You're Expecting*, had mentioned this, but she wasn't fully ready for *this*. He offered her the book, but she declined. Other than wanting to be a good house for Drew and Mason's kid, she had very little desire to know what was happening inside.

'No, I didn't, uh, forget.' Lucy guzzled back a ginger ale. She seriously needed to think about buying stock in this wonder drug. Ginger ale, saltines, and plain noodles were the only things she could keep down. Buying time, she chugged back a bit more. *Tonight, tonight. What was tonight? Oh no!* 'The bookstore.' She slammed her hand against her mouth.

A queer, woman-owned bookstore and bakery had opened on the west side of town. She and Jade had planned on going tonight to the opening night. Ugh, such a fail. Jade had been so excited. After being cooped up for a year without much of a social life she wanted to experience all these things, she told Lucy a few weeks ago. And Lucy had gone and forgotten.

Jade drew in her bottom lip. 'Yes. Doors open in a half hour.'

'So sorry. With me working offsite today, it totally slipped my mind.' True and not true. Having a Q1 kick-off party right after work was definitely a distraction. The holidays were always so busy for the bank, and the company waited until the first week of January to celebrate. Every year Lucy loved it. There was usually some terrible karaoke, free-flowing drinks, delicious appetisers. But today, being surrounded by the smell of buffalo chicken wings, bacon-stuffed dates, and garlic-stuffed mushrooms had pushed her over the edge. She sat at the corner of the bar, powered through, and chomped on celery.

Jade leaned against the counter and crossed her arms. 'You didn't respond to any of my messages.'

Lucy bristled slightly at the tone – one that she had heard a few times now. A sort of '*I'm irritated but don't want to make you feel bad*' tone. 'What? I didn't get any messages from you.' And now Lucy really wasn't appreciating the glare Jade was angling her way. Lucy ripped her phone from her purse and held it out to prove it. 'Here.'

'Lucy.' Jade exhaled a very annoyed, very exasperated sigh. 'Your phone is on do-not-disturb.'

What? Lucy fumbled and turned off the do-not-disturb. A rainstorm of messages popped onto the screen. A few from Jade reminding her of tonight, her co-worker sharing New Year's party gossip about two tellers caught making out in the bathroom,

Drew checking in, and a doctor appointment confirmation of Lucy's ultrasound next week. How had she forgotten to take it off the do-not-disturb setting? Not once all damn day. And not only that, she hadn't even noticed.

Her lip trembled.

'Whoa, whoa. What's happening here?' Jade met Lucy's gaze.

A flash of panic crept up Lucy. 'I'm not even halfway done yet with this thing, and is this how I'm going to be from here on out?' She was only fourteen weeks along, not even close to the halfway mark; it wasn't even 6:30 p.m. yet, and all she wanted to do was crawl into bed and sleep forever. Was the entire next year going to be like this?

'Hey, hey.' Jade held Lucy's shoulders. 'It's totally fine. Seriously. I almost forgot about it, too.'

No, she didn't. But Lucy needed this win to not feel like crap. 'I'm so scattered. I don't even understand how I forgot about tonight.' She was hot and cold, mad and sad, wanted to hit something and wanted to sleep. Her body twisted in every way, and her shoulders shook. 'I'm so sorry … but I just can't. I'm so freaking tired and feel like poop and my back hurts and—'

Jade pulled her in. The cedar bergamot scent rising from Jade was the only thing that didn't make Lucy nauseated. She rested against her chest as Jade stroked her hair.

Jade pulled back and planted a kiss on Lucy's forehead. 'It's no big thing. We can go some other night.'

'Other nights will not be opening night.' Lucy had really wanted to show her support. The community was friendly and open, but it wasn't filled with queer shops like San Francisco, LA, or Seattle. And the more they could rally, the more queer-friendly shops would open. And now she wanted to cry again. 'I think I cried ten times in my life up until I got preggo, and now I feel like I'm crying every day. What's wrong with me?' Her belly rolled, low and uncomfortable. She pulled away and dug in the cabinet for saltines.

'Isn't this normal? Aren't pregnant women like ... extra all the time?' Jade accepted a cracker and split it in half. She chewed in silence for a bit, breaking off a tiny piece for a whiny Chunky. 'So, listen, since we're not going to the opening tonight, I think I'll just head home and do some paperwork.'

Great, so now her girlfriend – her smoking-hot girlfriend – with her black skinny jeans and off-the-shoulder black sweater and freshly applied make-up wanted to leave for the night. Lucy hated that she was kind of relieved. She wanted a snuggle buddy but had limited energy for much else. They hadn't been intimate for almost two weeks and Lucy's pyjamas superseded sexy time with Jade. Twenty-year-old Lucy hated herself right now.

The saltines stuck against the roof of her mouth, and she nearly gagged again. 'Did you have time to break everything down by quarter?'

Jade shook her head and crouched down to Chucky.

Was she avoiding eye contact? Lucy tried not to butt in too much with Jade's salon business, but some things Jade did made Lucy want to pull her hair out. She didn't properly look at quarterly, or even monthly trends, which was so important for business owners. Lucy had this talk almost weekly when she spoke to small business owners at the bank. No matter what your business – wine, jewellery, specialty bakery, porn shop, whatever – it was imperative to study the numbers so that you could learn how to maximise profits. But anytime Lucy tap-danced even *around* the subject, Jade clammed up.

Lucy didn't want to say it ... *okay fine*, it was kind of, well ... irritating! Jade could make her business so much more successful if she just spent a tiny bit more time on logistics and less on doing hair. 'Why do you keep putting it off?'

Jade's face flashed red. She adjusted the shoulder on her sweater and stood from petting Chucky. 'Because,' she sighed, 'after working all day, dealing with customers and manager shit, I'm tired, too.' Jade's feet smacked against the floor as she grabbed her coat draping the kitchen stool. 'Hey, I'm just gonna head out. I'll call you tomorrow.'

'Okay, cool.' Lucy followed her and nearly sobbed when Jade shut the door. Yes, they had been friends for months before they got together. But once they did, they had never once parted without a kiss.

Until now.

Chapter 21

Jade

Jade swore at the snow piled on her windshield. She was a Midwesterner to her core, and normally, the white crisp flakes tapped into something satisfyingly primal within her. The substance, whether powdery, flaky, or full, dredged up the want to engage in a snow fight, or go sledding, or skate on a lake.

But today, the snow was more of a wet, clumpy, dirty slush. And she was over scraping her windshield. She wasn't even in Lucy's house that long, definitely not long enough for this white crap to coagulate on her car. She grabbed a brush and pushed off the snow, then flumped into her car and slammed the door.

Breathe, breathe. Jade shouldn't have snapped at Lucy like that. It wasn't fair. But ugh, they'd talked about this open house. *A lot.* How the hell did Lucy forget? *Nope, breathe.* It wasn't like Jade couldn't go alone.

Lucy hadn't been feeling well this month so most of the time Jade stayed in with her, cuddling on Lucy's couch with her and Chucky. And Jade loved it. Really, she did. But she'd been looking forward to the opening night all week – and she had *not* imagined going alone.

She pulled down the block, slush spraying beneath her tyres. A snowplough moved behind her and she inched over to allow it to pass, its blinking lights illuminating the snow-covered streets. The plough shook her car as it passed, and even the radio couldn't drown out its metallic scraping sound.

'Ugh!' Jade yelled to no one as she pushed her head against the back of the seat.

Was this level of irritation warranted for the queer bookstore open house? Probably not. But … it wasn't just that. Lucy had hit a nerve about the salon books.

A couple weeks ago, Jade finally dived into the books and started recording discrepancies. What with the whirlwind of a new relationship, she'd pushed aside Shayna's sinking profits, a vendor who marked up their products over twenty per cent without warning, and an electric bill that was supposed to be on autopay which oddly defaulted to paper and got lost in the shuffle. Being with someone special pushed pesky things down the priority list – like having a solid heart-to-heart with her former top stylist as to why she was currently ranking ten out of seventeen. At this point, Jade just needed to accept that for the second year, Shayna hadn't brought in what she brought in the first year. And maybe that wasn't that odd? People tended to hustle hard their first year in a salon as they fought to push their way to the top. Sometimes it was harder to maintain a top spot than get there in the first place.

Jade slid to a stop at the light and scolded herself for being distracted. Minnesota winters and space-cadet driving did not mix, and she needed to focus. She plucked her wool gloves off and gripped the steering wheel.

God, why had she stomped out like that? Elizabeth used to always complain that if anything got heated, Jade would bolt. Lucy didn't deserve that reaction, and as Jade turned down the block to her neighbourhood, a pinch squeezed in her chest.

Her girlfriend was having a damn baby for someone else. A freaking baby! Jade should be back at Lucy's rubbing her feet, running a bath, helping with dishes – not having a short fuse. She had no idea, nor desire, to know what it was like to be pregnant. And she had gone into this relationship with eyes wide open, knowing things would change for Lucy as they went forward. Jade should be more accommodating and not let these little things get to her.

Because these little things *were* getting to her, hard, and she needed to pinpoint why. Two nights ago, Lucy promised to get Jade's favourite eclairs from a local bakery and forgot. And last Monday, they were supposed to go see Kate McKinnon's latest flick, and Lucy forgot she had a doctor's appointment. Jade had to choke back her irrational irritation. Again.

She slunk into the house, tossing her keys on the counter. The candy stash in her drawer called to her, and she indulged as the chewy caramel melted on her tongue. She popped one more, put on her sweats and ripped off her bra, an unofficial declaration that she was not going alone to the bookstore opening. She was staying in for the evening.

Her phone rang. She dug it out from her cross-body bag and read the screen.

Amanda.

'Hey, lady, got a second?'

'Sure.' Jade slid her feet into her slippers and checked her watch. 'What's up? You're not still at the salon, are you?' The salon closed an hour ago, and if Amanda was still there, it meant that the stylists were not pulling their weight in cleaning. That had happened once last month, but after Jade gave them all a stern chat about being a team, she'd been under the impression that everyone had stepped up.

'Yes, but it's not what you think,' Amanda said. 'I forgot my laptop charger there. I have to finish an essay that's due tomorrow morning, so I swung by to get it before heading to the library. And, uh, Shayna was there doing hair on a couple of people.'

Huh. 'That's weird. She doesn't work Wednesdays.' No matter, though. Jade allowed the stylists to use the facility for family after hours. Even Amanda had done that. But they usually just stayed longer on the shifts they were already working, as opposed to coming in after hours on their days off.

'Jade … I, um, don't think they were family.' Amanda's normally confident tone wavered.

The skin on Jade's neck prickled. 'How do you know?' She lowered herself onto the sofa.

'I recognised them as a couple of clients she used to have.'

The prickle spread and Jade's heart dropped. Her internal organs were labouring double-time. There had to be an explanation. 'Did you say anything?'

'No, I didn't know what to say. She just looked up when I got there and maybe looked a little sheepish? It's hard to say. The space had such a funky energy, so I grabbed my stuff and split.'

A low but fierce throbbing had started in Jade's temples. She jammed her knuckles into her forehead to release the pressure and exhaled a quick breath. 'Thanks for letting me know. I'll look into it.'

As soon as she disconnected the call, Jade propped her elbows on her knees and dropped her head into her hands. *Dammit.* What a shit night. Her former top employee was definitely up to something, she had no text messages from Lucy, and she was a month behind on quarterly reviews for her staff. The only thing that could make today worse was if her ex called.

Jade stormed into the kitchen and filled a glass with an Argentina Malbec, grabbed a block of cheese (don't judge) and returned to the recliner. She snugged her favourite grey-and-white knitted blanket over her shoulders and stared out the window, the plate of food resting firmly on her crisscrossed legs. The fresh snow falling in the moonlight was beautiful, making the ground sparkle like white sapphires. She tried hard to focus on that and not the sick feeling that was rising in her chest.

The tart wine melted into a robust, velvety mix of plum and berry on her tongue, and the brie was a perfect offset. She savoured the creamy cheese, which she withheld from eating around Lucy, since she was avoiding almost all soft cheese right now. The cheese thing didn't make much sense to Jade – like how many pregnancies were actually affected by *cheese*, but whatever. It made Lucy feel better to avoid it, so Jade supported her.

Yep, Jade was doing anything possible to avoid thinking about Shayna. She sipped from her glass and rolled the wine on her tongue. She was pretty sure she knew what had been happening with Shayna but didn't want to face it. There was no chance that Shayna was doing *that* many re-dos. Confronting things like this head-on made Jade sick, but … she *had* to. I mean, she was the owner, dammit. The salon was her life, her career, *her baby*. Time to protect it.

Her night was ruined anyway. Between missing the bookstore opening, and the way she'd left things with Lucy, how much worse could it get? She grabbed the laptop and set it back on her legs. She had access to security footage from the salon but had never needed to review it. After multiple failed log-in attempts – and enough F-bombs to make a Gen X'er blush – she finally pulled it up.

She poured herself another glass of wine and scrolled through video after video. 'Nothing …'

No weird activity, except for an oddly large amount of people who tried to peek through the window after hours.

Sip and scroll, sip and scroll. She sank her teeth into another chunk of buttery brie and stopped. A terrible sensation seized her chest. Her neck felt cold, then hot. She leaned in as she watched Shayna bouncing through the door, followed by several people. The footage was from 8 p.m. last Wednesday, an hour after the place closed.

Amanda was right – Shayna wasn't with family. The man trailing Shayna was one of her clients, Tony. Not that Jade knew the names of all Shayna's clients, but she remembered joking with Shayna about how much he resembled Justin Bieber.

The recliner squeaked as Jade edged forward, looking even closer at the screen. *What the ...* she scrolled through the footage as the shop became alive until almost midnight. Five clients served. And not a single one was Shayna's mom, sister, or brother – all of whom Jade would have recognised.

The wine gurgled in Jade's belly. She frantically hit the back button, both hungry and terrified to find more incidents. Scrolling through videos, an icky voyeur-like feeling consumed her. Video after video of people laughing, chatting, hair flying on the floor, colour processing under the dome hair driers. Clients sitting in chairs, Shayna stuffing cash in her pocket, hugs shared for a job well done. Shayna going to the back room, cleaning, no fear on her face, just her usual smile as she wiped everything down, shut lights off, and locked the door.

An hour had passed. Jade's glass was now empty, and half the cheese demolished.

I ... can't believe this. Every week, sometimes twice a week, for almost a year, Shayna had stolen from the shop.

Jade's chin quivered as the screen spat out images of more clients, and more money shoved in Shayna's pockets. The glass trembled in her fingers, and she wanted to throw it against the window. The betrayal hit deep, in a dark place that she hadn't felt in such a long time.

'Right in front of my face ...' The words sputtered out, quiet yet echoing against the bare wall.

How had she not seen this? Or ... had she? Was there somewhere inside Jade that had suspected this? No, she couldn't have ever guessed that *this* was what had been going on with Shayna. This was Jade's livelihood, and she thought her stylists *respected* that. Her home, her business, her reputation. Sure, Jade skirted the rules about working on family after hours and she could have been fined, but that was a minimal risk. But with Shayna bringing in all these people ... It wasn't just about the lost profits. What if someone slipped on the floor and sued the shop? How much product had Shayna used? How many dollars had she taken right off the shelves?

Jade's throat burned. Her fingers, clenching so tight against her palm, cramped. When Jade bought the salon, Shayna was her first hire. She even volunteered to get the place ready, coming in with cut-offs and bandanas, schlepping gigantic cups of bubble tea for her and Jade. With music blaring, she'd painted, cleaned, and organised the products side-by-side with Jade and laughed with her over cheese pizza and exhausted limbs. Shayna was the first friend-ish person Jade had made since her divorce.

Jade's lip quivered again.

Once, during the first month of work, they'd gone out and thrown back a few drinks. They giggled at embarrassing stories, including one where Shayna nearly re-enacted a swan-dive faceplant across the salon her first month of working. Jade remembered thinking it was the first time since her divorce that she'd laughed. And now, Shayna was stealing from her. Not just once.

For over a year.

How much had she taken? Jade wanted to calculate it, but when she started adding it up, the knot in her chest tightened so hard, she couldn't breathe. She roughly knew. She could match it with the profits dipping. Thousands and thousands of dollars, gone. And it got worse – Jade had a profit-sharing mechanism in place for all the stylists. When they met the salon goal, they all got a percentage of the profits. So, Shayna had ripped that money out of their mouths as well.

Although Jade normally claimed she had no motherly instinct, some kind of deep, instinctual mother-bear rage roared. She flew out of the chair and paced the house, biting the edge of her finger. Deep breaths were doing nothing to calm the painful thud in her chest. She opened the door and let the cold slap her in the face. She stayed there until she started shivering and slammed the door.

She snatched the phone from the coffee table.

'Hey ...' Lucy's groggy voice answered.

'I can't believe this. I'm shaking right now.' Jade stomped through the house, a rabid animal circling her cage. 'Amanda called. I'm so fucking angry. I looked through all the security ... hours and hours of it ... I figured out what's been happening with Shayna.'

A pause and a yawn followed. 'You did? Oh ... what was ...' The final words were incoherent behind a heavy breath and mumbles.

A burst of anger and exasperation ripped through Jade. She knew it wasn't fair, but she couldn't help it. She inhaled a sharp breath through her nose. 'Did I wake you up?'

'Yeah, um, yeah. But it's okay. I'm here. Tell me.' Those were Lucy's words, but the tone of her voice was saying *Let me go back to sleep.*

Dammit! Jade really needed to talk to her girlfriend, who could talk her off the ledge. Maybe Lucy would put a comforting spin on this fucked-up situation and shepherd her through the numbers storm currently battering Jade's head. Lucy, with her positive energy and sing-song ways, could assure her everything was okay, that it wasn't as bad as she thought, and convince her to sleep on it and come at the problem with a fresh mind.

Another yawn.

'No worries. Go back to sleep. I'll call you in the morning.' *Dammit!* With her insides fuming, Jade barely waited for Lucy to say goodnight when she hung up. She paced the house with long strides, her gaze catching on the sink, which hadn't had a good scrubbing in forever.

Yes, good. Scrub the sink.

The citrus eucalyptus spray filled the room as she doused every inch of the sink and counter with the cleaner. Jade took out a fresh scrubber, the rough edges scratching against her skin. She pushed hard, scouring the cracks, the edges, and the grout until beads of sweat crept up her forehead.

Maybe Amanda could talk. But the second Jade picked up her phone, she set it back down. The last thing she needed to do was drag an employee into an HR-type situation. Although Amanda had long ago proved that she was the most trustworthy of all the staff, news like this could spread power-blow-dryer fast in a salon.

Think, think! Jade grabbed her keys, then set them back down. She'd only had one glass of wine but still hated driving with anything in her system. So, she did what any thirty-five-year-old, responsible, professional business owner would do.

She sent Shayna a text.

Tomorrow, come to work for a meeting at 9 before your shift.

She poured yet another glass of wine, an absolute rarity for herself, and stormed back to the bedroom.

Anxiety-filled dreams finally woke her at 6 a.m. The heavy comforter clung hot and sweaty against her skin. She wished she had Lucy sleeping next to her, although that happened less frequently than she hoped as they both realised they were creatures of habit and enjoyed the familiarity of their own beds. Besides, Lucy had a huge body pillow for some sciatic issues she'd developed with the pregnancy, and it got in the way.

Jade dragged her exhausted body to the kitchen and poured herself a coffee, but the acidic taste curdled her stomach.

A long shower, some dry peanut butter toast, and another cup of coffee did little to settle her stomach. She arrived at the salon at eight, where she stared at the blurred numbers from the quarterly reviews for half an hour. Backstock sorting was the next best option, and she flipped all the dye boxes right-side up, making sure to properly stock the colours and levels.

The door creaked open. Shayna stomped the snow off her boots and unravelled her hot-pink cable-knit scarf. Jade crossed her arms, begging if a god existed that Shayna would take one look at her, admit what she did, offer to pay back what she took, and quit. All the prep and mental rehearsals Jade had done the previous night bolted and her mind blanked.

Stay strong. Be strong. Do not waver.

'Hey, what's going on? Did the shipments get lost again?' Shayna's smile dropped at Jade's face. 'Dude. What's wrong?'

'I just, you have, I saw …' Jade strummed her fingers against her biceps and exhaled a hefty breath. 'I know what you've been doing here. After hours.'

Shayna opened her deep-plum lipsticked mouth, then closed it. 'I don't know what you—'

'Please don't. Please.' Jade's voice cracked and she hated, *hated*, that she couldn't be one of those people who landed difficult conversation with confidence. 'I'm really struggling with this and you're making it worse.' If she heard one more lie, she was pretty sure she'd break something in this small space. 'You know. I know. Do I really need to spell it out?'

Shayna was unusually quiet.

Fine. She wasn't going to confess. Then Jade had to spit it out. Her mind shifted to the fellow teammates who'd lost out on the profit sharing, to her broken trust, to the unfairness of this situation. She straightened her spine. 'You're fired.' The words cut, hard, in the air. 'I'm withholding your final paycheque to recoup a fraction of what you stole. I'd tell you to pay it back, but we both know that won't happen, will it?'

Shayna's tear-filled eyes lowered, and she shook her head. 'Do you even want to know why?'

'Would it matter?'

A long, tense moment passed. 'No. Probably not.'

Shayna's gaze stayed on the floor before she pivoted sharply and stomped out of the room. Jade bit back the urge to follow her and yell out passive aggressive comments about needing to watch her to make sure she didn't steal anything else on her way out. She heard shuffling and the clang of curling irons being shoved into a bag. Shayna returned a moment later, her head held high, her eyes focused on the wall in front of her. She slammed through the alley door.

And then, she was gone.

Jade sat down on the stool but leapt back up as her stomach churned and acid flooded her mouth. She rushed to the bathroom. So much for cool, collected confidence. She was going to be sick.

Chapter 22

Lucy

What was this miraculous burst of energy? Could Lucy bottle this up and sip from it when she needed it the most? She felt human. Alive. *Ah-mazing*. She couldn't believe that a mere six weeks ago she was so sick that she forgot about the queer indie bookstore opening, and today she felt like she could actually jog – which she never did, pregnant or otherwise.

'Morning, Erica!' Lucy bounced down the hall at work holding a decaf white chocolate mocha, her cross-body bag snugged tightly around her expanding chest and belly. 'Morning, Pamela. Yes, before you ask, the new account list is almost done and will be on your desk by ten.'

'Well, aren't you chipper this morning. Give me ten minutes to finish this coffee and I'll match your energy,' Pamela called out as Lucy rounded the corner.

Lucy moved to her office, flumped her stuff onto the desk, and cracked open the blinds. February had started with a week of dense, heavy clouds, but today, the sun had finally pushed its way through. The evergreen trees outside her window were laced with fresh snow from this morning, and the sunbeams made the snowflakes sparkle. After answering a few emails in record time and pulling an audit report, she heard the clicks of heels against the floor approaching.

'Knock, knock,' Pamela said as she also physically knocked and poked her head through the doorway.

'Don't you think it's a little redundant to both knock and say that you're knocking?' Lucy grinned and sipped from her drink.

'Redundant or efficient. All in the eye of the beholder, my dear.' Pamela rubbed a flattened hand down her blue power suit. 'I come bearing gifts.' She pulled out a colourful bouquet of tiger lilies and wildflowers.

Lucy's chest lifted. 'For me?' Her and Jade's technical four-month anniversary was today, but they hadn't celebrated the other ones, so this was out of the norm. Or maybe it was an early Valentine's gift? *Swoon.*

'Sure wasn't for me from my hubs. God knows it's been years since he bought me flowers.' Pamela set the vase down on the desk and waved as she exited.

Lucy ripped open the envelope.

Just a little something to let you know how much we love you! Hugs, Mason and Drew.

Her heart shouldn't dip with disappointment like this, and she felt like a total jerk-hole for frowning at the flowers like they'd personally betrayed her, but … she really thought they would be from Jade. Lucy hated that she felt so icky.

She and Jade were solid. Only six months had passed since they met each other over Lucy's lost wallet in the condiment section, but it felt like Jade had been in her life for years. And it had been forever, literally forever, since Lucy had a *real* girlfriend, so maybe she didn't know all the rules.

She definitely wasn't going to dwell on the fact that they still hadn't said 'I love you'. Should that have happened by now? She shook the insecurity away and shot off a thank-you text to the dads.

The morning flew by with a smattering of customer enquiries, putting out a few fires, and chatting with the marketing team about what made their bank unique. Just as she was about to get up from the chair to use the bathroom, her phone buzzed and she grabbed it from her purse.

Drew: *Still on for tonight?*

Lucy: *Yep! So excited.*

Double-date night was one of her favourite nights of the month, because it meant she was surrounded by her favourite people in the world. For the next few hours, she buried herself in work, until Pamela stopped by again. 'Were the flowers from Jade?'

Lucy's smile twitched. 'No, Mason and Drew.'

'Ah, that's super sweet. I'm sure they don't know how to thank you enough for everything.' Pamela crossed the room to Lucy's desk. 'How are you feeling?'

'I'm good. Great, actually.' Lucy tucked a few papers into a folder and handed it over. 'Woke up this morning and like, I don't know, I wanted to run a marathon. I mean, if I was a runner, which we all know I'm not.'

'Oh! I call this the second trimester honeymoon. It's this incredible space where your body finally accepts whatever foreign stuff is happening and floods you with a burst of energy. Enjoy it. It won't last.'

Lucy bit her lip. She still had so many questions about all things pregnancy, but the one time she went down a Google pregnancy rabbit hole, she got terrified and emotional and vowed never to look up any symptoms again. 'Can I ask you a personal question?'

Pamela clutched the folder against her chest. 'Of course.'

Lucy stood, moved to the side and rubbed her belly. 'Is this normal?' She'd put on close to fifteen pounds by now, and every single pound seemed to have gone straight to her belly, instead of evenly spreading out across her body like she'd experienced in the past when gaining or losing weight. Interestingly enough, she loved her body. She had no idea how sexy she'd feel in her skin while pregnant. 'I'm not even halfway through this thing and I'm *so* not one of those "did she eat a burger" or "is she bloated". I am legit in the "*there's a baby up in there*" stage.'

'Well, yes, you do look pregnant. But it's so hard to say what's normal.' Pamela tapped the folder against the doorway. 'Did I ever tell you my sister-in-law didn't even know she was pregnant for almost six months?'

'Wait, what? How is that even possible?'

'Well, she'd always had irregular periods. She wasn't showing at all and only gained like ten pounds. Hell, I've gained ten pounds in a few months before.' Pamela chuckled. 'It was the shock of a lifetime. So really, I'm not sure if there is a norm. What I do know is that you look amazing. Pregnancy suits you.'

Lucy rubbed her belly. 'It's pretty cool, right? I have a newfound respect for the female body.' She withheld adding a dirty comment about *always* loving the female body.

'Just take it easy, and make sure you're taking care of yourself. Let me know if anything gets too stressful around here, okay?' Pamela flickered her fingers in a wave and Lucy returned to the computer.

Four thousand trips to the bathroom later, Lucy glanced at the clock. Half an hour of work left for the day and she'd be busting out of here. She logged back into her laptop and started to answer an email when her phone buzzed.

Jade: *Can you call me? I have something amazing to tell you!*

Lucy shut her office door and dialled. 'Oooh, tell me everything.'

'You are never going to believe this.' Jade's normally even-keel voice was rushed and excited. 'I just got a call from the *Minneapolis Times*.'

'A good call?' Lucy lowered herself back into her chair. 'Or like, hey there, we're investigating the murder that took place in your basement fifty years ago.'

Jade chuckled. 'Yes! A great call. You know how every year they do the "best of" articles? Like, the best Greater Twin Cities restaurants, bars, bookstores …'

Lucy grinned at the infectious energy in Jade's voice. 'Yes …'

'I was nominated for Best Salon!'

'Oh my God, what?' Lucy squealed, then covered her mouth. 'You've only been open for like two years.'

'I know! I'm freaking out. They're going to do a full article on me and the other top three nominees, with pictures and everything.' Jade's breathless voice sounded through the receiver. 'And get this. They're having a banquet, and I'm invited as a guest of honour.'

'Like all white linens and fancy-pants people speaking in British tones and too many forks?'

'Well, the British accent is a no, but everything else yes. I'm already thinking about what to wear. Flats are a good choice, right? I mean, for the record, I can rock the shit out of heels. I just don't want to walk in all six-three and tower over everyone.'

'You mean like a goddess? Come on, you should wear heels and show off those spectacular legs.' Lucy grinned. 'I'm going to vampire-style devour your legs.'

'Um, okay.'

'Not sexy huh? It was a solid try, though, right? "A" for effort.' Lucy tapped her fingers on the desk. 'How about I'm going to eat through you like a filet mignon?'

'Getting worse.'

'I am going to lick you like a stick of butter.'

'Who licks a stick of butter? You know what, never mind. I don't think I can look at you the same if you say you do.'

Man, was Lucy happy for her girlfriend. This was the win Jade needed. She'd been so down lately, ever since she fired her employee last month. Jade had talked about it a little, with a quiver in her voice when she uttered the word 'betrayed', but she always refocused the conversation back to Lucy.

'This is amazing.' Lucy logged off the computer. 'When are they sending the photographer? What are you going to wear? What will you say?'

Jade's voice was breathy. 'So many details. They're sending over a confirmation tomorrow but sounds like the journalist will come in about two weeks, and the banquet will be in May. I'm so flipping giddy right now.'

Lucy tucked the phone between her shoulder and her jaw as she gathered items into her bag. 'We have to celebrate. Let's do something different. Skating? Sledding? Wine tasting?'

Jade laughed. 'You've literally just said three things that I'm pretty sure pregnant women can't do.'

'Ugh. Pregnancy ruins everything.' Lucy grinned. 'But ... quick update. Drew messaged earlier and he needs to meet us at the theatre.'

'Oh really, so no dinner first?' The sound of Jade stirring something sounded in the background. 'Do you want me to pick us up some takeout?'

All of Lucy's energy pooled in the most delicious places, and her legs warmed. 'We have two hours before we need to meet Drew and Mason at the theatre.'

'Yeah ...'

She licked the corner of her lip. 'I know *exactly* how I want to spend that time.'

Lucy swore she heard Jade swallow. 'I'm on my way.'

Forget work. The tingles were fierce. Lucy immediately logged off and rushed home.

Chapter 23

Jade

Sweat misted Lucy's chest. Jade licked, the saltiness satisfying her cravings, tingling her tongue. Lucy's breasts, fuller, spilling from her bra, her nipples darkening and hardening and Jade didn't know, she had *no idea*, how fucking hot Lucy's pregnant body would be.

Jade licked and sucked, pinched and groaned. She pushed, glided into Lucy, savouring Lucy's moans and squirms. Lucy kissed Jade's mouth, hungry, hard, and with superhuman strength, flipped Jade under her and crawled lower, trailing her tongue.

'Ugh, my stomach, shit, it's too hard, wait …' Lucy rolled to her side, used her fingers as instruments, and ground a palm in Jade's centre.

Jade rode the rhythm, breathless and wanting, with Lucy's beautiful round belly pushing into Jade. God, she was gorgeous, womanly, so full, so beautiful. Her fingers dipped, stronger, and Jade was getting close.

'I want to taste you. Please, my, ugh … my stomach … here.'

Lucy flipped on her back and shimmied down. 'Come up here. I need you in my mouth.'

Jade scooted up, squatting and hovering over Lucy. She swirled her hips, her breath full and raspy, as she gripped the headboard and moved against Lucy's tongue, her fingers, the way she sucked, then licked, knowing exactly what Jade needed. 'Yes, keep going ... so close ...' she mumbled, her thighs tensing, her limbs quivering.

Clamping her mouth on Jade, Lucy steadied Jade, cupping her ass with one hand, gliding her fingers with the other. Jade arched her back, clenching, letting out a scream as she released. Her heartbeat slammed against her neck, in her head, as her legs trembled.

Lucy released her hold, her lips grazing Jade's inner thigh. She stayed there, kissing the skin until Jade lowered herself and rested her head against Lucy's chest.

Lucy ran her fingers through Jade's hair, softly twisting until Jade's body calmed.

'Give me just ... a minute.' Jade wanted to bask in this sensation but also wanted to feel Lucy in her mouth.

Kisses covered her shoulder. 'Later, when we get back. We really should get ready to leave.'

Jade tossed her arm above her head. 'We have time.'

'Babe ... we've been at it over an hour.' Lucy smiled. 'Okay, fine. Honestly, even though I love Drew and Mason, I kind of just want to stay here.'

'Same.' Even though Jade had become close to the two guys, she could have lain here all night without a morsel of regret. 'Shower?'

'I guess ...' Lucy's belly grumbled against Jade's. 'Uff, I'm sooo hungry.'

The shower was tiny, but the water pounded down on their bodies, warming Jade. Even though they were supposed to be cleaning up and getting ready to go out, with a wicked grin, Jade filled herself with Lucy's warm lips, her fingers aching for Lucy's skin. *We have time.* Lucy moaned as Jade pulled a nipple into her mouth, savouring the grip of fingertips against her head, and Lucy murmuring 'harder'. She moved, hands on flesh, increased pressure, quicker, more intense. They had to leave soon, but she wanted Lucy. And she wasn't willing to wait until later tonight. She slipped inside her, and Lucy balanced herself against the wall.

They'd had a few rough weeks of not connecting in the way Jade needed. But now, things had shifted, and in this moment, Jade knew everything would be okay. Some sort of magical lesbian energy fairy had released its powers on Lucy these last few weeks, because she was insatiable. And Jade loved every second. She'd even spent most nights this month in Lucy's bed, because after the tantra sex sessions, she was boneless, exhausted, high off endorphins and lust, and couldn't trust herself to drive.

Twenty minutes later, with towel-dried hair and fresh clothes, Jade rubbed Chucky's fur as Lucy filled his food bowl.

After hopping into Betty Yellow, Jade glanced at Lucy as she tried and failed to zip her jacket over her belly.

'It's huge, right?' Lucy clicked on the blinker.

'It's not huge at all.' *Such a lie.* Her belly was crazy huge. How could bodies shift so quickly? Jade swore that Lucy's belly grew every day. Yes, Lucy was fun and sweet and easy-going. But she was also a woman, fed the same societal messages as Jade, and Jade wasn't sure if agreeing with Lucy about her massive belly was a smart girlfriend move. 'It's just … it's so much more prominent than even last week. I'm just amazed at how much it's … grown.'

Lucy turned down the heat. 'So, it's huge?'

'Stop.' Jade laughed as Lucy navigated towards Main Street. When Lucy pulled Betty Yellow into the parking spot and killed the engine, Jade jumped out to get to Lucy's side of the truck. She held her arm out as Lucy carefully climbed out of the truck. 'This is the first time I haven't seen you hop out of the truck.'

'I was thinking about that earlier. Is hopping bad? What if it shakes the baby too much?' Lucy pulled her scarf tighter around her neck. 'I'm going to ask Drew later. I swear he studies pregnancy as much as he studied for his master's.'

Jade held the door for Lucy. She hadn't been to a movie theatre in forever, and the savoury scent of freshly popped popcorn was already making her mouth water.

'Hmmm ... I'm so hungry.' Lucy clapped her mitten-covered hands. 'It smells so good.'

Jade pulled off her gloves and shoved them in her purse while searching the menu. She really should eat healthy, but damn if those blue raspberry slushies don't get her every time. She dug for her wallet when someone tapped her shoulder.

'Hey!' Mason tugged Jade in for a hug while Drew scooped up Lucy.

Jade really liked the fathers. Getting to know them these last few months, she understood why Lucy felt such a bond. Drew was funny and light-hearted, reminding Jade a bit of Lucy. He had a carefree energy, whereas Mason was more serious. But they were both overwhelmingly protective of Lucy.

'Holy ... what is happening here?' Drew stared at Lucy's belly. 'I saw you less than two weeks ago.'

Lucy rubbed her stomach like she was trying to release a genie from a bottle. 'I know, right? It's pretty cool.'

Jade bit back the urge to ask the men if Lucy's belly growth, along with her ramped-up sex drive, was normal. She moved aside for a group beelining for the concession stand and checked her watch. 'We better grab some snacks if we want to make the show in time. Don't forget, we have to factor in two bathroom breaks for Lucy just to cover the walk down the hall.'

'I'd like to say that's not true, but it's totally true.' Lucy tugged on her ponytail and peeked at the menu. 'Will you grab me a hot dog, popcorn with extra butter, Twizzlers, and water? A big one. Oh, maybe some nachos with cheese? You all want to share that one with me?'

Mason and Drew raised their eyebrows.

'Don't you dare judge me. I'm eating for two.' Lucy pulled her fists in and ducked like a boxer with a scrunched nose.

'Wow. That's intimidating.' Mason grinned. 'No judging … but I better help Jade.'

Jade mouthed a silent thank you.

As they waited in line, Mason loaded his arms with candy from the shelf and pushed his slipped frames up his nose. 'Think they have apple slices? We should offset this sugar intake with something absent of red #40.'

'I sincerely doubt it.' Jade tugged the strap of her cross-body and eyed the menu. 'How are you and Drew doing with all this baby stuff? I feel like I never get a chance to talk to you one-on-one.'

Mason's expression softened. 'I've never been more sure about anything in my life.' They moved a foot up in line. 'Now, ask me how we're doing at picking out a stroller, and we have a whole other issue. I did a thorough evaluation of all the brands on the market, cross-referenced safety, durability, reliability and costs, and chose the best one.'

Jade withheld her smile at Mason's very serious, definitely not-joking-around tone. 'And?'

'And Drew doesn't think it's *cute* enough. Honestly, who cares what it looks like? It has all the capabilities we need, and the functionality is superb. I married a diva.'

Now his smile returned. They set the items on the counter as a bored teenager rang up their loot.

Mason paid for the items and stuffed his wallet back in his pocket. 'How are you doing?'

So much better than last month. 'Great. Lucy seems to have a burst of energy, so we're going to enjoy that as long as possible. And the puking stopped, so I'm calling that a win.' Jade gathered the items and took a long, sugary sip of blue raspberry slushie. Just like drinking frozen cotton candy – *delicious*.

Mason slowed, then came to a full stop. 'No ... how are *you* doing? Not how is Lucy.'

The sincerity in his voice created a surprising lump in Jade's throat, and she felt pink rise to her cheeks. With the exception of Amanda, who seemed relatively unfazed by Jade's girlfriend's pregnancy, once people in the salon had heard the news, every question they shot at Jade revolved around how Lucy was feeling, changing, or how Jade felt in relation to Lucy's state.

The situation with Shayna had broken Jade, and she'd been in a funk for weeks. She had very few people to talk to about what happened, except Lucy, and she didn't want to drone on when Lucy was in the middle of a life-changing event. Of course, her stylists had noticed Shayna's departure. But when they asked her about it, Jade mumbled something along the lines of Shayna leaving to pursue other opportunities. Even with Amanda, Jade only brushed the subject.

'You know, today I'm actually super excited.' Jade took another sip of the slushie and winced at the instant brain freeze. She shoved her tongue against the roof of her mouth to alleviate the burn. 'The *Minneapolis Times* contacted me to do a story on—'

'Twizzlers!' Lucy called out, rushing to Jade and tugging the bag from her hand. She ripped it open with her teeth and popped one in her mouth. 'So freaking good. But I should probably stick with the hotdog first. Thanks, you guys, for grabbing these.'

'No worries at all,' Mason said, and tossed Jade a sympathetic smile.

Jade shook it off. Mostly. This was Lucy's time. She could tell Mason about the article later.

Drew stepped closer. 'Did you grab my M&M's?'

'Oh, sorry. Shoot, I forgot. I'll go back,' Mason said.

Drew tossed him an exaggerated, annoyed look, then grinned. 'Ah. I'll come with. Consider it your punishment.'

Lucy sank her teeth into the hotdog. 'I know, I know. They're so bad for me, but they taste so good.' A dribble of pork oil trickled down Lucy's chin and she swiped at it with her hand.

Jade refused to scrunch her nose, as much as she wanted to. Navigating a vegetarian/non-vegetarian relationship had a few challenges. When she was married, she and Elizabeth subscribed to the same diet lifestyle. Being with Lucy, Jade had to accept that Lucy loved meat almost as much as she loved Chucky.

'Here, let's grab some more napkins before you destroy your shirt.' Jade nudged Lucy to the corner.

'So rude.' Safely in the corner surrounded by napkins and sanitiser, Lucy scarfed down the hotdog in record time and pointed to her belly. 'Look at this. Pretty sure the baby is kicking. Here, feel.' Lucy guided Jade's hand to her belly.

Jade put her hand against Lucy's belly and waited for something to happen. Lucy hiccupped. 'Sorry, nope. I think that's just your meat dinner digesting.' Jade breathed a small sigh of relief. Obviously, Lucy was pregnant – her body was shifting right before Jade's eyes. But feeling a baby kick inside her girlfriend's stomach would make this situation even more of a reality, and Jade wasn't quite ready for that leap.

Lucy laughed as Jade continued to rub her stomach, kissing Lucy on the cheek.

A woman approached them holding a large bucket of popcorn and reached for the salt. 'I have to say, I think it's so sweet to see a couple like you have a baby. How great that a baby gets to experience the love of two moms!'

Jade's eyes widened, then she glanced at Lucy. 'Oh, it's um not, the baby is … ah …' Was it really appropriate to drop all the history on this bystander? Or should she just say thank you and leave it at that? Doing that felt strange, and diminished Mason and Drew's role. 'The baby, it's, ah–'

Lucy's hand gripped Jade's. 'My girlfriend is not the father.'

The woman tilted her head, looking confused.

'But I thank you anyway for the intention of the message.' Lucy grinned, and the woman nodded.

Jade's bystander status was solidified in that single comment. 'It never dawned on me until now, but I bet she's not the first person to think that.'

'I hadn't really thought of that either.' Lucy wiped her mouth and reached for another napkin. 'Thank God, though, right? Neither of us would make good mothers.' Lucy giggled at the comment.

Jade grinned, but the tiniest bit of her heart sank. Yes, she'd said this about herself before, and yes, she had zero desire for children, but why did Lucy think that Jade wouldn't make a good parent?

The men approached, and Jade followed, trying to push away the comment.

Chapter 24

Lucy

Lucy unwrapped a hefty Reuben with dripping sauerkraut and spicy mustard, and bit into the squishy sandwich. She thought last week at the movie theatre nothing could beat the hot dog, but she was wrong because this was freaking delicious. Oh, it felt so good to like food again. Swollen ankles be damned. This sodium sandwich was hitting every spot. 'You are a god among men.' She chewed some more, barely noticing that Drew had cracked open the window to take gulps of fresh air.

'God, sauerkraut smells like–'

'Ass?' She giggled.

'I was going to say rotten garbage.' He took a bite of his club and wiped his mouth. 'I'm glad to see your vulgar ways haven't changed even while knocked up.'

She couldn't believe she'd tipped over the halfway mark. Since the nausea left, minus some muscle cramping, she'd been feeling good. Per her doctor, she'd downed coconut water for the cramping. But holy hell, she had to get up almost five times a night to go to the bathroom. That *had* to be why she was so tired.

'You know what I was just thinking about?' Drew sipped his sparkling water. 'Do you need to check with Jade and see if she's cool with me seeing your vag when you're popping out the baby?'

Lucy grabbed a napkin. 'Why would I check with her? She may own a tabby, but she doesn't own this kitty.'

Drew winced. 'Does she have a cat?'

'No, but I thought the joke would land better if she did.' She snorted. 'Did it land?'

'It landed like a toddler flying a Boeing 747.' He dug a napkin out of the bag. 'So, Mason and I talked, and we should probably see if we have to revise any legal paperwork.'

'Revise?' Lucy pushed the food to the side of her mouth so she could talk around it. 'What do you mean?'

'I mean, you signed a million documents saying you were single, and that if something horrible happens, your dad is the one to make any medical decisions on your behalf.'

'Ah.' She pulled a dangling piece of sauerkraut from the sandwich and tossed it in the paper bag. 'I mean, the medical decisions should still be up to my dad. But, yeah … paperwork.'

It hadn't occurred to her until now that she should revisit the paperwork. Lucy loved being in a relationship with Jade. As her first real, true partner, she wasn't sure what to expect. But so far, things were easy, simple, and mostly fun. Having never connected with anyone like this, Lucy was navigating fresh waters and learning as she went.

Sometimes, though, Lucy felt like she did so much talking that Jade knew her better than she knew Jade. Their conversations were a delicate balance between Lucy asking questions, and respecting Jade's quieter nature by not prying.

'You're not single anymore.'

'Thank you for that update, Captain Obvious.' She saluted him. 'What constitutes being together enough where you have to file paperwork?'

Drew shrugged. 'I think that's something you have to define with Jade. Maybe talk to her and see what she thinks?'

A groan was on the tip of Lucy's tongue, but she refrained. Was talking to Jade about paperwork a good idea? Nothing like putting an extra stress on a new relationship by bringing up super unsexy paperwork.

Drew's eyes folded in concern. 'What's the matter?'

Lucy finished the last bite of sandwich and wiped her hands. 'We haven't said I love you yet.' Was that weird? They'd been together for a little over four months. She'd met Jade in late summer, and now they were headed towards spring. They'd talked about future-ish plans, like splurging and going to Italy in the fall. But things like moving in together, or buying a house, or saying *I love you*, were totally out of the picture.

Drew narrowed his eyes. 'For real? Like U-Hauling is straight up part of the lesbian culture.'

She rolled her eyes. 'Not all lesbians U-Haul, jerk. Stereotype much? I think, well, we're taking it slow.'

'Why haven't you said it?' Drew sat back and crossed his arms as several long pauses followed. 'You do love her, right?'

I think so? Wait, no, yes, she did. She was sure. Okay, *almost* sure.

Drew would never understand. He was the kindest, most gracious human, who told everyone he was close with how much he loved them. He ended phone calls to his family with 'I love you. Bye'. He told Mason he loved him after like two minutes and was *sincere*.

Whereas Lucy? She'd never been in love before. This connection, this need to be physically near someone beyond just the sex part, was foreign. She never missed hugs and kisses from partners when they left, or counted the minutes until they could snuggle and laugh together again. She always wished exes well, of course, and hoped they were happy. But she always felt separate from them, like Lucy could never match their happiness. But with Jade, it was different. When Jade was happy, Lucy felt those same flushed feelings. When she was sad, Lucy wanted to cry.

Of course, she also liked her routine and her space. And if she really loved Jade, wouldn't that mean that she'd want Jade with her every single moment?

Maybe she didn't know what love was.

What she knew was, when Jade was at her own home, Lucy went to bed thinking of her. When she woke up, she missed Jade's warm body.

Lucy did worry about how much of her clingier feelings were because of the pregnancy. If she didn't have all these extra hormones making her squirrely and emotional, would she still want Jade just as badly? Pregnancy brain was a real thing, and what if everything changed after this journey was over? Ninety per cent of their conversations surrounded pregnancy, birth, stretches, body aches, or laugh/crying when Lucy's inability to see her own nether-regions for a safe shave forced her to resort to waxing, which she determined was only one step down in pain from childbirth itself.

Drew jiggled the ice in his cup. 'How often do you guys sleep overnight with each other?'

'Lately it's been more. But before that, maybe one or two nights a week?'

'Are you serious? That's it? Mason and I were living together by this point.' He exhaled through his nose. 'I'm sure I'm being paranoid. I just don't want anything to get messed up, or if the courts got involved or something …'

Drew *was* being paranoid. Most likely. Tapping into the logical side of her brain, Lucy knew Jade wouldn't try to interfere with medical decisions or kidnap a newborn.

'It's a ton of pressure on a new relationship,' Lucy said quietly.

'It's not *that* new.'

He had a point. But a few times, the relationship had felt … under pressure. Like a weighted blanket had inched over them, and not in a positive way. Jade sometimes seemed to tiptoe away, like she was eyeing their relationship from a close distance. She clammed up when talking or switched subjects to turn the spotlight on Lucy. Admittedly, Lucy had no idea what it was like to be divorced, and the trauma that may stem from ending an important relationship. But Jade refused to talk much about her ex, so Lucy stopped asking.

Maybe Jade held back at times, but Lucy wasn't completely innocent, either. Giving so much of yourself was scary as heck. Even though Jade had reluctantly accepted a pregnant Lucy, what was going to happen when she wasn't pregnant anymore? Would Jade want to be with Just Lucy?

Ugh. Lucy needed to stop the cyclone of thoughts. She took a sip of root beer and adjusted the car vents to lower the heat. 'Whoa.' She slapped Drew on the arm. That gurgly thump was *not* indigestion. It was a definite, miniature, hi-ya!-style kick. 'Drew, holy cannoli ... I think your baby just kicked.'

'What!' His hand whipped to her belly.

'Dude! Wipe your hands. I have to go back to work and I don't want greasy mitt stains everywhere.'

'Sorry, sorry, oh my God.' He slapped a napkin across his hands, then laid both palms on her belly.

Nothing.

His gaze flickered between Lucy's eyes and her stomach. 'Should I FaceTime Mason?'

'I don't think you have to whisper.' *Come on, little one. Give your dad a kick.* Drew was not blinking, not breathing, and his heart was going to stop if this little guy didn't do something. She poked the side of her belly but was met with nothing.

'Can you make her do it again?'

The pleading in his voice was for the record books. 'Her?' Lucy raised her eyebrows. 'Wishful thinking for next week's ultrasound?'

'I feel it in my bones. I just know it's a girl.' He jiggled her belly and waited. And waited some more.

She took another sip of ice-cold root beer. A few seconds later … *pow!*

'Ah. Oh my God … I felt it.' Drew's hands pressed more firmly into her belly, his mouth frozen in an open-mouthed smile. 'Oh shit, Luce. This is real. This is the realest of real.'

When Lucy was younger, she phased through a solid crush on Sigourney Weaver and snuck movies she had no business watching when her dad was at work. The scene in *Aliens*, where the beast ripped from the dude's belly, didn't quite feel like this. But it definitely felt like she'd swallowed a fish that was now moving around inside, banging into her belly aquarium walls.

Lucy's body had morphed before her eyes. Her nipples were bigger, darker, her boobs were Eighties porn star status. Even her feet had grown a whole size. She'd expected change, of course, but not *this* much change.

After Drew guided her out of his vehicle and slung an elbow out for her to grip, he escorted her up the sidewalk to her building.

'Do you think my vagina is going to get all mangled during childbirth?'

He scrunched his nose. 'No! I mean, I guess, I don't think so? Is that a common thing?'

Was it a common thing? Maybe, in *this* case, she should do a little research: will the boobs shrink, will the vagina return to a pre-push size, will the brain fog end? *Will my girlfriend still want to be with me?*

Enough.

She schlepped back into her office and shut the door, letting the moment flutter through her body. Today was a very, very big deal, and she wanted to celebrate with Jade.

She pulled out her phone.

Her dad answered. 'Why are you calling during the workday?'

A smile crept across her face. 'Hello to you, too.'

'You know, back when I was working, you couldn't just make personal calls whenever you saw fit.'

She eased herself into her chair. 'Did you walk uphill both ways during the winter with Wonder Bread bags rubber-banded to your ankles so your socks didn't get wet?'

A loud huff echoed through the receiver. 'You think it's funny, but that's the original waterproof shoe and didn't cost no more than the one-dollar loaf of bread it came with. Nowadays, you all spend a hundred dollars to get a decent snow boot. I didn't even make a hundred dollars a week when I first started working.' The sound of water filling a glass was followed by several gulps. 'What do you need? I'm a busy man.'

'God, you're cantankerous.' She tucked the phone under her chin and fired up her computer. 'I want to take Jade out for dinner after work, but I don't want to leave Chucky. Can you come over and watch him?'

'You know dogs can be by themselves, right?'

As if on cue, the familiar sound of Chucky trotting around echoed. Hah.

'You're already over there, aren't you?' she said, barely suppressing a smile.

'You need to install a Ring camera,' he said. 'I could have been a dog-napper or murderer.'

'How many hours are you there, exactly, during the day?'

'I'll never say. But I'll tell you that your dog is fat and he's not getting any more jerky sticks from me tonight, no matter how much he begs.'

If she could hug her dad through the phone, she would. 'I love you.'

'Ya, ya. You too, kid.'

Chapter 25

Jade

Jade's eyelids snapped open. She reached across the bed, making contact with the warm imprint of a body now gone. Heavy breathing rose from the floor. What had woken her ...? Grunting sounds. Poor Lucy. Just shy of six months pregnant, and this past week it seemed her body was kicking and fighting as it edged into the third trimester.

'Where'd she go, Chucky?' Jade murmured.

The bathroom light was off. Jade blinked into the dimly lit room to peek at the clock. 3:15 a.m. *Oof.* Maybe it was time to return to sleeping in her own bed. Lucy had started tossing and turning at night, and more than once her freakishly oversized snake-shaped body pillow smacked Jade in the middle of the night.

She grabbed the top blanket, wrapped her naked body, and eased herself out of the bedroom. 'Lucy?'

'In the kitchen,' a groggy voice replied.

Lucy lazed a wave, her leg tossed up on the counter as she stretched her muscle and a half-drunken glass of milk next to her ankle.

Jade kissed her shoulder. 'What are you doing?'

'Did I wake you?'

Yes. 'No, I just noticed you were gone.' She yawned. 'Are you okay?'

'Not really.' Lucy grimaced along with some fire breathing and dropped her leg. 'My back is killing me. It's like this weird electric spiderweb shooting spikes down my hips and legs.' She heaved her other leg off the counter and groaned.

'Come on, come back to bed.' Jade pulled the blanket tighter around her chest, the winter chill in the room springing goose bumps up her arms. Tomorrow, pyjamas. 'I'll massage you.'

'You don't have to do that.'

'I know.' She ushered Lucy back to the bedroom. Lucy groaned as she eased back onto the mattress. After throwing on Lucy's way-too-short yet ultra-plush bathrobe, Jade pumped lotion into her hands.

Lucy shifted to her side and shoved a pillow between her legs. Jade pushed against her lower back and hips with firm pressure, and soon eye flutters replaced Lucy's gritted teeth. The dads were grateful for Lucy, of course, but did they *really* know about nights like this? No doubt Lucy hadn't told them, probably preferring to swap goofy GIFs and raunchy comments with Drew rather than admit she was restless and in pain and literally up at all hours of the night.

When Jade started the relationship with Lucy, she knew what she was getting into. Still, she'd be lying if she said it was easy. Watching her partner transform, shifting from her goofy self to cautious, fluctuating being misty-eyed and forgetful, was harder than she anticipated. For every time she was annoyed at Lucy for spacing out or not picking up on social cues, she was livid at herself for being selfish. And Jade wasn't sharing the way she should, she knew that, but Lucy had so much going on. Did she really need to hear about Jade's workplace drama or her favourite colour line getting discontinued? When this was all done, they'd have time. A lifetime, in fact. Right now was Lucy's time.

Lucy's muscles loosened under Jade's pressure. Her chest lifted and lowered, and when her breathing grew even deeper, Jade peeked at her face. Yep – asleep.

Jade eased away and slid back into a sleeping position. She put her index finger up to her lips, said 'Shhhh' to Chucky, then reached down to rub his head before closing her eyes.

Three hours later was not nearly long enough. How did parents of babies live with interrupted sleep? Jade dug a knuckle into her sawdust eyes, dragged herself into the shower, and left the house before Lucy woke up. She normally wouldn't get to the salon this early, but today was a big day. With the *Minneapolis Times* interview scheduled for this evening, she had a gazillion things to do – swing by the grocery store, grab a fresh flower bouquet, clean every inch of the salon until it sparkled, change clothes, refresh her make-up …

The fresh, overnight snowfall dusted the lawns and tree branches, and she cracked the window to breathe in the bone-dry, crisp air. Normally when snow fell this late in the season, she was officially over it and ready to see green. But even though it was April, the snow was a pretty, magical blanket.

She tapped her steering wheel, turned up the radio, turned down the radio, cracked the window even further, and breathed through her racing heart. *Interview.* She was getting interviewed by a freaking journalist, and now the steering wheel was turning slippery under her damp palms.

Elizabeth was always the eloquent speaker, not Jade. During family holidays, she gave the toasts and the speeches. In boardrooms, she commanded the space. She'd even been on a few business podcasts, and even though Jade didn't grasp the content, Elizabeth's delivery was flawless. She had that gravitational pull where people wanted to breathe her air, like maybe her star power would rub off on them. Jade both hated that trait almost as much as she was attracted by it, fluctuating between feeling ignored, feeling like someone had stolen her thunder, and feeling relieved that competent Elizabeth was by her side when she stumbled. If Elizabeth were here, she'd sit next to Jade, pepper Jade's words with commentary, and complete the story circle Jade had been mentally struggling with. But now, Jade was flying solo. She pinched the bridge of her nose and exhaled heavily through her mouth.

The journalist had sent a list of preliminary questions a few days ago. Things ranging from what made her salon unique to why she thought the community gravitated towards it, how she'd managed to grow the business so quickly, and what made her the proudest about her salon. One question, however, was what made her decide to move here from Chicago. She emailed and asked if she could strike that question as it was a 'personal family matter'. This interview was not the time to dive into her gut-wrenching divorce and need for a fresh start.

Jade cleared her throat. Rehearsal time. 'Honestly, I think the community rallied so much because when you step into the shop, it feels like family.' Ugh. Did that sound idiotic? She'd said this line twenty times in the past few days, but now she was questioning every word.

The word *family* didn't flow. She tried to ignore the drop in her stomach as her thoughts turned to Shayna. Since Jade had fired her, she had not heard one single word from Shayna. Every time Jade thought about the situation, she turned queasy. She really hadn't taken the time to process what happened, the betrayal, and the sadness that followed.

But she'd taken action. That was the most important thing, right?

She shook her head and pulled into the parking lot. 'The stylists try hard to learn the names of regulars, even if they aren't their clients. And the rumour is that I have the best tea cookies in town.' That was supposed to be funny, but maybe people would get confused. Should she talk about having the quickest balayage application in the Midwest, or keep it about the cookies? *Ugh.*

After turning off the ignition, she checked for mascara flakes in the vanity mirror. She paused and looked at herself. 'You did it,' she whispered with a grin. *Damn right.* Without Elizabeth, without her family, even without Lucy. The community had nominated her for this award based on her hard work, merit, their love for her salon, and Jade's grit. She had something that was truly just hers.

I fucking did it.

If the fresh snow hadn't been a potential safety hazard, she would've skipped across the parking lot.

A solid cup of coffee down, two clients completed, and the door jingled.

'Mrs Dieterman.' Jade held out her arm. 'I got fresh cookies for you.'

Mrs Dieterman whooshed away the comment and gripped Jade. 'Today's the big day, huh?' She had an uncharacteristic smile. 'Getting interviewed by the paper.'

Her chest fluttered, and Jade bit back a grin. Last week, after her weekly shampoo set, Jade had mentioned the article in passing.

And Mrs Dieterman had remembered.

Mrs Dieterman's gaze flickered up and down Jade, from head to toe, a deep frown on her face. 'Tell me you're not wearing this outfit for the pictures.' She sat in the shampoo chair and lowered her head slowly back into the sink. 'Promise me you'll wear a nice shirt, for God's sake. Not much we can do about that pink hair of yours, but at least a button-down should help.'

God, Jade loved her brutal honesty. Reminded her of her shoot-from-the-hip grandma, who was borderline rude, sure – but always full of good intentions. Jade laughed and tugged at her off-the-shoulder, ripped Nirvana sweatshirt with a black bralette. 'So … not this?'

Mrs Dieterman scowled but quickly softened. 'Back in the

day, the a.m. radio station interviewed me. That was a huge deal, you know.'

Jade lathered Mrs Dieterman's hair and began scrubbing. 'What were you interviewed for?'

'I had won a barrel shooting contest at the local county fair. Beat out the men, too. I ended up going to five different county fairs that year to compete and won four of the five.'

Wow. Mrs Dieterman's cool factor had just skyrocketed. 'No way. That's really impressive. Wish I would've been around to see it.'

Suds rolled down the drain, and Jade brought her back to the station.

'The attention after the interview surprised me,' Mrs Dieterman said, settling into the chair. 'I was a local celebrity, if even for a moment. You have all these news stations, and this internet crap. Back then, we didn't even have television. People glued themselves to their radio just like you kids glue yourselves to your phones.'

'Such a different time, huh?' Jade snapped the cape around Mrs Dieterman's neck and grabbed the rollers.

'So, I say, you better prepare yourself for some stardom.'

A blush swept Jade's cheeks. 'I don't think it will be quite like that. I suppose we might get a few new clients from the article, but …' *Or maybe more?*

Jade had come into her happiness last year, after mending her heart and stepping into her life here. Getting the salon off the ground, meeting Lucy, the dads, even Chucky … Jade was blissfully content. Her mind drifted, and for the first time in forever, she dreamed.

What if this article did kickstart something bigger? Maybe it would bring in so many clients that she'd have to expand or, *or!*, she'd open a chain. Years ago, she'd created a mood board, cutting out pictures from hairstyling and décor magazines, envisioning what a second salon's name would be. Jade the 2nd? Or Jade's

East? Jade Part Two? The thrill had energised her for weeks until reality set in and marriage issues took over. When she moved to Minnesota, Jade had tossed that board into the trash and scolded herself for being so naïve.

But what if this article, or perhaps winning the award, was the key turning point? Maybe that mood board would become reality after all. Maybe it was time to pull that dream out of the garbage …

'Well, I tell ya. I'm just real proud of you,' Mrs Dieterman said. 'Be as humble as you want, but don't sell yourself short on what a big deal this is. There are hundreds and hundreds of salons in the Twin Cities and beyond. Tough competition. And you are a damn finalist. Be proud.'

God, if it wasn't straight out of the 'what not to do with a client' handbook, Jade would've hugged Mrs Dieterman and squeezed for an uncomfortably long time. *Be proud.* Where had she last heard those words? She wracked her brain. Maybe when she was a freshman in high school and her team won the basketball championship? After bucking her parents' life plan for her, they definitely didn't say they were proud when she graduated from 'beauty school', or when she opened her salon, or started a new life.

But suddenly, these words were filling a hole that she hadn't realised even existed.

'Now, I bet that lady friend of yours is happy for you.'

Jade wrapped hair around a curling rod and tucked it against Mrs Dieterman's scalp. 'Oh yes. Super excited for me.' *I think.*

Lucy was ecstatic when Jade first told her. Hugs and kisses and some amazing celebration sex. But since then, she hadn't asked about it once. Although, once again, that selfish gremlin crept up on Jade's shoulder and tapped her. It was crappy for Jade to expect Lucy would talk about this in between appointments, sore feet, insomnia, and her work.

Jade rolled the standing dryer to Mrs Dieterman. After setting the timer, she went to her office, grabbed a yogurt, and checked her unread messages.

> Lucy: *Want to grab some dinner tonight at the vegan restaurant off 8th?*
>
> Lucy: *Yes, vegan. You heard me right. But that salt-and-pepper tofu was Da Bomb Diddy Bomb.*
>
> Lucy: *Ignore that last part. I meant to say the tofu was delicious.*

Jade took a bite of yogurt and held the spoon in her mouth as she typed.

> Jade: *The* Minneapolis Times *reporter will be here at 5, so it will have to be after that.*

Three bubbles appeared.

> Lucy: *Oh shoot! I forgot. That's right. Good luck, you are going to knock it out of da park.*
>
> Lucy: *No more da's. I don't think it's working for me. You're going to do amazing. Betty Yellow and I can pick you up at 6.*

The GIF she sent of a rainbow beam shooting from a woman flexing muscles couldn't shake Jade's instant urge to cry. Jesus, Lucy was the pregnant one, but Jade was getting emotional over the silliest things! Ridiculous. Pregnancy brain was a real thing, and she needed to cut Lucy a huge amount of slack. Drew had sent Jade an article about this phenomenon a few weeks ago with a message along the lines of giving her space-cadet girlfriend a break. The article dived in about extra hormones, lack of solid sleep, and increase in blood volume, making pregnant women foggy and forgetful. Jade inhaled through her nose, let the comment go, and plastered on a smile for her next client.

Later that afternoon, after she finished her last client of the day, she rushed to her office and changed. Not a button-down, much to Mrs Dieterman's eventual dismay. Jade still wanted to look like herself, but a more elevated, professional version of herself. So ripped skinny jeans, heels, a Stevie Nick's T-shirt and a black quarter-sleeve blazer for the win.

A knock at the door sounded, and she cracked it open.

'Damn, woman. You clean up nice.' Amanda flipped her long black braids behind her back. 'You ready for your photo shoot?'

'God, I hope so.'

'I just finished cashing out the last client, and the team is cleaning.' She flipped her wrist to look at her watch. 'She still coming in about ten minutes?'

'Yep.' Jade glanced in the mirror and plucked a chunky bang from her face. 'I have like two seconds to pomade and apply some eyeliner.'

'You nervous?'

Jade swiped black liner across her lids and added gloss. 'A little.' She dragged her pinky under her eyelid and moved to the left eye. 'What if I sound like a complete idiot?'

Amanda scrunched her face. 'I've never heard you sound like an idiot. You're wicked smart, a great boss, and funny to boot.'

'Are you trying to get a raise? 'Cause it's totally working.'

'I mean ...' Amanda smiled. 'But really, I'm serious. The crew has mad respect for you, the clients love you. Just be yourself, and you're gonna nail this.' She tapped her fingers against the door frame. 'I just think this whole sitch is really damn impressive. Queer Female Entrepreneur. You've already broken barriers, you know. Like, you punched through the glass ceilings. And now this. Besides, you're totally going to win. I can feel it.'

Between Amanda and Mrs Dieterman, Jade was two steps away from being a blubbering mess. She grabbed lip gloss from her drawer. 'It's just an honour to be nominated.'

Amanda rolled her eyes with a wide smile. 'Such bullshit.'

Jade threw up her hands. 'Okay fair. I really, really want to win.'

The door jingled, and Amanda's eyes widened. 'Okay, I'm sneaking out the back to leave you alone. Quick teeth check?'

'Yes, please.' Jade smiled and Amanda's eyes travelled her teeth. 'You're good. You got this. *Cannot wait* to read the article.'

Jade had no idea how much she'd needed a pep talk from a twenty-year-old. She shook out her hands, low exhaled, and walked to the front.

A woman was stomping the snow off her feet on the mat. As Jade approached, the woman unravelled a heavy knitted scarf from her neck and shook out her brown curly hair. 'This much snow? Come on.' Her smile was warm and inviting, and fine wrinkles feathered out from the corners of her eyes. 'Hey, there. I'm Caroline, from the *Minneapolis Times*.' Her gaze travelled the salon – from the dark leather chairs, to the multiple plants, to the huge, colourful paintings of scissors and a comb that Jade ordered from an incredible artist back in Chicago. 'This place is great. I can already see why people love it.'

'Hey, I'm Jade.' They shook hands. 'Great to meet you. And thanks. I really love this place, too.'

Caroline hung up her jacket and twisted her neck to look out the window. 'My photographer is parking now. Let's go through the logistics …'

For the next hour, Jade posed in various places. She attempted to strike a balance that represented her image – strong, confident, and authoritative, while also being warm and fun.

Caroline graciously offered to model so the photographer could get an action shot. Jade grabbed a roller brush and hairdryer and pretended to work.

Caroline took notes in an old-fashioned flip notebook, but

she also recorded everything on a voice memo app. She asked the questions that Jade had prepared for – how long she'd been in business, what she liked about Minnesota, a fun client story from the past year.

'I think we're just about wrapped up.' Caroline strummed her pen against the notepad. 'Any last words?'

As fun as this was, Jade also felt like she'd just given mental birth. How did people do this all the time? Being on, answering questions while trying to sound clever, but not *too* clever, was damn hard. 'I really appreciate all this. Minnesota is a tight-knit, family-orientated state, and ...' Jade grinned as she shrugged. 'I'm still an outsider. I've lived in Chicago my whole life, and I was worried I wouldn't feel like this place was home. But the city has wrapped its arms around me.'

Caroline clicked off the recorder. 'That's awesome. Perfect ending.'

The photographer said he'd load the truck and left the women momentarily alone.

'Thank you, Jade. This was so much fun. The article releases next Tuesday, and they'll announce the winners at the May banquet. I'll send the photo proofs to you for review.'

The door opened and Lucy stomped in, smacking her wool mittens together as snow dusted to the ground. She glanced between Jade and Caroline. 'Oh sorry! Yikes. I thought you'd be done by now.' Lucy took off her coat and hung it on the rack.

Jade grinned. She could not wait to tell Lucy everything that had happened in the last hour. 'Hey, no worries.' She gave Lucy a quick kiss, then motioned to Caroline. 'We were just wrapping up. Lucy, meet Caroline. Caroline, this is my girlfriend, Lucy.'

'Nice to meet you. Gah. I'm so sorry. I have to use the bathroom.' Lucy pointed at her belly. 'Baby shifted and is like hammer-dancing straight on the bladder.' She frowned at her words, then scooted away without waiting for a response.

Caroline tugged on her jacket. 'Are you two having a baby?'

God, no. 'No, she's a gestational carrier for her friend and his husband.'

Caroline plucked her scarf from the rack and dangled it in her hands. 'That's amazing. What a gift she's giving them, huh? You, too. Can't be easy to be the partner and not, you know, get a baby out of the deal.'

'Well, thankfully, I'd rather crack the ice on the Mississippi and take a long swim over getting a baby.' Jade chuckled and twirled the ring on her finger. 'The journey has been pretty daunting, but there are some major bonuses. I've become close with the dads, and I get to witness my partner being kind of a badass. Besides, when the dads bring the baby home, they won't have as much time for Lucy, so I'll finally get her all to myself. Win, win, you know?'

Caroline laughed along with Jade, thank God, because the words had somehow sounded ickier than intended. But they weren't entirely untrue. After birth, Jade couldn't wait to reconnect with the woman she'd first met at the grocery store.

'Sorry about that,' Lucy called out as she approached. 'I cannot wait until I can go a solid four hours again between bathroom visits like a normal human.'

'It gets worse.' Caroline laughed and stuffed her notebook into her bag. 'With my daughter at the end there, it felt like every twenty minutes. How far along are you?'

'Twenty-five weeks.'

Caroline nodded. 'So, you're a surrogate for your friend. He must be pretty special, huh?'

Lucy shrugged, then sat on the lobby chair. 'Yep. We've been besties since we met at St James in kindergarten.'

'St James?' Caroline nearly shrieked and pulled a chair next to Lucy. 'I went there. Many, many years before you, I'm sure. Was Sister Katherine still there?' She glanced at Jade for a snap, then returned her focus to Lucy.

Jade fiddled with her watch and took a step back. This

conversation was not for her. She didn't know if she should pull up a chair and listen or walk away. She grabbed a pen from the desk, needing to do something with her hand, and tapped it against her palm.

'Oh, yes. Sister Katherine is definitely one of those people who's gonna live forever. Too stubborn to die, you know? Oh, the memories.' Lucy pulled her hands into her chest. 'That woman is probably still there to this day, terrorising the children.' Lucy giggled. 'What about Father O'Neil?'

Caroline smacked the top of the seat. 'Right?'

'Right.'

Like some sort of Catholic-girl secret code, they swapped a look, then dived into stories about the creepy stairway under the tunnel they swore was used during prohibition, the locked room on the top floor that Lucy heard had confiscated Ouija boards, and the blood stain on the second-floor bathroom ceiling that had never been cleaned. Caroline was convinced it was to scare the children about the devil.

'Tell me more about the surrogacy journey,' Caroline said. 'Are you nervous about the birth and handing over the baby?'

Lucy rested her hands on her belly. 'I'm nervous about labour, sure, but handing the baby over is easy-peasy lemon-squeezy. Getting there is the hard part, and there was so much work and prep to even get to where we are today. Pushing this thing out will be the easy part.'

As Caroline peppered Lucy with questions, Jade's smile faded. A few minutes in, she stepped back, and five minutes in, she excused herself to go to the bathroom.

As soon as she closed the bathroom door behind her, tears welled. Jade frantically blinked them away. 'Stop it,' she murmured under her breath, fanning her reddened face. She was being ridiculous. Surrogacy was fascinating, and Caroline was certainly not the first person to be intrigued and ask Lucy questions.

But did Lucy need to be *such* an open book?

Jade shook out her hands and her shoulders, taking in gulps of air. Jealousy was not a good look. This appeared to be jealousy. But this didn't *feel* like jealousy. She couldn't pinpoint the sensation pricking at her insides, but it was terrible and gross. And familiar. Jesus Christ, what was wrong with her? She'd had this same feeling multiple times with Elizabeth, this fear of being invisible and unimportant. The fight inside between wanting to shrink into the corner so no one could see her, while screaming and pounding her feet to make people pay attention.

But Lucy was not Elizabeth, not even close.

After pressing a cold towel behind her neck, Jade forced a smile and returned to Lucy, who was scribbling in Caroline's notebook.

'I better get out of here,' Caroline was saying as Lucy wrapped up whatever she was writing with a flourish and handed the notebook back. 'Our photographer has been in the car this whole time, oops. I'm sure he's ready to head back to St Paul.' She stuffed the notebook in her bag and swung it over her shoulder. 'Thanks so much, both of you. Who knew it'd be a two-for-one type of night? I appreciate both your time.'

When the door swung closed, Lucy wrapped her arms around Jade's waist and nuzzled into her chest. 'How did it go? She was super nice. Did you answer all the questions?'

A half hour ago, Jade couldn't wait to tell Lucy every single detail. And now, the words stuck like thick peanut butter in her mouth, and she was struggling to formulate a sentence. 'Yeah, it went well. Sounds like …' She cleared the tackiness. 'Sounds like you two had a chat?'

Lucy's released her grip. 'Yeah, get this. She wants to do a story on me, Drew, and Mason. Crazy, huh? She's going to talk to her editor and then get back to me next week. I gave her my contact info.' She tapped her fingers together, her smile widening. 'What if we have an article out the same day? Wouldn't that be cool? I'm totally going to frame it and add a big fat, obnoxious heart around it.'

Jade tried to smile, she really did. But right now, she was using one hundred per cent of her effort just so she didn't burst into tears.

Lucy's face dropped. 'Hey, what's wrong?'

Now was not the time to dive into the inner workings of Jade's mind – which, by the way, she could barely decode herself. Jade put her hands against her stomach. 'Oh, uh ... man, that salad I had for lunch is doing something funky to my belly. I'm so sorry. I don't think I can do dinner tonight.'

Lucy's eyebrows clenched. 'Oh no. Are you okay? We can go home, order in, I can run to the store for veggie soup? Or I have a Costco-sized box of saltines in my cupboard, and a fridge full of ginger ale.' Lucy nibbled on her lip as she glanced around the salon. 'You still have that peppermint tea? I'll steal some for home, but since it's your shop and for your consumption, it's not *really* stealing. But that might settle your belly?'

Jade kissed Lucy's cheek, but her lips felt numb. 'Nah. Thanks, though. I think I just need to head home and take a bath.' She grabbed her keys and threw on her coat. 'You parked out front? I'll lock up behind you. I have to go through the back to get to my car.'

'Oh. Yeah, um okay.' Lucy pushed her arms through her jacket and grabbed her purse. 'You sure you're okay?'

No. 'Yep. Hopefully this is just a twenty-four-hour bug thing.'

Jade held her arm out to walk Lucy to her car and then rushed back inside. She shut the lights off, locked the door, and hurried back to her office. She didn't make it to the door before she burst into tears.

Chapter 26

Lucy

The room had a distinct, powerful sterile smell. Bleach, metals, and antibacterial soap nestled among the electric wires and freshly washed cotton. Even the first week of May's special scents, which she'd always loved – blooming lilacs, fresh cut grass after a long winter,. the budding of trees – were so acute they almost gave her a headache. For the past few weeks, Lucy had considered contacting the government to see if her acute smelling powers could lead to a part-time gig as drug-sniffing human, until she realised sniffing drugs was definitely *not* recommended during pregnancy.

With this new pregnancy superpower, cleaning supplies weren't the only thing reaching her nose. Drew's cologne and deodorant – a definite man smell she was not loving at the moment – permeated the space. She shifted the pillow under her neck and scooted up. At almost twenty-six weeks along, this proved to be more of a challenge than it had been just weeks ago.

Her bestie, who resorted to chewing his fingernails like he did back in grade school, looked on the verge of passing out. 'Don't be all weird now,' she said. 'You're the one who knocked me up.'

'Technically, it was the doctor, a bunch of tools, and Mason's swimmers.' He dropped his pinky from his mouth. 'But I get what you're saying.'

Someone rapped on the door, and a nurse poked her head in. 'The other father is here. Making sure he can come in while we wait for the doctor.'

'Yes, yes, of course.' Lucy adjusted her cotton gown. 'Let's be like John Stamos, the Olson twins, and the guy who allegedly did Alanis Morissette dirty, and get a *Full House* up in here.'

Drew shook his head, an extraordinarily pained look flashing across his face.

'That didn't land, did it?' she whispered.

He squeezed her shoulder. 'It never does.'

A moment later, the door flew open. 'So sorry I'm late. I can't believe I'm late.' A crease sliced across Mason's forehead, a rarity on his usual stoic face. 'I had to park on the fifth floor, and they were down to one elevator.'

'No worries.' Drew hugged him. 'The doc isn't even here yet.'

Mason glanced around the room. 'Where's Jade?'

Who knows? Lucy wasn't sure where Jade was, other than not here. In fact, lately, Jade had been more absent than present. She hadn't slept over in a week and had cancelled plans multiple times saying she was working late. Even when she did show up, it felt like she was trying to find an excuse to duck out early.

Maybe Lucy tossed and turned too much at night, and Jade was too polite to say anything? The interrupted sleep sucked for her, so she could only image it sucked for Jade too. But they hadn't had sex for well over a week and Lucy was getting itchy.

'Uh, Jade had some clients that couldn't reschedule, and she felt bad cancelling.' Ugh. Why lie? She'd never lied to her friends before, minus the one time she said Drew's skinny jeans looked good. Lying was a cardinal sin, a one-way ticket to devil-land per her childhood teachings. But in this case, it was necessary. Lucy refused to ruin this moment by going anywhere negative.

The men, thankfully, seemed distracted, and the doctor entered the room at the perfect time.

'Hey there, family. Big day today.' The doctor snapped on gloves. 'Are you ready to see how much your baby has progressed?'

'Yes, we're so excited.' Drew's voice was an octave higher than usual, and he cleared his throat. 'I know we were on the fence before, but Mason and I decided we want to know the baby's sex.'

'Sounds good.' The doctor faced Lucy. 'How about you. Feeling good? You ready for this?'

The level of dissociation was for the record books. Lucy was ready, but it wasn't to view the cells forming in her stomach – it was to watch the fathers' reaction to seeing their baby.

Was she curious to find out if the kid had sprung an extra limb or something? Sure. But other than that, observing a floating blob with a head was not what she considered a good time. She thought by now, she'd think differently, or even perhaps grow some sort of attachment – maybe even a fondness – to the foetus.

But no, nothing. Chucky would always be her one and only child.

After the doctor explained what to expect from the sonogram, she lifted Lucy's shirt. Poor Mason was looking everywhere but her naked belly. 'Mason. You can totally look at my stomach,' Lucy said. 'I mean, we've gone swimming like a gazillion times.'

'True.' Mason glanced down to her stomach, his eyes morphing into a cartoon-wide bulge. 'Wow. You got huge!'

'I retract my invite,' she said with a groan, but wished she could snap a photo of the sudden, beautiful light in his eyes.

'Sorry, sorry.' Mason held up his hands. 'It's just amazing, you know?'

Cold gel blopped on her stomach, and the wand travelled up her belly.

And, well, there it was. Floating around on the screen was a profile of a half-shaped human with a belly, head, ears, hands, and maybe toes? She squinted, gave up defining body parts and waited, again, to feel something.

Nope.

Until she looked at the dads.

Mason, sweet old statuesque Mason, pulled his lips into his mouth and gripped Drew's hands so tight that Lucy could see Drew's fingers turn white. 'That's our baby ...' His voice quivered.

Drew blinked at the image, taking a step closer to the screen. He ran his hand down his cheek as Mason stood firmly at his side, rubbing his back. 'Is everything ... ah ... normal? Good?'

The doctor smiled. 'Everything is looking good. We'll check for spine, bladder, heart, kidneys, limbs ...' She rattled off more as Lucy's mind wandered.

Drew and Mason were solid. They'd been like this since Day One, never faltering in their feelings, never questioning where they stood. Lucy had met Jade nearly seven months ago, standing in the grocery store aisle looking like a goddess and swearing at the vacant sriracha shelf. She loved being with Jade. She adored Jade. But she hated the way her heart tugged and shifted. Oh, no. Had the magic from the beginning disappeared? Right now, Lucy wished she was feeling towards Jade what Drew and Mason felt towards each other.

'Ready?' the doctor asked. When the men nodded, she continued. 'You are having a ... baby girl. Congratulations.'

Drew and Mason yelped. Lucy was unsure of who had yelped louder. He hugged Mason hard, as Mason buried his face in Drew's shoulder. 'We were hoping for a girl. We, of course, wanted the baby to be healthy and would love them no matter what ... but a girl!'

The joy from the men filled Lucy, and she wanted to savour this moment for eternity.

The doctor wiped Lucy's belly with a towel. 'Any questions?'

Oh no ... Pandora's box had been opened. As the men

peppered her with questions – like, how do the baby's kidneys compare to others, how much would she weigh at birth, did her brain activity look normal – Lucy noted all the things she wanted to ask her dad. Was this how her dad acted with her mom? Was he even in the room during any of the ultrasounds? She ached, wishing her mom was here to hold her hand, share her own pregnancy story, and maybe add in a small joke about her dad.

And dammit, she really wished Jade was here, sharing this moment.

'Did you eat chicken pot pie for dinner last night? Did you remember to make your yearly doctor's appointment? And did you see that they have yet another new *Jeopardy!* host?' Lucy chatted with her dad as she sat in her car in the parking lot outside the radiology department.

'Why are you calling me during the day?'

'I took the afternoon off.' She leaned her head back into the car seat. 'Explain to me something. How was it snowing less than two weeks ago, and now it's sixty and sunny. My brain can't comprehend that I'm looking at snow while wearing a sundress.'

'I'll tell ya, the farmers are none too happy about this. We needed more snowfall for the moisture. We don't need no drought comin' in like last year.' She could hear him slump in a chair and crack open a can. 'What do you need?'

Lucy needed *so bad* to hear something, anything, about her mom, and she needed her dad not to clam up. She needed Jade to be here, not wherever the hell she was, and for someone to hug her and assure her that everything would be okay.

'Well, shit. Are you crying?' Her dad's tone was much softer than the words.

She sniffled. 'It's just hormones. I'm fine.'

A long pause followed. 'Wasn't today some big day for you all? You got to find out if you're having a pink or blue.'

She grinned but bit her tongue. Explaining to her dad that the baby's sex did not equal a colour would do zero good. Well, she knew what he meant. 'When Mom, um, had me, did you find out my sex ahead of time?'

She tossed the question out softly, so that he could give a gruff yes or no if that's all he wanted to share, and they could move on. She listened to him take a long pull of his pop, and then heard the ting of the can as he set it on the table.

'Your mom was a nervous wreck. She wanted a kid so dang bad. A girl. She wanted to dress the kid up in ballerina shit and God knows what else.'

Lucy waited, begging, praying, hoping he'd say more. A moment passed, then two. She was about to change the subject when he started talking again.

'And you know, I was just wonderin' how many toes you had. I didn't care much even if you had eleven toes. I just wanted to see with my eyes that, you know, all things were good.'

So many moments passed, she thought for sure *this* time he was done.

Then he took a breath. 'So, we looked at the machine, and I'll tell ya. I was so damn relieved. The doctor said you were healthy, and all your insides were the way they should be, and I just remember being able to breathe after that, knowing you seemed good.'

Lucy tugged on her lower lip, refusing to let herself cry with this backstory goldmine. 'Thanks, Dad, I really needed this.'

'All righty then.'

The phone clicked off, and she held it to her chest. Her lips trembled and she replayed his words. She lifted the phone and hovered her thumbs over the screen. Why was she contemplating *not* texting Jade? Seemed odd for people in a committed relationship, right? Of course she should message her, or call her, and give an update.

Lucy dialled. Straight to voicemail. *Must be with a client.* She flexed her thumbs.

Lucy: *Had the ultrasound. Want to guess what's behind door number one?*

Three bubbles popped up. Then stopped. Then popped. Then stopped. Lucy waited. Three minutes. Six, ten. At the twelve-minute mark, she started the car and drove home.

Chapter 27

Jade

Jade stared at the orange, syrupy drink and gagged in solidarity as Lucy choked back the last bottle of the day. The twenty-seven-week, three-hour-long glucose test was no joke. Hopefully, the test showed Lucy did not have gestational diabetes and then she could happily eat ice cream until the end of the pregnancy.

'I can't do it,' Lucy groaned in between gags, wiping sweat beads from her brow. 'It's like orange cough syrup mixed with Sunny D. I'm one hundred per cent going to ralph.'

'Do people still say "ralph"?' Jade dunked a paper towel into a water cup and dabbed Lucy's neck. 'You got this. Tonight, you can make me try something that will make me gag.'

'Salty meats.' Lucy slammed the rest like a shot and slapped a hand over her mouth.

'I definitely should have added a disclaimer to that statement.'

Jade had not attended many of Lucy's appointments, unclear of her place in all the surrogacy stuff. Pregnancy was something happening *to* her girlfriend, *for* someone else. It was all a little removed from Jade. Of course she wanted to be supportive, but she also didn't want to step on toes. Unfortunately, it seemed like no matter what decision she made, she was letting someone down.

'Lucy.' The lab worker motioned Lucy forward for yet another blood draw.

Man, that was a lot of pokes. Jade had a sleeve tattoo, but getting blood drawn was a different level of pain.

Lucy hoisted herself up and followed the white coat to the back room.

For the appointment today, Lucy told the dads last week she could fly solo. But Jade was sitting next to her during the phone conversation and saw in Lucy's face that she clearly wanted someone there for moral support. And now, seeing what Lucy had to endure, she couldn't blame her for needing someone by her side. After this, she was taking Lucy out for a fat burger, a steak, or whatever carnivore-style thing Lucy might be craving for lunch.

Lucy returned with a cotton swab and bandage secured around her arm. She slumped in the chair and leaned against Jade's shoulder. 'I know what would make me feel better.'

Oh ... this could get interesting. She kissed the top of Lucy's head. 'Oh yeah, what's that?'

'Looking at your hot-as-hell boss photos from the newspaper.' Lucy pressed her mouth against Jade's ear. 'After I get my energy back, we are *sooo* going to play out an ice boss/secretary fantasy. I'm going all in. Plaid skirt, button-down blouse, suit and tie for you, everything.'

'That's a lot of clothes that will need removing.' Jade chuckled through her nose. 'Can't wait.'

She had to admit the *Times* photographer had captured some awesome shots, and Jade did, in fact, look like a boss. When the article came out last week, she devoured it, reading each line multiple times. She was in *the newspaper*! In a really great article, and she'd received so many compliments from staff and clientele. On Monday, when Mrs Dieterman arrived, she brought a stack of newspapers and asked Amanda to hand them out to everyone in the salon. She even skipped grandkid stories that day to talk about the article and the event in May when they'd announce the winner.

Lucy sat up. 'Even Mason said the article turned out great, and you know how stingy that man is with compliments.'

Learning everything about Mason and Drew these past few months, this statement was pretty damn accurate.

Lucy yawned and tipped her head back into the seat.

'You tired?' Jade asked.

'I feel like I'm getting sleepier these last few days. Although we have been staying up a bit extra at night. *Raaaar.*' Lucy did an absolutely horrible feline impression, including strumming her fingers in the air.

Jade glanced over her shoulder to make sure no kids were listening. Or actually anyone. But Lucy was right. After a brief dry spell, they had picked up the bedroom activities again – but the energy was no match to what they'd had when they first got together. Which was understandable, given how tired they both were at the end of the day. And logistic-wise, navigating the beautiful belly produced a few challenges. Although Jade was pretty sure she was nailing it, if she did say so herself.

Lucy dug out lotion from her purse and pumped a dollop into her palms. 'Are we still going shopping tonight?'

Relief coursed through Jade. She'd been looking forward to dress shopping all week but was sure Lucy would forget or be too sick after her tests. 'You still up for it?'

'Yep. Let's see what I can get this bad boy into.' She tapped her belly.

Tonight should be fun, and Jade double-crossed her fingers and toes that Lucy could keep up her energy. Jade hadn't worn a dress in years. Buying a fabulous cocktail dress for the banquet held a sort of *Pretty Woman* excitement. She wasn't sure who she'd be meeting at the ceremony, but the mayor of St Paul, along with prominent business figures, were scheduled to attend. Now was the time to dress for success, schmooze like her life depended on it, and win.

There, she said it. She wanted to win this award more than she'd wanted anything in forever. Being nominated was pretty cool. But this award represented so much more than the glass-engraved statue. Knowing she'd won Best Salon in the Greater Twin Cities area would represent that she'd finally made it – despite what her family thought, despite what Elizabeth thought, despite her own self-doubt. If Jade won, the award could never be stripped away. It couldn't leave her, or divorce her, or forget about her. A win was forever.

The nurse approached Lucy. 'Results are ready. Follow me, please.'

When Lucy struggled to heave herself up, Jade grabbed her elbow to help. 'I'll be right here waiting for you. Good luck.'

Lucy glanced behind her shoulder. 'You don't want to come back with me?'

'No, this is all for you.' She'd never intrude on Lucy's business like that. Besides, it probably wasn't fair for Jade to hear any of the results before the actual parents. 'Fingers crossed though. For both of us.' She winked. Last week, Jade had made a terrible pact: if Lucy's results showed she had gestational diabetes, Jade would give up ice cream for the rest of the pregnancy in solidarity.

She really, really didn't want to give up ice cream.

After she slunk in the chair, a woman two seats down leaned towards Jade.

'Are you and your partner having a baby?' the woman asked as her knitting needle poked against her round belly.

Shocking, how many times random people asked this question. In her entire life, Jade had never asked anyone about an impending birth. But this woman had a kind smile, and they were in the OBGYN office, so it seemed less invasive. 'Ah, no. She's a surrogate for her friend. I'm just the person who rides shotgun.'

The woman nodded and returned to her knitting. A few moments passed as she wrapped her yarn, and then she glanced up. 'That's quite the sacrifice for you.'

Huh? No way Jade had heard her right. Lucy was the one making the sacrifice, not her. 'She's happy to do it. And she's such a trooper.' Jade almost commented about how this woman must know about sacrifice since she was pregnant herself, but Jade zipped her lips. Golden rule, learned in the most mortifying way her first year of hairstyling: unless you see the baby's head, never assume someone is pregnant.

'That's lovely. But I meant that's quite the sacrifice for you. Giving up your partner for a year, for a life that you may not have chosen, and for little to no recognition. It's remarkable.' She unspooled her yellow yarn. 'Buy yourself a push gift, too.'

Wow. No one had ever said that to her before. Having a pregnant girlfriend *was* hard, even though Jade hated admitting it. Lucy was the one who had it really hard, with all the sickness, swollen feet, and aversion to smells. Wasn't it selfish of Jade to think about how tough it was for her? It wasn't right that she sometimes dwelled on an alternate reality in which, in the prime of their relationship, she and Lucy danced and travelled and did very naughty things in the bedroom. Instead, they had movie nights, long nights broken up by restless sleep, and nausea.

Jade knew what she signed up for and didn't regret entering into this relationship. And she was happy. Really, really happy. Right? *I think.* Yes, definitely happy. She adored Lucy ... she lov ... she coughed the rest of the sentence from her brain.

Lucy exited the room with two thumbs up and an exaggerated wink.

'Does this mean we get ice cream?' Jade asked.

'Yep.' Lucy gathered her bag. 'Clean bill of blood glucose health. Let's get some lunch and then go shopping. I cannot wait to see us all snazzied and jazzied.'

Lucy's purse vibrated, and she dug out her phone. She motioned

Jade to follow her as she made her way to the entrance. 'Hello?' Lucy's head bobbed as she listened to the other end. 'Okay, sounds good. Tomorrow? That's awesome. Thank you.' She tossed the phone back in her bag and gripped Jade's arm. 'That was Caroline. The surrogacy article is coming out tomorrow.'

The article. Jade had had a while to cool from the unexpected, heated feelings drudged up during Lucy's interview. After some solid soul-searching via several Ted Talks and a few Instagram reels with the right combo of heartfelt music and inspirational quotes, Jade could finally, freely admit that Lucy wasn't trying to steal her moment. Lucy was vibrant, fun, and bubbly, and had a really cool story. She deserved her moment, too.

Jade held the car door for Lucy as she lowered herself into the seat.

'How do Mason and Drew feel about you all becoming a three-ring local celebrity unit?' said Jade.

'Oh my gosh, whatever.' Lucy stretched the seatbelt and clicked herself in. 'There's going to be like ten people who read the article.'

Jade went around to the driver's side of the car. 'You know people love feel-good stories. Especially now with everything …' She didn't need to ruin a good moment with a political climate chat. 'Pretty soon, people are going to be asking for your autograph.'

'You're one to talk! You're totally going to win the award and I'm going to have to make an appointment just to see you.' Lucy dug out a bottle of water from her bag and guzzled. 'I need to pick up an extra paper tomorrow to give to my dad. It's a sweet story, and Drew and Mason are pretty damn cute, but unless it's a very slow news day, I don't think people will care.'

Jade hated to admit it. *Hated it*. But a part of her hoped Lucy was right.

Chapter 28

Lucy

Well, it was obviously a very slow news week.

Lucy had genuinely thought that outside of Drew and Mason's families, and maybe a couple of co-workers, no one would care about the surrogacy story. She wasn't the world's first surrogate. They had entire clinics devoted to this kind of family journey. But something was in the air – maybe the upcoming dicey presidential election, or spring approaching after a gloomy winter, or the lack of any current celebrity scandals. Whatever it was, people pounced on the story like toddlers on cookies.

Lucy blinked into the ring light, trying to remove the spots messing her peripherals.

'Dads,' the producer called, and Drew and Mason snapped to attention. 'Place yourselves here, one on each side of Lucy. Sorry, you're going to have to squish in.' He checked the frame and stepped back with a slight frown. 'Lucy, a little forward. Dads, a tad back.'

After the *Times* had run the story, the weekend local TV news station had picked it up for a segment. And then a Wisconsin news station asked for an interview, and a national online news source ran the story. And now here they were, two weeks later, getting shuffled to perfection in Drew and Mason's living room. The producer clapped his hands and motioned for the technician to attach their mics.

Mason adjusted his bowtie, Drew cleared his throat, again, and Lucy used every core muscle she had left to maintain proper posture.

'You doing okay?' Drew asked.

'Totally.' Lucy ran her tongue across the ridges of her teeth for a final lipstick check. 'I'm ready for my close-up, Mr Deville.'

'It's DeMille,' Mason whispered.

'No. Really? Like really, really?' Lucy cracked a smile. 'I've been saying it wrong all these years.'

'Who do you say that to?' Drew whispered back as the make-up person added one more sweep of powder to his forehead. 'Please say no one, ever.'

'I don't like you.' Lucy scrunched her nose and glanced to where Jade was resting against the corner wall, a soft smile on her face. Since the local media frenzy hit, Jade seemed a little withdrawn. Again. Still. More.

Or was she? Jade was here, wasn't she? Since the start of this baby-making situation, Lucy's thoughts hadn't been clear, and maybe she was sensing something that didn't exist. When the national morning show team reached out for an interview, Jade had snuggled in bed with Lucy and joked that she alone needed to do Lucy's hair because it would reflect poorly on her if her girlfriend's hair looked ratty on national television.

'Did you seriously just call me ratty?' Lucy had said with a grin. Jade had quickly retracted her words and reassured Lucy with a 'that's not what I meant!' and a 'you're the hottest woman alive' until Lucy was satisfied Jade had completed her penance.

The producer stepped in front of Lucy and checked his watch.

'Any refreshers needed on what we chatted about earlier in the week?'

'I won't swear.' Lucy grinned. Last week, along with the prep questions, the producer told them multiple times that the network had a three-second delay as a fail-safe in case someone swore. Then quickly followed with, 'But please, please do not swear.'

'I think we're good,' Mason said.

Drew leaned into Lucy's ear. 'You look like a hot mama.'

Lucy patted her beach-waved hair. 'I kind of do, don't I?'

'Everyone take a deep breath,' the assistant producer said and inhaled a huge breath while raising his palms from his belly to chest. 'You look great. This will be a piece of cake, and we'll be out of here in three minutes.'

Jesus, the lights were hot. Lucy picked a few strands of hair off her sticky forehead, and her belly knotted. Ugh, now her legs were cramping. And why was everyone in the room staring directly at her and not the dads?

Jade mouthed, *You got this*, and Lucy's shoulders relaxed. She focused on the monitor resting on the table. The morning show logo remained static, and a commercial played in the top right corner.

The producer adjusted his headset and threw up his fingers. 'And five, four, three, two …'

'Hello and welcome back. Today, we have a good news story all the way from Stillwater, Minnesota, about thirty minutes east of Minneapolis. Joining us today are Lucy, Drew, and Mason, a group of childhood friends who made a very special surrogacy pact years ago and are now in the midst of fulfilling that promise. Welcome all.'

'Hi,' Lucy said along with the dads, although she added a way too enthusiastic, elbow-to-wrist wave to her greeting. *Whoops.* She quickly dropped her hands to her lap.

The camera zoomed in on the host. 'Let's start with the woman of the hour. Lucy, can you tell us how you're feeling?'

'I'm great.' Lucy patted her stomach. 'The baby is kicking up a storm, I'm back to eating solids, and my feet have only gone up one size. So far.'

'Oh, the feet.' The host smiled. 'I remember that uncomfortable stage when I was pregnant with my children.'

'Do they shrink back? I don't want to be stuck at size ten forever. Oh gosh, no offence to any size ten-ers out there.'

'Let's hope so.' The host chuckled. 'Drew and Mason, what led to the decision to choose Lucy as your gestational carrier? That's a lot of trust to place in someone.'

'When Drew and I first started talking about surrogacy, we always knew Lucy would be the one.' Mason's legs tensed, but his voice was calm. 'Drew and Lucy have been friends since kindergarten; I've known her since junior high, and we all just click. Once Drew and I started dating in high school, we just became this unique type of family and stayed like this ever since. We're just thankful she said yes.'

'Lucy,' the host said. 'I imagine you get a lot of questions, especially since your story hit. How are you handling the media interest and the pressure that can come with that?'

Lucy recalled her notes from the prep session. 'Everyone has been so nice. Either I'm blissfully unaware – and it wouldn't be the first time I've been accused of that – or people have kept any "personal comments" to themselves.'

'That's great to hear,' said the host. 'For the dads, I understand there are more legalities and paperwork surrounding surrogacy than a traditional pregnancy. Can you walk us through that process?'

Drew took a breath. 'It took nearly two years of conversation, legal paperwork, doctor appointments, donor reviews, and shots, before we ever got pregnant. I think all three of us have a few more grey hairs than when we started this.'

'Speak for yourself,' Lucy said out of the corner of her mouth.

The host laughed. 'That's quite the journey. I imagine it would be daunting for anyone in your situation.' The host glanced at the notecard on her desk. 'So, Lucy, I read that you have a significant other, right?'

A spark of heat travelled up Lucy's neck and she peeked at Jade, who wiggled her brows. Sure, this was on the list of potential questions, but she secretly hoped it wouldn't be asked. Yes, they'd been in a relationship for months, but this interview would be searchable content for infinity. Was this the equivalent of getting the kiss-of-death tattoo of a partner's name on your body, and once the ink dried, something terrible happened? 'Yes, I have someone special in my life.'

The host smiled. 'I imagine the dynamic changes within a relationship when you're carrying for someone else.'

You have no idea. 'Well, I had to give up my dancing days, that's for sure.'

The beginning of their relationship looked nothing like what it did now. There was so much pressure now, that just hadn't been there when they first met. Was it because of the pregnancy? Or was this some step in the natural progression of a relationship?

'I bet.' The host laughed. 'For things like birthing classes, how do you handle that? Do all four of you go? Just you and the partner?'

Birthing classes. Drew had been pestering her, sending her emails with various classes around the area. He not so subtly tapped his knee into hers, and she understood his 'told you so' message.

'Oh no, my partner won't be joining. I've said to folks before that my girlfriend is not the father. She's totally hands off with the pregnancy stuff. That part of my life is for the dads, and the other part of me is for her. She probably won't even be in the hospital when I give birth.'

The host dipped her head. 'Interesting. Well, we all do what we feel is best. Thank you so much for chatting with us and wishing you all the very best of luck.' She turned to the camera. 'Coming up after the break, we'll talk to a local San Francisco twelve-year-old who has built such a reputation for his butterscotch cookies that he was invited to the White House. Back in a moment.'

'Great job, everyone.' The producer tugged off his headphones.

The assistant reached for Lucy's microphone, then unplugged the devices from the men. Lucy's mouth was bone dry and sweat prickled her chest.

'Oof. Am I stinky? I was sweating so bad, I swear. God, I'm thirsty.'

'You did great.' Drew stood and adjusted his pant leg while Mason ducked over to the producer. 'But for real, Luce. We need to sign up for the birthing classes soon. Promise me you'll look at all the emails that you've happily ignored this last month.'

'I wouldn't say *happily*.'

Drew glanced at Jade, who was scrolling through her phone in the corner. 'Are you sure Jade doesn't want to be part of the classes? Do you really think she won't be in the hospital room? You know Mason and I are fine with whomever you want there.'

Lucy smiled to cover the fact that she had no idea if Jade wanted to be in the room. 'Gotta go to the bathroom. Be right back.' She scooted out without another word.

Sure, there were conversations they hadn't had – like if Jade would join Lucy in the hospital, or during birthing classes, or nearly anything that had to do with the baby. They just … didn't go there.

Lucy felt emotionally detached from the pregnancy, and besides feeling the alien squirming inside, she wasn't that interested in what was happening. She'd do whatever Lamaze, yoga, or hypnotist class the dads wanted. It was their baby, and she was just housing it for a while. But for the level of dissociation Lucy felt, Jade was probably on Jupiter with anything baby related.

After her trip to the bathroom, Lucy returned to find the production team had already removed the lights and monitor and were loading up a bin. Drew and Mason were chatting in the corner, but Jade was gone. Lucy went into the kitchen, the other guest bathroom, but nothing.

'Have you guys seen Jade?'

Mason jutted his chin to the patio door. 'Yep, she's outside. Probably replenishing the vitamin D she depleted over the winter.'

Outside, Lucy didn't see Jade right away, so she tilted her head to the sky and soaked up the warm sun. She took a moment to breathe in the fresh spring air, with the smell of mowed lawn and budding trees. She crossed the lawn to the side of the house. Ah. That's where Jade was hiding – leaned up against the wall with her eyes closed.

'There you are.' Lucy hooked her arms through Jade's and hugged.

Jade stiffened under her touch.

'What's wrong?' Lucy unhinged her arms, then stepped back, her gaze flickering over Jade's expression.

The look on Jade's face was foreign, and Lucy's belly flopped in response. Squinted eyes, a flatlined mouth, red cheeks, and now, heavy crossed arms.

'Why would you assume I wouldn't want to be in the hospital with you? Or take Lamaze classes?'

Whoa. Her tone was a mix of hurt and pissed, and Lucy fumbled for words. Why wouldn't Lucy assume that? Jade never asked about those things, and was Lucy supposed to offer it up? This wasn't even her kid. 'I don't know. I just … in general you seem disinterested in anything about the pregnancy, so I just thought …'

'Disinterested? Disinterested!' Jade's hands punched into her hips.

Oh, yep. That tone was no longer hurt. Jade had gone from zero to ten. She was pissed.

Jade's nostrils widened, and she dropped her arms. 'I went to your appointments, I rub your feet, I don't eat certain cheeses around you, I ask you how you're feeling all the time.'

'Are you serious?' Lucy felt heat rise in her face. *That's* what Jade considered showing interest? Not eating brie? Jade could not be more indifferent if she tried. 'I mean, sure, you ask how I'm feeling, but you're not asking about *me*. You're checking off a list. You've never once asked what it feels like to have something shift inside you, or how it is to feel my hips widening, or if I'm worried about postpartum depression, or what it's like not having my mom here to ask why I have raging heartburn and if she had a secret potion she used when *she* was pregnant!' Lucy caught her breath.

Jade's jaw worked in a circle before she exhaled. 'You don't like talking about your mom.'

The comment may be fair, but Lucy's good old stubbornness reared its ugly head. She was not about to acknowledge the logic of Jade's statement. She may not like to talk about her mom, but Jade avoiding the subject was something *else*.

'Hey, you guys out here?' Mason's voice cut through their stare-down.

Lucy blinked. 'Over here!'

'Should we all go grab some brunch?' Mason paused a few feet away from them and looked between the women. 'Everything okay?'

Jade cleared her throat and pushed herself from the wall. 'Um yep. I've gotta get back to the salon. Great job all of you.'

Without a kiss, hug, or another word, she left.

And Lucy held back the sob choking in her throat.

Chapter 29

Jade

Jade stared at the screen of her phone with the same hesitation she'd felt these last two weeks. She and Lucy did not have a co-dependent relationship, which she valued. But at this point, their relationship was on the extreme end of the non-co-dependent side and had crossed the line into full-on avoidance.

For the past two weeks, since the incident outside Drew and Mason's place, they'd seen each other only a handful of times, skipping dinner dates because one of them was tired, or working late, or sifting through piled-up paperwork. Jade knew it was bullshit, and Lucy most certainly did, too. But neither one called it out.

As the sound of the salon springing to life echoed behind her closed office door, Jade's fingers lingered over the screen. She took a deep breath.

Jade: *Have a great day at work!*

Good God. Could the message be any more impersonal? If she swapped the exclamation with a period, it would fall directly into the 'friends-only' category.

Jade had zero doubt that she wanted to be with Lucy. But just because she *wanted* to be with Lucy didn't mean that was the healthiest choice. A future existed, she was pretty sure, and in ten more weeks they could figure out what that future looked like. Until then, these sterile messages would need to keep them afloat.

Lucy: *You too!*

Yep, like clockwork. This sad little message string summed up the last fourteen days of their relationship.

Jade had let go of her jealousy over the attention the media had showered on Lucy, who at this point was probably in the running for *People* magazine's next cover. The sting of her nomination being overshadowed by Lucy had faded, and she'd genuinely loved watching Lucy get interviewed by the morning show. The world saw Lucy's charming, selfless self, and during the interview, Jade wanted to scream her pride at being with such an amazing woman.

But when Lucy said that Jade wasn't interested in her world, and she *wasn't considered* as a partner in the birth, Jade's heart cracked. Did Lucy think Jade was unreliable? Unstable? Or maybe this was Lucy's way of showing she wasn't as invested in their relationship.

Jade reached into her mini fridge for oat milk creamer, added it to her coffee, and stirred. After pulling in a hefty, earthy sip, she leaned back and focused on the ceiling tiles. Besides the moment she'd first learned about Lucy's plan to get pregnant, Jade had supported Lucy. Choosing to be in a relationship with a pregnant woman should have demonstrated Jade's level of investment, right? But an obvious disconnect existed, and as much as Jade hated it, she had to confront it.

'Screw it.' She grabbed her phone and punched out a message before she lost her nerve.

Jade: *I think we need to talk tonight.*

Her pulse pounded in her neck as the three bubbles appeared.

Lucy: *Ok.*

Oof. Well, Jade had ripped the proverbial band-aid. Just like she'd done with Shayna.

Tonight, she and Lucy needed the mother of all heart-to-hearts to make sure they were on the same page, which required some vulnerability from Jade. She *hated* opening up. But Lucy was worth it, their relationship was worth it, and it was time.

Three clients later, Jade rinsed out the bleach bowl in the back room and flopped on a chair. She pushed her fist into her chin to crack her neck and let out a deep exhale along with the satisfying pops. Nerves over the impending conversation with Lucy had burrowed into her cells, and Jade bounced out of the chair and started organising backstock. Too bad her next client had cancelled, because now she had an hour to sit here and stew without the distraction of a complicated balayage.

The back-room door flung open, and Amanda gripped her hand against the door frame. 'Hey, lady, you have a visitor.'

Jade's eyebrows twitched. 'Lucy?' She checked her watch. It was around her lunch time, but she rarely made surprise visits.

Amanda shook her head, her Afro puff bouncing with the movement. 'Nope. Not sure who she is. Didn't give a name and I don't recognise her as a client.'

The phone rang and Amanda scooted away.

Jade washed her hands, balled the paper towel into the trash, and moved up front. Rounding the corner, her footsteps halted before her brain could process the scene.

Standing in the salon entryway, next to the blur of shampoo bottles and take-home conditioning treatments, was Elizabeth. And a baby.

Ringing filled Jade's ears, and the lights seemed to dim. What in God's name was Elizabeth doing here? With a kid? The moisture in Jade's mouth evaporated on the spot, leaving her tongue heavy and raw. She pulled in a breath, withheld a few choice words since it was her place of business, after all, and marched up front. 'What are you doing here?'

Jade's tone was sharp. Her look even sharper. But her insides were anything but. Here was a woman Jade loved for *years*. Committed her life to, and – in the beginning at least – she just *knew* that they'd grow old together and be that couple that died days apart from each other because they couldn't bear the idea of not being with the other person.

Elizabeth looked both the same and different. The blond pixie cut she'd been wearing for years remained untouched. Jade recognised the dark denim jean jacket. A memory flashed of them buying matching ones, which was the first – and only – time they ever wore anything remotely similar. Elizabeth was always a fan of power suits and sharp lines, whereas Jade was drawn to anything black and grunge.

But Elizabeth also looked different. The determined rigidity in her eyes was softer, and she had more lines creasing the edges. Dark circles rimmed her lower eyes, and yet, she looked refreshed. And it all suited her. Incredibly well. She bounced the baby in the front backpack thing strapped to her chest, and her hands patted the outside of the carrier.

'Hey, Jade.' Her voice was sheepish, quiet, and an atypical blush rose to her cheeks. Which for some unknown reason got Jade right in the heart. 'Can we talk?'

Nope. She peeked at Amanda, who was doing a terrible job pretending to type on the computer. Jade's face burned so hot she was sure she might pass out. 'Uh, sure. Yeah. Outside?'

She didn't wait for an answer and moved to the door, holding it open for her ex. A vacant city park bench provided the spot. Jade sat at the farthest edge and scratched the back of her neck.

Elizabeth dug a pacifier from her diaper bag and clipped it to the side of the carrier.

Neither said a word. For way too many moments.

'How did you get a kid so fast?' Jade cut the excruciating silence, even though there was so much more to say.

Elizabeth popped the pacifier into the baby's mouth. 'Funny how things work out, huh? I'd been waiting for so long. A birth mom changed her mind last minute and selected me instead of a different family after an icky interaction with the dad. We met a few times and clicked, and well … she chose me.'

Jade peeked at the baby, at the smattering of black wispy hair poking out on its head, at the brown eyes and deep black eyelashes flicking its round, chunky cheeks.

She waited to feel something. She didn't.

'The kid's cute.' Jade was officially at a loss for words, and Elizabeth was being quiet and vague. She needed to spit out the reason she was here, or leave. Jade really couldn't handle this. Not now, probably not ever. She had a business to run, a girlfriend she needed to resync with, and probably some backstock that needed reordering.

'I named her Jayden,' Elizabeth said with a smile, while focusing on the baby's head.

Jayden? Was she seriously naming the kid something that close to her own name? A sickly bubble rose in her throat. 'Why the hell would you do that?'

Elizabeth's eyes grew wide, then narrowed. Then, her mouth cracked, and she laughed. 'Jesus Christ, your face. My God. I'm just kidding, but that reaction was priceless. Her name is Amber. Thank you very much.'

Against her better intentions, Jade let out a giggle. 'God, don't do that to me.' She slapped her hand against her heart. The baby fussed and Elizabeth bounced her knee.

'Why are you here, Liz?'

Elizabeth slowed her rocking and straightened her shoulders.

'I'm visiting my brother. He moved to Minneapolis, if you can believe it. Took a job at Target headquarters.'

'Wow. Good for him.' Jade could hardly believe it. Elizabeth's brother had talked about doing this very thing for over a decade. After declaring that half his paycheque went to the store anyway, he told everyone he wanted to leave Chicago to work at Target. He'd been saying that since Jade met the guy. *Wow ... so he made the leap. Good for him.*

When she and Elizabeth divorced, Jade cut off contact with Elizabeth's family. But every now and then, she missed her former in-laws. She couldn't help but feel a little proud that her former brother-in-law had finally got up the nerve to follow his dreams.

Time was dragging by at glacier-speed, and Jade needed to move this along. Being next to Elizabeth, Jade's insides were tightening, moment by moment, and she didn't like it. There was a pressure in the air, like clouds rolling in during a bright summer day, and you weren't sure if they were going to turn into a vicious storm, or a needed rain reprieve. Jade folded her arms and strummed her fingers against her skin. 'Look. I don't mean to sound like a total dick, but what do you want?'

Elizabeth's eyes shifted, and she patted the baby. She opened her mouth, closed it, and opened it again. 'I miss you. And ... I should have never let you go.'

Jade's heart leapt.

Well, shit.

Chapter 30

Lucy

Lucy's insides begged her to pace the house, but her swollen ankles had very different ideas. So, she sludged to the patio bench in the backyard to enjoy the last of the afternoon sun and pressed her toes into the floor to swing while Chucky chased a bird.

A car door slammed and her heartbeat picked up speed. Earlier today, when Jade said she wanted to talk, Lucy didn't know what to expect. But it probably wasn't good. She and Jade had been misfiring for weeks now, but Lucy didn't want to call attention to it, hoping it would all magically fix itself. She assumed these were typical fluctuations in a relationship, but deep down she knew something was off.

If she and Drew ever disagreed, which was rare, they called it out on the spot. They'd hash through the details until it was time to hug it out, at which point they went back to arguing about which *Schitt's Creek* one-liner was the best ('*Ewww, David, obviously*'). She knew Drew would never leave her. Maybe that's why she didn't mind confronting him. But did this mean she thought Jade might?

Lucy strained her neck to see if she could spot Jade inside the house, through the screen door. 'Out back!'

Footsteps approached and the screen door flew open.

'Dad?' Lucy started to stand, but her dad waved her back down.

'I told ya I had to come into town for parts.' He tapped his baseball cap lower to cover his eyes and took a seat opposite her under the shade of the tree. Chucky beelined his way towards him, accepted a rub on the head, and retreated to circle the yard.

'Yes, you did, but you never said you were going to stop by. Everything okay?'

Her father was quiet as he stroked the stubble on this chin, but that wasn't abnormal for him. 'Ya, well, I figured I needed to make sure you hadn't popped nothing out yet.'

Dad. A man of the most profound words.

'I'm only thirty weeks. I still have a couple of months.' She grinned and kept swinging.

Growing up, she had friends whose dads were full of life who took her skating, sledding, and to the park. Drew's mom was a former theatre major who landed a role in a 'very off' Broadway show when she was in college. She was *sooo* chatty and vibrant, and Lucy loved being around her. Drew's mom dropped the words 'I love you' as casually as if she was asking what your favourite snack was.

Her dad was as different as a Minnesota summer was to a Minnesota winter. He may not express himself the way Drew's mom could, but Lucy felt his love to her core.

A cramp started in her lower belly. She pressed against her stomach and breathed it out.

Her dad's fingers gripped the chair. 'What's going on? You're not popping it out now, are ya?'

She rolled her eyes. 'No. I've been having Braxton Hicks for a while, though.'

'What the hell are those?'

The worst thing ever. 'It feels like someone attached duct tape to my uterine wall, then rips it off.'

'Jesus Christ, sorry I asked.'

The first time the Braxton Hicks started, she thought she was in labour. These early contractions weren't painful really, more bothersome. She called Labour and Delivery, who guided her in timing the cramps to determine if they were 'real' contractions. Lucy did that, while searching what Braxton Hicks were, and called BS that so many people online said 'trust me, you'll *know* when it's labour'.

Her dad watched Chucky do laps as his beard scratching intensified, and a moment later, he sniffed. *Sniffed?* 'Dad? What's going on? Are you feeling okay?' The uptick in her pulse now thudded in her ear. He was healthy, right?

A weighty exhale left his mouth, and he stared at her stomach. 'Uff, you look just like your mom.'

One sentence, but the tone behind the words packed a heavy emotional punch.

He pulled his hands into his lap and stared at his fingernails. 'I never saw her happier than when she was lugging around that huge belly. She'd always rub that thing. I had to go out and buy her headphones, and she wrapped that thing around her belly and blared some classical music right into her stomach. I damn near worried you were going to come out without working ears.' One quick chuckle escaped. He returned his gaze to his fingers and scraped at his nail with his thumb. 'But that woman was so damn stubborn. Just like you. She didn't listen to me none. So, I bought all these baby books at a garage sale, and at night I laid my head by her stomach and read to you. Don't say I never did nothing for ya, kid. I saved those eardrums.'

Hot tears stung Lucy's eyes. He read to her when she was a bump? What did her mom think? The tears fell, and she wiped them with her palm.

'Oh yep, there I did it. Made ya cry.' He motioned like he was going to stand but then sat back down. 'I don't like talking about these things 'cause I don't want to make you all sad.'

'These are happy tears, I promise.' Lucy wiped again and sucked in air through her nose. 'You never talk about her. I want to know so much more, and you never say anything.' What was this, pregnancy courage? They had their unwritten rules, and she abided by their code of silence. But she was hungry, desperate, and if he clammed up, at least she had tried.

Too many moments passed, and Lucy wondered if she'd crossed the line. *Dammit.* But she'd savour the visual of her thirty-something-year-old dad coming home with a pile of garage sale books on a mission to save his daughter's eardrums.

'I thought all you pregnant ladies wanted ice cream and pickles. That's what the movies said, ya know. But ice cream hurt your mom's stomach something fierce. She was like that girl on *The Exorcist* when she tried some.' A grin cracked through his flatlined mouth. 'You know what she couldn't get enough of, though? Pineapple. She even got those damn canker sores but powered through and ate 'em up like the world was ending.'

A sob escaped Lucy as the tear gates burst wide. 'Thank ... you ...' She buried her head in her hand but tried to breathe through the overwhelming emotions, so she didn't totally freak him out.

Her dad lifted himself from the chair and patted her once on the back. 'Now don't go gettin' yourself all worked up. Probably not good for either of ya.'

'I'm good, I'm good.' She pulled in choppy breaths. 'Please tell me more.'

She didn't want to push her dad too much for more info, but now that he'd cracked open a fraction, he seemed less reluctant to share. Maybe all these years it really was his terrible way of trying to protect her from feeling sad.

He sat back down and stared at a hummingbird nestling

itself on the branch. Chucky plunked himself at her dad's feet, exhausted from playing. 'Remember the table saw I had in the shed? That's what her snores sounded like …'

For twenty minutes, her father opened the memory floodgates. He talked about going on a wild goose chase looking for 'shea butter' for her itchy belly, checking the dairy section of all the grocery stores in town until some nice woman told him it was lotion. He chuckled, talking about how cranky she got when their window air-conditioner had broken down and he put wet blankets in their deep freezer to give her some relief. He said he thought he never gripped the steering wheel as tight as he did when he brought her to the hospital, but he was wrong, because he damn near busted a knuckle driving home with tiny Lucy in the backseat.

For every word, every syllable, Lucy felt like he was wrapping her in a warm blanket. For so many years, she'd needed to know more about her mom, terrified that the memory of her would fade. This conversation was everything she needed right now.

Her dad patted the front of his jeans and stood. 'You know she's watching you from wherever she is. She's got her soap operas on one channel and you on the other.'

The soap operas! Lucy grinned, remembering the only thing that could distract her hyper-involved mom. 'You think they have *Days of Our Lives* on rotation in heaven?'

He snorted. 'You remember that?'

Lucy followed him into the house and held the door open for a panting Chucky. 'I mean, Marlena was the devil. Any idea how much that sears itself into a young kid's brain?'

She filled Chucky's water bowl and grabbed a pop for her dad for the road.

'Well, kid, I better take off here.' He reached into his pockets and pulled out a treat for Chucky, who greedily gobbled it up. 'Don't be giving him any more treats tonight. I don't know what in the world you're feeding this dog.'

She threw her hands around her dad. 'I love you. Thank you for today.'

He gave her one small squeeze and left.

The clock showed Lucy had about ten more minutes to close her eyes and replay every word her father had said before Jade arrived. Tonight, after she left, Lucy was going to write the stories down in her journal so she didn't forget a single word.

Chapter 31

Jade

On the bench outside the salon, Jade blinked at Elizabeth. There was no way Jade had heard Elizabeth right. Did she really just utter those words? *'I miss you and should have never let you go.'* She just lobbed those out into the universe without a care in the word, like those words didn't have the power to shatter everything that Jade had worked for the last two years.

Elizabeth wants me back. Two years ago, Jade had begged to hear these words. When she slept on the couch, when she packed her belongings, after she moved, she ached to hear her wife say any variation of this. 'What do you expect me to do with that information?'

Elizabeth pulled the corner of her lip between her teeth. 'When I look back at my life, you were the constant. The rock. And I think it's taken me until now, and having Amber, and seeing what really matters in this world, to know I should have never let you go. I don't want to do this without you. Listen to me, though. I *can* do this without you. I'm perfectly capable. But I don't want to and *that's* the difference.'

Jade snapped her jean fabric against her leg. She wished she could take in Elizabeth's words and feel flattered, or happy, or healed. Instead, she felt nothing. And Jade's lack of emotional response told her everything she needed to know. 'I guess I appreciate that?' Those weren't the right words. She didn't even know if she appreciated the declaration, or if this would mess with her mind later tonight when she'd recovered from the shock. 'But my life is here now. I'm happy in my new world. I have a successful business, and new friends, and an amazing girlfriend.'

'I heard.'

When I lifted a brow, Elizabeth added, 'I ran into your sister a while ago. She told me.' Elizabeth locked her gaze with mine. 'Pregnant, huh?'

The words dropped like a block, and a flash of white heat shot through Jade's veins. She wanted to yell that the baby wasn't hers, they weren't raising it, and it was a totally different situation than what had happened in their marriage. But Elizabeth had not earned the right to know anything about Jade and Lucy's relationship. 'You are *not* trying to make me feel guilty.'

'No one can *make* you feel guilty.' Elizabeth plunked the dropped pacifier back into the baby's mouth. 'Your feelings are your own and I'm not responsible for your emotional response to my words.'

In an instant, Jade was back in her marriage. The two years she spent deprogramming from their relationship ickiness was undone. A smattering of pedestrians walking around them, and the occasional car honk, did little to stop her from sinking into the swirling memories – eating dinner alone, ignored calls, failed resolutions because Elizabeth didn't have time to discuss their problems. 'You never needed me.'

Elizabeth stopped bouncing her knee and her mouth twisted. 'What?'

Trying to offset the rising sickness, Jade filled her lungs. 'Our whole marriage, I was nothing more than a prop, someone in the background to elevate you, someone you could tell your dreams to. You never *needed* me.'

A stillness filled the air. Several moments passed. Elizabeth's slightly open mouth twitched, but no words came out. 'Well,' Elizabeth finally said. 'I need you now.'

Like a bolt had just struck her in the chest, Jade hopped off the bench and paced. Such simple words tossed at her so easily. God, the tears she shed, begging to hear these words. Begging to hear a *fraction* of these words. The nights she sobbed into her pillow, the days she couldn't get out of bed … Jade should either say 'thanks for sharing' or 'too late now' or 'fuck off' but none seemed like the appropriate response. Black spots invaded her peripheral vision, and Jade's stomach turned queasy. She eased herself back to sitting and inhaled several shaky breaths to fight off the nausea.

'It may not sound like it,' Elizabeth said, 'but I really respect that you have a girlfriend and am not trying to be that other person. But, you *know* me. I know you. We were together for over a decade. We saw the worst in each other, but we also saw the best.' Her fingers played with the baby's feet. 'If you gave me a second chance, so many things would change. Amber showed me what love and family is all about, and I'm so fucking sorry I didn't grasp that when we were together. I have spent so many months replaying things over and over in my head, and I know exactly what I did wrong. I promise you that I can be the wife you need. I know the love between us isn't lost forever. It's simply … buried right now. But with a little bit of time, and me proving myself to you, I know we can uncover it. Together.'

Nope. No, no, no. Jade needed to put a fat, hot stop to this conversation immediately. Everything about this felt disloyal to Lucy. Sure, it might be cathartic for Elizabeth to get this off her chest, lighten her internal load, the verbal equivalent of chopping off waist-long hair to a pixie. But Elizabeth had a kid and was being more vulnerable than she'd ever been during their entire marriage, and Jade wanted nothing to do with it.

'I took a step down from my position at the company, threw out my five-, ten-, and twenty-year plans.' Elizabeth shifted and held the carrier with both hands. 'I work fewer hours. I'm no longer tied to climbing the corporate ladder. My values have changed completely. I never prioritised you, I see that now, but now you'd have top priority, alongside Amber.'

The pleading look in Elizabeth's eyes tore into Jade, and she snapped her gaze away. She kicked a small rock into the street and tried to take a few moments to gather her thoughts. Now was not the time to reiterate that Jade had zero interest in being a parent, that even if she were single, the baby was an absolute, hard no. Jade flicked her tongue against the sticky roof of her mouth and cursed herself for not bringing a water bottle.

'You never saw me.' Jade's voice was a hoarse whisper.

Elizabeth's head titled like she didn't hear her. 'I don't understand.'

Jade hated the way her insides felt like they were splitting. This is all too much, too vulnerable, too *late*, and yet Jade needed to purge this from her system. 'You never saw me. I was a mirror. A reflection. I was there to amplify you and your accomplishments. You never saw *me* for *me*.'

Elizabeth's facial expression didn't move. And then, suddenly, it cracked. The baby fussed and she rose, shifting her weight between her hips. 'That's not true.' Her tone was dense but not sharp. 'You never *let* yourself be seen. I asked you countless times about work, life, dreams, and you'd just shrug and say "fine". You were always so worried about not being needy that you … I don't know … over-corrected. You refused to let me in. You refused to let *anyone* in.'

Oh, no, no, no.

This couldn't be true. Could it? Jade shook her head, her thoughts swirling and colliding. No, *Elizabeth* was the one who didn't give her time and attention. Elizabeth was the one who pushed her dreams onto Jade. Elizabeth was the one who was the star, and Jade the bystander. Right?

Fuzzy memories emerged. Elizabeth asking her about cosmetology school, filling out financial aid papers together, baking a truly terrible chocolate cake when Jade graduated. For every missed anniversary, there was a surprise birthday party. For every quiet dinner conversation, there were thoughtful random gifts, like that vinyl Nirvana record Elizabeth found during a work conference in Portland.

Shit. This was too much. Jade was outside, but somehow she needed more air. She hopped off the bench. Her watch beeped, indicating she needed to return to the salon. But her head was heavy and clouded and she needed to sit somewhere that didn't smell like baby powder and Elizabeth's signature Chanel N°5.

And then, the smallest string threaded its way up Jade's chest and stitched her heart. It took several moments, but everything Jade had been holding in for so long felt like it was set free. Elizabeth's words had unlocked something buried and indescribable.

'I have to go back to the salon,' Jade said.

Elizabeth nodded and remained silent but slung the diaper bag over her shoulder.

A few steps in, Jade stopped, turned around, and put her hand on Elizabeth's arm. 'I'm sorry this might not have turned out the way you wanted. But for whatever it's worth, I think this was something I needed.' She dropped her hand. 'I'm really happy you have your baby. I meant what I said in my support letter last year, and I can see it here – you're a fantastic mom. The kid's lucky to have you.'

Tears filled Elizabeth's eyes, and she swiped a lone trickle with her thumb. 'Take care of yourself, Jade. You deserve all the happiness in the world.'

Elizabeth pivoted and marched away, and Jade stood on the sidewalk biting back tears.

Chapter 32

Lucy

The *beep beep* of a car locking sounded, and soon footsteps were outside her front door. Lucy's chest tightened, and she tried to breathe through the tension. After her gut-wrenching last hour with her dad, she wasn't sure how many more emotional conversations she could handle in one day.

'It's open!' Lucy readjusted herself on the couch and stayed sitting. Getting up and down these last few weeks was no joke. She didn't know how she would handle two more months of near-immobility.

Jade stepped into the entryway, swiping a chunk of bangs away from her face. 'Hey.'

'Hey.' Lucy tried to read her expression, to brace herself for whatever Jade wanted to say for *their talk*. Lucy may be relationship-inexperienced, but when anyone – a boss, a co-worker, a friend – said 'We need to talk', it was never good.

Sadly, Jade's face showed nothing except a tired half smile. She toed off her shoes on the mat and inched across the room.

Without a word, she curled onto the couch next to Lucy and laid her head on her chest.

Lucy dangled her fingers in Jade's hair, and she kissed the top of her head. The ticking of the analogue clock and Chucky's snoring were the only sounds. For every inhale, Lucy's insides softened. They were going to be okay. This wasn't the end, and whatever was happening, they'd figure it out together.

'Elizabeth stopped by today.' Jade spoke into Lucy's belly, making no motion to look Lucy in the eye.

Um ... come again? Her freaking ex, *who lived in a whole other state*, just randomly popped by Jade's place of business? Was she needing some fresh highlights or something? *Be cool, be cool.* For the ex to stop by, it obviously was something huge.

Jade rarely opened up about her ex. The most she'd ever spoken about the woman was the night Lucy and Jade confirmed they were together, when they bared their souls and secrets. 'Wow. Okay.' *Say something comforting and kind, not something weird and jealous.* 'What did she want?'

Fail.

Jade draped her arm across Lucy's lap. 'It's a long story, but ultimately she wanted to show off her new baby and see if she and I still had a chance.'

The tightness in Lucy's chest came fast and fierce, and her breath seized. *Oh my God ... what?* The ex wanted to get back together with Jade? Obviously, because Jade was incredible, but *actually* get back together? Heat filled Lucy's chest. *Okay, okay. Think.* Yes, she and Jade needed to talk and figure stuff out because they'd been so hugely, grossly misaligned lately, but Jade wouldn't be sitting here, snuggling against her, feeling all warm and cosy if she was going to get back together with Elizabeth, right? 'Huh.' Lucy chewed on her lower lip. 'So, um, what did you say?'

Jade sprung up from her lounging position and rested her gaze on Lucy. 'What do you think I said?' Jade looked almost hurt, which Lucy hated to admit was the most beautiful look she could've asked for at this moment. 'I told her that I was with you, and she and I would never get back together.'

The air returned to Lucy's lungs, and for the second time today, tears sprang to the surface. 'You did?'

'What else do you think I would have said?'

So many things. They were not on the same page lately, and it was obvious. Maybe Jade regretted leaving her old life. Lucy was a totally distracted, semi-hot mess of a girlfriend, and they had way less history than a decade-long marriage. 'Honestly, I don't know.' She needed to spit out what was lingering in the air, but talking like this was so miserable that she wanted to run and hide in the coat closet. But whatever was happening between the two of them, it needed to get out. 'I, uh, I think there's something going on with us, and I'm not sure what it is. But I'm really sorry for whatever I've done.'

Jade gripped Lucy's hands in hers and sighed. 'No, shit, Lucy. It was me. I just ... this' – Jade waved between their chests – 'this funkiness was all me. I kept thinking it wasn't me, though. Honestly, I blamed it on you, the baby, the hormones, the fanfare around the surrogacy, literally anything that removed the responsibility from me. I hate that it took talking to Elizabeth to see what I've been doing.'

I'm so confused. 'What do you mean, what you've been doing?'

A choppy exhale left Jade's lips, and she pinched the bridge of her nose. 'Do you remember me talking a while ago about how when I was married, I felt invisible? Like I was just along for the ride with Liz, but she was the star, and everyone was focused on her?'

Oh, no. Lucy already saw where this was going. And how in God's name was she so obtuse that she hadn't put two and two together? The bigger Lucy got, the more attention she received, the more she talked to other people, *the more she ignored Jade.* Lucy put her hand against her mouth. How did she do this?

How did she take the one thing that Jade mentioned was such a sensitive spot on her psyche and do the exact same damn thing to her? But also, why didn't Jade say something? My God. She'd been holding on to this for so long.

Actually, nope. Lucy wasn't doing this. Although communication was obviously good, Lucy should have been more in-tune with Jade and her needs and not make her draw a map. 'Oh God … Jesus, Jade. I'm so sorry. I did what Elizabeth did to you, didn't I?'

'No, don't say that. This is not on you, at all.' Jade shifted on the couch and rubbed Lucy's shirt fabric between her fingers. 'Even though seeing my ex was not exactly the highlight of my year, she brought me so much clarity. I've been unfair to you, expecting you to be a mind reader. Honestly, I've been unfair to myself, too. I never speak up the way I should. I never let you know what *I* need, what *I* want.'

The house was four million degrees and Lucy needed water, a fan, and a shower. Her fingers trembled. 'What is it you want?'

'*You*, Lucy. I want *you*.' Jade's throat rolled with a heavy swallow. 'I love you.'

'You do?' The words came out choked, terrified somehow, like Lucy was sure she misheard Jade's declaration, like she might take them back and leave. But seeing the sincerity in Jade's eyes, the way she nodded and kissed Lucy's hand, feeling those words tingle all the way to her toes, Lucy knew it was true. *Jade loves me.* Oh, the words felt so good. Lucy had always wanted to know what it would feel like to hear those words, if it was the way the movies showed, if the stars really burst in the sky, if the sappy music queued. And now she knew. It was *better*. They felt like a warm, plush, rose-scented blanket wrapped tightly around her, holding her snug.

Lucy grabbed Jade's cheeks, contorting her belly in the most uncomfortable but necessary way to kiss her mouth, to cement this moment. For so many years, Lucy was unsure of a lot of things. If she was a good enough daughter for her father. If she'd make a good oven for Drew and Mason's kid. If she'd succeed at her job, and ever make a real connection outside of Drew, if she'd be happy, truly happy. But what she was no longer unsure of? Jade. *Jade loves me.* Lucy wanted to hear the words again. And again, and again, and again. 'I love you, too.'

Ah, the release. *This* was what love felt like. This was what Drew talked about when he raced to Lucy's house as a freshman after the first time he and Mason kissed. This was how her dad felt about her mom, how Lucy finally, finally understood how hard it was to talk about her because of the pain he felt that she was gone. The words, the feelings had been there for a while, but saying them out loud was so freeing, so rejuvenating, so freaking beautiful. And right here and now, Lucy vowed to tell Jade this over and over again, because if she thought hearing the words felt good, it didn't even compare to how it felt to say the words.

For the next two hours, Lucy and Jade talked. They talked so much that Jade refilled their water glasses twice and Lucy was still parched. Jade dived into what it felt like during her marriage, how she didn't realise the lingering effects dampened her relationship, how she had been holding back, probably trying to protect herself, trying to avoid what she felt with Elizabeth. But by not opening up, Jade was a self-fulfilling prophecy.

Over pizza, Lucy told Jade the stories about her mom. Lucy admitted she wasn't sure if her previous inability to connect to someone romantically was because of who she was, or if it might be extended trauma from losing her mom so young. Lucy laughed about the pineapple, had a debate about *Days of Our Lives* versus *General Hospital*, and snuggled into Jade's arms when she got weepy again.

As they slipped into bed, Jade nuzzled into Lucy's backside

and laid her hand on Lucy's belly. Before Lucy fell asleep, Jade whispered it one more time.

'I love you.'

And for the first time in her adult life, Lucy drifted off to sleep with a completely full heart.

Chapter 33

Jade

Jade seriously regretted wearing heels.

All she'd done was leave the house, drive to Lucy's, and walk up her porch, and her toes were already on fire. How did people balance their weight on such a small strip of material?

But damn, they looked good. Much like waxing, beauty before pain, at least for today.

Getting ready in her own house and then driving to Lucy's was a little odd. Sure, she'd been doing it for the vast majority of this last year, but after *the talk* a few weeks ago, their relationship had shifted. Jade felt like she'd shed the years' worth of baggage she'd been lugging around, Lucy was somehow way more intuitive to Jade's needs, and Jade started stepping up with all things pregnancy. Jade felt like she'd practically moved in with Lucy by this point. She'd even brought her bamboo plant to Lucy's so it wouldn't die if several days passed without Jade going home to water it.

She creaked the door open, and Chucky bolted her way. 'Hey, boy. No slobber on me tonight, please.' She rubbed his head. 'Where's your mama?'

'Be out in a minute!' Lucy yelled from the bedroom.

Jade set her clutch on the side table, then thought better of it, and moved it to the centre of the kitchen island in case Chucky mistook it for a toy. She peeked at her reflection in the entryway mirror. A rogue mascara flake rested on her cheek. She swiped, then ran her hands down the fabric of her black spaghetti-strapped dress, tugged on the thin rainbow belt, and exhaled.

Tonight was the night. She'd been waiting so long for the Best of the Greater Twin Cities announcement. But the need to win – the almost *desperation* to win she'd felt before – had evolved. Of course, winning would be validating. But the award no longer felt like it had the power to define her self-worth.

The click of low heels against hardwood echoed from the hall. Jade turned and the air zapped from her lungs. Lucy stared back with a timid grin, long waves curled around her face, make-up on point. And that dress. *My God.* A deep rose, form-fitting chiffon gown with cap sleeves. All belly and boobs and beautiful. 'Lucy. You're so gorgeous I can't even handle it.'

Lucy gripped the side of her dress and performed a very clunky, very pregnant, very slow pirouette. 'Ah, this old thing?' She bowed. 'Well, *you* look hot as fuuuudge. How are you seriously my girlfriend? I want to parade you around with a sign that says "I'm with her."'

A blush swept over Jade.

'And Christ, you're tall.' Lucy stepped towards Jade and measured the top of her head against Jade's chest with a hand. 'My face is going to be right at your boobs.'

Jade wiggled her brows. 'Why do you think I'm wearing heels?' She dipped her head for a kiss, but Lucy put a hard hand against her chest.

'Air kisses only. It took me like an hour to apply this make-up. No matter how much I love you, if I smudge anything, someone's going down.'

No matter how much she loves me. The words would never

get old. 'Ha, fine. Deal. But when we come home, I make no promises.' Why had she waited so long to break the 'I love you' seal? Ever since last fall when they watched the riverboat and tourists, she'd felt it. When she'd stormed out of the diner with the delicious pie and terrible coffee after her conversation with Mr and Mrs Dieterman, she'd known it then too. Then, finally, the love floodgates opened, and now she could hear the words every day and never get sick of it. 'Need to go to the bathroom before we leave?'

'I'm good for the next ten minutes.' Lucy double-checked Chucky's food and water. 'Be a good boy. Papa will be here later to keep you company.'

Jade snatched her clutch from the kitchen island and held out her arm. 'Your dad's coming? I thought he couldn't make it.'

'Yeah, that's what he said until I told him we wouldn't be back until after ten, and he said I neglect my dog.' Lucy tucked her arm into Jade's. 'I've literally not left Chucky's side all day. He even helped me get ready.'

Jade dug out her keys. 'He was an excellent assistant stylist. I may have to hire him at the salon.'

'You hear that, Chucky? Finally, you'll be pulling your weight around here.' Lucy locked the door and stepped down the porch. She paused before lowering herself into the car. 'You ready for this?'

Jade grinned. 'Right now, I feel ready for anything.'

Perhaps ready for anything was an exaggeration as Jade stared at the strumming harpist – yes, a real-life harpist wearing a white gown, no less – as they strolled into the ballroom. Perfume and food scents surrounded them, people with tuxedos and gowns chatted at standing hors d'oeuvres tables, and servers weaved in among guests and tables, carrying trays of rose-stemmed champagne flutes.

Lucy let out a low whistle. 'Damn. This is fancy-pants, huh?'

Her neck stretched as she scanned the edge of the room, where easels held pictures of the nominees. 'Come on, let's find your photo.'

Jade gripped Lucy's fingers. They snaked their way through the rice-light lit room, past the white table-clothed tables with flower centrepieces and silverware, until Jade saw her board.

A large black-and-white photo, her favourite from the article, sprawled before her with the massive headline: 'Jade Hudson of Jade's on 7th, nominated for Best Salon in the Greater Twin Cities.' Tingles crept up her neck.

Lucy dug out her phone and nudged Jade towards the easel. 'Let's take a picture of you in front of your picture!'

'No, I can't. That's weird, right?' Jade clenched her teeth. 'Are other people doing it?'

Lucy angled the cell phone. 'Who cares? I'm so damn proud of you. Who knows how many moments like this you're going to get?' She glanced at a couple strolling by and pointed at Jade. 'This is my girlfriend, right here. How lucky am I?'

Oh God, she's so wonderfully embarrassing. Jade smiled through the rose flushing her cheeks and posed. The excitement in Lucy's voice, one level louder than usual, made Jade want to scoop Lucy up and smother her with kisses. *So, this is what it feels like to have someone who is truly in my corner – who doesn't think their light dims when mine shines.*

'I'm hungry.' Lucy dropped the phone into her purse and sniffed the air. 'Can we grab some food?'

'We're at table fifteen.' Jade pointed to the table near the exit. 'Why don't you go sit and I'll grab snacks.'

Lucy rubbed her stomach. 'Make it a double serving, please.'

As she moseyed away, Jade waited to make sure Lucy found the table okay. Lucy wasn't helpless, and she still had six weeks to go before her due date, but the past few weeks, Jade had been feeling an extra surge of overprotectiveness. She was probably spending more time worrying about Lucy's safety than running her salon. Satisfied Lucy was situated properly, Jade scooted to the appetiser table and loaded up their plates.

A woman approached, grabbing tongs from the platter. She eyed Jade, who was double fisting two heaping plates with crostinis, chicken skewers, fruit, and mini grilled cheeses. 'This is not all for me.' Jade grinned. 'I'm bringing some to my girlfriend.'

With a chuckle, the woman raised her hands. 'Hey, no judgement here. You can eat both plates if you want to.'

Jade jutted her chin towards Lucy, who had leaned back and was tapping her fingers against her stomach. 'My girlfriend's appetite is pretty insatiable right now.'

'Ah, eating for two. Congratulations.'

For the past half year or so, anytime someone made a comment like this, Jade wanted to snap-correct their assumption. But tonight, her insides glowed with the magic of the evening, her pride in Lucy, her pride in herself, and for once, she didn't have the urge to clarify. 'It's definitely an exciting time. And you're right – she's a champ.'

Jade grabbed a few extra napkins and manoeuvred her way to the table as other attendees took their seats. After she finished crunching into the crostini, and Lucy polished off the chicken, Lucy rested her hand on her chest and winced.

'You okay?' Jade asked, pausing before her next bite.

Lucy poked a finger into the top of her belly. 'Yep. Ugh. I cannot wait for this heartburn to stop.' She dug in her purse and popped a Tums. 'It's not like I'm eating your crazy sriracha or anything. This is freaking chicken.'

'I stand by my testament that sriracha is the best condiment ever created. I think once you have the kiddo, we should have you try it again.' Jade filled up a glass of water from the pitcher and handed it to Lucy. 'We don't have to do it on eggs this time. We'll do something like noodles or rice.'

'Hmmm. Let's see how adventurous I am when I'm not lugging this thing around.' Lucy guzzled the water, then fanned her face.

'Hot flashes. Yet another thing. This better not happen again until I'm in blissful menopause. Everything is sweating, even my kneecaps.'

'It's definitely kind of hot today,' said Jade sympathetically, even though the air conditioning in the banquet hall was turned up so high that Jade had goose bumps to her toes. She laid her hand on Lucy's belly and inched lower. 'Stop making your auntie sick or we're never going to babysit.'

'Babysit?' Lucy's neck jerked. 'Would you actually babysit?'

'Well, obviously.' Jade rubbed her girlfriend's belly one more time before sitting back up. 'I mean, Drew and Mason are your friends. This butternut is going to be in our lives, and babysitting is fun.'

'Fun?'

'Yeah, 'cause you can give the kid back at the end of the night.' Just because Jade had never wanted children didn't mean she didn't like kids. Would she work at a daycare? No, definitely not. But she was a kick-ass aunt who loved spoiling her niece and nephews whenever she had the chance.

The lights dimmed and the screech of an active microphone cut through the chatter. A woman stood at the podium, smiling. 'Hello, everyone! Welcome to the thirty-fifth annual Best of the Greater Twin Cities!' A roar of claps erupted. 'I am thrilled to be the host this evening, honouring the best of the best in all areas of business.'

Jade's breath hitched and she took in a heavy breath through her nose. The night was *finally* here. Although she'd never expected anything like this to happen to her, Jade's body was warm with validation. Even if she didn't win, this was a nod to all her hard work, her effort. Against all odds, *she'd made it*. As the host spoke about the history of the awards, previous winners, and the nomination process, Jade straightened her back, trying to fully absorb every word so that she'd never forget it.

Lucy interlocked her fingers with Jade's at the table and moved her mouth to Jade's ear. 'I'm so proud of you. You've worked so hard for this.'

Jade's heart felt like it was going to explode out of her chest. She kissed Lucy's forehead and focused back on the podium as the host called out the nominees for Best Restaurant. She clapped for the winner and concentrated on the thank-you speeches. For the last few weeks, she'd prepared a bit of what she would say if she won. She didn't want to be presumptuous, so she hadn't written anything down, but she had rehearsed some potential remarks in the car on the way to and from work. But looking at the two men at the podium accepting their award, both holding a notecard with shaky hands, she nibbled on her lip. Dang it. They didn't look presumptuous, they looked *prepared*. Ugh.

Her heartbeat kicked up a notch and thudded in her ear. Only Best Tattoo Parlour, Best Independent Bookstore, and Best Coffee Shop until her category arrived. *I'd like to thank my amazing staff, and the customers who trust us every day ...* Jade silently recited what she'd practised over and over until the people on stage blurred. She pictured herself at the podium, standing tall.

Okay, dammit. She really wanted to win.

An elbow to her shoulder snapped her back to the present.

'Oh, sorry. I'm trying to grab your ice.' Lucy dug into Jade's glass for an ice cube and held it against her neck. Red splotches had spread against her cheeks and chest as she shifted with a grimace.

'Are you okay?' Jade whispered, turning her back to the stage so she could see Lucy more clearly. Underneath the red splotches, the rest of Lucy's skin seemed unusually pale. Her chest lifted in heavy, short breaths. Jade touched Lucy's face. 'Are you sick? What's going on?'

Lucy grabbed another ice cube. 'I'm just super hot. Maybe the baby didn't like the grilled cheese or something. I think I just need some air.'

'There are fewer people in the lobby. Let's go there.' Jade pushed back her chair and tucked her hand under Lucy's arm to help her up.

Lucy shook her head. 'Nope. No way. This is your big moment. There is no chance I'm going to make you miss hearing your name called.' She grabbed her purse. 'I'll go by myself. My body is just being super dramatic right now.'

'Absolutely not.' Jade stood and helped Lucy up. God love Lucy, but if Jade let a potentially sick Lucy sit alone in the lobby, the only award Jade would win tonight would be Worst Girlfriend Ever. She grabbed her clutch and headed towards the door, her arm on Lucy's elbow as they weaved between tables.

'And the winner for Best Tattoo Parlour is–' The door clicked behind Jade before the winner was announced, but she was crossing her fingers it would be the woman-owned shop a few blocks west of Hennepin Avenue that she'd visited when she first moved to Minnesota.

With only a few handfuls of people chatting in the lobby, the air was cooler, *thank God*. 'Let's go over there.' Jade pointed to a vacant seat in the corner.

Lucy nodded, her fist pushing firmly against her lower back, as she waddled after Jade. 'How many more minutes until you need to go back in there? Maybe five? Ten?'

'We're not even going to worry about that right now.' Jade helped lower Lucy to the seat and squatted in front of her. Oof. Her face looked pinched, almost in pain, but the blotches in her neck seemed a little lighter? Jade gnawed on the inside of her cheek. 'Do you think maybe we should call a doctor or something? Or Drew?'

'Nah. I'll be fine in a second.' Lucy bobbed her head towards the door. 'I can't hear what the announcer is saying. Can you? Maybe we should just prop the door open a little so we don't miss the announcement.'

Jade scooted in beside Lucy and touched her hand to the back of Lucy's neck. 'Your neck is still pretty hot. Should I get you some more ice?'

'Are you purposefully ignoring me?' Lucy squeezed Jade's thigh. 'You have got to stop this fussing, okay? Go see what they're saying in there! They have the bookstore and coffee shop one next, right, then yours?'

'I'm not *ignoring* you.' Jade grinned and peeked at her watch. Maybe in five minutes she would crack the door and see where they were at, but right now, Lucy was top priority. Something seemed off, and Jade didn't want to spook Lucy. 'I just want to make sure you're okay, that's all.'

'I'm totally fin–'

Plurp, plurp. A sound reminiscent of when Jade pulled the drain plug from her tub whooshed from Lucy's belly. 'What the hell was th–' Liquid gushed from Lucy's legs and onto to the floor.

Lucy's eyes widened. She glanced at the floor, back at Jade, back at the floor.

The room narrowed, everything outside of Lucy turning a murky grey. *No, no, no … now? This wasn't … was it?* A few solid moments passed before Jade flew up. 'Was that …' The veins in her neck felt tight, pulsing against her throat. Should she get towels? Did the banquet hall even *have* towels? Should she carry Lucy to the car? Call 911? *What was she supposed to do?* No, this wasn't right. Lucy still had like almost two months to go. Was this bad? This was bad, right?

'I, uh, I think my water just broke.' Lucy's eyes glazed over before panic filled her face. She gripped Jade's arm. 'Holy shit, Jade. Jade! My water … oh, we need to call … we've got to get to the hospital … is everything gross? Oh, no – can someone clean …'

Even Lucy's scattered thoughts were more coherent than what Jade's brain could process.

She was so wrapped up in the moment, Jade didn't realise a commotion started behind her until someone passed her to get to Lucy. 'Are you okay? Did your water just break?' The woman from the appetiser table was just squatting in front of Lucy.

Lucy's mouth was practically hanging open, her eyes glazed and confused. 'I think so?'

The woman looked at the puddle. 'I would say definitely.' She rested a hand on Lucy's shoulder. 'I've had four of my own. You got this.'

A hand touched Jade's arm, shifting the swirling tunnel vision and muted voices into sharp focus.

'You're the partner, right?' the woman asked. When Jade nodded, she stood. 'Let me help you get her to the car.'

'Can you stand?' Jade asked, ready to carry Lucy Tarzan-style if that was called for. When Lucy nodded, Jade gripped her around the waist and heaved her up.

The room burst into action, people asking how to help, someone rushing towards them with towels, another person holding a cup of ice while walking behind Lucy as they moved to the exit.

Lucy's body shook in Jade's arms, her breath coming out in spurts.

'It's too early!' she gasped. 'She's not supposed to come out for like six more weeks. I don't know what to do. I'm not ready.'

'There's nothing you can do, but you absolutely got this.' Jade glanced at the woman helping them, who tipped her head in a nod. 'Baby girl's ready to join the world.'

'We didn't even take the birthing classes yet!' Lucy seized Jade's arm. 'I never learned about the breathing and hypnotist and baths or anything!'

Jade knew this, of course, but didn't want to say anything to add to Lucy's panic. After Lucy convinced herself she'd forget everything if she took the courses too early, they had actually signed up for the Lamaze classes. They were supposed to start Monday.

'You'll be fine, I promise,' said the woman, keeping stride

with Jade, then opening one of the big double doors that led outside the hall. Jade felt a breath of heat from outside on her face. 'Women all over the world give birth every day who've never taken classes. Trust your instincts, breathe for yourself, push when you need.' The woman grabbed the cup of ice from the person behind her, but when several people rushed over, the woman shooed them away. 'Give her some space, please. Now.'

Jade had no idea who this woman was, but she was absolutely her new best friend. Okay, wow. It was hot outside. She glanced around the valet space. *What in the hell am I doing?* 'My car. Shit. We took the elevator.'

'Okay, no worries.' The woman's calm voice was in direct contrast to Jade. 'We'll go sit in the shade and make a call to labour and delivery to find out her next steps while you get the car. I'll stay with … what's your name?'

'Lucy.' She pushed her name out through gritted teeth.

'Lovely name.' The woman tucked an arm around Lucy. 'I'm Amelia.'

Lucy sucked in such a large breath that Jade's heartbeat stopped. 'Amelia? That's my mom's name.'

'Ah. Meant to be then, I suppose.' Amelia smiled and dug out an ice cube from the cup someone had handed them in the lobby. 'Why don't you suck on this for a while and stay hydrated.' She glanced up at Jade, who was frozen firmly in place, with a solid case of decision paralysis. 'Better grab that car.'

'Right, right. Okay, I'll be right back.' Jade kissed Lucy on the head and scurried back into the lobby. *Holy shit, the baby is coming!* Jade could not remember a time when she was so simultaneously terrified and excited.

Twenty feet in, she plucked off her heels, gripped her clutch purse, and sprinted to the elevators.

Chapter 34

Lucy

Lucy's belly bumped up and down as Jade tore through the hotel parking lot, gripping the steering wheel with white knuckles. 'You doing okay?' Jade asked her for the hundredth time, her eyes only leaving the road for a split second. 'Are the contractions bad?'

So far, Lucy wasn't even sure if she was having contractions, or if the pressure in her belly was from the aftereffects of her water breaking. 'No ... I'm okay.'

Jade stopped at the edge of the parking lot. 'Which hospital? Stillwater or Minneapolis?'

Oh God. Now what? Lucy didn't know. Her OBGYN and the dads were in Stillwater. She was currently in Minneapolis. The labour and delivery department told her to choose whichever she was most comfortable with when she asked this same question. Her chin trembled. 'I don't know. I don't know ...' Too many decisions, too much pulling in her belly, too much sticky dress fabric adhering to her skin.

'I'm going to pull over to a parking spot. Call Drew, get his thoughts, and then we'll bolt.'

Jade whipped the car to the left and put the blinkers on as Lucy dialled.

'Luce. We have a strict texting-only friendship. Which must mean ... you're calling to tell me Jade won her award?'

Shit. Jade was missing the biggest night of her life, and it was all Lucy's fault. The baby wanted out, early, she hadn't taken those freaking classes, her chest hurt, and basically everything was going completely opposite to their plan. What if she couldn't do it? Why didn't she read that damn book that Drew had begged her to read? The trembling in her chin moved to her lips, and she choked out a bumbled word.

'Lucy? Are you okay? What's happening here?'

'My water broke and ... it was everywhere, and I don't know which hospital to go to and we're in Minneapolis, but I don't know anyone here, and ...' A sob erupted from Lucy, and Jade gripped her shoulder.

'Are you serious? Are you okay? Is Jade with you?'

Lucy conjured up more jumbled words until Jade grabbed the phone and put it on speaker. 'Drew, she's okay. But I need to know, now, which hospital you want us to go to. We're thirty-five minutes out from Stillwater, about fifteen from the nearest Minneapolis hospital.'

A deep inhale sounded over the phone. 'Ah, ah ... Stillwater.'

'Got it. On our way.' Jade handed back the phone, slammed the car in reverse, and sped out of the parking lot.

This is happening. Drew must be so scared for the baby, and Lucy couldn't say a single thing to alleviate his fears. 'I'm so sorry, Drew. She's so early. I don't know if I caused my water to break or what. I don't think I can stop it from happening, but maybe the hospital can add more back in?' The amniotic fluid was gone, the remnants sticking to her bare legs, but maybe they had new technology or something.

'This is not your fault.' He sighed. 'Everything's going to be okay.'

They'd been friends for too many years, and even though her thinking was muddled from being in labour, she knew his fake voice. She was immediately thrown back to when her mom had died in the bike accident, and he'd used those same words. *Everything's going to be okay.* He was worried. She was worried. Jade's pale face and parched lips showed she was worried. 'The birthing classes. We didn't do them. We should have, and you told me, but I didn't listen—'

'Stop it. You can do *anything*, including having a baby without classes.' He paused. 'I have to call Mason. We'll be up there right after you. Jade's gonna be there with you and we'll be two seconds behind, got it?'

Lucy nodded, but her throat felt too tight to verbalise a response.

'I love you, Luce. We love you so much.'

Car lights, bridges, and orange construction signs zoomed by as Jade weaved through the traffic. 'I'm so sorry for tonight,' said Lucy. 'You're missing everything because of me.' Her lip trembled. For everything Jade had sacrificed during their entire relationship, this evening was supposed to be one hundred per cent solely focused on Jade and not on Lucy and the baby. She deserved to have her moment and Lucy was ruining everything. 'Do you want to go back? Maybe I … we … can get me an Uber or something?'

'*Lucy.*' Jade touched her thigh for a quick moment before white-knuckling the steering wheel again. 'This award is just an award. For real. This … all this right here … this is *life*. I would never, ever leave you. Don't even give it another thought.'

A deep knot tugged at Lucy's lower abdomen, and she winced.

Jade flicked on her blinker and passed a car. 'Contraction?'

'Yeah.' Lucy clocked the time and shoved an ice cube in her mouth from the cup Amelia handed her earlier. Was it five million degrees? The vents were not blasting enough air, and Lucy was a second away from melting into the Prius's seat. She rubbed an ice cube against her hair line, closed her eyes, and tried to take calming breaths.

Less than thirty minutes later, they were squealing to a stop in front of the emergency entrance door and Lucy lurched forward.

'Jesus Christ, I'm sorry. You good?' Jade whipped off her seatbelt and bolted from the vehicle, not waiting for an answer. 'Can someone help me, please?' Panic laced her shouts, and she waved people towards their vehicle. 'Somebody!'

Another cramp, deeper this time, seized Lucy's gut. 'Gahhhh!' She gripped the door handle. 'Dammit, that hurts.'

The emergency doors slid open and two people in scrubs burst through, one pushing a wheelchair. Jade reached both arms into the car and lifted Lucy to standing. A moment passed as Lucy attempted to steady her sea legs. Nausea flashed through her, and she grasped Jade's hand.

'Hey there.' A man in blue scrubs pushed the wheelchair next to her. 'Looks like we might be in labour. Did your water break?'

'Well, I didn't spill a milkshake on this dress.' Lucy pointed at the bottom half of her stained gown. 'It broke about forty-five minutes ago.'

The nurses guided her into the wheelchair and a barefoot Jade followed them up the sidewalk.

'I'm sorry, but you have to park your car,' the man said.

Jade's head frantically shook. 'I am *not* leaving her.'

God, I love this woman. Lucy reached for Jade's hands. 'It's okay. The pain is at like a two. Go park and meet us up there. You don't want to hold someone else up if they're having an emergency.' She kissed the top of Jade's hand. 'I'm totally fine.'

That was the largest load of bullshit ever to leave Lucy's mouth. Everything was on fire. Her head was hot, burning from the inside out. Her belly raged, and her knees trembled. Nothing about this moment was fine.

Jade pulled her lips into her mouth. 'Where are you taking her?'

'Triage in labour and delivery, sixth floor.'

'Got it.' Jade planted a kiss on Lucy's forehead. 'I'll see you in two minutes, tops. Okay? Don't worry about a thing.'

'I'm good. Go.'

As the electric hum of Jade's car took off, Lucy rolled into the hospital with two strangers. Independent her whole life, right now, she felt alone. She wanted Jade to hold her tight and tell her everything was okay. She wanted Drew and Mason and her dad to answer the doctors' questions, because one thing was certain – she couldn't do this alone.

The receptionist checked her in at record speed. As Lucy stuffed her ID back into her wallet, another cramp seized her stomach. *Oof.* That one kicked things up a notch, a solid 2.5, and she clocked the time. Fourteen minutes since her last one. She restarted the timer.

Several nurses surrounded her. One helped her into a gown as the other tapped on her keyboard. 'Chart says you're 33.5 weeks. Is that accurate?'

Even though she already knew how early she was, hearing the nurse say it, fear flooded Lucy's system. She blinked at the vitals screen, hoping it would provide a magical message saying everything was fine. 'Is the baby going to be okay?'

The nurse showed no reaction. 'Right now, let's focus on you. But we'll do everything for your baby.'

That's not a yes! That was not anywhere near a 'baby is going to be fine' type of reassurance. Lucy lowered herself onto the stretcher, and soon, wands and ultrasounds and blood pressure cuffs had been efficiently attached to her various body parts. 'Wait, it's not my baby. Is that in the chart?'

The nurse cocked her head, eyes narrowed. 'What?'

'I am not the mother!' Lucy yelped, then leaned back as spots overtook her vision. Did they know she was a surrogate? Did that change something somehow? Do they have all the paperwork? And where was Jade?

A knock on the door came from behind the curtain. 'Permission to let Jade Hudson in?'

Thank God. Tears filled her eyes, again, for the millionth time. 'Yes, yes. And when Drew and Mason get here, let them in. They're the dads.'

Jade burst into the room and wrapped Lucy in her arms. Lucy shook against Jade's familiar scent and comforting touch. Several breaths later, her racing heart had calmed somewhat. 'What happened to your dress?'

Jade tugged at the dangling spaghetti strap hanging from her arm. 'Your fierce grip from when I helped you out of the car.'

None of this was how tonight was supposed to go, nor how the birth story was supposed to go. 'I'm so sorry about tonight. It was such an important event for you and this ... I should have offered for you to stay.'

'Darn.' Jade rested her hip against the cot. 'I really should have called you that Uber and met you here after the ceremony.'

'Really?'

Jade let out a small chuckle and tucked a piece of hair behind Lucy's ear. 'Lucy, I'm totally kidding.' She pressed her lips against Lucy's forehead. 'There is nowhere else I'd rather be. Truly.'

The nurse strapped a blood pressure cuff on Lucy's arm again and watched the vital machine. 'Blood pressure's good.' She recorded the information. 'We're going to roll you down to labour and delivery. Questions before we go?'

Only a million. 'How long until I push?'

'Hard to say. Could be an hour or twenty-four hours. We won't know until we check your cervix and see if we need to boost contractions.' Her index finger scrolled across the mouse. 'Have you thought about pain medication? There's nothing in your charts that indicates your wishes.'

Lucy avoided Jade's surely heated gaze.

Throughout the paperwork process, the question about what

type of pain medication she may or may not want arose often. Lucy knew about epidurals, of course, but the idea of getting a massive needle shoved into her spine terrified her more than labour itself. But then the doctor explained opioids, local anaesthesia, even laughing gas, which she'd thought was only for the dentist. Who knew there were so many options? But Lucy hadn't done the proper research – which she was totally kicking herself for now – on the possible effects of drugs on the baby.

Throughout the journey, Jade barely had any opinions – except for the medication. She was adamant that Lucy take some pain management, touting all her clients over the years who used various things, and the babies turned out fine. When Lucy pushed back, Jade cracked. 'I can't stand to think of you being in pain,' she'd said.

'Lucy? Thoughts on medication?' the nurse repeated.

'I'm not saying no, but I'm not saying yes.' Lucy looked at Jade's flatlined lips. 'Can I just wait and see how bad it gets?'

'Of course.' The nurse nodded and added the note in her computer.

Lucy turned to Jade. 'Can you call my dad, tell him what's going on, tell him not to worry, and ask him to stay with Chucky?'

'Of course.'

The contractions held steady at ten minutes apart. In the labour and delivery unit, the nurse helped Lucy into the bed. 'We've got yoga balls, a bathtub, towels, and heating pads. You can walk around, squat, roll on the ball, whatever will help you. As long as your vitals stay stable, you're free to do whatever you need for relief.'

'Thank you.' An odd calm before the storm settled. The nurses were right – there was nothing Lucy could do now but accept her fate. She sucked on an ice cube and peeked at the army of goose bumps on Jade's arms. 'Can we get my girlfriend a sweatshirt or something? A blanket?'

'I'm fine. Please don't worry about me.' A shiver tore through Jade. 'I mean, only if you have one available.'

'On it,' the nurse said. 'I'll grab something and then leave you two alone for a little bit.'

As soon as the nurse left, Jade hurried to the bed. 'Are you okay?'

The creases crossing her forehead gutted Lucy, and she kissed Jade's hand. 'I'm banning that word from here to eternity. I promise that if I'm not, I'll say something.' She glanced out the hospital window at the swaying trees. 'Thank you for being here. I couldn't have done this without you.'

'Yes, you could have.' Jade pulled the chair next to the bed and rested her head by Lucy's lap.

Lucy closed her eyes and relished the moment, knowing that in just a few hours, all their lives would change forever.

Chapter 35

Lucy

'Ahhhhhhhh!' Lucy screamed into the tearing contraction as Jade absorbed Lucy's death-grip on her hand. Drew was on Lucy's other side. Searing fire ripped through her belly, and she attempted to 'he, he, whoooo' through the pain.

Mason wiped a cool towel against her forehead and held out a shaky cup of ice.

Almost five hours into the escalating contractions and the baby was stuck, refusing to budge. Lucy's abdomen ached, her whole body felt torn and shredded, her eyelids were heavy, her energy depleted. Voices hovered, the dads and Jade offering words of encouragement, but Lucy couldn't focus. Fingers inspected her insides, and at this point, she barely noticed.

'You're dilated to five. This is good. You're moving along.' The nurse snapped off her gloves and tossed them into the trash.

The pain was unbearable, and she was only at a *five*? Did that mean it was going to get five times worse? Panic seized her chest and her vision clouded. *I can't do this.* How could any woman do this? The movies, the books, everyone she'd talked to – nothing had prepared her for this.

'Gah!' An unexpected contraction ripped through her, crushing her pelvis, moving her five-minute reprieves between contractions to less than four. Ringing sounded in her ears, and the room blinked in and out of focus. She pulled Jade's hand into her lap. 'I can't do this. I can't do this! It hurts too much.'

Jade squeezed her hand back and pushed sweaty, matted hair from Lucy's forehead. 'You can do this. You are a goddamn warrior.'

Mason and Drew were now watching helplessly from the corner, their mouths moving in quiet conversation, their worried eyes focused on Lucy. Lucy watched them warily. Drew, probably the designated point man, approached the bed. 'Lucy, I know … we know … all medical decisions are up to you.' He swallowed and glanced back at Mason, who thumbed his glasses and gave him a brief nod.

Lucy already knew what he was going to say, the same thing they'd alluded to for the past two hours. They wanted her to take pain medication, but her brain was cloudy, and she was terrified she'd make the wrong decision. What if the drug hurt the baby? What if it came out high and went through withdrawals because of her selfishness in not being able to withstand what women worldwide endured? And now her best friends would have a drug-addicted baby on top of having a preemie and then she *truly* would have ruined everything!

'Take the drugs, Lucy. Please.' Drew's voice cracked, and he sucked in a breath. 'Please … I can't see you in any more pain …' One dry muffled sob escaped, and he covered his mouth.

Lucy couldn't think between the contractions. She heard murmurs of 'blood pressure elevating' as nurses joined the room, a doctor checked in on her status … people flitted in and out of her spotty peripheral vision. Drew stood at the end of the bed, dragging his hands down his cheeks as Mason whispered to the nurse.

'I don't know what to do.' Lucy clung to Jade's arm, her teeth gritted, her belly compressing, preparing for another searing wave. 'What should I do?'

Jade wiped Lucy's matted hair from her face. 'I can't make this decision for you. I want to, but I can't.' Jade dropped her hands, her gaze holding Lucy's. 'You've got to do what's best for you. Not the baby, not the dads. *You.*'

Another contraction tore through Lucy and she ground her teeth so hard she was pretty sure her molars cracked. Her heartbeat thudded in her ears. 'Give me the drugs.'

Two more hours passed, hushed words, screams – her own – and more unbearable contractions. Jade at her side, Jade by her feet, Mason gripping her shoulders, Drew squeezing her hand. And then, Lucy felt it – a drop, quick, sudden, pushing against her bladder and pelvis. *Now?* Right now of all times and she had to go to the bathroom? 'Nurse?'

'Yes, what can I do?'

Lucy looked at her love, her bestie, her friend all staring back. 'You guys go to the corner. Private convo.' Her snipped words carried the weight of a drill sergeant, and they immediately split. 'I have to go to the bathroom. Like, really bad, right now.' Lucy started rising from her position.

The nurse laid a hand on her shoulder. 'It's time. Baby's ready.'

Frantic, Lucy shook her head. She was *not* getting it. 'No, like *the bathroom.* Not the baby.'

'We need to get ready to push.' The nurse radioed the doctor and put on a gown.

Why isn't she hearing me! 'Please, you don't understand. I'm … ugh … I have to poop!' God, this was so embarrassing, but not nearly as embarrassing as shitting the bed with an audience. Another contraction and Lucy yelled. The meds softened the pain, but she could still feel her insides stretching and squeezing.

'Lucy, that's what it feels like.' The nurse leaned closer to her ear. 'I promise, if you do poop, I'll cover for you. No one will know.'

Fuck it. 'Fine. I gave you a fair warning.' The exhaustion was so deep, seeping into her bone marrow. Her body felt tense and limp and strong and weak all at once.

'Dads, partner, it's time,' the nurse called out.

Hurried footsteps, latex gloves, a doctor putting a gown over scrubs. In a snap, Mason was at Lucy's shoulders. Drew moved to the foot of the bed, whipped off his shirt, fully prepped for immediate skin-to-skin. Hands guided her to grip under her knees to yank towards her chest. Voices called out inaudible instructions. Her lungs couldn't fill fast enough. Screams, shaking limbs, a ring of fire screeching through her bottom, more screams, breaths, someone yelling 'push!' and 'breathe!' blanketing her and … release.

Lucy flung her head back into the pillow, the veins in her neck on the verge of popping, and the sweet, sweet sound of a baby crying filled the space. Through snipping, hushed words, and wet kisses planted on her forehead, she blinked at Drew. He sat, holding the baby against his bare chest, as nurses added blankets on top of the baby. Mason crumbled next to him, fat tears rolling down his cheeks, one shaky arm thrown over Drew, one on the baby's back. 'Thank you … thank you, Lucy …'

Tiredness overwhelmed every cell in her body, but she forced her eyes open, telling herself to brand this image into her brain, the moment she'd dreamed about for years. This was what pure, unconditional love looked like. Overcome with emotion, she sobbed. Jade pulled her into her chest, stroking her hair, kissing her head. She heard Jade tell the guys Lucy would be fine and to keep focusing on the baby, and whispered into Lucy's ear how proud she was.

More footsteps came, a beeping of a machine, nurses and the dads talking. Lucy tried to focus, but everything muddied. A kaleidoscope of worried faces blurred – Drew handing the baby to a nurse and tugging his shirt back over his head, Mason nodding frantically, the nurses scurrying and radioing with quick, sharp voices.

'What's … going on?' Lucy mumbled, her tongue thick and heavy. 'Jade, what the hell is going on?'

The nurse placed the baby in the incubator and in a second, the room cleared, minus Lucy, Jade, and one nurse, who picked up an armful of soiled linens to dump in a bin, and then continuously checked Lucy's vitals. Where was the baby? The look on Mason's face … God, she was so tired; she tried to grab Jade's hand but went limp. Her brain fuzzed, shorted, the words stuck in her throat.

'Jade … please …'

Jade took a deep breath. 'Something's wrong with the baby. They took her to NICU.'

Chapter 36

Jade

A rustling of sheets and a short moan stirred Jade awake. She squinted into the dark and checked the time. 6:04 a.m. *Oof.* She pushed down the sheets and crossed the room.

Lucy blinked and yawned, the IV in her hand tugging. 'Ouch.'

'Hey, you,' Jade whispered as she sat on the chair next to Lucy's bed. She swiped her thumb against Lucy's cheek. 'How are you feeling?'

'What time is it?' Lucy asked, her voice groggy, hoarse.

'Six.' Jade filled a cup of water from the pitcher and handed it to Lucy.

Lucy winced as she sat up, and Jade withheld from wincing, too. Seeing her partner in so much pain broke Jade, and she prayed she never had to witness that again. After watching Lucy give birth the night before, Jade not only had enormous respect for her girlfriend, but also for anyone who'd given birth. Her sisters-in-law never talked about their birth stories, her mother certainly hadn't, and the only reference she had was movies. Jade had no idea there were so many variations to how labour could go, no idea of the medical trauma that took place every day.

'How's the baby?' Lucy asked, sipping the water.

Yet another thing Jade wasn't prepared for – watching the men she'd grown so fond of rush out of the room with terrified faces, unsure if their daughter was okay.

'She's stable. She's a fighter.' Jade caught Lucy up on the events. A few hours after they'd taken the baby to the NICU, Drew and Mason stopped by separately to check on Lucy, who was sleeping by then. They explained that because the baby was born so early, she needed to be incubated for a few weeks for her system to fully bake. But all signs pointed to everything being fine.

Later, Jade tried to get more information from the nurse, who said nothing. The moment Lucy had given birth, HIPAA laws kicked in and the code of silence began.

Lucy lazed a hand on top of Jade's. 'Did you win?' Her voice was hoarse, barely above a whisper, and her eyes flickered with hope.

Oh, wow. Jade had no idea if she'd won or not. Since Lucy's water broke, the award was the last thing on her mind. But something inside Jade filled with the words. Even in Lucy's crisis, fighting through pain and fatigue, she hadn't forgotten Jade.

'I don't know.' Jade pressed her lips against Lucy's forehead. 'But let's both agree it will be a night we will never forget.'

Lucy's eyes closed and heavy breaths filled the air. After confirming Lucy was peaceful, Jade slipped back into the guest bed and tugged the blankets up to her chest.

A quiet knock on the door jostled Jade awake, and she glanced at where Lucy was sitting up, eating eggs.

'Morning,' Lucy said between bites. 'Can you grab the door?'

'How did I sleep through all that?' Jade rubbed the corners of her eyes. She slid out of bed and opened the door. Standing in the hall, yawning, with dark circles under their eyes, were Mason and Drew, holding flowers.

'Is she awake?' Drew whispered.

'I'm awake,' Lucy called from the bed.

Drew squeezed Jade on the arm and stepped past her to get to Lucy.

'How's she doing?' Mason whispered.

Jade couldn't wait to have a full conversation with Lucy to actually gauge how she was doing. She seemed fine-*ish*. Tired, achy, and she needed help going to the bathroom. But mentally, Jade would find out later. Lucy claimed she could hand over the kid without a problem, but expectations and reality didn't always align. 'She's okay. Been sleeping off and on. Crashed pretty hard last night.' Jade waved him in and closed the door.

'Good to hear.' Mason stepped into the room, beelined for Lucy, and opened his arms for a hug.

Lucy put up her hands. 'Fair warning. I've been through labour, childbirth, and recovery, and still haven't showered.'

Mason waved away her concerns and embraced her anyway. 'How are you?'

'I'm feeling good.' Lucy slid the tray table to the side. 'Sore, tired, but other than that, I'm fine. Enough about me. How's the baby?'

'She's doing great,' Drew chimed in and pulled up a chair. 'Everything is as expected the nurses said. They think she'll go home in two to three weeks.'

Mason patted Lucy's hand. 'Would you like to see some pictures?'

'Yes!' Lucy adjusted the bed to a higher sitting position, then took the cell phone from Drew. As she scrolled, her hand covered her mouth. 'Oh … you guys. She's so beautiful.'

Mason glanced at Drew and nodded. 'Go ahead.'

'Mason and I would like to introduce you to … Lucille.' Mist filled Drew's eyes. 'We wanted to honour you, and everything you've done, with her name.'

The air in Jade's lung hitched at the beautiful tribute. The dads had been so grateful and caring towards Lucy this entire journey, but this added gift solidified their bond for life. In the past, Jade wasn't sure how she would've reacted to such a testament towards a partner. But now, she wanted to join in the biggest, fattest group hug.

Lucy looked between the men, her eyebrows squeezing, and a hand against her heart. Her lips trembled. 'I don't know what to say …'

While the three of them chatted, Jade slipped out of the room, promising Lucy she'd be back in a bit. This moment belonged to them, not her. But Jade didn't feel excluded or forgotten on the sidelines. She felt whole.

Jade wandered the hospital halls, tugging the robe they had given her to cover her dress, and went to the gift shop. She purchased slippers, a sweatshirt, and some gourmet chocolate for Lucy. And then, she had an idea.

She pulled out her phone and noticed a missed message from Amanda.

> *Thought you'd want to know … you won! Some woman named Amelia called the salon to leave you a message. She said she sat with Lucy after she went into labor. Hope you, Lucy, baby, etc. are all good. Congratulations!*

A grin tugged at Jade's lips. Besides the fact that she'd been wearing her dress from the banquet, she had not thought about the award ceremony until Lucy brought it up. But she was proud. Her girlfriend had given birth, her friends had a daughter, and she had freaking won Best Salon.

Now, there was only one more thing to do.

Jade paid the Uber Eats driver and headed back up the elevator. In the hall, she bumped into Drew and Mason, who were just leaving Lucy's room. The men wrapped their arms around Jade in the best group hug of her life.

'Take good care of her,' Drew said, a smile crossing his tired face.

The events from the last thirty-six hours were finally starting to settle, and to her surprise, Jade found herself choking up. She'd been so focused on what life would look like post childbirth, and how Lucy would feel, that she'd never allowed herself to imagine how *she'd* feel after the transformation. But one thing was certain – Lucy's happiness was still top priority. 'I will.'

'But also' – Drew held up a finger – 'let her take care of you. This entire process was hard on you, too, and we haven't forgotten that.'

'Just don't let her cook for you.' Mason grinned. 'Unless it's grilled cheese. Remember that time she tried to make asparagus hotdish?'

Drew groaned. 'How could I forget?'

Jade gave each man one more quick hug, and then stepped into the room.

'How am I still so hungry?' Lucy asked as reached for her water cup. 'I thought I was eating for two, but this might be the new norm.'

God, I love this woman. Messy, dishevelled, un-showered, her make-up from last night smeared across her face, and she was still the most beautiful woman Jade had ever seen.

'Luckily, I come bearing gifts.' Jade revealed the bag she'd been hiding behind her back and dangled it in the air. 'Close your eyes.'

'Whatever it is, I already love you.' Lucy grinned and put her palms to her eyes.

Jade lined up the containers on the TV tray and slid the tray over Lucy's lap. Her heart was skipping way too quickly for the small gesture. 'Ready? Open!'

Lucy's eyes scanned the spread – a mound of prosciutto, salami, soppressata, and chorizo. 'Salted meats? You got me salted meats!'

She dug into the salami and moaned as she chewed. Amusement tickled Jade that something as simple as an animal protein could elicit that response. 'Ah, I really, really, *really* love you.'

Two years ago, Jade could never have dreamed she'd ever feel as fulfilled as she was right now. She grinned at Lucy, devouring her salty meats with such pure joy, and let herself bask in gratitude. She had opened herself to up to love, and the results had exceeded her wildest dreams.

Lucy layered a prosciutto around a small slice of mozzarella and wiggled her brows. 'Want to try some?'

'Nope. Not even a little.'

She grinned at Jade in between bites and swallowed. 'Next week, vegan restaurant. Maybe we can even start Meatless Mondays. It might kill me, but for you, I'll give it a shot.'

Knowing Lucy the way Jade did, this offer ranked only one step below her offer to carry for her friends. Jade planted a kiss on Lucy's lips, the closest she'd been to cured meat in twenty years, but it was totally worth it. Everything about Lucy was worth it.

'Can't wait.'

Epilogue

Lucy
Twelve months later

The blinding sun busted through the bedroom shades without any consideration for those who might still be sleeping. A soft hand swept Lucy's long hair from the back of her neck and lips pressed against her nape. 'Luce?'

'No.' Lucy pulled the pillow over her head.

'*Lucy*.' Jade's lips moved to the top of her spine. One kiss, two kisses, three kisses … She trailed her mouth down Lucy's back.

A soft, traitorous moan released from Lucy. 'Still no.'

'Lucy. Sunshine. Green.' The kisses stopped and a firm hand squeezed her tush. 'You have to get up. It's time.'

'Grrr …' Lucy tried to groan, but a soft giggle escaped instead. 'Seriously, who schedules a one-year birthday party for 10 a.m. on a Saturday?'

Jade laughed. Because *clearly* she also knew the start time was ridiculous. 'The dads are very serious about keeping Lucille's nap schedule, aren't they?'

That was the understatement of the century. The nap schedule, the all-organic homemade food, the acceptance of Jade's terrible advice on vegetarian cooking ... they even made the poor kid eat sweet potatoes and peas for God's sake! The second the baby could have dairy, Lucy was sneaking her some ice cream.

'That nap schedule is designed with complete and total disregard for every other human on the planet.' Lucy rolled onto her back. 'Drew and Mason are *so* turning into those dads. What's next? A participation award for every month she doesn't get potty trained?'

'Um, I think that is a few years away,' Jade said.

Lucy wiggled the sheet down, past her naked chest and to her navel. 'Are you *sure* you want to leave ...'

'Mmmmm,' Jade murmured and licked the corner of her lip. 'Nope, sure don't.'

Lucy would never, ever get sick of the way Jade looked at her, the way her hazel eyes darkened until they were damn near ravenous. She thought when Jade moved into her house a few months after Lucy gave birth that their sex life would eventually slow.

She thought wrong.

'You fight so dirty, Ms Green. But I promise I'll make it up to you when we get home.' Jade licked then blew into the crook of Lucy neck, in the place that always made Lucy squirm. 'I'll take Chucky for a walk while you're in the shower and put the gifts in the car, okay?'

Lucy grinned and dragged herself out of bed. Was she excited to see the little peanut? Definitely. Did it still suck getting up at 8 a.m. on a Saturday to get ready? Yep.

These last six months had been such a whirlwind for both her and Jade that sleeping in on the weekend was a reward. When Lucy got the bank managerial job right over the holidays, it was simultaneously everything she dreamed of with the hours she feared. After many, *many* heart-to-heart talks and even a few couples counselling sessions (*who knew you could pre-emptively do couples counselling before any issues started?*), she and Jade both committed to maintaining a healthy work-life balance, and prioritising their relationship as much as possible, which was proving a tad difficult for a while with both of their rising careers. But finally, these last two months, things have settled into a routine.

A beautiful, most often, *delicious* routine.

After winning the award for the Best Salon of the Greater Twin Cities, Jade's salon started booking out longer and longer lead times. An investor even approached Jade about opening a chain, but she declined for now. However, she did expand the store hours and hired an assistant manager to help with the paperwork and basic manager duties so Jade could cut back on her hours. For the first time in years, Jade worked a solid nine-to-five with no weekends.

And trust Lucy when she says they waste *no* time on the weekends making sure they are still aligned.

An hour later, Lucy rolled Betty Yellow into Drew and Mason's neighbourhood. When she turned the block, her breath hitched. '*Jesus* ...'

Jade covered her nearly cartoon-wide grin with her hand. 'Don't even say it. They're just ... excited.'

'I mean, obviously. But *wowza*!' Not that Lucy expected anything less but leading up to the house – starting from the mailbox through the driveway and up to the entrance – it looked like a jumbo jet-sized pink piñata had cracked open and rained down on the property. Lollipop lawn ornaments, a balloon arch that rivalled a high-school prom, a chalkboard 'happy birthday' sign, a bubble machine ... and they couldn't even spot where the party was being held.

Lucy actually kind of loved it. Sure, it was a lot, but she loved every time she and Jade visited their home; the place bounced with joy. Lucy interlaced her fingers with Jade and tugged. 'I cannot wait to see what the backyard looks like.'

'Oh my God, me too,' Jade said, picking up her pace. 'Do you think they actually–'

'Got the pony?' Lucy chuckled. 'Honestly, I've known Drew my whole life, and I still don't know if he was kidding.'

Over the last year, Lucy watched as the love of her life fell in love with the men. They all bonded more than Lucy could've ever dreamed, and Jade especially gravitated towards Mason. But, not as much as Jade gravitated towards Lucille. Jade was a full-on doting auntie superstar, sucking up every second she could with the baby.

Oh wow … okay, if the front yard was pretty spectacular, the backyard was downright phenomenal. In front of them lay a pink-and-white wonderland: a cotton-candy machine with a guy in a white chef hat scooping cones for kids, white-linen–clothed tables with pink-and-white place settings, balloons, flowers, a cake that rivalled Harry and Meghan's wedding cake, and more bubbles. So many freaking bubbles.

Out of the corner of her eye, Lucy saw Jade scan the fifty-plus attendees until she locked eyes with Lucille, who was tucked into a white baby gown with a pink bow wrapped around her bald head. Jade dropped Lucy's hand like it was sticky and beelined across the law. 'Ah! Sweet girl! Come to Auntie,' she said, holding out her arms. And of course, as always, Lucille's face lit up the moment she saw her Auntie Jade.

'Oh, hi guys, good to see you, too,' Jade said to the dads and smooched the top of Lucille's head.

Seeing this side of Jade brought so much sparkly joy to Lucy that sometimes she felt like she'd tip right over. Of course she loved Lucille, just like she'd love any of her close friends' kids. No more, no less. But Jade *loved* Lucille, with a straight-up capital L.

After the birth, everyone seemed to ask Lucy if she had a special bond with the baby, and she'd always smile and say, 'Of course! She's my best friend's baby.'

But the truth was no. Yes, she loved Lucille, but there was no bond, no connection, no longing that folks warned her about when she first signed up to be a surrogate. And it was perfect.

'Well, since I'm not going to get my daughter back for the foreseeable future since Auntie Jade is here' – Drew grinned and jutted his head to the house – 'can I steal you for a few minutes, Luce? I need some help grabbing some things in the kitchen.'

'Sure,' Lucy said, knowing dang well this was code for chat time.

Fruit platters, extra punch bowl ingredients and charcuterie boards lined the kitchen island. She blew out a low whistle and grabbed herself a glass of punch.

Drew did a quick scan around the corner like he was on a covert mission. 'Everything in order?'

'Yep.' Lucy took a sip of the strawberry lemonade and stood on her tiptoes to confirm Jade hadn't somehow snuck in undetected. *Good.* She was still out in the yard, bouncing the baby on her hip, and laughing with Mason. Yes, *laughing*. She clearly cracked the Mason code and was one of the only people besides Lucille who could make him crack up. 'The jeweller called, and I get to pick the ring up on Monday instead of Tuesday. Can I still drop it off right after?'

Drew nodded. 'Of course. But are you sure you can't just hide it somewhere?'

'No way,' Lucy said. 'With my luck, between Chucky and Jade, one of them might uncover it.' For the last few months, she'd planned out all the details of the proposal – with Drew's help. After designing a beautiful band with channel-set jade (*of course*) and a lovely round diamond, Lucy panicked about keeping it at home. Everything was perfect – from the quaint bed and breakfast she booked on Lake Superior, to her dad taking Chucky for the weekend, to the macaroons from Jade's favourite shop downtown. The last thing she wanted was Jade – or Chucky thinking the box was a toy – pre-emptively discovering the ring.

'Okay, I got you. I'll swing by your house for a visit on Friday before you leave and slip it to you,' Drew said.

'That's what she said,' Lucy said then scrunched her nose. '*Whyyyy?* Why does that joke never work when I say it?'

'I promise someday it will land. You just keep practising, and – oh crap, they're coming,' Drew tugged on Lucy's arm as Mason and Jade weaved their way through the crowd. 'Don't act suspicious.'

'Gah! What the hell? Now I'm for sure going to act suspicious when I don't want to act suspicious. *Shhhh* …' Lucy swatted his hand and waved at the three of them, sliding open the patio door. 'Hey, you guys, is the party over already?'

Jade rightfully rolled her eyes at the terrible joke. 'No, the princess here needs a diaper change.'

'And Auntie's volunteering?' Drew said, taking Lucille from Jade.

'You know I love her,' Jade said, handing over the baby. 'But I draw the line at diaper duty.'

That is a very fair call, and no one could be blamed. As the men walked Lucille back to her room to change her, Lucy took this opportunity to plant a kiss on Jade's perfect, lush lips.

Lucy sighed into Jade's mouth.

Jade. Her love. Her life. And … her (hopefully) soon-to-be wife.

Everything was perfect.

A Letter from Dana Hawkins

Hi there!

Thank you so much for reading *My Girlfriend is Not the Father*, which is my most personal story to date. Although this story is not an autobiography, I did draw heavily upon my personal experiences from when I was a surrogate for my best friend and his husband. I drew so much from memory, so if laws, policies, or medicine injection schedules have changed ... please don't come for me!

Being asked to be a surrogate, to have the fathers trust me so implicitly to house and care for their little nugget, is one of the greatest honors of my life. During the multi-year process, I remember talking to my *incredibly* supportive spouse about how I couldn't imagine navigating the surrogacy process as a single person and made a few laughs (cries!) about not being able to "shoot myself in the butt" (let me tell you, the angle is really, really hard!) My spouse joked about how this would be the ultimate icebreaker on a first date. Thus ... this story stuck in the back of my mind for years until I finally took the plunge and wrote it.

I hope you enjoyed the book! If you would be so kind to leave a review, this is the most effective way to support authors.

I consciously choose to write stories where coming out is not an "issue" and that being LGBTQIA+ is nothing to "overcome." Creating a world where my characters live in a safe, affirming, celebratory space while navigating their relationships and real-life issues fills my heart. I am keenly aware the queer community continues to live in fear and is subject to discrimination, violence, anti-inclusive legislation, and more. I write novels that create a reality I want to be a part of – a hate-free world.

Please follow me on my socials to find out about upcoming projects. Thank you for taking this journey with me!

Dana Hawkins

Website: www.danahawkins.com

📷 d.hawkinsauthor

Acknowledgements

To my real-life "Drew", "Mason", and "Lucille" (names changed for privacy), thank you for trusting me all those years ago with this responsibility and letting me be part of your lives. To "Drew", who knew thirty (*ahem*) plus years ago when you asked me to a school dance, we'd create an unbreakable bond. I love you!

To my agent, Jenna Satterthwaite. When you called and offered representation based on this book, the sparkle in your eyes, enthusiasm, and validation that I created something special meant the world to me. Your unwavering support and the safe space you've created for me has unlocked my creative process more than I ever dreamed. Your championship, leadership, and kindness are unmatched. Are you an agent? A therapist? A superhero? How you do what you do, I'll never understand. Thank you for taking a chance on me.

To my spouse. Thank you for always being my biggest support in everything I do. Seriously. I am constantly amazed by how much you support me.

To my kiddos, Tanner, Kiki, and Joey. You are my life. I love you, my babies!

To my mom, Esther Dusha. Thank you for also shooting me in the butt back then, for being in the hospital with me, "Drew" and "Mason" when "Lucille" made an unexpected early arrival, and my spouse was out of town. And of course, thank you for reading all of my books!

To Erica Dusha. Thank you for also being in the hospital with me when I had "Lucille", and I still apologize for the exorcist style-level of vomit you had to endure. Oops. Your support over all these years means more to me than you'll ever know.

To Jennifer Gatewood. My critique partner and friend, extraordinaire. Thank you for not being sick of me yet. Please don't ever leave me! Your continual encouragement, guidance, and support mean everything to me. Shoulder shimmy for life!

To S.E. Reed. Thank you for making me believe I can do anything. Your friendship and encouragement lift me up on my lowest days, and I am forever grateful for you. I am so beyond lucky to have you in my life.

Katharine Bost. You are the queen of editing and critiques. Getting feedback from you is like opening up the huge box under the Christmas tree. Thank you for helping guide this story!

To the team at HQ. Thank you for everything you did to bring this story to life.

And to Team Jenna. You all are amazing! What an incredible support system.

Thank you to those who continue to read and celebrate queer stories! It's more important than ever not to silence voices.

Dana

Dear Reader,

We hope you enjoyed reading this book. If you did, we'd be so appreciative if you left a review. It really helps us and the author to bring more books like this to you.

Here at HQ Digital we are dedicated to publishing fiction that will keep you turning the pages into the early hours. Don't want to miss a thing? To find out more about our books, promotions, discover exclusive content and enter competitions you can keep in touch in the following ways:

JOIN OUR COMMUNITY:

Sign up to our new email newsletter: http://smarturl.it/SignUpHQ

Read our new blog www.hqstories.co.uk

𝕏: https://twitter.com/HQStories

f: www.facebook.com/HQStories

BUDDING WRITER?

We're also looking for authors to join the HQ Digital family! Find out more here:

https://www.hqstories.co.uk/want-to-write-for-us/

Thanks for reading, from the HQ Digital team

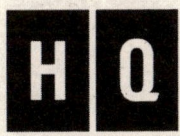